THE CARNIVALE OF CURIOSITIES

THE CARNIVALE OF CURIOSITIES

AMIEE GIBBS

THORNDIKE PRESS
A part of Gale, a Cengage Company

LIBRARY OF CONGRESS CIP DATA ON FILE.
CATALOGUING IN PUBLICATION FOR THIS BOOK
IS AVAILABLE FROM THE LIBRARY OF CONGRESS.

ISBN-13: 979-8-88579-113-7 (hardcover alk. paper)

Published in 2023 by arrangement with Grand Central Publishing, a division of Hachette Book Group, Inc.

Printed Number: 1   Print Year: 2023
Printed in Mexico

*To anyone who has ever whispered a
wish in the dark*

PROLOGUE

It took three hours to kill Charlotte Bainbridge.

An egregious amount of time for an exsanguination, he knew. Any slaughter-man worth his salt would have scoffed at anything beyond eight minutes from first slice to last drop. But this instance demanded less of speed and more of precision. And though his hands had known blood, he was not an habitué of the abattoir. He was an artist.

Haloed by gas lamps, Mr. Pretorius continued his work in near silence. The only noise to be heard was the iron creak of the gibbet where a life-size Automaton hung amid overburdened shelves and cabinets full of the ephemera of the stage. If anyone had said to him fifty-odd years ago, when boarding the belly of a boat from Barbados in the afterglow of emancipation, that he would one day find himself in the understage of an English theater, with the fresh body of a dead girl, he would have laughed.

So it beggared belief how only that morning his little shop, nestled back behind the ropes and pulleys and hydraulics of the understage and dedicated to the props and contrivances that dazzled the eye and confounded the senses for the Athenaeum's productions, had been transformed into a death house worthy of any hospital in the city. Only a few hours had passed since the audience had exited and the theater stilled before his precious workbench was pushed to the wall and in its place a mortuary table appeared. Trays, surgical instruments, and foul-smelling fluids had disordered the orderly chaos of his hammers, levels, wrenches, and wiring. It all seemed impossible, and yet —

He tested the needle's integrity against the meat of his thumb as his old Nani had taught him and, hovering over her body, threaded the sharp point through the open incision on her neck, lacing the fine silk over and across the wound until the flaps of skin were neatly stitched closed. A faint trickle of fluid escaped over his fingers, but a quick, tight knotting of the silk stanched the leak.

"I have said this before, Pretorius, but it bears repeating. You have one of the finest set of hands in London." Aurelius Ashe approached the table where Charlotte's body lay. His soft leather boots barely made a sound on the carpet of damp sawdust on the floor. "These sutures are barely noticeable."

The great illusionist's stage vestige had been swept from him but none of the swagger. He stood straight-backed, hands in pockets, with kohl still smudging his dark eyes.

"The best I could do," Pretorius said, dropping the needle into the tray on the table. "I had hoped to leave her unmarred. If I could have figured out another way —"

"My dear Pretorius, you know that no one ever leaves here *unmarred.*" Aurelius studied Charlotte's prone body. Pulling his hand from his pocket, he let his fingers hover over the dead girl's face, never quite touching her skin but running a hair's breadth above. Down along her cheek, he traced her jawline until his sharp nails touched down on the stitches at her throat.

With any good magician or thief, hands were the tools of the trade. One hand ready to distract while the other picked the pocket. For Aurelius Ashe, the distraction was built in. Indelibly inked onto the back of his hand was the image of a wheel. Taken from the tarot, this Wheel of Fortune moved along his skin with each motion. Not in the natural way that skin moves over active muscle and tendon but as a wheel over ground. On the wheel spun, until his hand stilled.

Pretorius's own hands had taken him farther than his skin told him was allowed. Brown, callused, and hard as horn with fingers thick and suited for the labors Aurelius required. The pinkie of each hand was spatulate with nary a nail, an old injury that had left tips flattened, crushed, and absent of feeling. These were not the hands of a magician, and for that he was grateful.

"I warned her, as I did our mutual friend, that she would not be the same. Concerns were dismissed," Aurelius said, slipping his fingers through her hair. "Look at her, the sleeping lamb. Not a care in the world."

Pretorius noted the gentleness applied. It might have been a comforting gesture if it was not a precursor to the violence to come. Not to Charlotte, who was well past feeling, but to Aurelius, for whom there was no god to offer a single mercy with this private performance.

"Now, as to your thoughts on there being

10

another way . . . you know as well I that any alternative would not have been in her best interest. We discussed this and you agreed. Do you no longer trust me on this matter?"

"I might question your methods now and again, my friend, but I've not lost my faith in them nor my trust," Pretorius said. "Even when they make me a murderer."

"That's a bit harsh." Aurelius's head darted up. "You know I never make anyone do anything. I only offer the means."

Pretorius shook his graying head with the impishness of a fox at a rabbit warren. "Maybe we should have thought of bringing *this* to the stage."

"There are some things in life, Pretorius, that do not need an audience. Not even you. Dim the lights," Aurelius said as the first wisps of the gray clouded his dark eyes.

Stepping away from the table, Pretorius crossed the shop to where the Automaton hung. Reaching behind the gibbet, he turned the central valve he had installed to lessen the flow of gas to the lamps. The shop fell into soft golden shadow as the hiss dropped to a whisper. It was craven, he knew, to remain at this safer distance, but if this turned out to be the one time that Aurelius failed, well . . . there was no need to risk them both being taken by this dangerous trick.

The first words of an ancient tongue, fluent to Aurelius but foreign to his own ears, churned the quiet room like a rush of water. Pretorius looked at the Automaton.

"No audience means you too," he whispered, gently turning the gibbet until the inanimate eyes no longer faced the spectacle at the table. He might have looked the fool for doing so but he was not about to risk one of his creations should the trick go astray.

Few people knew that magic was real. Even practitioners of long standing often dismissed the existence of magic as nothing more than card tricks, distraction, and sleight of hand. Entertainment for pleasure, for money, prestige. After all a magician's greatest trick is getting you to believe what they themselves often do not. For Pretorius, magic, like faith, was not to be instantly doubted as false, although he was of a mind that preferred what could be seen, touched, and explained by taking something apart and rebuilding it. There was truth in the precision of science, and his understanding of the world came from the tangible not the fantastic.

Magic was not a game to be played lightly. As Aurelius Ashe had shown him, it was only the most daring practitioners who attempted to harness its darkest secrets. Many lost their lives, their sanity, or both in the gamble to understand and to perhaps amass power for themselves. While he had no desire to enter the realm of magic, he no longer questioned the validity of its existence. Too often Aurelius had succeeded in doing the unimaginable. Still, every man had his vulnerabilities, and luck didn't last forever.

Pretorius chanced a glance back at the table in time to see Aurelius's shoulders shudder and his strained body lurch over Charlotte. The temperature dropped in the shop like hail. Pretorius's breath rimed the air, droplets coating his beard, and the impishness that had taken him before passed in the wake of the serious undertaking.

He couldn't watch his friend's sacrifice any further. He looked instead at the grate in the ceiling where outside the dull roll of Southwark echoed down through the ventilation ducts. He wished again that he had torn up the letter that had brought the man, who in turn brought the girl, *this girl,* to their door. The thrum of horses and wheels and the vague shouts of the streets at night. *Life!*

But those noises soon gave way to a cruel,

deathly rattle, and Pretorius whirled around in time to see Aurelius stumbling back from Charlotte. His shirt was sweat-matted to his chest and back, and remnants of a dark fog trailed from the corners of his mouth. The gray that had clouded his eyes retreated and returned to black, hollowed and haunted as the universe. The demon claws had held and slowly the shop warmed again.

Pretorius pulled his watch from his well-worn waistcoat pocket and began to count the seconds.

One — Two —

His eyes shifted from Aurelius, slumped down on the dusty floor utterly drained from the act, back to the table where the dead girl lay. Old Nani's last words to him before he boarded the boat to England bit at his ear.

'Do your best to be a free man, but if you must serve another, choose your master wisely.'

Taking a breath, the watch ticked down.

Three —

Slowly Charlotte stirred.

CHAPTER ONE

The wind blew from the east the night the ship was first sighted along the south bank of the River Thames.

There were no horns, no whistles, no bells to sound her approach, only two stories of sleek black hull slicing the water like a bat's wing through the dark.

Giant wrought-iron wheels saddled either side of her, each partially hidden behind a half-moon paddle box painted black, a match to the hull, and sprinkled in silver stars. The wheel's wooden paddles were sheathed in bright copper that glistened in the spray and splash, each turn a damning rebuff to any who stood in her way.

The nightly sifting of every sharp-eyed Mud Lark on the river halted as she thundered toward port.

"You see anyone?" one boy asked at the

15

river's edge. He hopped foot-to-foot amid the thick of the stink, hoping to bring relief from the cold swirling around his ankles. The dank bandage wrapped around his left foot offered no relief; the linen only sopped the water, creating a thin barrier between the soft mud and his bare skin. A pair of boots hung around his neck from their laces. The muddy soles bounced off his hollow chest but he didn't dare leave them on the bank, as they would be gone as quick as the tide. It took losing something precious one time to learn that honor among thieves is a lie.

"Looks like a ghost," said another as the ship towered past, roiling the low tide mist in her path as either an act of pure entitlement, an honest oversight, or simple disregard for the safety of anyone else on the water. The tall black funnel protruding from the heart of the ship's body caught the young hungry eyes.

"That there ain't a ghost, my lads."

The boys turned toward the approaching creature, whose hulking form draped in thick canvas trousers and a thicker long coat was more bogey than man. His grease-matted hair fell across his pallid skin and into a pair of moon-gray eyes that reflected his subterranean life. He was every bit the imagined monster parents warned their children of on the darkest nights, but the hardened Mud Larks did not flinch at his company.

True, it was rare to see Old Tosher Jim or any of his ilk topside of London trawling as they did in the tunnels beneath, living and often dying away their days in filth. There was, however, one sure lure that would bring these men to the surface, away from the noisome sewers, and that was the promise of copper. And this incoming ship had enough copper on her to fill a tosher's belly for a year.

An explosive bellow of steam shot high into the sky, painting the night a momentary white.

"And again we are to see our share of devils." He sat his bull lantern on the bank like a votary amid the shit and rubbed his rough hands together, jostling the treasures in his bulging coat pockets.

The boys eyed the old man. "You saying you know who's on that ship?"

Tosher Jim ran a grimy hand back through his hair. Flakes of dandruff and dried mud drifted onto his shoulders. "Aye, I do. Demons and dreams is what she brings, which is why I say that you lads are best keeping to the river. Take it from your Old

Jim, steer wide and forget seeing that ship or any of those who sail on her."

"And if we don't?" asked the boy with the boots dangling at his neck.

The tosher retrieved his lantern from the river's filth. "What's your name, boy?"

"Michael Mayhew," the boy said, with as much firm conviction as the silt sifting between his toes.

"Well, young Michael my lad." He smiled, clamping his free hand onto Michael's thin shoulder. "Don't and be damned."

In validation of Tosher Jim's threat, the dark ship woke. Flames flickered in her deckhouses as the gas lamps within sprang to life. Within minutes, much of the lower hull illuminated against the river like a Turner waterscape. MANANNAN was emblazoned across a large brass plate near the tip of the bow.

Lost in the spectacle, few noticed the tide rising. Soon their opportunity to search the shore for nails and scrap would be lost until the next day's low.

Who could look away, though, when the stars speckling the paddle boxes began to spread across the hull until the random pattern shifted into words:

It had to have been a trick of the eye, this moving of stars, and even the sudden presence of a tall figure at the bow did little to assuage this doubt. He stood stock-still with one hand held out over the water. Balanced in his palm were three spheres of light that he flung high into the air. As each rose, the next higher than the first, the spheres exploded in a flash of fire and spark to the delight of the watching Larks.

He heard the children murmur and squeal, but from where he stood the air was so deadened with grease and fog that even following the tails of the flares he could barely see the spires of the bridge, let alone the faces of his audience. A hint of unease, quite untraceable to any reasoned source, nagged at him. Pulling his heavy coat close, he waited, half hoping that his signal would go unanswered, but knowing as sure as the paddles that sloshed the filth-thickened waters that luck was not to be with him.

The *tick tick* of the watch dangling from his waistcoat pocket counted the minutes until three flares of light shot over Tower Bridge. He followed the stripe of light as the last retort sliced through the darkness with a distant boom. A chill cut through him. No amount of clothing could cure the touch. Nevertheless, he pulled his scarf tighter.

As he hurried back to the deckhouse, a shadow crossed him. It was a dark sliver that danced away as quickly as it had come, far too quick to see the shape of its meaning.

CHAPTER TWO

17 October, aboard Manannan
Dear Mr. Ashe, I have in my possession something you might be interested in . . .

"It never ends," Aurelius Ashe said, hearing the salon door open. He did not bother raising his eyes from the picture in his hand. "So many offers and every single one the same. . ."

"Nothing promising then?"

"This one" — Ashe flipped the picture like the third card of a three-card trick — "clearly a fake and not even a particularly good one." He threw it down, nearly upsetting the pile of neglected letters that teetered on his desk.

"Ever since that damned Mermaid they've been crawling out of the woodwork with whatever piecemeal chimera that can be thought of. I ask you, Lucien, do they take me for a repository for every odd bit of claptrap?"

"Can you blame them?" Lucien pulled the damp scarf from his neck and tossed it across the red leather chaise. The stink of the river was a ghost on the wool. "As long as people enjoy seeing the strange there will be those seeking to profit, no matter what form it comes in." He pressed his hands to the column radiator, wrapping his fingers around the filigreed cast-iron pipes until his skin scorched. A smile crossed his lips as the chill drew from his bones. "Look what it's done for Barnum."

"Then let Barnum continue to store the tat away in his American Museum." Ashe sniffed, dismissing the name of the impresario as he did any other inconvenient thought. "I haven't the need for humbugs."

"You never did like him."

"On the contrary, if anything I find his ambition admirable, and I would never begrudge a man who seeks to put coins into his coffer. It is, however, a matter of taste. I am not above a little deceit, but I do believe in offering authenticity rather than being a purveyor of hoaxes. It cheapens the art, the name, and in my opinion the experience."

Had it been anyone else words such as these might have been viewed as jealousy, but from the lips of Aurelius Ashe, it was merely the honest observations of a carnival king with whom few would argue.

"Our paths crossed once, you know, Barnum's and mine. Long before all of this" — he waved his arms — "and I saw his potential as clear as I see you. He has done well for himself, better than I expected with the encouragement given, but I had still hoped for more from him. Who knows, the man does have vision. He might still conjure up something even greater."

"Not everyone has your skills," Lucien said.

Ashe leaned back in his chair, his hands folded across his stomach. Tattooed to the back of each was a tarot image. The Wheel of Fortune on the right hand, on the left the Magician, while the wisdom of the world was etched across his handsome features as deep as the arabesques on the wood paneling behind him.

"It is from the thin air and the high hopes of our patrons' imaginations that I build. If it can be dreamed, Lucien, if it can be believed, then it can be seen and realized."

"If only for a moment."

On the corner of the desk, an intricate brass orrery shone under the lamplight. The planets slowly spun in their orbits.

"Sometimes a moment is all one ever gets. Or ever needs."

Lucien had learned much of the Carnivale's business from watching Aurelius, who was always astute, often cunning, and without exception fair in his dealings. These were all skills to be learned. But the man seated comfortably behind the big desk held an intangible quiet confidence that would take a lifetime to acquire if he hoped to be half the magician and twice the master.

"You've made the announcement?"

"Yes," Lucien said.

"And?"

"And Pretorius answered. He knows we're coming in."

"Good, good, good, good."

Lucien remained by the radiator, where curious fingers of heat crept up his spine. "How long are we staying in Southwark?"

"In two nights we should run the first show. After that we'll have to see. I prefer to wait until after November to set course again, perhaps even to the New Year. Avoid the first and the worst of the Atlantic storms. Why?"

Lucien shook his head. "No reason."

Ashe leaned forward in his chair. The oil lamps bathed the polished rosewood walls in a warm golden glow, gilding his pale skin and firing his dark eyes.

"Something bothering you, Lucien? You're

rather subdued tonight."

"No, no . . . I . . . I had hoped only for a longer stay in Tangiers. The warmth. The sun." He shrugged. "I've never been fond of English winters."

Ashe's eyes narrowed. "I taught you to lie better than that," he said, his broad smile creasing his bearded cheeks.

And he had. It was the first lesson Lucien had learned, though he was not a constant practitioner. Not like the Harlequin, and certainly not like Aurelius himself, who could unspool a fiction quicker than a thread from a bobbin. The only thing he was quicker at was ferreting out the truth.

"Your objections to returning to South-wark are well noted but they do not change the fact that I have business to attend to here. I have neglected London for seven years in deference to you. I'll not address the troubles that came before that."

"You usually show more courtesy when prying into my thoughts."

"When a man is an open book, he had better expect his secrets to be read." Aurelius sank back in his chair. "Not that your grief is any great secret. You have taken to wearing it like a second skin." He swept his hand back through his thatch of long dark hair, into which winter was beginning to

25

creep. "My question is, how much longer do you plan to continue this nonsense?"

It wasn't the cruelty of Aurelius's dismissal that seared but the casualness. "Nonsense!" Luce shouted. "You call what happened to my mother —" Rage choked him until his eyes burned.

"No, I call your tiresome mourning nonsense. Lucien, if every person decided to avoid a place because they could not put to rest their ghosts then the cities would fall to the rats because there would be no one left to sustain them."

Aurelius ran his eyes over Luce's face, hoping to see a chink in the stone. "I am not entertaining this any further. Southwark remains the nearest to a home that we have. Ghosts and all, this is where *we* began, where *we* are bound. It is where our theater stands —"

"I've no issue with London proper, but there are other stages, Aurelius, other theaters across the city. We could sell out The Royal Albert, Covent Garden. Why limit ourselves to only The Athenaeum?"

"She stands at the Newington Crossroads, which has proven convenient for my purposes. There are some rules even I must follow, nature of the beast and all. Besides, The Athenaeum is an experience unparalleled by any other circus, sideshow, or theatrical act. To speak of another venue diminishes not only us, but also all that Pretorius has created. His life's blood runs through every inch of iron, oil, and brick in that building."

The planets of the orrery spun a smooth click that resonated through Luce deeper than Aurelius's words could reach.

"When you are running the Carnivale, as I hope one day you will once I tire of it, you can then perform anywhere that you choose as you and I do not live by quite the same dictates. Don't think me callous, Lucien. If it would bring you some semblance of peace by all means lodge here on ship for the duration of our stay. Spend your evenings, your days in Westminster or Piccadilly, but you will be on The Athenaeum's stage for every performance."

Luce's earlier rage, while no longer boiling, still simmered under the skin. "I wouldn't dare dream of being anywhere else."

"We are born into places, Lucien. Not of our choosing, but they are the places that never quite leave our bones, no matter how far we run or how much we succeed. For better or worse Southwark, for all that she is and will be, runs through you like the

27

pitch in your veins."

"And when my time comes for the Carnivale, am I to inherit everything that entails?" Lucien retrieved his scarf from the chaise and wrapped it around his neck.

"That is some years away to be of any concern now. Whether or not you will walk fully in my shoes is yet to be seen," Aurelius said. "But I have confidence in your abilities. How far they will take you will be determined by how much you are willing to accept and learn. A role played like any other."

"Only one with real consequences and repercussions that last long after you've left the stage."

"Few of which will be yours," Aurelius said. He laid his hand on the desk. The robed magician inked on the back held a wand above his head with one hand while the other, empty, pointed to the ground. Only the most observant eye would have caught the figure's hands change position until the wand pointed at the ground and the other opened to the sky. "As above, so below, Lucien. Where the two meet is where magic resides. All pure fancy until made real."

"One day, Aurelius, someone is going to come wanting —" Lucien tucked the ends of his scarf into his coat. "I'm afraid to think of what you have already been asked to do and have done."

"If I were to stop and think every time about the repercussions of something that I had done or intend to do, well, what a dull little world that would be. Besides, we are merely a theatrical troupe, a band of illusionists and players who serve at the audience's pleasure. Tell me, where is the harm in giving people what they want?"

"You know the cost."

"Only because I set the price." Aurelius smiled, but any humor had faded by the time it reached his black eyes.

Lucien left the deckhouse with Aurelius's words still stinging.

The side-levered engine thumped a steady tattoo in the ship's belly. The steps thrummed under his feet as he made his way belowdeck.

"Damn!"

"Dita?" he called into the galley. "Y'aright in there?"

"You mean aside from the tea all over the floor?" she muttered, falling to her knees to sweep the leaves into a small neat pile. Her heavy black skirts pooled around her. She favored the somber color nearly as much as the mourning queen herself, but unlike Victoria, Dita preferred a little flair to her underpinnings, as proved by the lace of her red underskirt that peeped out from under the pool of black.

"Better the tea than the milk, eh."

She jerked her shoulders and stared up at him from beneath a cloud of thick salt-and-pepper curls. Dita du Reve, the Romani Oracle of Budapest by way of Ipswich, if the truth is to be told. Her grandfather was the last member of the family to set foot in Hungary since coming to England, but Aurelius was not one to let a small fact get in the way of better fiction. She was a natural empath and an instant favorite. Her forecasts had increased the company's fortunes exponentially. If Aurelius was the Father, then Dita was the closest thing to a Mother the company had. She was the comfort when prejudiced tongues inflicted cruelty, and as a seer she was the answer to all that you feared to ask. "Hand me a cloth. Wet it first."

Lucien passed her the damp towel then slumped down at the table. "Aurelius?" He gestured to the spent leaves.

"He likes a reading when we near port."

"See anything of interest?"

"What are you on about?" she said, scooping up the leaves.

"Are we going to have a good run? Any promising offers coming Aurelius's way? Did you see anything?"

"If I had, I wouldn't be telling you, now, would I? What I see during a reading is shared between the seeker and seer alone. Not for nosy nibs such as yourself." She tossed the cloth into the sink. "Now, you look as if you could do with a cuppa."

"Have we something stronger?"

Dita picked up the kettle. He watched her hook the handle over the faucet's neck and turn on the tap. Water pattered into the metal basin from the rim of the kettle.

"Biscuits? Though I can do up something more substantial. We've some ham left or I could do you a ploughman or a cheese and pickle."

"Tea is enough."

"Are you sure? You missed supper. Again." She turned the tap off and removed the kettle, pouring off some of the water into a teapot before setting the pot back to the burner. A small plume of blue flame hissed against the kettle's steel bottom as she placed it on the stove.

"At this rate, you'll be wasting away to nothing." She poured the hot water out of the pot, leaving the china body warm to the touch.

"Dita —"

"It's not like you, Luce, love, this loss of appetite. You ill?"

He smiled at the warm familiarity of his name. He often wished that Aurelius would be less formal toward him, but some natures weren't meant to be changed. "I know that you can't help yourself and bless you for it, but trust me when I say I'm fine."

"Is that so?" She walked over and took Luce's face in her hand. There was an unmistakable aura around him. It was an otherness that even among curiosities spoke to an abstraction from the world where the rest resided. Whether on the stage or in passing, it was plain to see why eyes tended to follow him like a procession. Utterly desirable yet decidedly unattainable.

A whisper past twenty-five and surpassing six feet, Luce wore his lean frame like a hand-tailored suit, comfortable, well fitted, and not a stitch out of place. Beneath a thick mop of cinder-black curls, which had never quite been tamed by hand or brush, was a set of fine features that had been etched with the sort of easy charm that guaranteed notice, and it was only by grace that he was mercifully unaware of what his

32

presence commanded in others. He had a broad clear brow and strong jaw that offered a pleasing symmetry and a pleasant open expression with a wide, engaging grin that contradicted the serious turn his thick black brows suggested.

But it was in his eyes that the magic lay. They were a brilliant, burning blue, a glance of which was so piercing as to be endured for only a limited frequency should one have the fortune, or misfortune, to fall under his gaze. That was the reflection of his true gift. Lucien, the Light-Bringer. Lucien, the Lucifer.

"Paler than normal. A week's growth of beard on your cheek and the puffiness under your eyes says to me that you have not been sleeping. And you have barely eaten a decent meal in three days. Need I say more?"

She released him, but the imprint of her fingers remained. "I'm beginning to think that I'll need to tie you to that chair and force a meal down your throat. Oh, and, pet, cuss me one more time and I'll swat you with that there spoon."

"I didn't say anything."

"You were thinking it. Now, are you going to tell me what is troubling you? Or would you prefer I have a look about that pretty head of yours on my own? By your consent or not."

"Am I not allowed a sleepless night?"

"Were you a man prone to them I'd not question it. But as I've never known you to suffer that ailment I have to wonder" — she turned to answer the whistling kettle — "what fancies keep you awake."

"Dita, there's nothing to —" He traced a circle on the ring-stained oak table.

"Tell me."

With two little words she ended his protest. Luce sat back in his chair. He nibbled his lower lip until a paper-thin strip of skin tore free. After Aurelius, he did not wish to draw a scolding from Dita as well. A bittersweet sting touched his tongue and he quickly licked away the beading blood.

"Do you know that my quarters measure exactly ten feet by fourteen? Do you know how I learned that? By pacing it out every night since leaving port last. I do that until I am near asleep on my feet." His voice dropped to a whisper. "If I work myself to exhaustion, I'll fall into bed and that will be all until the next night when I do it again."

"Should have come to me sooner, love. I could have fixed you a tonic that'd have you sleeping like the dead."

"Even when it's the dead keeping me

awake?"

Dita gripped the edge of the sink, her back tensed. There was no need to turn, no need to meet him eye-to-eye. She had trod this fragile road many times, but it remained as slippery as fresh-fallen snow. "We've not even hit ground yet and that damned woman is already —"

She had not intended to be so sharp, but the subject always managed to bring out the worst in all of them, as damaged souls often do.

"I know what you think, love, what you believe, but —"

"I know what I did. Blood's on my hands and no matter the years, it's not going anywhere."

"You didn't do anything, Lucien." She pried the lid of the tea tin open with the butt of the spoon and scooped two heaping tablespoons of loose leaves into the infuser. "How many times are we going to peel back the skin on this? What happened that night was an accident. You were only a boy."

Luce looked up at her. It was only a glance, but the grief in his eyes crept into Dita's chest and tugged hard; tugged until it felt like her heart would unravel. She watched this fragile man dissolve into a boy of ten years, haunted by a tragedy he had no hand in crafting and the cause of which she would never forgive Aurelius for.

She poured out a cup in front of him. The warm scent of bergamot lingered as the droplets slowed until the shimmering circles stilled in the cup.

"I saw her face, Dita. In the fire."

"Darlin', whatever it is you think you're seeing or remembering is a trick of the mind. Aurelius and I have told you what happened that day. Have you spoken to him about any of this?"

"You know what it's like trying to talk to him. He acts as if I should forget what happened." He sat the cup back to the table and looked at her. She had a pleasing heart-shaped face with eyes the color of figs, but tonight both heart and eyes were drawn and tired. Tiny lines crept from the corners of her eyes to touch the dusting of gray at her temples.

"It's this damned place." She brushed the curls back from her brow. "A resurrection of grief everywhere you turn."

"You read people, Dita. You see futures, but you also see pasts, and all those connections in between." He hated doing this to her but he had to put this ghost to bed at least for a night. "I've never asked this of you before but please, would you do a reading of me?"

"No, love, I won't. My going into your head and sifting up memories that are best left settled is not going to change anything for you." She settled down into the chair opposite him. "Private thoughts and private pains are what I deal in. Telling lies to make someone happy while telling truths and making others sad. All this mourning and what does it get you?"

Reaching across the table, she wrapped her fingers around his wrist. Heat flowed under his skin but she held firm. "Oh, my love, you have been through the wars," she said, her warm eyes looking into his. "Suffering wounds a lifetime will never heal."

She squeezed his wrist once before releasing her grip. "It's time to bury your dead, darlin', and not look back. *She* can no more hurt you than those worryin' shades ever could."

"Luce! I saw the flares! Are we coming into port?"

The boy bounded into the galley and tumbled into the chair beside Luce, brushing his shoulder against him as he reached for a chocolate biscuit.

"Georgie, ask don't take," Dita scolded.

"Sorry, Mum," he said, sinking back into his chair, stolen biscuit firmly in hand.

Georgie had come to the carnival one night near Warsaw. An unexpected acquisition hand-delivered to Aurelius by the boy's grandmother. Born covered head-to-toe in fine, inch-long light-brown hair, what she had seen as an abomination, Aurelius had seen as potential, and gladly took the child; adding to his growing menagerie of performers that had come to include an aerialist of unparalleled skill, a juggler with the unique habit of vanishing before one's eyes, conjoined child tumblers, an automaton, and a delicate dancer so small that on first glance she was often mistaken for a doll.

Ten years on and Georgie's hair had grown to eight inches on his face and nearly three inches everywhere else. Only the soles of his feet and the palms of his hands remained bare.

"Of course we're near port," chirped a voice from the door. "Luce wouldn't have sent a signal if we weren't."

As if summoned from a thought, Angelique sauntered toward the table. Her soft pink skirts rustled a bold inch above her ankles, showing off her dainty slippered feet. At eighteen, boldness was part and parcel of her personality. And her survival. At only thirty-four inches tall and less than two stone, The French Fairy, as she billed herself, made an immediate impression on everyone who met her as much from her dancing as from her appearance.

"Cuppa, dear?" Dita asked.

"Yes please," she said. "Luce, if you would?"

She held her arms above her head, allowing Luce to wrap his hands around her waist. Gently he lifted and stood her on the table. Despite her diminutive stature, the tiny parts of her body flowed in perfectly formed harmony, every inch a woman in miniature. Exceedingly beautiful with delicate pixie features, she made the perfect poppet on- and offstage.

Dita placed a child's tea set on the table. Angelique sat down cross-legged near Luce's arm. "So what are we talking about?"

"Memories," Dita said.

"Nothing," Luce responded.

Angelique rolled her blue eyes from one to other and was about to question deeper when Georgie interjected.

"Will you do us a trick, Luce? Please?"

"I don't know, Georgie. Have you been giving Dita any extra grief lately?"

"No . . . not too much," the boy said.

"I wouldn't say that." Dita winked.

"Mum?" Georgie's thick brow furrowed in fear of missing out on a treat.

"Hand me three cups, Dita. Please," Luce said.

"As long as you're careful with them," she said, setting down three china cups on the table.

Luce flipped the cups and beneath one placed a chocolate biscuit. "Are you watching carefully, Georgie? Do you know under which cup the biscuit is?"

"I know." Georgie nodded, pointing at the center cup.

"Are you sure about that?" Luce moved the cups quickly. His fingers were feather-light as he moved one cup around the other, back and forth in a figure eight. But Georgie kept his eyes on the center cup. Even Angelique, who had seen this trick at least two hundred times, couldn't help but watch again as rapt as Georgie.

Luce stilled the cups. "Think you still know where the biscuit is?"

Georgie nodded. "Center cup. I never took my eyes off it."

One by one, the cups were flipped upright. Georgie's eyes widened in anticipation, but when the center cup was lifted, it revealed nothing. The biscuit was not beneath any of them.

"I . . . I never took my eyes off the cup," Georgie said.

"Should have been watching your pockets instead," Luce said. He reached over and plucked the biscuit from Georgie's jacket. "You were so focused on the cup that you lost sight of what was happening around you. And that can be a dangerous thing. It's important, Georgie. You have to stay aware using all of your senses, not just your eyes. They are the easiest to deceive."

"Do it again," Georgie asked. "I want another try."

"Maybe tomorrow." Luce patted the boy on the head. "We disembark in the morning so tonight we've packing to do."

Luce stood up and walked toward the door.

"We've more to talk about, Lucien," Dita called after him. "I know what scares you."

"The shades? The shadows —" He paused.

She stood from the table and reached into the cupboard above the sink. "I've seen them too, pet." She tossed him a bottle of Powers single malt. "Sweet dreams."

CHAPTER THREE

18 October 1887, Ports of London,
  Southwark

The color filling the sky over the wharves and warehouses offered no kindness to Southwark. The light breaching the grease-sodden air did little to soften the edges of the packets, the clippers, and the storm-worn coastal traders that moored snug in their berths.

Between the drifting islands of brown filth, the thick gray waters of the Thames were a rancid scar across the city's breast.

Luce rubbed the whiskey-infused night from his eyes. He could barely hear his own breath over the pulse of the water purging from the sewer mouths into the river. Not that he was eager to take the air, as a constant vapor of sulfurous yellow blanketed the dock, adding to the already sickly glow of the lamps that bled from the windows of the buildings along the waterfront.

Despite the early hour, clerks were preparing for the day's business.

From shop to ship to shop porters hustled, hauling buckets of herring, haddock, bloater, eel, and anything else the Irish Sea and Atlantic could offer.

On deck, footsteps sounded, followed by the slow rattle of the gangway lowering to the dock, scattering the children, some as young as six, who crawled amid the barges. The grand ship from last night kept them near, especially the promise of those copper-sheathed paddles.

Yet none of the young Larks dared draw close. Perhaps Tosher Jim's warning had not lost its power in the daylight, though it was likely the well-dressed West Indian with the dusty hair standing sentinel on the dock that kept the birds at bay.

Mr. Pretorius had come to meet the ship. It was unknown as to whether that was his Christian or his surname, as he was only ever called Pretorius by the troupe and that was name enough. His face was a warmer, darker shade of the rosewood that graced the interior of the deckhouse, well worn but with young eyes, though winter had nearly taken full hold of the wires of his dark beard and his brow. He grinned up at the grand ship, *Manannan,* his child of iron wheels and gleaming copper. In one hand he held his hat, a shiny worn John Bull topper whose brim bore the scars of candle grease. With his free hand he drew his watch from the pocket of his second-best suit. The long silver chain glinted in the sparse morning light.

It struck a strange chord with Luce, seeing this old Hephaestus outdoors and in daylight. One stood a better chance of running into the queen herself rambling along the docks.

But that was how Pretorius preferred it. A creature of solitude, he happily whiled away his days and nights in the comfort of his workshop, where the sole sign of life was a cheerful whistle and a hammer strike as he tinkered at contrivances.

In the nascent days of the Carnivale, long before there was a ship, before there was even a theater, when the stage was nothing but an abandoned storefront, Pretorius served as Ashe's architect. Given the freedom to construct what he wanted with no expense or extravagance too great, theirs was an ideal partnership — a meeting of minds, tastes, and imaginations that expanded far beyond the cheap confines of a Southwark stall to a world stage of their own. Because if Aurelius Ashe could envision it, Pretorius could build it.

Ashe is the blood of the Carnivale. Dita its heart. Pretorius is its bones and Lucien its spark. A refrain Luce had heard whispered of the troupe along the show circuit for years. Yet few knew how true those words were. Lose one part and the Carnivale would fall.

A brisk breeze kicked a chop on the river and Pretorius's long coat billowed around him like a bell. These chops, both large and small, were part of the unforgiving nature of water, a not-so-friendly reminder of how capable it was of inflicting great harm on those who ventured across. The same could be said of city streets, especially those of Southwark.

Luce waved at him from atop a paddle box. Pretorius pocketed his watch and called to a group of men who lingered on the wharf. The men flexed their arms to drive out the cramps made worse by the cold, and prepared to earn their wages hauling props, parcels, and luggage from the ship.

"It's always a bit sad making ground."

"Yes, making ground is always sad."

Luce looked down from his perch to the two heads peering over the ship's starboard side. Danny and Davie O'Kearne.

45

The twins stood arm in arm, bound as much by the blood they shared as by the thick band of flesh that fixed them to each other's sides. They shared a liver; that much Aurelius had discovered since they joined the troupe four years ago.

As they stood before him, it was hard to imagine them as they had been the night that Aurelius had rescued them from the ten-in-one show in Brighton, where Dita had first discovered them. A pair of scrawny birdlike babes, small for their age, with huge eyes and dirty feet. Connecting them was a scarred band of skin, and the story of each of those raised white scars roiled the fire in his veins.

An egregious woman by the name of Bridget O'Kearne, or "Auntie O'Kearne" as she was called by those unfortunates she displayed, had operated the ten-in-one. A purveyor of living oddities, the twins were her starring act, although *act* was a poor choice of word as they did little more than stand on a dais shirtless while the audience gaped. There was money in the strange and the stranger the better and that band of skin that stretched between the two promised almost three square meals and near to a month's rent with every showing.

Each of us are born into our lot and each

46

must make the best out of what we are given. The best any of us can do is to hope. The worst any of us can do is to give up. We can do no more. We can do no less.

Mothering words courtesy of Dita that became something of a Curiosities motto. And for young curiosities like Danny and Davie, understanding that there was solace to be found in the fact of their difference, of being unlike anyone else, made the days bearable.

Luce had never learned exactly how Aurelius procured the boys' freedom, but that particular ten-in-one and "Auntie" O'Kearne had disappeared from the show circuit. There were rumors: O'Kearne had taken the twins and run out on the rent, leaving in her haste only a few meager belongings and two cups of tepid tea on the table, one full the other half drunk, as a reminder that anyone had been there at all. Another was that of a fire spurred by an overturned lamp as the burnt rug and sooted walls suggested and yet no bodies nor damage to the remaining rooms of the cramped dwelling. Nine families in a seven-room house and no one heard, saw, or smelled a thing. When her body turned up a week later in the Thames, bloated with burns on her hands and a stomach-churning

47

terror in her near-lidless eyes, a search of the waters revealed nothing of the twins.

It was a relief when nearly a month later, the tow-haired pair showed up on the Carnivale's stage, in the pink and brimming with joy. Aurelius never spoke of how the twins came to be in his care. Few dared to question, despite suspicions that he knew more about O'Kearne's death than he would ever admit. Soon the instance was forgotten. But on the rare occasion when her name was mentioned within earshot, a glance nothing short of conspiratorial would pass between Aurelius and Dita, which never failed to bring a smile and a warm embrace to the twins now safe under her watch.

"Have you gotten your things together?"

Their towheads turned in unison. "We're packed and ready," Danny said.

"Ready and packed," Davie echoed.

"Then hurry along and find Dita. See if she needs any help."

He watched the two run off in a well-choreographed trot, nearly knocking into Pretorius as they bounded belowdeck.

"Careful, boys," Pretorius called after them. He straightened his jacket, brushing the ever-present dust from his sleeve. "Lucien, is Aurelius in the deckhouse?"

"All morning."

"Good." He turned to the man who followed him. "Tell your men to bring the cart 'round and start unloading," he directed. "Try to be finished by noon. And if you have any questions direct them either to Lucien" — he pointed — "or to Madame du Reve. You'll find her belowdeck."

Orders given, Pretorius quickly slipped into the deckhouse.

"Wonder what himself and Aurelius have up their sleeves now."

Luce jumped down from the paddle box. "Wouldn't know."

Timothy Harlequin appeared from thin air not more than three feet from where Luce landed. Clad in shades of shadow, he stood stock-still, his tall, wiry frame as tense as a cat on the prowl. Only his quicksilver eyes darted left, then right before fixing on a distant point on the river's bank. After a moment, he moved forward.

"Rumor has it the old man has a new prospect."

"Listening at closed doors again?"

"Perish the thought," Harlequin said. "Although if asked. . ." He tipped his dark gray-banded Wide Awake bowler back and ran a long-fingered hand through his dark-auburn hair. A persistent strand lingered on his high pale brow. The long, thicker strands fell over a curious pair of horned protuberances that curled back like a ram's on either side of his head.

"Not necessary," Luce said. "I'm sure we'll know soon enough. Besides, there are more pressing matters to attend to. Like making sure everything and everyone arrives at the theater in one piece. Think you might be bored enough to help out with this today?"

"I'll be doing my part, no need to worry. I was thinking, though, that after we get everything settled in that you might be up for a parlor jump or two tonight. Maybe a turn at a bit of 'smithing? What do you say?"

"I would say that you are mad for even suggesting it."

"C'mon Luce, I need a bit of fun. A little Bacchanal" — with his slight brogue, this came out as *bag o'nail* — "wouldn't hurt you any either. We can keep it small and easy. A quick run through Whitechapel or Spitalfields, like the old days. Stop by a couple of public houses, down some libations, and then bug hunt outside the boozers at closing when the drunks are reeling in the street. You amuse them and I'll do the rest. It never hurts to keep a hand in."

It was a dreadful habit of Harlequin's, this

need for petty crime to satiate his mood, but mischief was in his nature and when he desired pretty things, he would not be denied. Timothy Harlequin, a living testament to Aurelius Ashe's desire for authenticity. To not only seek out a real Púca, a genuine shape-shifting trickster of Irish lore, but then have the audacity to set one loose on the stage: The potential menace to every unsuspecting city they would appear in was beyond the pale. But Aurelius often sought the things that others feared. And what real harm was there in picking pockets or the occasional house break if it dispelled the thought that the Carnivale would ever stoop to humbugs for cheap entertainment? Any devilment to keep Harlequin's tedium away was a fair trade to maintain a reputation. As for the audience? They did not need to know the truth. They only had to believe.

"You're not tempting me this time. We draw enough attention as it is. Last thing needed is you dipping into the pocket and purse of every geezer who passes by, especially as we have just docked. Think, for once; if things start going missing, expensive things, it won't take much for the suspicious to start pointing convenient fingers in our direction. It will be Prague all over again."

"Prague was a hundred years and a day

ago." Harlequin leaned against the wheel-box, an easy grin spreading across the generous Vandyke-framed mouth that made him look even more the rogue than he was. "Thieving may never be particularly respectable as occupations go, but there are times when it is essential. I'm surprised to see you of all people being struck down by a conscience at this late date. Bit like locking the barn once the horses are out."

"Neither of us is a child anymore, Timothy. We have a good thing here running what we have. Aurelius —"

"— Never cared what we did after hours as long as it didn't interfere with the show. And by the by, he is the biggest con out of all of us and you know it. Hell, you know how this show began. Or have you forgotten those early days?"

"No, but we don't have to relive them either."

"You being apprehensive about returning to Southwark doesn't change the fact that the city runs through you. The good, the bad, and all in between. Like Aurelius said —"

"I thought that you weren't listening at doors."

"I confess. I'm not very truthful." Harlequin grinned. "Do what you will, Luce, but you had best remember that once a thief, always a thief. There is no changing the past. No changing a single part."

With a snap of his fingers, Harlequin was gone, dissolved as a whiff of smoke quick as he had come.

Luce stood alone on the deck. His empty stomach churned, but not from the hawkers' shouts or the wafting heat of the open-air cooking assailing his senses.

The morning's fog had thinned enough to lift what anonymity the dockyard still held. Soon the scrutiny would begin and the idea of being watched and gawked at grated. Once he and the others left the safety of the ship to make their way to The Athenaeum, the public's eyes would be on them.

Mentally, Luce wound his way across Southwark. He knew the quickest route to the theater, but it went past the market stalls. Harlequin's parting *'once a thief'* raked his shoulders. He had preached to Georgie last night about awareness and environment and now the test was his.

The clattering and scrapes of shifting boxes echoed belowdeck. Luce saw Aurelius and Pretorius exit the deckhouse. The pair were down the gangway without so much as a backward glance before ducking into a waiting hansom.

"So it is down to me to see everyone safely there, is it?" he shouted after the cab.

Luce walked down the gangway to wait on the wharf for the haulers. But no sooner had his feet touched the dock than he noticed the boy. Most of the Larks were gone, but this one clung close, plucking whatever resolve he had to investigate the ship.

A gin-hollow sixteen if a day, the boy was little more than a flea-blown heap of rags. He had about him an expression that harbored sensitivity more than youthful daring. He did not have a shirt despite the cold. Only a thin frayed jacket and chilblains on his bare feet. His boots hung by their laces around his bony neck.

His trousers were rolled to his scabby knees and caked in mud that had congealed to an offensive stiff crust but it was still more cloth than Luce had seen on many on the river, reduced to pitiable sods who walked nearly naked to the thigh in search of their haul.

"How'd you get that?" Luce pointed to the dirty bandage binding the boy's left foot.

"Nail."

Luce nodded. He knew why the Larks worked barefoot. Lockjaw and infection be damned, it was better to find the nails and pieces of glass if they stuck into the feet than to miss one and starve. The potter's fields were full of the trade's collateral, and judging by the boy's malnourished and stunted frame all bets were off as to whether he would pass five foot one before passing to the grave.

"What's your name?"

"Michael." The boy wobbled closer. "Michael Mayhew."

Lame, possibly gangrenous. The reek of decay had sunk into his bones, flesh, and clothing. He would be lucky to live another month let alone see the New Year. "What of your parents?"

Michael shrugged.

Luce nodded. Stories such as these were all too well known. By choice or circumstance so many Larks on the river had long lost touch with their families, they had to band together ones they made among themselves. "Nobody looking for you then?"

"Not hard enough, if anyone is at all."

"The river's not been too good to you, has it?"

Michael did not quite know what to make of the man. He did not look like a demon or devil as Tosher Jim prophesied. He was just a man, a gentleman stranger taking rare notice of a Lark, with a half-kind word instead of a slap. The only certainty to be had was that he was talking to the man whom he saw on the ship's bow the night before. The man who threw light into the sky.

"She's not killed me yet," he said bold as he could.

"No, you've still some life in you. For now." Luce dug in his pocket and pulled out a pound coin. "That leg strong enough to haul equipment?"

"Yes, sir."

"Then get yourself aboard and talk to that woman on deck. Tell her Lucien sent you and she will show you what to do. Do a good job, Michael Mayhew, do as you're told and never question what you're asked or what you see, and you might find yourself a permanent home."

Luce tossed the coin to Michael, who grasped it tight in his stink-blackened hands as if it were a rope. The coin was warm against his skin.

CHAPTER FOUR

*18 October 1887, Decimus House, Regent's
Park, London*

Across the city nestled safely away from the
wharves and the rough of Southwark, a
woman of uncommon gentility spends her
morning gazing out her bedroom window.

It was a singular glass, large and wide, that
offered a glorious view of the grounds of
Regent's Park on clear days and the shadowed pitch and moonlight on even clearer
nights. On this day, seated in the gray morning haze, it was difficult to see much of
anything. Between the leaded, stained panes
and the heavy fog, the grounds were little
more than a smoky sheet.

On brighter days, the houses blessed with
this view oversaw wonders of architectural
design, where the elaborate Corinthian and
Ionic met the simple street Doric. Regent's
Park was a green escape from the uncount-
able number of densely clustered alleys and

courts that defined the labyrinthine slums within and around the cities of London, Westminster, and the wretched borough of Southwark as the hellscapes they were.

On the days when a London fog fell, not even Regent's Park was spared. All the black soot and brown brick dust of the East End, the Dials, and Charing Cross rained down on the green grass and the white walls of Decimus House like an accusation against the woman within.

Charlotte Bainbridge turned away from the window back onto her room, which was of a pleasant sort, warm and cheery with a brightness that emanated as much from the tended hearth and smooth white bedclothes as from the temperament of the occupant herself.

It was much larger than her needs required, which made her feel undeserving of her situation. She had run far from the two rooms she had shared with her mother on the edge of Charing Cross, two rooms that could easily fit within this one, but in her heart this previous life followed like the filth in the fog.

The Roses had been more than gracious with their generosity, almost as a point of pride over a girl three days from the street at the time her path crossed theirs. And she was not ungrateful, but being a beneficiary of fortune did not diminish the feeling of being an imposter.

She sank down onto the bed. It was on days like this, shadowed and gray, that she missed her mother most. Even those two rooms, soot-stained as they were, held a warm spot in her. In sunshine it was easier to shelve Mary Bainbridge into the farthest recesses of her memory, locking away her soft face and small frame, locking away the needle that pumped like a piston in her hardened fingers as she stitched and sewed until the candles waned for a master Charlotte never knew.

On the gray days, though, especially ones that followed a bad night, she longed to see those red-rimmed eyes that peered over the stacks of linen and piecework and somehow managed to look on her with love.

Thirteen years and three days. Had so much time passed?

Charlotte ran her thumb across the thick strip of satin that bordered the coverlet. She closed her eyes and smelled again rag oil and coal.

'Where is my mother?'

'She has gone the way of Guy's,' the Widow Rausch, a spindled twig of a woman, had said the day she came in her mother's place

to collect her from the charity school. *'Don't be expectin' her to be coming back out. My own William went the same way, as much from stubbornness as from the cough and ague, and he was a fourteen-stone man. I doubt a little thing like your mam will fare any better.'*

There had been little reason to doubt the woman as she had already buried two husbands and three of her seven children.

'Am I going to her?'

'Did you not hear me, miss?' Rausch's eyes hardened. *'She's in a place you cannot go.'*

It had taken two nights of tears to fully comprehend the possibility that she would never see her mother again. By the end of the third night the realization was set in stone.

'It's no matter of mine, miss, about what you're to do, so you might best be savin' those tears. You billet a night or two longer in the attic but I can't be takin' you in without some payment. Not when I've still four of my own to keep fed.'

The old woman's eyes shone like twin spits. *'You're a strong girl, a clever one, and if Mary's done right by you, she will have been trainin' you up.'*

Training up! Her mother had not trained her for anything. She could barely thread a needle and never on the first try. She did not have her mother's quick, agile hands. Beyond the maths tables, reading, and writing of the charity school, the only other thing that her mother had taught her was to be kind and that kindness would be shown in return.

' 'Course the alternative for a pretty little girl like yourself, why I believe that you could very nearly name your price.'

From that night on, Charlotte dreamed in harlot's colors with the feel of the Widow Rausch's hard fingers sunk deep into her cheeks. Satin greens, blood reds, and crisp blues swirled through her mind, shivering on the corners in the Dials.

'So this is our young Charlotte.'

The man who addressed her had appropriated the best chair in the front room of the Widow Rausch's small parlor. He was distinguished looking to her ten-year-old eyes, although she could not pin an accurate age on him. He was thin as smoke with a sunken look on a face that once might have been thought handsome but had now firmly settled into something more reliable. He wore a finely tailored black suit that was neat and modest with only a hint of his journey borne in the dust on his polished leather shoes.

'*Come closer my dear,*' he beckoned, '*no need to be shy.*'

'*Charlotte, mind your manners and do as Mr. Rose has asked,*' the Widow Rausch had said.

A smile grew as Milbrough Rose studied her face and seemingly memorized her features.

'*I think that you will find her to be a good and obedient girl. She is quite charitable, clever for a whiffet of ten, and quick to understand her duties —*'

'*You needn't sell this girl's merits to me, madame. I would not suppose her to be anything less than what she is. The Mary Bainbridge that I knew would not raise her child to be anything else.*'

He had sat back in his chair without another word and resumed his tea with a focused enthusiasm that was matched only by the speed of which the Widow Rausch bundled Charlotte and her belongings into the large black carriage. In a kick of dust the only home she had ever known fell away; her life measured by the single carpetbag at her feet. Her whirlwind entrance to Decimus House had been calmed by a tall woman with a kind but dry face and two children to either side, a boy and a girl.

62

The circumstances by which she had joined the Rose household were not questioned, and any fears dissipated that first day when young Florence, only four years older than herself and the loveliest creature Charlotte had ever seen, had taken her hand and kissed her cheek with the promise of being the best of friends. On the breast of Florence's dress was an embroidery of violets on a field of pale blue. The flowers were very fine and run through with threads of yellow and white, and the hand that made them was unmistakable.

"Charlotte?"

Her back stiffened at the sound of his voice, and the daydream of her past dissolved into the recess of her mind. Odilon Rose, the master of Decimus House, son and heir of the Rose fortune and, more important, the Rose name, stood in the doorway.

"Odilon, you startled me. I thought that you would be at the bank at this hour."

"Home for tea. Have you not been downstairs today? It is well past noon."

"Is it? I . . . . I must have lost track of the time."

Odilon sauntered toward the bed. A lean man, not unlike his late father Milbrough, he had a far sturdier constitution but little of the kindness that the elder Rose had possessed around the eyes. He wore his dark hair slicked back and his beard neatly trimmed. He ran his hand along Charlotte's cheek, his forefinger glancing the edge of her lip as he cupped her chin. A faint whiff of talc and citrus underlaid with musk emanated off his skin. She closed her eyes to his touch.

"If you are not well today, then it is best that you keep to your bed. I will have Mrs. Adelaide bring you your tea. You need your strength for what is to come."

Charlotte looked up into his eyes. They were a deep indigo that had a way of looking past your skin to the bones beneath. His hand remained on her chin though it took every ounce of restraint not to pull away. "What is to come?"

"A cure." Odilon leaned down and kissed her forehead. "I have plans to meet with a man very soon whom I believe can help you."

"But the last round of doctors —"

"Failed us. Which is why I am consulting this specialist." Odilon's fingers slid to her throat, gently folding around the curve of her neck as his thumb remained pressed to the soft underside of her chin. "Now are you going to be a good girl for me and do as I say?"

'*Do what is expected of you without question. Stay diligent, Charlotte; observe obedience, offer and accept charity without shame or judgment, and you will always be secure. You will always be loved. That is all that we can ask for. That is what matters.*' Her mother's words rang in her ears as the heel of his palm rested heavy on her clavicle. '*That is all that matters.*'

"Of course, Odilon. I can think of wanting nothing more."

It was like the weight of a hundred years lifted when his hand relaxed and stepped away from her.

"Excellent." He nodded, walking back toward the door. "I'll stop in and see you before retiring tonight. Oh, and there is no need to lock your door. I have all the keys."

Charlotte stared at the door as it closed behind him. She clutched the edge of the coverlet and could feel her fingernails pressing into her palms. "All that matters," she whispered to herself.

CHAPTER FIVE

21 October 1887, Athenaeum Theater,
  Southwark

Two frenetic days of moving, unpacking, and staging all had been leading to this. A capacity crowd despite the exorbitant fee and lack of publicity, as Aurelius was not one for advertising. He preferred word of mouth. The ship alone was often enough to set tongues wagging. Plastering a city in playbills and broadsides was in his opinion the height of vulgarity. Leave that to the Barnums and the Silver Kings of the world.

The only allowance made was the placement of a single announcement in the *Times.*

Ashe & Pretorius proudly presents
The Carnivale of Curiosities
Two-Week Engagement
Athenaeum Theater, Southwark, London

The strategy always worked. The audience always found them. No matter how dirty or dangerous, the less fit the place for finer folk to venture, the more they came in droves.

Southwark was not an exception. It was itinerant and criminal and where the Newington Crossroads met, nestled amid a rabbit's warren of aged buildings, the old panopticon stood.

An imposing four-story circular building, The Athenaeum was initially a debtors' prison until the '42 act of Parliament caused it to go the way of Marshalsea, falling into disuse and regret, until Aurelius clapped eyes on it and set Pretorius to renovate.

Luce watched from the wings as a gaggle of London's finest preened and postured their way to their seats. Men trussed up in black tie like exquisitely dressed tailor's dummies tended to ladies who whispered behind fans; pointing long gloved fingers at the near-bare stage and red silks strung high above.

Their curiosity was not unexpected. The Athenaeum was a novelty. For those newcomers who were expecting the proscenium stages and baroque elegance of the St. James or Covent Garden were soon surprised to find themselves being led not to tiered seating or private boxes but rather to banks of rich velvet seats ringing the stage's perimeter like those of an arena. The stage itself was a miracle of imagination. Fashioned as a set of exaggerated clockworks that shifted and pivoted on hydraulic lifts, it was as much an actor as any of those who coursed her boards.

Affixed to the wrought pillars and scaffolding were incandescent mantles that Pretorius had improved upon to meet his standards, which better lit the theater in a soft greenish-gold glow that added to the otherworldliness of the space. The entire house came to resemble a gilded cage in which all the patrons were displayed as much to each other as to the players, who would soon take the stage.

Proximity was everything to Aurelius Ashe. To be close to the audience was a must.

And the audience was meant to see and to be seen.

"And they call us freaks."

Columbine's breath kissed his neck like a blade. She linked a strong thin arm through his, pressing her shoulder into him. Wired and wound as a spring in anticipation of tonight's performance, she was full of an energy borne through and through and equal only to the elegance in which she carried herself. Her buttery blond hair hung in a single tight braid, pierced through with a series of silver and gold rings.

"There's more spectacle going on out there now than what we'll bring to the stage."

No one spoke truer than Columbine when it came to spectacles. Since childhood, the stares and whispers had followed her like a rumor. Despite the gloves and the veil forced on her, or the rare times when her mother in desperation rubbed her skin over with soot mixed with a penny's worth of india ink trying to make her as black as a Sudanese night, nothing took. The alabaster would bleed through like fear and make her once again a ghost. Among the West Indian and African families that populated Canning Town, where superstitions surrounding albinos thrived despite the time and distance from their ancestral homes, this absence of color had made Columbine and by association her family outcasts among the outcast.

"Paying us for the privilege of being seen?" Luce asked.

"Seen by the right people," she added. A curl had loosened itself and dangled along her brow and for a moment she was the adult vision of Longfellow's horrid little girl.

"Speaking of, I see *they* have arrived."

He followed her gaze to the boisterous party that were making their way to their seats. Every season that the Carnivale performed, a notable coterie of devoted followers came and would do so each night. In the seven years since the last of the London shows, the anticipation of the crowd had not wavered as the men and women expressed their admiration for their favorite performers by mirroring the colors of their costumes in their own clothing choices.

The most notorious was the woman dressed in shades of black and flame, the colors favored by Lucien. Florence Suskind stood as Diana sighting the field, assertive and assured in her stance as she rested her hand on the back of one of the seats. At this angle, the curves of her body were highlighted by the burners, gilding the lines from her graceful neck to her shoulders to the cinching of her waist. She showed a bold expanse of skin, unadorned by jewels and aristocratically pale, which made the color of her dress that much more jarring against her flesh. Of solid red silk and black striped satin, the skirt had three draperies of striped satin and gauze edged with fire-singed Mechlin lace. The bodice cut a V along her chest and the sleeves fell to her delicate white elbows. A black crepe rose was a cinder in her hennaed hair.

Luce was not surprised to see her. She had come to nearly every performance of the London run and then followed the Paris shows three years ago and each excursion called for more extravagance. Tonight was an overt contrivance. She would do anything to stand out. Anything to be seen by him. Anything to be remembered.

"My, my, my, but she has outdone herself tonight," Columbine teased. "And yet she still can't capture the eye of her chosen prey."

"Who says that she hasn't?" Luce shook away the tousling fingers from his hair as she kissed his cheek.

"If so, then you are the cruelest man in London." She smiled. "You'd best get ready. We start soon."

Columbine slipped away as quiet as she had come, leaving Luce to watch as the seats filled. He was about to follow when he noticed a far more familiar figure.

Pretorius, dressed in his best suit, walked alongside another man with whom he engaged in conversation. It struck Luce as odd, as Pretorius was never far from the riggings during a performance, least of all a first night. It was incongruous to see Aurelius's tinker acting as cock of the walk but he played it well, far more at ease than the man whose company he kept.

The stranger's bewilderment was as evident as the money invested in his fine suit. Luce thought he detected a hint of fear when the man scanned the theater as Pretorius gesticulated, pointing out the finer details of his restorations.

Perhaps an investor, or maybe the man brokering the new acquisition. There had not been any more talk of a new act since taking up residence two days ago.

The two men took their seats, near the front that had been especially reserved.

It was almost time.

Luce let the drape fall as he slipped off into the darkness of the wings.

CHAPTER SIX

21 October, opening night

The house lights dimmed and the raucous chatter waned to a titter. As eyes adjusted to the half-light, women waved fans lightly across their décolletage and shifted in their velvet seats against the binding stays of their corsets.

Those who had attended previous shows trembled, despite the heat of the close bodies. Those attending for the first time found the excitement contagious.

One minute passed. Then two and then . . .

The slow hiss of a tambourine silenced the last of the talk, as the throb of a drum became the heartbeat of the theater. The thin melody of a flute picked up the metallic tink of the tambourine's bells as a soft strum of strings rode the gentle plinks of a pianoforte.

Music streamed from everywhere and

nowhere. The melody, melancholy and medieval, unfurled as ribbons over the audience, lulling them as the charmer does the snake, until a loud hiss of steam caused the nervous patrons to jump and the illusion to break. A whine of metal and the stage rotated with a heavy thunk until a single spot of light illuminated the lone figure who had taken center stage.

Aurelius Ashe kept his head bowed, hands firmly gripping the ebony walking stick in front of him as the lights began to brighten. Rings glinted on his fingers.

"Ladies and gentlemen, allow me to bid you welcome!"

His voice rose no higher than conversational but carried across the theater with an emperor's strength.

"You are probably wondering what to expect tonight considering the lack of scenery, but do not be alarmed by our humble stage. Reality does not need dressing and illusion . . ." He waved his hand in a fluid motion, slicing from the air a mass of white butterflies that fluttered up into the red silks. "Illusion favors blank slates to project herself upon."

The audience stirred. Ashe tipped his hat to the applause, the tail of his cream frock coat sweeping his legs as he walked the

74

stage. Not one eye was missed in his tiger's coursing, certainly not those of Pretorius and his guest.

"Tonight you will witness extravagances that will test lines between reality and illusion. Tonight the greatest, the most astounding aggregations of marvels and miracles have been gathered under a single roof. From Paris, Warsaw, and the streets of London, expense has not been spared in the search for these wonders."

A spark grew in his kohl-lined eyes.

"And now, fair ladies and fine gentlemen, take a breath and remember this moment as you are, for I guarantee you will not leave this house quite the same as you came." A broad grin creased his powdered cheeks. "Shall we begin?"

With a flourish and a flash, Aurelius slipped from the stage. In his wake strode a lone figure. The man walked a rapid pace, head moving up and down, toward center stage. At his mark, he came to a sharp stop.

He stood in silence as the spotlight fell across his painted features. Pretorius beamed at the audience's astonishment. The Automaton remained one of his greatest works, his own *David,* so perfect an artifice that it was often mistaken for a live man instead of a construction of metal, wood, glue, and lacquer.

The machine's costume was a lavish confection of heavy white cotton with a waist-length jerkin scalloped at the neck by a black frill. Matching frills edged the jerkin's long puffed sleeves, and appliquéd across the front was a large black satin circle with an *A* and *P* embroidered in silver thread at the center. Painted on his white lacquered cheek was a small black heart.

In his hands, he held a hurdy-gurdy, which he slowly cranked as his long white fingers pressed a gentle tune from the keys. Absorbed in the mechanical man, few had taken notice of the large ornate box that was slowly opening behind him.

With each crank of the instrument echoed a hiss of steam as the box lid opened to reveal within a pedestal on which stood a diminutive figure. Dressed in a loose white frock, she perched en pointe as the pedestal slowly turned.

A black ribbon bound her long curls. With her face painted the color of porcelain, exaggerated eyes, and rosebud lips, Angelique looked every inch the doll she pretended to be.

To the delight of the audience, she quickly fluttered down to the stage to dance, leaping and spinning as the Automaton played.

Angelique brushed her hand along its arm and it began singing, perfectly in tune. She touched its knee and it began posturing, keeping perfect time to her own dance.

The odd pair continued to dance as Pierrette and Pierrot for nearly twenty minutes before the audience erupted in applause. Luce sat alone in his dressing room. Georgie and the twins would take the stage next. Then. . .

Luce sighed and powdered his already pale skin. He had considered shaving but it was an effort he did not feel tonight. From down the hall he listened to Harlequin talk and Columbine laugh. They were always so easy before a performance. Not a care in the world.

He stood and walked over to the wardrobe. From within he pulled a long red-piped black leather coat, the hem of which was seared until the leather had scarred and bubbled. Slipping it on, he stepped back and sat on the edge of the table before the mirror.

The stage would have fallen dark in anticipation. Music filtered backstage, light and fresh as spring.

For Columbine.

She would be climbing to the silks above the stage. Harlequin would be waiting stage

77

right for his cue.

Luce closed his eyes.

The heat started as a white spark behind his eyes and ran in a synapse across every nerve in his body until the first flicker rose from his palm, not as an orb of light but as a raw flame, pale and blue, that quickly engulfed his hand.

Footfalls clattered in the hall on a wave of boyish laughter that died at the doorway.

It had only been two days since the coin touched his palm but for Michael Mayhew the river seemed a lifetime ago, nothing more than a bad dream. A moral lesson. Amoral lessons.

What a shift the world had since made!

He gamboled along the back hall, passing door upon door. He kept one hand pressed to the wall, imprinting its feel, memorizing each grain in the wood just in case it was a dream and he'd wake tomorrow to the bleak gray Thames.

'What's this now? Shy are you? You've nothing I've not seen before,' Dita had said before stripping him down to the nip and pushing him back into a bath of hot water before a single case had been unpacked.

The heat had stung his cold skin back to feeling, and as for his foot Dita had drained the wound of its milky-green pus and drenched it in friar's balsam. He had barely a limp now and could wear a boot again without pain.

Michael tapped his foot on the floor and laughed. But at the dressing room door, his laughter fell silent.

A life on the river had prepared him for anything, or so he had thought. Seated on a table's edge, a globe of blue fire cradled between his hands as a pair of enormous fiery wings enveloped him like those of his own namesake angel, was Lucien.

Two days had not given Michael nearly enough time to know or understand each of the performer's acts. He knew that tiny Angelique danced, the twins tumbled, and Columbine was an aerialist. Harlequin could disappear and Georgie played violin. The master Aurelius was a conjurer and he had assumed Lucien the same, as he had seen him perform card tricks for the children the night before.

But standing here in the dressing room doorway, seeing for the first time Lucien's true abilities on full display, was as terrifying as could be expected to anyone who lived in a close city built on wood, coal, and gas. And if he was wrong about Lucien, could he be wrong about the others?

The expected smell of burning flesh was oddly absent, and there was not the slightest flinch from the man himself though the flames caressed his skin like a lover, all facts leading to assumptions that this was merely a trick, an illusion; it would certainly make sleep easier if Michael was able to force that belief. And he could almost do so, were it not for the heat and the crackle of the flames that emanated from the man.

"You needn't be afraid. I assure you I have exceptional control."

Luce opened his eyes, breaking the charm. The flames dropped to ash at his feet. He looked over the boy, slight as a lapdog and equally as skittish. He could hear the boy's heart thumping away as he clung tight to the doorjamb.

"You a'right there? Or has the cat got your tongue?"

As forbidding as he found Luce to be, he was nevertheless the man who had given him the coin, who had given him a chance. *Never question what you are asked. Never question what you see.*

He gathered his courage and looked him dark eye to blue. "Begging your pardon, Mr. Lucien, but you're wanted on stage."

Despite this timidity and tendency to jump at sudden sounds, the boy had adapted, taking quickly to his duties and to Pretorius, with whom he spent most of his time. It was always pleasing when hunches bore fruit. Luce smiled and slid off the table. The hem of the leather coat dusted the back of his legs as he strode toward the door.

Michael wedged himself as tight as he could between the door and wall.

"You'll learn that I have a ritual, Michael, from which I never waver," Luce said, laying his hand on the boy's shoulder, the heat fresh under his skin. "Before each show I take a few minutes to get into my head, to stoke the fire until I hear the music. My music. Once that begins I can then look in the mirror, and in that moment I am the Lucifer." He slipped on a leather diavolo mask that fitted the upper portion of his thin face like a second skin. His hair curled against the horns. "But until then, I'm only Luce."

The lights flickered as a soft melody played. A flutter of air shivered through the silks above. With slow deliberation they dropped and from within Columbine unfolded like a paper lantern.

She needed to do little else, as her dress alone was a necessary scandal that would keep the audiences talking. It would have been impossible for an aerialist to perform while confined in the day's fashionable heavy skirts and high necks. Instead, she wore a thin shift of blue-and-white gossamer that was little more than a suggestion of fabric, belted tight to her waist. An intricate embroidery of white flowers adorned the midnight silk corset. The laces were a brilliant yellow. Beneath the shift, she wore a pair of thick stockings dyed to match midnight.

There was an audible gasp as she took flight. The silks bound her arms as she circled above their heads. There was no net, no clear indication of safety measure, but this woman glided high above without a care, pausing her flight only to flip or spin. More than one woman and a few men averted their eyes in fear of a fall.

But Columbine never faltered.

Masked Harlequin appeared in a puff of smoke, devil sticks in hand to the audience's delight. Quick as silver, he bandied about the stage, teasing, joking, seducing. One moment here, the next there, sometimes appearing seated in the audience much to a woman's surprise. He appeared and disappeared so quickly many thought that there had to be multiple men playing the role.

Columbine danced overhead, swooping and sweeping just out of Harlequin's reach. Playfully she teased the hapless man until the music darkened and a hellmouth screen that had gone unnoticed unfolded like a concertina.

Steam billowed and from the cloud, Luce stepped out. He threw three fire orbs into the air, narrowly missing Columbine in their flight. The orbs exploded in a shower of sparks, lighting the theater but fading before any spark could alight on a patron.

The duel began with Harlequin juggling his devil sticks with gyroscopic precision. With each stick flip, Luce answered with a fiery display. First, a butterfly, then a hissing snake followed by a rose; each display was more intricate than the one before and led up to the finale, which was an incomparable work of living art created in fire.

The dragon was everyone's favorite. The most elaborate and draining of his designs, it started small, no bigger than a robin's egg of a flame in the palm of his hand. But the fire was quick to turn, shifting from an innocuous flicker to a living thing as the egg cracked and a tiny figure emerged.

A little coaxing and the fragile blue creature rose, growing at will until it outsized Luce's hands. The dragon unfurled its wings and launched into the theater, eyes red and spitting fire as it swooped over the cowed audience before returning in a spray of flames to consume his master. But it would come too late. For as the Lucifer stood with fiery wings outspread, the Harlequin had stolen away into the silks above, taking with him his beloved Columbine. Defeated, the flames fell to ash and the Lucifer returned to his lonely hell as the stage darkened, the story told.

The house broke into a wild tumult. As one body, they rose from their seats in applause. Normally staid men and women alike rushed for the stage doors like a band of unhinged revelers in the hope of getting one more glimpse of the players.

Pretorius casually stood amid the crowd, dusting his sleeves free of any wayward ash. His guest remained seated, dumbstruck by what he had witnessed. It took a tap on the arm to rouse him from his stupor.

"Shall we?" Pretorius asked, gesturing toward backstage.

CHAPTER SEVEN

Stage office, The Athenaeum

Pretorius navigated his guest through the crush, slipping nearly unseen through the doors leading to the dressing rooms.

Before a hand could be raised the closed door at the hall's end swung open, revealing the master of ceremonies himself seated at his paper-littered desk.

Ashe waved the two men in.

"Please do sit, Mr. Rose, no need to stand on ceremony." He motioned to the armchair that had slid forward. "Don't be afraid."

"Mr. Ashe sees fear as bad form. Especially on first meetings," Pretorius said, leaning back on the edge of the desk, his hand a narrow inch from the orrery. "And this is Mr. Josiah Emmett. Rose sent him along instead, quite to my surprise."

"Did he now?" Ashe sat back in his chair, hands folded across his stomach. He had stripped his stage role with the ease of the tailcoat now tossed across the armchair. His waistcoat hung unbuttoned and as careless as the loose puff of silk tie around his neck. "That sets a tone to this relationship before it has even started, doesn't it?"

"If you knew my employer you would understand how irregular this is. Odilon Rose prides himself on professionalism and punctuality. I'm afraid that this evening is an unfortunate anomaly."

"Lucky for you that unfortunate anomalies are part of my business."

Pretorius smirked in amusement at their guest's growing discomfort.

"Intriguing, is it not?" he asked, noting Emmett's curious gaze crossing the orrery. "It's been fitted with an astrarium, so not only is each spin of the planets carefully mapped but so too are eclipses and transits." He traced the brass base with the tip of his finger. "A single bump could throw the spectrum off like a pebble can a wheel. It is these causalities, Mr. Emmett — cause and effect, control and chaos, and all of the entanglements that can follow across time and space — that keep one mindful of one's own small actions."

"You've an interest in physics, sir?"

"I have an interest in everything." Ashe leaned forward, his elbows coming to rest

86

on the desktop. The powder on his face had cracked into thin brackets around his nose and mouth. "So where is our Mr. Rose tonight? I'm in the habit of dealing with the organ grinder, not the dancing monkey."

"I beg your pardon —" Emmett sputtered.

Ashe grinned. From a stack of papers, he pulled a letter. The envelope still bore the red stain of a thick waxen seal. The paper was of the highest quality: cream in color, weighty, and finely textured.

Dear Mr. Ashe, he began,

As I am certain that you receive many requests for an audience, if you could see your way to allowing me one hour of your time tomorrow evening, I would be forever in your debt. There is a matter, of no small business, that I wish to discuss. You come recommended as a man of taste and discretion.

"From the tone of this letter I was under the impression that our meeting was of a vital nature."

"I can say, sir, in no uncertain terms that that is indeed the case —"

"Yet he couldn't be bothered to come after *he* initiated this meeting. A meeting that *I* acquiesced to."

"Unfortunately he has been unavoidably detained. He extends his sincerest regrets, I assure you, but he is a busy man."

"Implying that I am not?"

Emmett flushed under his stiff collar. "Not at all. Clearly your time —"

"This is fine paper. Superior quality, wouldn't you agree, Pretorius? Unpretentious yet tastefully expensive." The page dangled between Ashe's fingers. "It is the little things that reveal the most about an individual." Slowly he tore the page into three long strips. "Proof that money does not guarantee common courtesy."

He took the three strips and began folding them together. One over the other until they were a compact square. "I don't like being kept waiting, Mr. Emmett. It leaves a taste."

"I assure you that I have been authorized with the utmost confidence to act in his stead."

"Well then, in his stead" — he unfolded the torn letter to reveal it a whole and unblemished sheet — "perhaps you could illuminate me on what it is he requires? What is his business?"

Emmett removed his gloves and tossed them into his hat. The timidity he had first displayed evaporated into a deep shade of wile. "You will have heard of teratology, I think, considering your close relationship to the *lusus naturae.*"

The Latin rolled sour off his tongue and its tone was not lost on Ashe's ears. "Crudely known as the study of monsters and a peculiar interest for a financier to have."

"It is far from being the average gentleman's hobby, I agree. But then Mr. Rose is not the average gentleman." Emmett smiled. "The writings on classification and nomenclature, while interesting, remain theoretical and incomplete."

"Surely you are not coming to me for a specimen from my troupe for his entertainment." Ashe eyed him. "Not when for the right price a body can be purchased, living or dead, for practical study — even that of a curiosity."

"But I'll not find what you have, Mr. Ashe, if the word of the man who recommended you can be trusted."

"And what is that?"

Emmett's thin lips slithered into a grin. "You once had in your company a child —"

He fished from his waistcoat pocket a folded paper. Carefully he unfolded the page and leaning forward slid it in front of Ashe. For a moment, he thought he saw hesitation in Ashe's eyes, but it was only a fleeting reflection.

Ashe smoothed the page with the palm of his hand, mindful of its delicacy and age. It was a single sheet demarcated into four squares from the fold. Yellowed and soft from frequent handling, the simple typography remained clear and familiar.

Ashe handed the bill to Pretorius. "The Lazarus Boy."

"Is the claim true?"

"That child was swallowed by the years long ago," Pretorius said, dropping the bill on the desk.

"So he is dead?"

"I didn't say —"

"You came by a recommendation?" Ashe said, cutting Pretorius short. "Who?"

"Linus Noanes."

The dropping of Noanes's name had sucked the air from the room and Pretorius watched Aurelius. A glance, a shift of his shoulders, or a lift of his brow and this Emmett would be tossed out on his ear without so much as a by-your-leave. Of all the associates whose paths he had crossed over the years, Noanes was the last name he expected to fall from the man's lips.

Emmett smiled. "He predicted that there

might be an ill reaction. Bit of a back friend, I take?"

"He would have had to have been a friend first," Aurelius sniffed.

"I recall him mentioning that you had stolen the show —"

"We had a contract."

"Binding?" Emmett asked.

"I know of no other kind," Aurelius said, a glint in his eye like that of a cat stalking prey. "And no, the Carnivale was not stolen but reborn in my image."

"Ugly times," Pretorius said. "For all involved."

"After how things were left, I wouldn't have thought he would have dared to utter my name," Aurelius said. "How did you find him?"

"Mr. Rose is a resourceful man and he has been searching many years for proof that this boy existed. It was only a matter of time before someone came forward to set us on a proper direction. This Noanes was most convincing in what he had to say. Most convincing."

"Undoubtedly." Aurelius leveled his eyes on Emmett. "What did he say, exactly?"

"That one night a boy, or rather a body, came into your possession like a resurrectionist's prize. He was sparse in detail,

91

but after three days in your workroom, the boy walked out" — he eyed Pretorius — "in your company. Sir. Noanes offered no explanation other than it had to have been a miracle of God or the hand of the devil."

He tapped the flyer on the desk. "You can imagine the implications, if this is true. A cure for death. Of course such a claim would be easy to fake."

"Easiest thing in the world." Ashe nodded to Pretorius, who took the opportunity to excuse himself.

With Pretorius absent, fear crept along Emmett's spine. There was something reptilian in the way Ashe stared at him.

"You know you are not the first to come asking." Ashe leaned forward, spreading his hands on the desktop. "Not just about the boy but of all the acts. Over the years many have found their way to my door wanting access to my. . . family. To my secrets," he ended on a whisper.

"I can assure you that no one wishes any harm —"

"So tell me, what did you think of our little performance?"

Emmett shifted uneasily in his seat.

"If you find that chair uncomfortable, I can provide another."

"It is perfectly comfortable."

"Then answer my question. It is quite simple, Mr. Emmett. What did you think?"

"It was perhaps the most perfect display of legerdemain I've ever seen."

"But . . ."

"But while unsurpassed in skill, these acts are nonetheless tricks and illusions crafted to entertain and to manipulate."

"Fair enough," Ashe said, nodding. "Though if you had suspended your disbelief if only for a moment you might have found the evening more enjoyable. My guess is that either you lack the imagination to appreciate the art, you genuinely don't believe in it, or you prefer not to."

"I subscribe to reason, Mr. Ashe. There is no reason within magic. Only deceit. Which is why I do not take Mr. Noanes's word as an absolute, and Mr. Rose, being first and foremost a businessman, requires proof that you are not another charlatan."

"You think us liars, cheats, and thieves out to pilfer the pennies from the smallest child to the deepest purses of the elite. Victimizing your precious society for whatever we can take."

It was a venomous accusation, accompanied by the persistent feeling that his mission was dredged in Emmett returning to Rose a failure. But then Ashe laughed a low, deep, and unfriendly chortle that dispersed the growing tension like a pricked balloon.

"And you'd not be far off," Ashe said. "Mr. Emmett, your doubts are both valid and entitled. It is true that our industry relies on distorting reality for profit. However, I can assure you that *that* is not my business. You ask for proof and that is the mark of the astute businessman. Were I you, I'd request just that."

A slight creak of a floorboard alerted Emmett that the two were no longer alone. The door swung open and Pretorius returned with Luce in tow.

"Ah, Lucien, allow me to introduce Mr. Josiah Emmett."

"The fire artist, yes," Emmett said, rising and taking Luce's hand. "You were extraordinary, sir."

"Thank you."

Emmett felt the heat as Luce's hand enclosed his. Just under the skin. Boiling.

Feeling the other man's distress, he quickly released his grip. "Apologies, but the dragon always takes it out of me."

Emmett looked at the tips of Luce's fingers. The skin was raw, red, and split where they had bled fire. A blood-purple blister centered his palm. "My God . . ."

"Looks worse than it feels."

"You're not in pain?"

"Nothing I'm not used to." Luce tucked his hands into his pockets.

"How?" Emmett asked.

"Naughty Mr. Emmett, you should know better than to ask a magician his secrets. Now, we all know that your business does not concern this act," he said. "Lucien, our friend here has been making inquiries into another. An old act. Would you be so kind as to open your shirt?"

Luce looked at Aurelius, but the old man's eyes told him all he needed to know. He unbuttoned first his waistcoat, then his shirt, exposing his chest. A raised white scar ran down his sternum and curved across the third left rib to his side. From the thin silver chain around his neck dangled a small cross that rested just above the start of the scar.

"Noanes had it wrong. He wasn't quite dead when we brought him to the shop, although it was not long afterward that he succumbed to his wounds. You see, Mr. Emmett, we can fix what is impossibly broken. For the right price we can even fix death."

Emmett sank back down into his chair.

"It was a gas explosion," Aurelius said. "Lucien had the misfortune of being at the wrong place at the wrong time. A large bit of iron pierced his chest. It was quite dreadful."

"Left old Luce here with a severed artery and broken ribs," Pretorius said. "Tore his back all to hell when he landed in shattered glass, metal, and brick."

Pretorius traced his finger along the massive scar. "Took me three days to craft the heart. Glass tubing and brass, mostly, to rebuild and support the remaining muscle and give the blood a place to go. I found that embedding a small bit of flint, binding it in copper wire, and connecting it to a cog created a highly effective timing mechanism to stimulate a heartbeat."

The more Pretorius spoke of the operation, the more animated he became, Emmett noted. It was the most that he had heard the man speak since they met.

"Each rotation strikes the flint, causing a spark, which shocks the muscle to pump and recirculates the blood. All and all not that different from building an automaton, I found. We're all just a mass of moving parts. Bones, muscles, and organs can easily be replaced with cogs, pistons, and cams. And having a few bits from a willing corpse never hurts either." Pretorius winked.

"Invaluable as always where mechanisms are involved."

Pretorius bowed his head. " 'Course, once I was finished stitching up the boy, the master Mr. Ashe here took the lead, bless him for that, and used his best trick. Willed our Luce alive he did."

"Am I needed any further?" Luce asked, his shirt and waistcoat openly askew after his display.

"Mr. Emmett? I leave that question to you."

Emmett shook his head, drawing his eyes away.

"You see, Mr. Emmett, science is magic and magic is art," Ashe said as the door closed behind Luce. "For years, I have been asked by fellow gentlemen of the trade, by doctors and scientists, even a publisher or two, to document my feats and commit to paper my memoirs and secrets."

He fixed the man with a cool stare. "The grand argument being the amount of money people would pay for the validation that magic is indeed real. Each time I have dismissed the idea, although I have passed an odd evening with a story told over a glass of port and then only with the best and most trusted company."

Ashe absently tapped on the desk. Emmett watched his hand, the Wheel inked into the skin. The jeweled eyes of the skull ring on his third finger winked in the light with each tap.

"Perhaps one day there will be a record offered for posterity about how I brought a dead boy back to life. Until then, that remains a tale the public is better off not knowing, and it has not been an act that I've chosen to repeat."

Ashe's hand stilled on the desk. "Now, Josiah Emmett, do please take your report back to your master and tell him I agree to his meeting Lucien but it will be for a price to be determined. We will consider it a private performance. If, and only if, Lucien decides to allow himself to be studied while we remain in London, that is his choice and his alone. As long as nothing interferes with his performance. But this particular offer has a rapidly closing window."

The orrery shifted and the planets spun.

"Tomorrow. Rose must come in person. He and I will settle the terms. No substitutes."

Ashe's dark eyes grew harder and his lips tightened to suppress a growing rage and great disgust. "And one more thing, tell Rose that I've only agreed to this because I'll not have a Hunter seeking his Giant among my company. I know his kind and I will make it clear that he is not to make a plague of himself. Now, sir, fly away back to your master."

Emmett removed his gloves and returned his hat to his head. "Until tomorrow then, gentlemen. Good evening."

"I don't care for this," Pretorius said as the door fell shut behind Emmett. "If I'd had any idea that Noanes was involved, I'd have chucked the letter no matter whose signature it was. I only showed it to you because I recognized the name."

"Don't worry yourself. It is always better knowing about snooping interests."

"It could get messy, Aurelius. Maybe I should have the ship on standby."

"You're suggesting that we run? Before I have had one word with the man himself? I think not, Pretorius. I've run once in my life and I didn't care for it. I'll be damned if I ever wear a coward's colors again. We stay."

Pretorius sank down in the chair still warm from Emmett's exit. "Wonder how much Noanes already told him."

"Spinning a tale is one thing. Getting someone to believe it is quite another. And I think I've cast enough doubt on Noanes's character tonight to give anyone pause. But his reaching out to me says that he knows enough to do so."

"You think he'll come? Rose, himself?"

"Has he an alternative? Sounds desperate for something, so he will be here. As to the rest, well, we'll have to wait see how far he wants to go. And how much I'm willing to give."

"Wait we will, then." Pretorius tapped his fingers on the chair arm. Idle fingers were the devil's playthings, his old Nani had warned, and he never let his hands still save for sleep. "Bit of a surprise to see Luce wearing that cross."

"He's been wearing it for some time now."

"It doesn't bother you?"

"She was his mother, Pretorius. If it gives him some sort of comfort, who am I to take what's left away?"

"I wouldn't think you would even want that much remaining after what she did —"

"An act as much my fault as anyone's." Aurelius leaned back in his chair and watched the orrery spin.

"Do you worry that one day he'll learn about what really happened to him? His reaction?" Pretorius looked around Aurelius's private office and all the work he had put into the room — into the whole building. "I hate to think of the damage he could do."

"So long as you and Dita, Harlequin, and myself keep our cards close then all should be well. The powder has been kept dry this

100

long, so I see no harm in his keeping a token when we've rid him of the worst. That is all that matters."

"You've acted as any good father would." Pretorius nodded approvingly.

"I will see him through this world and the next, Pretorius."

CHAPTER EIGHT

"The old man can be hard. Well done on holding your own."

Luce glanced at Emmett but remained half turned at the head of the hall outside of Aurelius's office. He refused to meet the man's eye. "You've nothing of circus or show about you, sir. You're not a kinker or a boss. If I were a sporting man, I would wager a disgruntled father or husband, a copper, or a quack. So which are you?"

"I represent an interested party."

"Ah, well that makes things as clear as stink. Interested in what?"

"My employer's interest is in you."

"Then he should buy a ticket." Luce turned to the ratlike face staring up at him. "I don't know what Aurelius is promising or selling you but I'd advise taking your business to Hyde Park."

"No, that is not where my employer's proclivities lead," Emmett said, flustered by the implication. "I should clarify that the display requested of you pertained only to who you once were."

"Who I once was? I see . . ."

"I'm not a stranger to the theater. Makeup can be clever and begging your pardon, I have to be certain before I report my findings. I did not wish to insult Mr. Ashe with my doubts. He is a formidable man, but so is my employer, and Mr. Rose has looked a long time for the boy. The dead boy. The Lazarus."

"Yes, the boy." Luce nodded. "This charmed lad is undoubtedly the most wonderful marvel of any age. More incredible than any to grace this stage. For as you can see, 'tis real 'tis true, that when the heart is lacking, glass will do."

He pulled open his shirt. "So come one, come all to see this Boy Lazarus! Three days he counted among the dead until a spark of flint and the turn of a cog returned him to the living."

Emmett stared at his exposed chest. There was something of the harlot in the way he bared himself. The cross glinted against his skin.

"Well, go on. You want to know so badly."

Emmett's faint eyes traced the jagged scar, initially looking for traces of glue or gum.

But the skin was clean; a bit marbled in color, tight and near translucent to the left of the scar. Smooth and pale to the right.

He recalled Pretorius mentioning corpses and he wondered if this were not the skin of one. Emmett hesitated, feeling the ghoul before laying a tentative hand on the raised ridge.

"Bit more to the left," Luce said.

Emmett followed the cue until a bit to the left he felt it. Not a thunderous engine racketing away but rather a far more subtle bit of clockwork; a deep, metronomic rhythm underscored by fire. Mechanically precise, unnaturally so in its unvarying pace. He felt the skin rise for only a second as the cog rotated under his hand.

He pulled back with the speed of a scalded cat.

Luce shook his head. A slow inward sort of smile reserved for things kept deep within crept across his lips. "Satisfied?"

"More than I expected it to be," Emmett whispered. "Forgive me if I've made myself disagreeable in my reaction. Insult was not my intent."

"And what were you expecting?"

Emmett paused. "I . . . I don't know. Another humbug. We've seen so many over the years." His small pale eyes grew harder

104

and brighter. He did well suppressing his disconcertion, reducing it to a display of tight-lipped tension.

"Is it uncomfortable? It is a miraculous piece of machinery but fused to flesh . . . the way it presses into the skin . . . is there pain?"

"When I was younger I noticed," Luce said, buttoning his shirt. "The cog mostly but now I don't feel much of anything."

"You don't worry about the mechanism breaking? The glass? The whole heart must be fragile."

"Aren't they all?"

Luce fixed his inquisitor with a cold stare, the humor slipping from his lips. "You've asked a good many questions tonight, Mr. Emmett. Now I would like to ask you one. How did you find us?"

"As I told Mr. Ashe, you were recommended. Though a show such as this is not going to be kept secret for long."

"It's not the show that I was speaking of. I've not been Lazarus for a good fifteen years. We stopped the act because too many interested parties came sniffing around. So we killed the boy, figuratively, and dead he's been until now."

"That is a concern best left between my employer and Mr. Ashe." Emmett's mouth tightened to the thinnest line, the corners hooking into a near-rigor curl.

"You're very good at deflecting, I'll credit you that, and you do seem an intelligent man. Your requests of proof clearly reveal a man of reason so I hope you recognize that while Aurelius possesses greatness, that does not in any way mean that he possesses good. Remind your employer of that before he accepts any promises or enters into any agreements."

Emmett's mind raced in full awareness of Luce's watch, seeking the slightest break with the extreme attention. "Is that a threat?"

"More friendly advice. They can do what they claim. They can fix anything and more." He held up his hand. The wounds were less angry, healing over with astonishing speed. "But there is always a price."

Emmett watched as a small bud of flame flickered from Luce's forefinger.

"Best be on your way, Mr. Emmett. Mind how you go."

For a moment Emmett stared at the flame, seduced by the elegance with which it danced on Luce's skin. It was hypnotic. Tilting first to the left and then to the right, following Luce's breath. If a question had been pressed at this moment, he might have confessed all. But Emmett held his tongue against the impulse.

Luce watched Emmett's lone figure disappear down the empty corridor. In less than five minutes, he would be out of the theater and onto the square, bringing the course of his stay to just under half an hour.

He smiled in the half-light. "You shouldn't be here. It is not the action of a proper lady. Not without an escort."

She emerged from the shadows in a rustle of red satin but remained at a distance. A glove mercilessly twisted in her hands. "Is it true?"

Luce could see where her eyes fixed, but as he drew near her gaze shifted to meet his. She was indeed lovely, but no matter how much she painted herself or under how many layers of flame she wrapped herself, there remained something childlike about her. He plucked the cinder rose from her hennaed hair.

"Have you a cab waiting? The streets aren't safe for a lady to be on her own."

"Is it true? What you said about —"

The press of his lips to hers stopped any further questions. Being this close she could smell on him charred cedar, amber, and clove? Or perhaps it was only residue of the pitch in his veins that had seeped through

107

his skin from the performance.

He gently folded his long fingers around her wrist, feathering small circles across her skin with the tip of one finger.

"Go home, Florence," he whispered, breaking the kiss. He released his grip on her but left in his wake a single finger mark on her inner wrist. The burn was slight, an angry pink that would be quick to fade but would scar a skin as fair as hers. "It would be for the best if you did not return. I'm certain your husband would agree."

With that he pocketed the cinder rose from her hair and took his absence, leaving her to find her way out of the theater.

Before donning her gloves, she traced the burn as she would a cherished gift. It was tender and fresh and offered a pleasure that only pain could bring. She smiled, his secret hidden away in the corner of her lip.

Meeting Aurelius Ashe had been an unnerving affair, but the exchange with Lucien had left Josiah Emmett thoroughly shaken. As a man who doubted the validity of magic witnessing the rise of the cog in that young man's bare chest, the horrendous scar and the flames on his hands elicited questions with no easy answers. What sort of man could perform a feat such as that? Could he trust what his eyes believed but his mind rendered impossible? Belief battled reason as he ascended the stairs of Decimus House.

Before he was able to pull the bell, an aging butler, whose thinning hair plastered his skull in graduated shades of gray, met him at the door.

"Mr. Emmett, you've been expected. If you would follow me, please."

Emmett was led up an imposing staircase to a small antechamber at the far end of the house. A single knock and the door fell open into a room painted a deep shade of wine. Emmett was a familiar guest of Mr. Rose and many times had frequented this room. Yet these four walls still unsettled him.

Between the shadowy portraits of the eminent dead and the cracked leather of dusty texts that choked the air with age, there was much about this room to shiver the spine. However, if one had to choose, the blame would fall square on the two cabinets of pathological specimens and medical instruments, the centerpiece of which was the complete skeletons of cephalopagus twins.

Enhancing this evening's discomfort was the protracted silence of the three men seated at the large round table that stood anchored by a heavy oak pedestal at the center of the anteroom. Their presence was a surprise considering the lateness of the hour. Linus Noanes, the man who had put them on the trail of Aurelius Ashe, was joined by two companions, whom Emmett was happy to keep at an arm's length.

Emilian Kosh, the second man at the table, had something of the traveler to him. His long dark hair, greased and dank as the city air, fell roughly into a tail at the nape of his neck. He had the beginnings of a beard and a face that bore the hallmarks of a brutal life. His nose had been broken more than once and his hands, though dexterous, wore scars from years of knives and fists.

It was his skill with the knife that first caught Noanes's eye when he was looking for acts long before the carnival became *the Carnivale.* A steady arm and a clean throw promised fair entertainment. Add the danger of a living but willing target whose life was at the mercy of a blade and you had the beginnings of a popular draw. Until Ashe came along with his more sophisticated flair.

He twiddled a penknife in his hands, picking the edges of his nails with the point while the third man, known by the single name of Skym, sat with the self-possessed silence of a monk. An emaciated figure, his skin slid across his bones like that of a well-cooked chicken. He had once passed his days performing as a Thin Man but he had long since slipped away from the stage.

"Gentlemen," Emmett said, approaching the table. "I was unaware that there was a need for your services this evening."

"Ask himself there. We've been here an hour now and not word one from him."

Himself in question was Odilon Rose, who was seated at his desk apart from the others and had yet to acknowledge Emmett's presence. Several slow minutes passed before he raised his head from the paper in his hand to fix eyes on his newest visitor.

"A carefully chosen reticence I assure you," he finally said, removing his pince-nez. "Have you news?"

"We have found him." Emmett took his place at the table. "The Lazarus Boy and the Lucifer are one and the same."

"The Lazarus *and* the Lucifer." Rose clucked his tongue. "You are certain? We've been nearly duped before."

"I felt the mechanism move. I could practically see it through his chest. Moreover, it was described to me in detail how it was constructed and then implanted, right down to the copper wires and flint. There is no doubt on the matter. They can fix any-

111

thing." A half-second pause as the memory of a flame danced on the tip of Luce's finger. "For a price of course."

"Mr. Noanes, you have been holding out on us. So the boy you saw trundled into the shop that night is today the man gracing the Athenaeum stage. And here I thought that your revelation of him being Ashe's son was your only surprise. I'm beginning to wonder what else you're hiding."

Noanes looked over to Rose. Gin soaked his breath and the collar of what was once a fine white shirt.

"I'm sorry," Emmett stammered. "Son? Lucien . . . Ashe. Why was I not told this?"

"Emmett, please," Rose said. "Did Ashe present him as such to you? No? Why do you think that is?"

"I don't —"

"Because he doesn't want to lay the cards on the table. So why should we?"

"Nevertheless, it might have been useful to have known that before going in there."

There was a silence followed by a slight shift of the chair as Rose leaned back. He pressed his fingers to his lips, absently stroking them in thought. He was an impossible man to read. Inscrutability had been bred into the Rose family as speed is to an Arabian steed. It had long proved to be an ideal trait for a financier, as any show of emotion could put one at a dangerous disadvantage whether it be in a boardroom or a drawing room. And while he was not quick to win friends, he did garner respect, loyalty, and the occasional twinge of fear from those he dealt with.

"It has been requested that you come tomorrow evening," Emmett said as the silence continued. "Ashe will only discuss your proposal in person. And he stressed that there is only a limited amount of time for consideration."

"What is your impression of the man?"

Emmett shifted stiffly against the antique horsehair chair. "He is impudent and outrageous and not the sort to suffer fools lightly. Nevertheless, he is astute so I believe he would be willing to enter into your venture for the right price and, considering the nature of his business, judgment withheld. He understands secrecy so I do not think you would need worry that he would ask too many questions. I think that he will be a challenge and not easily intimidated."

"Scared the piss out of you, didn't he?" Noanes grinned, his tobacco-stained teeth like flint corn.

Rose cast his eye across the men seated around the table. "Gentlemen, do you agree with Mr. Emmett's estimation? Truthfully if you can."

"Aye, Ashe is gentlemanly as he comes across, but don't be fooled. He is a master showman and a cunning one at that, so whatever it is that you have in mind best to ask yourself what it is worth to you. Ashe's first priority is himself and his gain, and he charges a steep price."

"Thank you for your concern, Mr. Kosh, but my business is my own and I am not paying you to question my interests —"

"You're hardly paying me at all! Definitely not enough to be mixing myself up again with that lot of devils. The day I left his stage I swore would be my last ever seein' any of 'em again. Truth of it is you will never meet a more wicked bastard this side of hell than Aurelius Ashe, hand to God I swear by that. He'll see through on his promises, make the things that you wish to happen, happen — real acts of magic even — but you best watch your back when it's time to collect because he'll take it back blood and bone without so much as dropping his smile. Though you might fare better, seeing as you work in a similar way."

"That's a damned impertinence! Might I remind you as to whom you are speaking?" Emmett said.

"Emmett, please, let us not be too hard. Mr. Kosh is entitled to his opinions, although his full judgment might be clouded due to the nature of his previous acquaintance with the man, which remains understandably sensitive." Rose fixed his eyes on the man. "Young women can be fickle creatures. Present to them a man of Ashe's standing — a man who is worldly, ambitious, monied — and he is bound to make a husband look the less by comparison."

The penknife stilled in Kosh's hands. It would only take half a second to plant the short blade into Rose's neck.

"Oh, forgive me but our Mr. Noanes here has been the fountain of information of late. Of course only with the right encouragement. About eighty proof worth, if I'm thinking of the correct bottle."

Kosh eyed Noanes, who merely closed his under the scrutiny of the table.

"Still, to be made a cuckold," Rose tutted, "and by your employer. What that must do to a man."

"It weren't like that. Until he got his hands on her, my girl was a good God-fearing lass. But it all changed after. Everything changed."

"Steady my lad," Noanes hissed under his breath.

"Mr. Kosh, are you suggesting force was used to procure an end?"

"Nah, that's not him. He has a way of talking that leaves little need of further convincing."

"It sounds as if your wife went to him willingly, and if Ashe is as powerful a man as it is claimed, I might have considered it beneficial to all," he goaded. "Besides, you gained a bastard."

"I gained an abomination. And she were a right dirty puzzle after. She wouldn't have me no more. Only *he* would do for her, at his convenience mind you. And she waited for him, beck and call. Had that son of a bitch kept his hands to himself" — Kosh glared at Noanes — "we might not be sitting here and my Isabel would still be with us."

Rose smiled at the easy provocation. "Calm yourself, Mr. Kosh, it is not my interest to open an old wound unnecessarily, but as you can see I feel it prudent to collect as much information as I can about those with whom I engage, including those in my employ. After all, forewarned is forearmed, as they say. Information has often proved beneficial to me, as you are well aware. I'm sure that you can understand that given the matter I hope to engage

116

the man's services for, it is imperative for me to know as much as I can about Aurelius Ashe. Untidy family ties aside, I want to know every other infraction he has made, every lie, every cheat, every crime —"

"Every crime?" Noanes asked. "Tall order."

"If he has so much as looked cross at the queen I want to know. No one is that careful. Which is why in this instance you three can aid me best. You have all been in his company. You lost your livelihood to him. Kosh, both his wife and his job. And you, Mr. Skym, you have been quiet on this matter. What did Ashe take from you?"

Skym thought a moment before stretching his long thin fingers flat on the table. "I know where my loyalties lie. And they aren't with Aurelius Ashe. Nothing for me to stay for."

"You want to know the nature of the man? I've tried figurin' that out myself." Kosh bowed his head. "Truth is, for the most, the show circuit is by and large a con. Yeah, there are authentic players. Jugglers, acrobats, knife throwers like myself, and human oddities and genuine freaks" — motioning to Skym — "but among them and us are the fakes. It's all for show. The illusionists, there is nothing to them and at the end of the day all we're doing is running a game for the flatties, but there's no harm, no foul. Ashe isn't like that. He's made it real. All of it. The Harlequin, I've never seen anyone do what he does, all that disappearing and reappearing out of smoke and thin air. Walking through walls as if they were paper. I tell you it ain't human and you'll not be convincing me that that's a work of God's hand any more than the fire that bleeds from the boy."

"Still no love for the by-born? *If* he was that. He could be your son."

"Lucien Ashe is no blood of mine." Kosh could barely contain the bile in his voice. He ran his thumb across the knife blade.

"It's all well and true that there is a strangeness to them," interrupted Noanes. "Ashe is a dangerous man. Only a damned fool or a damned soul would think of tangling with him. I've no love for the man and my reasons to hate run as deep as Kosh's here, but to the man's credit, he'll not be the first to betray. But if you cross him or he thinks that you have, then —" Noanes ran his finger across his throat, mocking a slash. "But he does have a weakness. An exploitable one."

"Go on, Mr. Noanes."

"You see, Mr. Rose, we're not like you and

your kind. We're not a settled lot because there's no cure for circusing. Once a man has been bit he makes his home where he can and his family with whom he finds. Ashe has found his. Untidy as it has been, he will go to any length to protect them. Particularly the one you want to see. He holds Lucien first in his heart."

"Ashe was adamant that he not have his company hounded," Emmett said. "That was one of his stipulations to your meeting."

"You will find the company equally loyal to him. And equally dangerous. Best tread with caution," Skym said.

The severity of the threat laced through the Thin Man's warning was effective on only one in the audience. "If I may speak frankly, I'm not fond of this scheme." Emmett sank back in his chair. "You and I have discussed this matter at length and after having met the man and his son, I must ask again if you've truly thought this all the way through."

Rose's eyes rolled like thunder over Emmett. "I assure you that I have never known my mind to be more decided."

"There are many unknown factors in this endeavor, with no guarantee that it will prove a success. You are putting your trust in —" Emmett paused, painfully aware of the three seated around the table. "Perhaps there are some things best left to their own course."

Rose smiled, his lips drawing back over an exquisite set of teeth.

"Your concern is both touching and unnecessary, Emmett. I am well aware of the risks, but I am equally confident that Ashe and his man Pretorius have the skills required to fulfill this particular task. And should anyone decide to become ambitious beyond the needs of the matter at hand, you have my sincere assurance that those parties will not live long enough to see their profits."

"You're not suggesting —"

"That is precisely what I am suggesting. And you needn't look so stricken, Mr. Kosh. I imagine this is not the first time such a solution has been called on."

Kosh refused to meet Rose eye-to-eye. He turned instead to the knife in his hand and to the way that the light ran along the blade like past deeds.

"And despite the casual accusations that have been made against Ashe, Mr. Skym and Mr. Noanes here certainly do not have the cleanest hands in London," he continued. "As I said, I never make an investment without doing my research first, gentlemen, and taking out insurance to bar against any ugliness that might arise. I have no qualms in taking whatever steps are necessary to eliminate any potential liabilities. Have I made myself understood?"

Noanes's face had grown red and he looked down the gin blossom he called a nose. "Perfectly, Mr. Rose."

"Very good. Then we shall consider this meeting closed. We will be in touch. Oh, and Mr. Noanes, if you and your compatriots would please leave by the back entrance by way of the park proper. Appearances, you understand."

"I could go into any public house between here and Whitechapel and find more reliable thugs than those three," Emmett said after the men had absented the anteroom.

"Tell me, what was Ashe's reaction to Noanes's name?"

"He was not pleased. It unsettled him, not greatly but there was a shift toward wariness."

"You see, then, they have their uses." Rose stood, hands thrust into his pockets. "And what of mine? Did Ashe make any note of *my* name?"

"By profession only. If otherwise, he hid it well. He made no connection between yourself and your parents nor any allusion to having known them at all."

"Good." Rose smiled. "I look forward to seeing his face when he does. I've the strong impression that he is not a man who wants his secrets known and the longer he is left guessing as to what Noanes has shared, the more cooperative he'll be."

"They said he was dangerous and I have to agree. There was something about his nature, his confidence —"

"Dangerous? Emmett, the man is an illusionist by trade, a trickster and a liar. He is going to exude confidence if he is to maintain his status and allure. He has elevated what should be no more than a penny entertainment to something — well, you've seen with your own eyes those who attend his shows. Only the best of society come out to see him and his band of merry freaks, yet he performs on a stage in one of the most repulsive areas of London. I have heard that even Princess Beatrice has attended a show. In Southwark!" He slammed his hand down on the desk. "They all dance attendance on him, which is why I made him wait."

"Leaving me to dance instead," Emmett said. "Another detail you left absent."

"He lured my parents to his door, the

soundest people I have ever known, and I needn't mention the hold over my sister. Clients and acquaintances all have attended one, two, sometimes as many as five showings. I have resisted — despite my own curiosity — as such entertainments do not meet my taste. But I have observed the effect on those who have."

"What have you seen?"

"An unusual pattern of good fortune. Certain clientele who, after mentioning attending a performance that included the opportunity to meet the proprietor, all saw in a matter of days, months, a sudden influx of money from a fortuitous windfall. Or a much-longed-for engagement or a promotion. Look back to my father's rapid ascension within the bank. How does one go from head clerk to board member and president within a year? Not impossible, to give credit to the man, but highly unusual even with his connections."

Emmett shook his head. "The two events are not mutually exclusive."

"But damned convenient."

"So you believe that Aurelius Ashe is some sort of kingmaker?"

"No, but I do think that he holds the keys to accessing those who are."

"And how does any of this help Charlotte?"

A smile drifted across Rose's lips. He rose from behind his desk and sauntered over to the glass case containing the skeleton twins. "Noanes said it himself, Ashe is a showman. He is the shiny lure that brings in the catch, so it wouldn't serve him well to admit that his greatest achievement, the Lazarus Boy, was nothing more than a medical fraud. That would not look good for anyone, if that were to become public knowledge."

"I saw things this evening that frankly I cannot explain. And I saw the grotesque scars on his son's body that were not any product of theatrical makeup. They were real."

Rose ran a finger along the edge of the case, his eyes stuck to the empty sockets that looked back at him like voided moons. "I don't doubt that you did. I merely doubt that the son was as dead as Noanes claimed him to be. Mesmerism, hypnotism, illusions — I'll credit the man with any of those skills. But raising the dead." He shook his head. "Dead is dead, Emmett. There is no coming back from that. I'm not discounting that there was a grave injury and that this Pretorius did craft a false heart, but I think that Ashe has access to someone of great medical skill and that is *the* someone that I need to meet. How do you implant a heart? A heart, Emmett! And keep the patient alive? I need the man who can do that."

"Do not take this as impertinence," Emmett cautiously broached, "but you have already met with every reputable and venerated physician affiliated with the Royal College, as well as guest speakers and visitors, on the matter of Charlotte's disorder. Do you not think that someone would have stepped forward by now with a proposal? To date all have said that she is incurable because there has not been enough progress made in the field."

"And there have been some among these same educated men who have gone on to whisper in private to me that her affliction may be of a supernatural origin. Her malaise, paleness, fatigue, dyspnea, weight loss" — he counted off — "the very same symptoms that can be plucked from the pages of any penny dreadful. That I have not yet been advised to stake her to the ground upon her death is a wonder. So as I see it putting unquestioned faith in these men is no different from finding out what Ashe can offer."

"What about the harm to Charlotte? Speaking as your solicitor, I have to think of the ramifications should something go horrendously wrong. You are proposing entry into a dangerous unknown. At least in a hospital there are trained professionals and assurances that all is aboveboard and the care given and procedures attempted are steeped in science. There remains some primitive thought within the profession but most physicians are broader-minded than that. Bringing in someone like Ashe, a magician of all things! With the thought that he might have access to some brilliant but possibly mad doctor! What do we really know about *him*? What is our recourse? Why the risk?"

"Charlotte is mine, Emmett." It was a quiet declaration yet it bore more force than the north wind. "She entered this house as Father's ward, but she became my purview."

Rose cast a glance to the large portrait of a regal woman, dressed in pale lilac, that dominated all of the other portraits in the room. Catherine Rose. Her dark auburn hair was tastefully up swept from her neck and face. The great portraitist Sargent had so perfectly captured the cold indigo of her eyes and the translucence of her marble skin that she practically leapt from the canvas.

"It was Mother, God rest her soul, who directed me to watch over Charlotte. To do with her as I saw fit for as long as we both lived under this roof, a state that I see neither of us vacating. So while I do appreciate your concern for her well-being —" Rose grinned and for a moment, cast in the glass, the twins smiled back in the shared conspiracy best suited to children. "— do not think that you can dictate how I oversee to her needs."

Emmett settled back in his chair. "And if Ashe refuses, what then?"

In three languid strides, Rose was stood before him. "Have you not yet learned that every man is persuadable? Charlotte has her charms as your discreet glances would attest."

Emmett could feel the heat of blood rise in his cheeks.

"She is dying. By appealing to the man's sympathies in this manner, it would be cruel to refuse. Should he not be moved, as I said earlier, Mr. Noanes has been a fountain of information, though I suspect he is wisely holding some cards back. There is more to be plumbed, more to be used, and perhaps it is best not to give the entire game away. I know I never do."

"I certainly hope that I never have the misfortune of falling from your grace, as you are a man I would not care to have as an enemy." Emmett stood to leave. Normally he pitied the person Rose would lure into his trap, but this time, the feeling was less pity for the victim and more fear for his employer. There was something about Aurelius Ashe and in what he himself had felt tonight that made Noanes's warning ring true.

It ain't human. It was troubling.

"I saw Florence tonight. At the theater."

"Did you?" Rose said. "And how is my sister? In the rudest of health, I'm sure."

"She was skulking in the shadows backstage. After the show. She didn't think that I saw her. I had just parted from Lucien Ashe, for whom I believe she was waiting. I said nothing, but with your current plans, I thought it best you should know."

"I shall have to have another talk with her." Rose smiled. "Thank you, Emmett, efficient as ever."

CHAPTER NINE

21 October, Seven Dials, London

"I'm telling you, the man's got balls of solid brass if he thinks he can tether the devil to his lead."

Noanes shouted over the roar of laughter from the raucous group of young men leaning on the bar. It was a brisk night down the Dials and the two women behind the bar dispensed drinks as quick as they could, pulling pints and spirits from the glossy array of bottles shelved before the mirrored wall. They were as fast with their hands as with their repartee, their agility inhibited only slightly by striped-yellow corsets that cinched their already ample bosoms almost to their chins.

"He's in for a rude awakenin'. The way he dismissed us from his sight with barely a listen to what we had to say. Out the back entrance through the park. 'Appearances, gentlemen,' as if we were common tradesmen. He has no idea what he is getting himself mixed up with." He emptied his dram of whiskey in one gulp. "And you — you were free with the information. Was it wise telling Rose all about Isabel? He preys on connections like that, especially if he thinks you want them hidden. He's going to own us forever."

"I told him no more than you did. Now he thinks I'm a damned fool and he fully knows you're a feckin' drunk! He asked for the truth, so I told it. But only as much as I thought necessary."

"Yeah, there are some things he might be better off not knowing," Skym said, nursing his pint. "Rose will find out soon enough and then on his head it will be."

"He'd not believe it. Besides, where did not knowing get us? We lost it all to Crossroads." Noanes swallowed back the rising rage. "That's what pride gets you."

"Yeah, and thanks to that pride and a generous purse we've a night ending at the best establishment the Dials can offer." Kosh slid another whiskey in front of Noanes.

"And it's a purse I'd like to keep filled, thank you kindly."

"I don't think we'll have an empty coffer anytime soon," Kosh said.

"Oh, what makes you so sure? Aurelius sights one hair out of place and he'll eat him alive."

"Rose might be a posh prig but he's a ruthless one, which is all the better to our advantage."

Noanes eyed Kosh narrowly. "What are you getting at?"

"Rose is as dirty as they come. He might play the gentleman banker for his precious appearances but he's a filthy crook. Both he and that Emmett are up to their eyes in schemes and here we are in the middle, called on to serve when things get a bit sticky, and we make a pittance compared with what they reap."

"Bite the hand that feeds?" Skym said. He slipped a pinch of tobacco into his mouth, shifting it into his cheek until the lump showed under his thin, veined skin. "Did that once before. Didn't get us far."

"Whatever scheme Rose has going that he needs to indenture himself to Aurelius Ashe, well —"

"It involves that girl of his," Noanes said. "I always thought there was something odd about that arrangement. Ward, my aunt Fanny. For a man who concerns himself and takes advantage of others' peccadilloes, it's pretty damned brazen to keep your whore under your own roof in plain sight."

"Who's going to challenge him? His victims are scared to cross him because he knows too much and enough people in the right places. Not one of 'em would have the guts to turn the table on him even if it meant their freedom." Kosh took a long draught off his glass.

"Nobody is going to take freedom over ruin," Skym said. "Too much care given to what others think."

"Hear me out. Ashe won't say no to what Rose is planning, especially if it concerns a girl in need. He has a weakness for the pretty, fragile things." Noanes could barely contain the thrill that was coursing through him as the pieces fell together in his mind. "Rose is looking for a miracle but he hasn't any idea the door he's opening up and I'm not going to be the one to tell him. Like you said, he's not going to believe it anyway."

"Because if he knew the truth of what Ashe is, he'd run a bloody mile before ever conjuring his name." The knife was in his hand before he even knew it, so common it felt that it was an extension of himself. Kosh stroked comfort from the blade.

"Rose won't like the terms. He will try to

winnow out by any way possible," Skym said.

"Two ruthless men, each trying to control the other. They'll destroy each other."

"And we'll be there to pick up where they left off. I don't see Mr. Emmett being much of a challenge and Pretorius cares only for the theater, which would leave us Rose's 'clients' and all those who benefited from Aurelius's help. That's a long list of deep pockets." Kosh raised his glass. "Gentlemen, we can be back on top where we belong."

"Rich men."

"Free men."

"By the breath of God, I do like the sound of that." Noanes grinned. "Mary, love." He waved at one of the women behind the bar. "Come on, let's 'ave another if you'd be so kind."

After Mr. Emmett had retired to his own home, Odilon Rose walked the silent halls of Decimus House alone with his prospects. Every nerve in his body stood on alert at the idea that after so many years Aurelius Ashe was within reach. Emmett's confirmation that the Lazarus Boy not only existed, but was in fact the man's son, erased any doubt that he was on the right trail.

He holds Lucien first in his heart.

Rose allowed himself a few seconds to gather his thoughts. One breath. Two. By the third his heart had returned to a normal pace, though his mind continued to spin.

He had not been forthright with Emmett about every aspect of his family's ties to Ashe. Yes, it was true that his father's fortunes turned for the better following his parents' attendance at the Carnivale. The family prospered well beyond anyone's dream. But it was not without sorrow. That was one thing he neglected to inform Emmett of. That every time fortunes rose, there followed a fall.

Odilon continued along the second floor before pausing at a locked door.

His late mother Catherine's room was sacrosanct, and he had not entered since the night of her death. Proud, ambitious, admired to the point of fear, he had adored every aspect of her. Until sorrow came. Louisa Sorrow Rose, her third and last child, whom the Lord, if he had been kind, would have taken before her first breath rather than allowing her to linger for days in her monstrous condition. Louisa remained a grief that his mother would wear like her finest gown.

He pressed his hand to the door, the grain

smooth and cold. It felt the same now as it had five years ago when his mother had taken to her bed.

Three days she fought a fever. Despite twice-daily bleeding, cold compresses, and sleep, she showed no recovery and he had taken to lingering at her door, waiting to be needed and listening to her delirious ranting.

But on the night of her third day of confinement, delirium turned lucid and through the door he heard her speak.

"I remember but when you said you would not . . . I came to you because something had to be done . . . I did but . . . yes . . . yes. No, that I did not agree to . . . you have twisted . . . It was not to be him. I did not intend . . . The girl . . . it was to be her."

Opening the door, Odilon found her in conversation not with a guest but with herself. She was bolt-upright against the pillows, hair a wild nest and eyes wide to a horror that was hers. She stared intently at the emptiness at the foot of her bed.

"Mother?"

"I understand, but why Louisa? She was innocent . . . That was cruel of you. What did I do for her to deserve that? What did I do that was . . . How can you deny her . . . she bore your marks . . . No."

"What about Louisa?" Odilon asked, sliding to his knees at her bedside. "Who are you talking to?"

"You seek my confession when you forced the sin! . . . Look at what you made of me, Mr. Ashe!" She raised her hands. "Do you see the blood? Now look to your own hands and the indelible stain that is as much yours as mine. We did this, you and I."

Odilon reached for her only to be rebuffed. "The doctor, I'll go for him."

"What? . . . What do you have there?" Her hands fell limp in her lap. "Oh. . . please, no. . . not that. I will g—"

Her eyes grew wide and wet with tears. Odilon touched her hand and for half a second she turned to him as if to a stranger. "Run, boy . . . cling to God and run! He has loosed a hound. . ."

Odilon drew back from the door, heart pounding. Her scream still rang his ears in the moment before she had fallen back onto the bed, chest sinking under her exhalation as if a great weight had plummeted and pressed the air from her body. Blood frothed at her mouth, her eyes blind and empty to the ceiling above.

Aneurysm, the doctor would diagnose, but he knew better. She had died of fright with the name of Ashe on her lips and a howl in

136

the wind.

It had taken these last five years to methodically piece together as much of the puzzle as he could. Still pieces were lost, information unconfirmed, but enough had been found to push forward. It would be a killing of two birds with one stone. Use Ashe for what he was worth, see to Charlotte's cure, and then afterward, while still within a finger's reach . . .

He grinned at the thought. Louisa was the ember that set the fire that burned through the family. But it was Aurelius Ashe who lit the match and he would finally have vengeance for what was done to his family, even if it meant tearing the fleshy pound from the man's bones strip by strip.

Rose climbed the stairs to the third floor. Reaching the door near the end of the hall, he tried the knob, pausing at the lock and fumbling the keys from his waistcoat. The floorboard creaked as he opened the door. The room was dark save for the triangle of light that stretched into a square as the door swung wide and exposed the sleeping occupant.

It was good that she slept. She needed the rest, though he had partly wished she had not yet retired. He walked toward the bed. The pale light softened features sharpened of late by pain. It was a cruel affliction, leukemia. *Weisses blut.* White blood. No matter the language, it remained an ugly word.

On the bed table stood a glass with water and a bottle of Fowler's solution. There had been so much promise in that little bottle. He leaned down and kissed her. There was a faint taste of the tonic on her lips. Medicinal. Arsenical.

A familiar prickle lifted the hairs on her arm as the door shut and the key turned in the lock. Charlotte blinked into the dark. She wiped her mouth with the back of her hand to rid the taste of him from her lips.

CHAPTER TEN

22 October, early hours, The Athenaeum

It had not been entirely a lie, what Luce had told Emmett about pain. He did feel it, but what he felt was a phantom: the heat and the cold, the tingling and the touch and every so often an ache deep in his chest where muscle met mechanism. In the spot where the memory of the missing half resided. Once, mere months following the surgery, the cog had seized and an eternity had passed in a series of seconds, for time has a way of measuring itself not by the quality of the sensation but by the quantity.

The moment had left him gasping. It had felt as if a knife blade were scraping between his ribs, the tip exploring the tissue in a series of prods before the cog slipped and the rotation had resumed.

Harlequin had been there. The two shared a bed then and though only a boy of ten himself, he had wit enough to hold Luce down and steady him until the pain ceased and his breath returned before he faded off to summon Aurelius.

Luce shifted on his narrow bed. The pillow was cool against his cheek. Slipping his hand under his shirt, he traced the underlying gear.

Ten. Nine. Eight. He counted back the seconds until he felt the ripple of the cog turn before falling into an unsteady sleep penetrated by a quicksilver gleam.

The scissors were cruel but steady in Pretorius's hand as he had snipped the loose skin, widening the wound to better see the damage. Every tug and tear was an exquisite act of pain, far beyond anything Luce had felt before in his short life. Heavy bleeding had forced Pretorius to rely more on touch than sight but once his fingers were in and he felt the sheared shards of rib impaling the remnants of the heart, he knew what needed to be done.

How bad?

I'll need to rebuild from scratch. Going to need a few parts.

Send for our friends to pay a visit on Crossbones.

Luce started out of his dream in a sweat. He reached for the lamp but paused, hand in midair.

To the denizens of Southwark, the East End, and the rooks of St. Giles, where one was as likely to have one's pocket picked as to have one's throat slit, a heightened sense of vigilance ran as thick in the blood as the grease in the air. Anything out of sort, any creeping doubt was cause enough for the alarm to ring.

Whomever it was, was close enough to cause the scars on his back to itch.

"Timothy? That you?"

A spark and his palm burned gold. A large marmalade cat, who had acquired the name Nicodemus the first night he had turned up and appropriated the foot of his bed, blinked into the light before settling his head back onto his six-toed paws.

The room was a panic of shadows as the flames danced across his fingers. But amid the panic, she stood.

His eye fell on the door that was ajar, the door that he clearly remembered locking before going to bed. It was there that she was nestled, in the dark void between the jamb and the hall, peering at him. She wasn't in flames, as he remembered, but whole, and it was only the hollowness of her pale face and the blackness where her eyes should be that spoke to her being anything but living. He heard her rasping,

141

her mouth moving without words. He attributed the noise to her burnt lungs. But by the light of his hand, he could see the gash that choked its way around her throat, a single slash that snagged her breath on the ridges of the wound.

Seconds stretched into minutes before he slipped from the bed and padded over toward her. She cowered as he reached to her, the fire on his hands driving her into the shadows. "Mum." The theater was still with only the hiss of gas and the faint tick of the gear in his chest to be heard. More than once his eyes tricked him into seeing other shapes and other shadows that all retreated as quickly as they had come but still silence.

"I'm sorry, I'm sorry." His voice quavered before the all-too-real sound of a door, creaking open then quickly closed on remote footfalls that coursed down the narrow alley.

If there was someone among the shadows, he never saw as he retreated to his room, bolting the door behind him.

Luce washed quickly. Each droplet of water was a relief as it carried away the sweat and memory of the night. A fine line of dark stubble defined his jaw, but he would wait until evening to shave.

He retrieved a shirt from the trunk. Well worn and not nearly his best but it would do. After smoothing his hair as best he could, he headed downstairs.

"You look like hell," Dita said.

"You're too kind," Luce said, crossing the kitchen. He stopped at the counter and pulled down from the shelf a bottle of Powers whiskey.

"Bit early for that, don't you think?" Dita reached up and brushed the hair out of his eyes. "You didn't sleep again."

Luce shook free of her hand. "Do you ever stop playing mother —" The sparks of white dangling from her ears caught his eye.

"My God, you couldn't help yourself, could you?"

"When it's there for the taking . . ." Luce turned as Harlequin faded into view. He was rocked back in his chair, one booted foot propped up on the table, a broad grin creasing his face like that of a debauched Romantic. His old green silk dressing gown gaped open over his white shirt.

"Hope you took more care leaving that house than when leaving this one."

"What are you on about? I didn't go anywhere last night. I happened to liberate a fine lady of those baubles at the show.

143

Along with two bracelets and" — he slipped his hand into the pocket of his dressing gown and retrieved a gold watch — "this. You want it?"

"I heard you leave. I heard the door leading out to the alley close."

The chair legs hit the floor as Harlequin leaned forward. His quicksilver eyes fixed firm on Luce's own blue. "I don't need doors, Lucien. Remember?"

"Boys," Dita said, setting the table with coffee and hot meat pies. "Now, what's this all about?"

"You're saying you weren't roving about last night?"

"I can assure you I wasn't."

Not one taken by any delicacy of nerve, he was nonetheless shaken by Harlequin's denial.

Timothy was something of a ghost himself, a hobgoblin trickster who could be whatever he needed to be at any given time. Whether he chose benevolence or malevolence was a matter of mood or circumstance, and these particular talents allowed him to haunt house and street, pocket and purse. That was his reason for being. It was his purpose in which he took great pride. He might not always be truthful but he never told outright lies. Not to him at least.

144

Luce slumped down into the chair across the table caught between bewilderment of his certainty about Harlequin's presence and the unexpected realization that he was indeed speaking the truth.

"Lucien, are you saying that someone was here?" Dita asked. "I didn't hear anything and I was up reading well past midnight."

He was on the verge of answering but his mind drifted back. Her ragged breath was back in his ear and the quick footfalls exited down the cobbles of the alley outside.

"Well I — I don't know. I thought I heard someone."

"It was probably Pretorius down in the shop. You know he keeps late nights. Could have been cats," Harlequin said before taking a bite of pastry. "Could've been anything. Could've been nothing. Either way, we've little worth taking if there were thieves. I don't know many who would want to traipse about in here after dark. Never know what might be lurking in the shadows. This is a house of unhappy memories, as you know."

His tone was noncommittal, cool, and calm, and Luce was not sure he completely agreed with Harlequin's theory but it did seem the most reasonable. There were indeed two Southwarks. Two Londons. Two worlds for that matter, where the flesh lived uncomfortably close to the shade and vice versa. And on occasion, as he well knew, there was a crossing of the realms.

"Of course we'll have a look 'round for any signs of robbery, just in case," Dita said, laying her hand over Luce's. "I'm worried about you, love. You have been a bit off ever since we landed. Did you have another dream?" She squeezed his fingers. "Another visit? Or was it Aurelius's visitor?"

Luce offered a crooked half smile, leaned over, and kissed her cheek. "It was an odd night all around."

"I think that you are not being completely honest with me. Or yourself for that matter. You know what I've always said about bottling things up —"

"— that one way or another the bottle will break and all will spill out. For better or worse."

She brushed an errant curl from her cheek, lodging it behind her ear. "You used to talk so freely with me. What's changed?"

Luce pressed his hand over hers. "Nothing, I —"

"Am I interrupting?"

Aurelius stood in the doorway. His red dragon brocade waistcoat was undone, and shirtsleeves rolled to the elbow revealed the

Gordian knot that embellished his left forearm in rich black ink.

Dita looked at Luce. "No, not interrupting anything at all," she said. "Coffee, my love?"

"Please." He sauntered over to the table and seated himself at the head. "I'm glad you're up, Luce. We are being paid another visit this evening, as our Mr. Emmett will be returning and bringing with him his employer, one Odilon Rose."

"Odilon Rose? The banker?" Harlequin said. "What would he want with us?"

"I don't know yet, but I've a feeling it's big and that it in some way concerns our Lucien. You will be present for our meeting?"

Luce looked at his father, the residue of Emmett's cold hand still on his skin. The gear shifted.

"Wouldn't miss it for the world."

Aurelius smiled. "Never doubted you would."

It had not been an easy night but Charlotte Bainbridge was determined to make an appearance at breakfast. She made her way slowly from her room and down the long hall of Decimus House, each step a show of sheer will. This betrayal of her body was the latest in a series of cruel acts life had bestowed on her but she acted the good Christian, counted her blessings with a smile, and did her best not to complain save to the devil late at night, when her bones ached the most.

Carefully she maneuvered her way, keeping one hand on the wall for support but cautious not to press too hard, lest her hand mark the paper. It would greatly displease Odilon if his precious walls were damaged in any way, and he had an eye that could spot a single fingerprint amid the proliferation of vivid green vines and gold leaves.

It was by taking this care that she noticed the door to Odilon's office ajar. Unusual, she thought, as he like his father before him always kept the room locked when not in use.

"Odilon?" she said, pushing the door open enough to peer inside. She had been in this room less than a handful of times but the impression remained: an unmistakable sort of dread that could follow a man to his grave, heavy with the scent of turned loam, yellowed paper, and oppression.

Curiosity proved greater than pain, and Charlotte stepped farther into the office.

The green fronds of two large ferns offset the blood-red walls but did little to shake the chill from the skeleton twins housed in glass that watched her, or from the rows of worn books. The portrait of Catherine Rose loomed as large from the wall as she had in life. Charlotte shuddered. Even in paint, the woman's eyes had the power to lift the hairs on her arms. She inched past the round oak table to Odilon's desk.

He was never a man of sentimentality. There were no personal objects nor any semblance of clutter beyond the needs of business displayed on the mahogany desk. Papers, many bearing the embossed monogram of T. Rose & Co., were neatly stacked to the right of a pen-and-blotter set. But among this order, one paper stood out from among the others.

Little more than a scrap, it lay in the center of the desk as if left with the reader's intent to return shortly. As Charlotte drew closer she could see that it was an aged news clipping, barely legible save for the word *fire* in bold black lettering.

"Is this how ladies spend their mornings? Snoopin' about places they shouldn't be?"

Charlotte spun like a rook in a net to meet a man dressed in the shabbiest coat and trousers she had ever set eyes on. Frayed cuffs, dust on his shoulders, and shoes whose soles were held together by a prayer.

His thinning hair was plastered against his head in a sheen of grease that practically dripped down into his thick muttonchops. A pair of beady dark eyes leered at her over a bulbous and bumped nose. He stood dead-center in the door like a malformed lump of pig iron, barring any escape that would result in her having to touch him as she passed.

"Who are you? What are you doing here?"

"The name's Noanes, miss. And I'd be tipping that there hat to you were it on my head."

Quick as she had been to enter the office, this was the first that she noticed the hat on the floor near the foot of the oak table. "Tradesmen are not allowed upstairs," she said, the strength of her voice stronger than that in her knees.

Noanes laughed and stepped up to the table. "Good thing I'm not a tradesman then."

"You cannot be here. Please leave, sir! Or I'll call for Mr. Rose."

"No, I don't think you will," he said, picking up his hat. "Your Mr. Rose is a particular fellow and I've my doubts that he would appreciate you nosing about his personal papers or whatever it is you were —"

"Is that an accusation? Are you calling me

a thief?" Charlotte huffed. "Who are *you* to have the right to question where I go in my own home?"

"Beggin' your pardon, miss, but this care you're taking in not being seen, while no matter to me, I would hate to accidentally let it be known that you were creeping about —"

"Odilon Rose would never take the word of a man like you —"

"You would be surprised by how much of my word he is willing to take. Why, last night —"

"Last night?"

"Had a chinwag of business with your man, sitting right here at this table. So good it was I came back this morning for another chat. That's how I lost my hat," he said.

"What sort of business would Mr. Rose have with a —" The glare in Noanes's eye unnerved her from saying what she wished to say. "I find it odd and . . . and impertinent that this weak association of yours has led you to believe that you can wander freely about this house. I can assure you that Mr. Rose —"

"Gave me full allowance to retrieve my belongings. And much as I'd enjoy spendin' the day with a pretty lady like yourself" — his eyes threatening over the course of her body — "I've somewhere to be." He returned his hat to his head, tipping the brim to Charlotte before turning back to the door. "I wouldn't linger in here too long, miss. Do give my passing regards to our Mr. Rose."

Noanes slipped out the door as quietly as he had come and Charlotte cradled her arms around herself, hands feverishly rubbing away the touch of his eyes.

CHAPTER ELEVEN

22 October, The Mint, Southwark

The morning swung on a pendulum between light and dark. Days like this proved to be a thief's paradise and many a helpful hand, whose province relied on the cover of night, took full advantage of the false dusk to stray into unguarded pockets. It was hard to stay wary when a man could not see more than two feet ahead of himself.

Luce had run these streets since boyhood. He knew them better than most. He and Harlequin had been terrors making even the best battalions look like bumblers with their thieving prowess when neither one had yet passed the age of eleven. Of course, when one partner can be invisible, the advantage was decidedly yours. Now on days like this, even he could fall prey to the fog, his eye tricked into mistaking the alien for the familiar, and it was only the assurance of the map within his head that kept his stride at a steady pace. Tempting as it was to create a flame, he knew it was wiser to keep his hands firm in his coat. No need to draw unnecessary attention.

In lieu of a lamp, the orange glow of a coffee stall's coal furnace acted as a beacon. A group of children, the oldest a bruise-cheeked girl of eight, warmed their hands by the fire. Off to the right stood a woman. Once she might have been thought the loveliest in London, were it not for the scar that ran across her pale cheek to her plump lip. Heavily made up, her black hair was piled and pinned atop her head. A violet ribbon laced its way through the tangled mess. She wore a skirt nearly the same shade, though rough at the hem and muddied. It was the only splash of color against the otherwise filthy gray street.

A cup nested between her thinly gloved hands and she smiled at him over the rim. "Give us a cuddle, love?" she called, catching his eye as he passed.

Silvia Marquette. Seven years since he had last seen her but their greeting was as familiar as a dance.

"Or a shilling for a frolic?"

"And for a kiss?"

He had asked the same of her the first night they had met, when he had slipped out of The Athenaeum after a show. He had been eighteen. She a few years older and wearing her finest, a skirt the shade of flame that made her stand out as if her face alone were not enough to catch the eye of any rich cullies leaving the theater. That was before the scar that she now wore like any other accessory, and while she had caught many eyes, only one man had ever caught hers.

"Always one for you darlin'." Silvia lowered the cup and her shawl fell back from her shoulders, exposing the white swell of her small bosom, the best a corset could make with the little flesh it had to work with. Equally exposed was a second, uglier scar that cut a clean line along the side of her neck. A near twin to his own hidden away under his shirt. She stood on her toes and pressed her lips to his.

"Bit early in the morning for you to be out, Sil," he said, breaking the kiss.

"Bit early for the whiskey as well," she replied, winking. "Besides, a girl's got to eat, pet." She shrugged her shawl back up to her shoulders. "When did you get back in town?"

"Three days ago."

"And you didn't call on me? That's enough to make a girl think she's lost a fella's favor."

"After the way I left? What could I say? Coming across you like that all I could think of was that you were going to die and I was going be accused of . . . I'm sorry, Sil. I couldn't take another —"

"You were young. Scared and gashed up as I was, all that blood would have broken anyone. Considering what you went through with your ma —"

She offered a smile, face lighting up like the sky after a storm. There was an abundance of life in her and true affection in her bright eyes. He considered her one of his dearest friends, one of the few who lived outside the troupe and did not turn away from his own scars, as another woman might.

"But you left me with your man and he fixed me right up. So what's there to forgive?"

The scar rode on her smile along her cheek. It had been a deep, ugly gash and the damage could have been far worse had Luce not found her. Pretorius had done a good job on the stitches, keeping them small and tight.

"Keeping yourself safe?"

"He's not been back, Luce," she said, her voice softening as if the culprit might be within earshot. "I have not seen hide nor

156

hair, not that I would recognize him. I only remember the blade."

"You know that at any time you can come to the theater. Pretorius will help you."

"And risk losin' my spot in the Row. I've worked too hard to earn my lodging and while it might not be much, it's mine. Darlin', I've been on these streets since I was a young girl. I didn't need rescuing then and I don't need your rescuing now. Besides, this" — she touched the scar — "is part of the trade."

If she weren't so steadfastly independent to the point of pigheadedness, he might have convinced her to join him at The Athenaeum during his stays. But he knew better. Liberty came first and liberty she would have.

"So we're still friends?"

"Yeah, still friends." She ran her hand up his arm, gently squeezing when she reached his biceps. "So what do you say? We can make it quick. I've missed you."

A torch waved before his eyes, suspending the *sorry darlin'* on the tip of his tongue.

"See ya on your way for five pence, sir —"

A pair of enterprising linkboys decided to take equal advantage of the conditions to ply their services to passersby. It was a novelty, as these boys were rarely seen in

157

the sun. Dusk was when they made their sweeps, swarming from the cracks and crevices of rookeries all over London. They raced the streets like packs of thieves into the closes and parks, clutching flints in their thin cold fingers as they offered their torches.

"Don't listen to 'im. I'll do for four —"

"Now, lads, that is a generous offer, but as you can see —" Luce raised his hand. Dead-center of his palm a perfect flame flickered to life. The boy's eyes widened as that single flame sparked several that danced up along his fingers until Luce's hand was engulfed. "I'm not in need of your good services."

Silvia laughed as the boys ran off in terror, their torches forgotten as they fled into the thick. "You best be getting on yourself, love, before those two come back dragging a copper in tow. Last thing either of us needs."

Luce shook his hand, extinguishing the naked flames. He gave Silvia a quick peck on the cheek before leaving her to the fog as he continued along The Mint.

The foot traffic grew sparse with the fading line of shops and businesses. In the absence of the gaslit storefronts, the fog grew malignant. The street was dingier here. Lonely, narrow footpaths and alleys branched from the main thoroughfare, causing him a moment's pause.

There was not a single place in Southwark that shined, not a single place that had not been touched by human desperation. However, here along the south bank, where poverty was a contagion, misery bled from the dilapidated buildings that the poorest called home.

He stood a moment listening to the whining houses. If he closed his eyes he could almost hear the ground sink and settle, upsetting the already corrupted wood and brick substructures. It wasn't more than six months ago that a house in the Giles rook fell, taking with it well over a dozen souls, mostly children, whom scavengers continued to uncover nearly three weeks after the fall. There was not a doubt that it would happen again, there were only the questions of when, where, and how many this time.

A deep breath and he started again, quickening his step as he left the maze of houses. He bumped by a figure darting from the opposite direction. Several times in the course of his walk, indistinct shapes and unidentified shadows swept along the street, which harked back to the night before and what he heard in the dark.

Fear was not something he experienced

often. The fire that ran through his veins was enough to ward off anyone who dared cross him. But fire didn't deter shades and there was something about them that nagged at the back of his mind, reminding him that it was only by the grace of Aurelius that he had escaped their realm and still they were waiting for what was rightfully theirs. And *she,* well, she would never let him go or forget any more than he could allow himself to. That was the balance he walked so it was reassuring when he made the casual brush with the tangible, to still be among the living though he was quick to check his pockets before passing.

He had not gotten far before the miasma of human filth gave way to a moldering reek of damp earth, rot, and neglect. It was a smell that stuck to the back of the throat that could not be cleared no matter how hard one tried.

Send our friends to Crossbones.

The cemetery was relatively open, the only plot of open land for miles within the borough. There was a wall and a gate and the fog eddied the lumps and depressions that made up the grave-choked ground. Crossbones stood unconsecrated, as beyond the pale as its residents who were outcasts and paupers. It was also referred to as a

160

single woman's churchyard, as many of the dead were prostitutes whose sinful, unrepentant lives had deemed them unworthy of proper burials in St. Saviour's yard. That was until the grounds became so overcharged by bodies that the iron gate was forced closed in 1853. A bit more than thirty years ago and one ill-advised attempt later to sell the grounds, rightfully quashed by the Disused Burial Grounds Act, fresh graves continued to appear. There was no harm in these burials. Who was to know or much care if one more misbegotten soul had their bones laid out among the thousands already there?

He hated the place. Hated the presumption held of those women consigned to this churchyard. It was an insult to *her* to be buried here.

The gate stood open and to the far right, deep in the yard, Luce spied a spark of red. Or so he thought, for the speck was gone as quick as it had come. The area was notorious for theft and prostitution, but beatings were common as was the odd garroting. Most recently Pretorius had warned of a nasty spate of stabbings, a fact that kept him acutely aware of every noise. Day or night the constables never patrolled The Mint unless necessary and then never singly.

This lack of constabulary had resulted in vigilante law presiding more times than not. More times than not these vigilantes' intentions only worsened the matter.

Luce rested his hand on the gate, mindful of burrs and sharp edges. The risk of infection from a place like this was a certain reality. "Hello," he called.

The reply was a speeding arc of silver. The knife landed with a thump into the spongy ground less than an inch away from a rat, monstrous in size and none too impressed, that slipped with a hunched hop run under the exposed roots of a stump.

It was a purposeful miss and a cold tickle of adrenaline spiked the hairs along his arms. Luce pulled his hand back from the gate. Fire flicked in his palm. He recognized the blade by its handle. Ivory and silver. He would have known it anywhere.

The speck of red glowed again, closer this time before fading on a breath of smoke.

"No need for that now is there, Laz? Or is it Lucifer? What is it you're called these days?"

Luce swallowed against the churn in his gut. "What the hell are *you* doing here?"

"Aw, now, is that the best welcome you can give?" Emilian Kosh slipped from the fog with the ease of a ghost. The cigarette was a beacon of his stride. "You seem surprised to see me."

"Considering I'd taken you for jailed or dead," Luce said.

The older man offered a throaty cackle, phlegmatic from years of smoke, city air, and whiskey. "I could say the same about you, but something tells me you haven't had to fall back on thieving too much. Judging by the fine cut of that coat, I'd say business has been exceedingly good. You don't even stink of the street."

"Aurelius isn't going to take you back into the company if that's what you're sniffing around for. You parted ways with us, Kosh. With all of us. And for the better it was."

"Back? Who said anything about me wanting back in with you lot? I served my time and more than paid the price for doing so. No, I'm onto something far more lucrative."

"Scavenging bones? Not much money in throwing anymore?"

"I like to keep my hand in a lot of pies." Kosh flicked away his cigarette. He maneuvered across the porous ground. The damp earth tilted and slid under his feet but he maintained his balance. Practice had made him sure-footed. He reached down and plucked the knife from the ground. "But as you can see, the knife is never far."

The two stood less than a yard apart. Luce had the height advantage but Kosh had a quick hand and a strong arm, so if there were one more stabbing who would notice?

Kosh's face split into a wide crooked grin. "Tamp down the fire, boy. If I'd have you for dead, you'd be so already."

Luce flexed then tightened his fingers, dousing the flame in his fist.

"Besides, you shouldn't look down your nose at resurrecting. This old boneyard has served you well enough, eh?" Kosh drew close and tapped him on the chest.

The lightness of the touch did little to mask the man's innate violence. Luce remembered all too well coming through the door as a boy to greet his mother only to find himself staring up at the ceiling a moment later, hand to his eye, cheek, or mouth, depending on the man's mood. There was never a need for provocation. Everything depended on the man's mood. He had never once seen the blow come. It was a gift old Kosh had, having hands sensitive enough to throw a knife with such quick and clean precision that he could slice a hair in half at a distance of ten feet but could still lay a beating on a body with nary a mark left behind. How his mother had been married to this man was a question that eluded him.

The fire stirred but Luce kept his hands firm to his side. He looked into Kosh's eyes. Despite the years, nothing had changed in their dark depths. Still cold, still cunning, and long drained of either respect or regard. Emilian Kosh, Knife Master. Emilian Kosh, Occasional Resurrectionist. Kosh, the Constant Thief.

"If it's not for the bones then why are you here? You been following me?" Luce said.

"The only thing I follow are certainties. Like knowin' you'll find your way back here eventually. All I had to do was stop in and wait. Sooner or later, you'd be here. Ever since your mum went into the ground. You're too damned predictable and that's a dangerous thing."

"You waiting to find out how dangerous it can get?" Luce asked, the fire licking at his skin below the surface.

"Nah, I'm here to ensure that you play nice this evening when my current employer pays his call."

"Your employer? What are you on about —"

Kosh's widening grin was a knife to the back, to the heart, and to any soft place that would cause the most damage.

"It was you who told Rose about us,"

Luce said.

"For his own reasons he has taken an interest in you and Aurelius. So when the question came up, Noanes and us —"

"And what is it he wants? His emissary last night was vague to say the least."

"Not privileged to know, I'm afraid, and I'm not one to be askin'."

"How'd you come to be tied up with him? I can't see you running in the same social circle as Odilon Rose."

"You'd be surprised how all sorts mingle. Rose might be a posh prig but he's a ruthless one, and for a man to attain and maintain his position there are times when certain services are required to ensure that there's no hindering of business by some petty problem. Sometimes people need a bit of encouragement. It's not all that different from working for old Aurelius, am I right?"

"Never thought I'd see the day when Emilian Kosh would be at the beck and call of a master's hand."

"We can't all be the boss's bastard. Lucky for you, I guess. The rest of us need to make a living where we can." Kosh snuck a glance over his shoulder back toward the graves. "Funny that for all the fondness he showed her, I always thought Aurelius would have dug deeper in his pockets for somethin' decent for your mum. I mean for the mother of his child, at least leave her in the grace of God at St. Saviour and not some hole in a slattern's field. But I guess consecrated ground proved a problem for a man like him."

"If you were so concerned you could have paid."

"She weren't my concern anymore."

"Despite her still being your wife?"

The knife's point kissed the soft skin under Luce's chin before he could move.

"Once," Kosh hissed. "She was once my wife. Correct yourself there."

The years had not hampered Kosh's extraordinary speed and it would be a matter of whim as to whether the cut was deep and clean or shallow and messy. The pitch rose in Luce's veins.

"You know your own blood, boy, and I knew day one you were none of mine. No matter how hard she tried to pass you off as such. Everybody knew what she got up to. One snap of Aurelius's fingers and she was slavering to him like a bitch in heat. Christ, she was a lousy liar about that. Thinkin' she could come to my bed after being in his."

"Which you never let her forget," Luce

said. "Night after night, cutting her on stage —"

"Had to show the authenticity of the blade."

"Other throwers demonstrated the sharpness by slicing paper or puncturing balloons. You used her like a strop."

"Better for the show if demonstrated on flesh. Keeps the audience on edge when they know the danger should I miss. Besides, I wanted Aurelius to feel every last cut. Every scar I put on her body, each time he touched her, he would think of me."

The blade pressed warm into Luce's skin and he knew that a single twitch was all it would take to be having this day's tea with his mother and St. Peter at the gate.

"Put it away, Kosh, I'm tired of playing. We both know you aren't going to use it. After all, I'm the one your boss wants to meet and I think he'd be sorely disappointed if I didn't show."

"You always were a clever little shit," Kosh sneered. He flicked the knife away, nicking Luce's chin.

"Still fancy the sight of blood, I see," Luce said as Kosh's eyes betrayed his pleasure.

Kosh barely registered the look on Luce's face before glancing back into Crossbones. The fog had thinned to a ribbon trailing the ground though the sun had yet to find a footing against the dead air above.

"One brilliant act, that's what Noanes said we needed. One brilliant act to put us on the map, make rich men of us all. Ashe was to be the answer to our prayers. A magician unparalleled. Well, look where that devil's deal got us and where it got you."

"We done here?"

"Tell Aurelius to give Rose what he wants and you'll not see me again. If you don't —" Kosh trailed the knife along his neck before slipping it back into his pocket.

"Kosh, if you so much as consider coming near me or any of my family again —"

"Then what?"

"You'll burn." In Luce's hand was palmed a glowing ball. "I couldn't do a damned thing against you when I was a child. But now —" The flames danced on his skin, jerking and waving as they crept up his arm to meet the flaming wings that had begun to unfurl from Luce's back. It was enough to turn Kosh's blood to water.

"Pray then that it will not be necessary for our paths to cross again." Kosh backed away and started up the street. "Tell him, Lucien. Whatever scheme Rose has going that he needs to indenture himself to Aurelius Ashe," he shouted back over his shoulder.

"Whatever it is, give it to him."

Luce watched him slip into the rookery maze. In less than five yards, he had vanished amid the ruins like vapor. The flames dissipated around him, the ash falling and joining the filth at his feet.

CHAPTER TWELVE

Less than ten minutes after passing the stalls, Luce was rushing up the Athenaeum steps. In less than five, he was standing in the kitchen in the middle of a disaster.

A splintered leg dangled from an overturned chair. Crockery sat in a shattered pile in the sink. Dita was on her knees trying in vain to sop up the remains of the breakfast tea from around the pacing feet. Only one other time could he remember seeing the kitchen in such disarray or the rage of the man at the whirlwind's center.

"You were supposed to be keeping an eye on him!"

"Is that my job now?"

"You are my eyes and ears, Timothy Harlequin," Aurelius railed. "Eyes and ears!" A thick vein throbbed on his brow. His skin was flushed face-to-neck in an ugly swathe of red.

Each shout twisted the dishcloth tighter

171

in Dita's hands.

"Are you hearing yourself, Aurelius?" A quick flicker of apprehension crossed Harlequin's face. He could at any moment vanish, should he wish to, but that would only make matters worse. Aurelius's temper was akin to a single ember capable of a burn that could last hours, days, years, even until the inevitable eruption. To disappear now would render a repercussion he would rather not meet later.

"I am not *his* keeper. I cannot be expected to be so when —"

"Excuses! You throw excuses at me?" Aurelius closed in until the two stood toe-to-toe. "Don't tempt me, Timothy, or have you forgotten how precarious the thread is that binds you here?"

"What's happened?"

"Lucien, thank God," Dita said, lifting her head. Her eyes widened when they lighted on his bloody chin and filthy clothes. "What on earth has happened to you?"

"Never mind me, what's going on here?" Luce looked first to Aurelius and then to Harlequin, who had yet to meet his eye.

"There's been an incident," Aurelius said.

It was a statement lost on Luce as a flicker of movement had caught his eye. He pushed past his father and walked straight toward

172

the fireplace. A good fire burned though it was lacking in cheer. One of the many stray cats Pretorius had the habit of adopting languidly stretched and splayed his six-toed feet toward the fire. Beyond the iron grate, the twins Davie and Danny crouched on the floor. Teacups sat to either side of them, cooling as they had lost themselves in the spinning of a thaumatrope.

Luce could see the picture disk twirl on the strings in the twins' hands. It had been one of his favorite toys when he was boy. One flip of the disk and the illustrated bird was free. On the second spin the bird was caged. Spinning and spinning from free to cage to free, it was a simple illusion that tested the persistence of vision, which for some was the very heart of common magic.

A chair was situated inches from the hearth, along the arm of which Angelique, still in costume from rehearsal, sat, with a small bowl and rag in her lap. The water in the bowl was a tepid shade of pink and the rag stained a pale red.

"No." Luce's steps grew tentative. "No, no no no."

Installed in the chair, Georgie sat with a mug of tea gripped tight between his hands. A blanket draped across his shoulders. The bare patch of skin on the boy's cheek was

173

raw. Blood beaded where the hair and flesh were cruelly torn away. The skin would scar, the hair possibly gone forever.

There were scrapes on his knuckles, and the finger marks on his neck would by evening be an ugly, angry shade of purple.

Angelique dipped the cloth in the bowl. "He slipped out not long after you left," she said, gently pressing the cloth to his cheek. "He was grabbed in the fog. I'm thinking an enterprising sort on the look to make quick money by selling him back to us. Or selling him on."

"We're too known for someone to attempt that."

"Don't be naive, Luce," Harlequin said. "There are places that we're not known at all. Places that have never seen anything quite like Georgie."

Timothy was right. There were rumors on the circuit of private collections where possessing a living curiosity was something of a status symbol. The stranger the deformity, the better, especially if one was talented. Any one of them would fetch a high price to an astute broker. It was a dark thought that Luce did not wish to entertain.

"He wouldn't be sitting here if that were the case." Columbine calmly sat at the table. Even offstage, she defied convention by

174

wearing men's trousers, though carefully altered by Dita's hand to fit her slim frame. "No, I think you will come to find this to be something far more vulgar."

"Whatever happened we've not been able to get much out of him." Angelique dropped the cloth back into the bowl. Couldn't risk Dita's wrath for messing up her dress before tonight's performance. "But judging by the damage done it was a bit of a barney."

Luce knelt down and touched Georgie's shoulder. He felt a tremor run the length of the boy's thin arm even under the thick wool blanket. "What were you thinking, Georgie? You know better than to go out alone. Haven't you been listening to anything I've told you?"

The boy remained silent. His eyes lost on the fire.

"Easy, Luce, don't blame him. He's been through enough," Dita said. She had stopped scrubbing and was looking directly at him. In her eyes he spied the glisten of tears. "He couldn't have known what was waiting out there."

"You could have."

Dita sat back hard on her heels. With three accusatory words he had struck harder than if he had used his fist. "That's a damned bloody cheek! You know that is not how it works for me. I need to attune to one person and only one at a time. You think I would sit by and let a child be beaten if I could see it coming?"

"I don't know, Dita. You have before."

"That's not fair, Luce," Harlequin interjected.

Aurelius squeezed Dita's shoulder. "And you damned well know it," he growled.

"Yeah, all too well. I've been on the receiving end of my fair share of beatings and *she* wasn't any help to me then. And neither were you."

"Lucien —"

"You're quick to castigate Harlequin's failings but where were you, Aurelius?" He turned on his knees to face his father. "You know what it's like out there in the streets. We're lucky because outside we don't look any different from them! No one knows what we are until we show them. But Georgie, the twins. They're children. They're vulnerable. And they need us to keep them safe."

"I know why you're angry and I wish I could change what happened to you and to Georgie, but even my eye strays from the ball from time to time." Aurelius's breath was steady but his jaw clenched, suppressing a rage that bore through the room.

176

"Which is why I rely on the company as a whole, as a family. We look out for our own because we are all that we have. And we will have our failings, few and far between I hope, but failings nonetheless, and that is when things like *this* happen. It could be much worse on us next time."

"There won't be a next time." Luce took Georgie's chin in his hand and gently turned his face to meet his. "Do you know who did this to you? Would you recognize them again?"

"All he'll say is 'skin and bones,' " Danny said.

" 'Skin and bones' is all he'll say," echoed Davie.

Skin and bones. A chill trickled down his neck, lifting the hairs like quills. The twin's singsong rode around the room on the back of an unfortunate creature Luce had longed to forget.

The Thin Man had scared him as a child, unsettled him still. As far back as Luce could remember Skym would sit silent with those red-rimmed yellow eyes endlessly staring from beneath his drooping eyelids. He had first taken him as mute as he rarely spoke, choosing instead to allow his expression to convey his thoughts.

Not that those moments when he finally

spoke were special as every word that dripped from his hard lips was laced with contempt and anger.

"Pardon?" Luce said.

"I said, near as can be reckoned he was following you," Harlequin said, edging away from Aurelius and drawing Luce out of his reverie. "Fog was thick. I guess he thought it was safe."

"And no one noticed he was gone."

It was not a question but a flat statement that acknowledged the guilt of them all.

"Lucien, what more can I do? There are boundaries —"

"Don't," Dita said, touching Aurelius's hand. "Let him be."

Harlequin leaned against the mantel. "You look like hell yourself. What happened?"

"Ran across an old . . . familiar of the company," Luce said. The words fell like lead. "Emilian Kosh. He sends his regards in the only way he knows how and hopes that all goes in his employer's favor tonight."

"*Kosh* is mixed up with Rose?"

"I don't think that banking is the only business this Rose is involved in judging by the company he keeps."

"So the old bastard still has teeth." A bitter laugh escaped Aurelius. It was louder than he had intended but it was a reflex of realization. "If he has Kosh and Skym still under his thumb after all these years then he's more clever than I've ever given him credit for."

The color had cooled in Aurelius's face and the composure he wore as casually as last season's suit had returned. The fire crackled as the wheels turned in everyone's minds. It was not much of a leap to under-standing, as Columbine had accurately stated, that the meaning behind Georgie's beating was in fact vulgar. The blows were delivered by those who had a long-standing familiarity with the company.

Luce sat back on his heels. He knew without needing to look that Aurelius's eyes were on him. They had hands of their own that were easy enough felt whether they were ten feet or ten miles away.

"Why take the risk? This attack on Geor-gie when we have not even met with Rose. To what purpose?"

"Same as Kosh's meeting with you. It is a warning that if we do not act in accordance with his employer's wishes then we are guaranteeing worse to come. They were able to get to our most vulnerable despite our watch." Aurelius shot a hard glance to Harlequin. "Noanes has gotten bold."

"Noanes was wicked but he wasn't violent.

That's not the man I remember," Harlequin replied.

"He's obviously *not* the man you remember."

Luce's response was quick as light and held something just as gossamer in its fold. Perhaps it was a memory, some half-suppressed malevolence, but whatever it was remained something he chose not to betray. He ran his hand along his chin. The blood had dried to a thin hard crust along the edges of the cut. "However, crawl into the purse of a rich man and it's bound to bolster anyone."

"And when you've men like Kosh and Skym in your employ you needn't dirty your own hands with these practical details," Aurelius said. "A more unsavory fellowship I've not come across in some time. About the only good qualities held by those two are the ability to follow an order and to not ask questions. Qualities that once served me well in my own time, continue to serve Noanes's needs, and are key to his relationship with Rose."

Harlequin shook his head. "Things seem to be moving toward a dangerous extreme. In all of your past dealings, I've never known anyone to take such advance actions before."

"You're working under the hypothesis that Rose is in compliance with what his hounds are at."

"You think him unaware?"

"About as unaware as I am of your exploits." Aurelius cocked a brow. "Never mistake knowledge of an action as compliance with or condonation of it."

"And you call me the eyes and ears."

"Don't worry, Timothy, I've never cared what you or anyone in this company gets up to, as long as it doesn't reflect badly on us. Rose, and men like him, follow a similar philosophy and though he might not be a man who has to play nice he is certainly not one who needs to resort to this." He waved his hand toward Georgie, who shrank back against the shadow. "I will assure him of that tonight. That is perfectly within the boundary."

Luce looked resolutely at his father.

"The easiest thing in the world to do is to make an enemy, Lucien." Aurelius inclined his head toward Georgie. "I've been expecting something like this for some time now. Although not nearly as violent and not against the boy. That was bad, but as you said a rich man's purse can embolden anyone. For men like Linus Noanes, whose life can be read in the gin stains on his shirt and the holes in his pockets, I suspect that for the first time since we parted, he and the others feel protected enough to act."

"Act against what? He knew what he was getting into when he signed your contract. It's not our fault if he failed to meet his own expectations."

"There were some things that were not expected, Lucien. Your mother for one, although I offer no apologies to that."

"Hearts can be wanton things." The cloth lay limp in Dita's hand. "But that doesn't mean you should always give in." She leveled her eyes on Aurelius. "Of course, by the same token it doesn't mean you shouldn't, especially under extenuating circumstances. I won't deny your mum's sufferin', Luce. She wasn't treated well and I can't blame her for turning to your father for what he could provide, but none of that excuses —"

A quick flash of Aurelius's eyes held her tongue.

"What we are saying, Lucien, is that Noanes, Kosh, and Skym created their own unhappy fate because they chose to do so and they will not be satisfied until we all share in it." Aurelius shook his head but his focus remained on Georgie, who had yet to turn his head in acknowledgment of anyone.

"He doesn't have to perform tonight. Dita," he said, his voice turning to silk. "I would be sincerely grateful if you would stay with him, though. He will be in need of constant comfort this evening to restore some semblance of safety."

"Did you think I had plans to leave the child on his own?"

"Get him to talk to you and then tell me everything he says. If he remains reticent, do what you must. I want to know what he saw and what he heard. I need to know what exactly happened in the fog."

"I will do what I can but I'll not press him, Aurelius. He's lived it once and I won't have him live it again."

"Then live it for him." Aurelius cupped her cheek in his hand. "Go inside his mind and bring out what I need." His nails scraped her skin. "You have a far gentler touch than I do."

She looked into his eyes but met only blackness. "Do you want me to make him forget afterward?"

Aurelius released her. "No, I think it's best that he is left a reminder of this unpleasantness. Lucien is right. The child needs to be wary in this world."

"The scar won't be enough?" Luce stared at his father. "Does he have to remember how he got it?"

"Scars are vital, Lucien. They are the proof of not only a life lived but also one survived. But sometimes we also need the memory of what caused them."

"I'll do what I can," Dita said.

"Good. Excellent. Well then, I've much to do before the evening comes, so if you will excuse —"

"So that's it? The bastards strike one against us and we wait for them to do it again?" Luce stood up. He had the very real desire to bolt and ferret them out himself. All three of them. It was an idea that had fired his mind and would not go away. "Maybe we should send a message of our own."

Luce felt Timothy's hand on his shoulder. "What you're thinking is not going to help matters any."

"Listen to him, Lucien." Aurelius stopped at the doorway, his hand paused on the frame. The Gordian knot on his forearm twisted and tightened with the flex of muscle beneath. "What would retaliation serve? Despite what has happened today, I will not have you, or any of you, strike out against a single citizen of this city because you think that a lesson has to be taught. Doing so makes you no better than the cowards who hurt this boy. Also, it would draw unwanted attention and suspicion, and there is too much at stake to risk that. Soon enough we'll know all and then —"

"And then what, Aurelius? You had the opportunity to end this once before."

"Allowances were made due to circumstances, but I assure you that a more-than-suitable punishment was delivered on Noanes and his men." He turned and Luce saw something in his father's eyes that gave him pause. It was something far beyond the mere ferocity of rancor. "As to this occurrence, it is pricking thumbs, my boy. Pricking thumbs."

With a bitter grin he was gone, and in his absence Lucien felt the weight of ghosts, of all those ephemeral little afflictions of the past that rose repeatedly no matter how deep he dug the grave.

CHAPTER THIRTEEN

22 October, Decimus House

"I should like to scold you, sister, but I'm afraid that it would be a wasted effort," Rose said as he sliced through the kipper on his plate with a surgeon's skill.

Florence Suskind looked coolly at her brother over the lip of her china cup, watching as he flayed the flesh from the bone with practiced ease. Odilon Rose was a man who ate with care and attention, not with enjoyment, an apt representation of how he attended to nearly all the facets of his life.

"I really don't understand what all the fuss is about." She returned the cup to the saucer. "I attend the theater all the time."

"Theater is one thing. Lingering at stage doors long after the performances are over is a different matter." He licked the salt from his lips before wiping his mouth on the napkin. "Dressed as you were —"

"It was all a bit of fun, if you can remember what fun is. My friends and I —"

"Yes, your 'friends' —"

"I'm not sure what you believe me to have done, Odilon, but I can assure you that no matter what transpires over the course of an evening it is no concern of yours."

"You have a position in society. You have a position as the wife of an eminent judge. You have a position as a Rose."

Florence smiled. King's pawn advances on the queen. It was an old opening, predictable but effective.

"My husband is an old man," she countered, "to whom if I show a single night's kindness a month, he will allow at least the remaining twenty-nine or thirty nights to be spent as I wish and with whom I wish, which is a more-than-satisfactory arrangement. And I've done nothing to discredit his name, or *yours* by association."

"Yes, I suppose I should be grateful that you are not an acolyte of the late Lady Lamb. Nevertheless, it would be for the best if you did not make such a spectacle of yourself. You were seen."

"I'm seen by many people —"

"Backstage . . . in the company of a curiosity."

Her wrist burned where Luce's finger mark was imprinted. "Yes, that must have been right after Emmett left him. They seemed to be involved in quite a discussion. So tell me, Odilon, what scheme have you brewing that would require the use of curiosities? Are you planning to add to your collection? Or is it something more perverse?"

He knew he should be more forgiving of his sister's shortcomings and of her challenging temper, as she suffered from the terrible affliction known as boredom: a chronic condition that affected women of her station from time immemorial. But that was no excuse for risking one's reputation for a night's passing fancy.

"That is purely business —"

"I know your business, darling. As you pointed out, I am a Rose." She leaned forward and laid her hand on his, her thumb tracing the bones of his wrist. "I see things too and have hosted my fair share of teas at your behest."

The sound of the door swinging open brought their conversation to an abrupt halt.

"Charlotte, dear." Odilon tossed down his napkin and rose from the table as she walked slowly toward them. Florence nodded and returned to her cooling tea. "I wasn't expecting you to be down today. Another difficult night?"

Charlotte sat down in the offered chair and Odilon quickly tucked her in. A plate, knife, and fork were placed neatly before her but the mingling of fish, eggs, and the beeswax of the polished oak table put off her already diminished appetite.

"It was not the best," she said. She had allowed herself ten minutes in the hall to recover from her encounter with Noanes, hoping it enough time to calm herself. She reached up and touched her neck, a habit since childhood. Whenever her nerves got the better of her, she would reach up and touch a long strand of hair, twirling the end around her finger. It was a small source of security but since her illness, her long dark-mahogany locks were cut to an inch above her shoulders. Too short to twist into the intricate ringlets and chignons that crowned Florence's pretty head.

Odilon stood beside her. "May I?" Charlotte nodded and he took her hand in his, gently turning her wrist upward and unbuttoning the cuff of her blouse. He rolled her sleeve upward, exposing her pale skin and dark bruises. In the crook of her elbow, a patch of pinprick hemorrhages nested.

He had a curator's touch, caressing her bare arm as if it were a piece of fine porcelain, checking for flaws and estimating the value. She was thinner and a whisper paler than the day before. Each day the bloom of health fell further from her cheek like the last petal from the rose. The only color she still held was the fever of her green eyes and the perpetual red stain on her lip. It was a remarkable alteration.

"You may cover up," he said, returning to his place at the table's head. "I do wish that you would partake of something, Charlotte. You need to keep your strength up. Will you at least take some port? I've had it brought up from the cellars."

"Thank you but . . ." Tears brewed in her eyes. "My head . . ."

"There, there, it's all right, dear," Florence said, pressing her hand over Charlotte's. "There's no cause for tears. Here, take some tea. That will bolster you, and then perhaps some clear broth."

Charlotte's head buzzed as the heat of the tea reached her nose and she felt for a moment that the world was about to fall from under her feet.

"You're trembling," Odilon said after a few moments. "Your cup clatters in the saucer. Florence, take her back upstairs and sit her by the fire. And Florence, one last thing. I do not wish to see you at The Athenaeum tonight."

"I have a ticket, Odilon —"

"And I have work. You would be a distraction."

"So I am to give up my evening so that you can go forth with whatever dubious plan you have? Perhaps I should warn them to proceed with caution."

"Perhaps I should warn you not to cross me, sister dear, not on these matters. You should know better than that."

Charlotte glanced from Florence back to Odilon. The two were of such similar minds and moods with nearly unbendable wills. It set her nerves alight to see them disagree and she secretly waited for the day they would again come to blows. Some things from childhood were never outgrown.

"It is a coward's game, Odilon, browbeating a woman."

"Yet still I ask if I will be seeing you this evening?" The question was loaded with as much malice as the words could quietly fit. "Am I to be forced to ask it again?"

Florence lowered her eyes. "No, darling. I feel a slight headache coming on and I believe that I shall stay in."

"That's a good girl." He ran his finger along her arm with tender familiarity. "I'm sure that your husband will be pleased to have your company. Imagine, twice in one month."

Once the door closed, Odilon sat silent. He refreshed his tea and sat back in his chair. He brought the cup to his lips and sipped. His face remained an impenetrable mask, betraying nothing of the fierce mood of his mind.

CHAPTER FOURTEEN

22 October, afternoon, The Athenaeum

"I know what I heard," Pretorius shouted from beneath the stage to Michael above. "Gears grinding. I won't have it, boy. It will not do."

"Mr. Pretorius, I'm not seeing —"

"Then look a bit harder!"

Luce sank back into the velvet seats of the second row and watched Michael check the riggings and the lights while Pretorius muttered beneath the floorboards, clanging about the pipes and the steam hydraulics, ensuring that all was running free of issue in advance of the night's performance. There was not much risk of malfunction, not even with Columbine's silks, but it was a compulsion of Pretorius that he check each device to ensure all ran as smooth as clockwork. In light of today's occurrence, the rumors of trespass, he needed to see with his own eyes that nothing had been tampered with. In such a dark churning space of complex machinery and rope, he would not risk a limb or a life.

Luce swirled the whiskey once in the bottle before bringing it to his lips. His head fell back against the seat as his mouth filled with the warmth of aged oak that slow-burned down his throat before it settled.

A repressed memory crashed back into his mind with an immediate and harsh vengeance. It only needed a stimulus and today, seeing Georgie beaten and bruised, made the pictures in his mind as vivid as the day that *it* had happened.

It was not intentional, it couldn't have been, because he didn't even know that he had it in him. It had been terrifying, the entire experience. The way his body felt under the first tremor that vibrated his veins and scorched his bones. His fingers had bled from the heat but it had come on so quickly that he hadn't felt any pain. That would come later, when Kosh would beat him within an inch of his life.

It wasn't the first beating laid on him but it was by far the worst. Kosh would have possibly killed him had Aurelius not stepped in. His mother was of no help. She was too frightened of his "gift." She never held his hand again, and when she looked at him fear and suspicion would edge her eyes where the flames still burned. Timothy Harlequin arrived at their door the next day. Another nine-year-old, same as himself, only with a pair of horns and the uncanny gift of being anywhere at any time.

Luce opened his eyes. "You'd not make it long as a thief. I could hear you from the hall."

Angelique stood in the aisle next to him. "You left abruptly. Are you all right?"

His eyes drifted toward her. "Never better."

"I can see that." She took the bottle from his hand and curled up in the seat next to his. Her feet dangled well above the floor. "Do you want to talk?"

"How's Georgie?"

"Shaken, but Dita and the twins are with him. He'll be better in a day or so."

"I'd hoped against hell that he wouldn't ever go through that. He was supposed to be safe with us."

"You were a bit hard on Dita, weren't you? She loves Georgie as if he were her own, and you know as well as I that there is no guarantee of safety. We can take all of the precautions in the world but —"

"It's my fault what happened to him." Wires closed around his heart. Or so he felt, and he flinched at their unexpected tightening.

"Why would you say that? Because you were not there to prevent it? If so that's a guilt we all share. You said as much yourself." Angelique tucked her legs up under her skirt. "We can't overlook Georgie's own actions in this. He knew better than to go outside alone. I think you're placing too much on yourself."

She looked at him thoughtfully. "Though what I don't understand is what Aurelius meant saying he'd been expecting this. What is that all about? Who are these men?"

"Part of a past best forgotten." Luce blew an exasperated breath between his lips as his head bounced back against the seat. "Trust enough that they are dangerous, love. Best to keep your distance."

"Lucien would not be the best person to pose your questions to, my dear girl. He would have only been a bairn at his first encounter and ten at his last. Too young to understand that particular period of time."

Aurelius sauntered down the aisle. His mood and manner had returned to their usual status of collected calm, a relief to them both. "But his estimation is not wrong. They are dangerous men in their own way. In fact, taken together the three could stand shoulder-to-shoulder with the vilest scum in London."

"I'll drink to that." Luce reached for the bottle but Aurelius was quicker.

"I don't think so. You've a performance tonight and I need you sober. And I'll be performing tonight as well, so I might need you to open the show."

"You're going on?"

"With Georgie under par, we are absent an act. I'd have Dita do it but she needs to stay with the boy."

"I don't think I have ever seen you perform a full act on stage before," Angelique said.

"It has been many years, *mon cher,*" he said with avuncular warmth. "Needs must, though. I can't very well send a broken child out on stage, and the show must go on. Especially tonight. For better or worse, blessing and curse."

"I cannot imagine why anyone would attack a harmless child?"

"Why? Why indeed. I believe that we are now seeing the true man, truer to form than when I first met him nearly thirty years ago."

"Who is he?" Angelique quizzed on.

"My dear, Linus Noanes was, is, and would still be the worst of bosses *if* he were still stalking the stage. He was the proprietor of a cheap ten-in-one a short jump from Newington Crossroads, where the entertainments changed with the frequency that one might change one's socks. Work-shy and bone-idle, he preferred to drink his profits rather than reinvest in the show and, more important, in his performers. For him, it was cheaper displaying medical specimens and pickled punks as there is no need to feed a fetus in a jar."

Aurelius took a long draw from the bottle. He despised such entertainments; the lack of dignity in the display of unfortunates appalled him. "As for the real curiosities, not that there were many, one whom I recall was a man by the name of Osbourne. He hadn't much by way of arm and leg, being little more than a torso and head. Miracle that he had survived at all but he had spirit. His act consisted of being propped on a table or in a sling and he had the amusing ability to roll cigarettes and light them using only his mouth. After this feat, the audience was then encouraged to touch his body, to prove to themselves that he was a living human and not some modified dummy. It was less about feeling the flesh and more the heat that made him real, that proof of life. When he died, Noanes took what he hadn't drunk and had him embalmed, put in a case, and kept on display."

The color faded from Angelique's face. "How awful, how bloody awful."

"Child, you have no idea the cruelties I have seen in my time." He cupped her small chin in his palm. "And may you never have to."

"Why would you ever help a man like that, Aurelius?"

"I have seen pious men corrupted by their own piety because they thirsted for power only to sink into the pit while I have offered my hand to a desperate man two steps beyond the gutter, only to be refused because he wished to hold on to the only things left to him: his soul and his humanity. But what our Mr. Noanes asked for intrigued me, because it was not the mundane longings of wanting love or money or fame that always find their way to myself and my brethren." Aurelius shrugged. "No, what Noanes wanted was magic itself."

Angelique watched Aurelius's eyes pool black. She shrank into her seat as a single red spark centered in each where the pupils had been.

"Noanes hasn't the sense God gave a goose. He was another drunk mumbling into the night," Luce said, propping his feet on the back of the seat in front of him to his father's disapproval.

"Perhaps I shouldn't have engaged him, but I saw a rare opportunity. A small idea that has allowed me to make more deals with this company, this theater, these players" — he twined a curl of Angelique's hair around his finger — "than I could have ever made waiting at the crossroads itself."

A bellow of steam burst from beneath the stage. The hot white cloud enveloped the three as the hydraulics pumped and the center of the stage elevated with a hard thunk.

"Pretorius!" Aurelius spun back with the look of a feral beast and stared up at Michael Mayhew, who was perched on the stage's lip with a shocked expression reminiscent of one who had been in the wars and had left the fields with the horrors intact. "What in blazes is that madman doing?"

"I . . . I don't really know, sir," Michael stammered. "I'm only handing him tools as he asks." In evidence, Michael held up a hammer and some strange metal device of Pretorius's own making.

"If you must know, I heard a grinding last night coming from the gears." Pretorius popped his head up out of the gap made by the elevation of the stage. Grease streaked his forehead and bled down from his brow to his nose from the steam. "I'm only thinking of the show and the safety of the company. Speaking of, Mayhew, be careful when passing tools down to me. I've not time to rebuild these pistons or your hand today."

"I didn't hear anything last night."

"And that's why I do the mechanics. I can always hear the cries of my children." And like a badger, he popped back down into the hole on the stage, out of sight and out of mind.

"The man's as mad as a bag of rats." Aurelius shook his head. "But where would we be without him."

Angelique folded her arms around her knees and tucked them tight up under her chin. Her eyes had grown pensive. "If everything was such a success, why the animosity now? Why part ways in the first place?"

"You need look no further than what was done to Georgie to find that answer," Aurelius finally said. "There was a crude and depraved brutality in the man that did not fit with our growing family. In the end, it was best for all to part ways. Though he is not forgotten nor has his debt been forgiven."

The glances between father and son had

not been lost on Angelique. She shifted, stretching out her legs so that her feet dangled off the lip of the seat. There was a reticence in her eyes as she looked at them both. So much alike, yet one was at peace, and the other haunted. "Why do I feel that I've been given a fraction of the story?"

"My sweet, sweet girl," Aurelius said. The Gordian knot on his arm twisted as he gripped the back of the seat he leaned on. "Always question more, always question intent, and never lose that sense of doubt."

"And if I do so, then perhaps one day I'll find the chinks in the walls and finally find the truth of you. Of both of you."

It was Luce's turn to squirm. "Until this business is over, until we leave London, don't go out alone. Angelique, I mean this, please: I don't want you running into any of them."

"Sound advice," Aurelius echoed. "I would encourage that everyone use caution."

Angelique smiled. "I was born in a Paris brothel and grew up on a dance hall stage. I know the world better than most. I can take care of myself."

Imperceptibly a penknife appeared in her hand from where she had it secreted on her body.

"Though she be but little, she is fierce." Aurelius grinned at the tiny yet surprisingly sharp blade.

"Though she be but little, she is fierce."
Aurelius grinned at the tiny yet surprisingly
sharp blade.

CHAPTER FIFTEEN

It was apparent to everyone seated in The Athenaeum that tonight they would be witness to something exceptional.

The first indication was the breaking of routine. As was customary following his introduction of the show and of the performers, Aurelius Ashe would exit the stage with a tantalizing flash. But as he stood alone on the stage, instead of the brilliant burst of sparks, the Auer burners began to flicker. Dimming then brightening then dimming with what seemed the whim of a god's breath before snuffing out completely, leaving the audience in darkness.

Time could be counted by the heartbeats of the men and women who anxiously sat enthralled. After a minute passed, nearly two, when every held breath seemed to exhale at once, a soft amber glow emanated from the center of the stage where Aurelius stood. The light illuminated him, and as he raised his arms the light followed, blurring against the darkness like velvet.

"Ladies and gentlemen, you may have noticed that tonight we are breaking with convention. It is not my habit to join in a performance." He grinned into the dark. "But habits are meant to be broken."

A fierce crack of lightning exploded the darkness and the entire theater burned a brilliant white as chains of electricity surrounded Aurelius before shattering with a swing of his arms like glass.

He bowed and basked in the audience's applause, modestly rebuffing the whistles and howls by drawing his finger to his lips. One soft "Shhh" felled the din.

"Now, my dear friends, my next act requires an assistant. Might I find one among you gentlefolk?"

The Auer burners rose with the hands in the audience and Ashe scanned the crowd until he lit upon a slight soft-eyed young woman whose nervous hands were clenched tight together in her lap.

"You," he said. He nodded as she looked up from her seat, her dark chignon dusting the back of her neck. She shook her head, a flush beginning to infuse her throat as every jealous eye was on her. "She appears to be shy, friends. Shall I give her a hand?"

Before she could further refuse, Aurelius held his hand out to her and slowly she rose from her seat. Not by her own volition, as the surprise in her eyes made clear. Her feet, her body did not move in the pedestrian manner, but rather she was lifted from her seat.

For several moments she slowly spun above the audience with the turn of Aurelius's hand, rising, floating, and falling with the tilt of his wrist. The expression on her face met at a point between fear and near-religious ecstasy before Aurelius drew his hand back toward the stage and she followed. The train of her gown drifted through the air until her feet settled back firm to ground and she found herself standing in front of the Illusionist himself.

Again the audience erupted to then be silenced with a wave of Ashe's hand.

"We have not been formally introduced," he said. "I am Aurelius Ashe, your humble servant. Might I have your name?"

"Vi . . . Violet," she stammered, regaining her breath but her mind still spinning.

"Violet." He smiled. He walked behind her and turned her toward the audience. His arms circled her without touching and she felt herself cradled safe in the space they made. "You have nothing to fear, my dear.

And you will be rewarded for you participation," he breathed into her ear.

His hands hovered before her face. "One so beautifully named should always have flowers." He spoke softly but his voice echoed across the theater. He quickly ran his hands down along her body, leaving in their wake a trail of flowers. Roses, carnations, lilies, and her namesake violets laced across her gown until there was no semblance of fabric to be seen. From head to toe, she was elegantly garlanded in petals.

Murmurs of excitement ran like rumor through the audience and Violet looked down in amazement as Aurelius stepped back to study his work like a couturier. "I don't know. Lovely as she is, I think that she is lacking something. What do you think, ladies and gentlemen? Do we need a little sparkle?"

He again waved his hands, the gems of his skull ring's eyes catching the light as the petals of the gown began to shimmer as each leaf sprung a gem. A ruby. A diamond. An amethyst and an emerald, until the dress was frosted in stones.

It was a moment unlike any that anyone in the audience had seen before, and from the euphoric tears of many it was an experience never to be had again. Aurelius escorted the young lady back to her seat. Her gown rattled with gems. As she sat down beside her companion, before parting Aurelius took her hand and planted a gentle kiss along her knuckles.

"You shall want for nothing now," he whispered, catching the eye of her gentleman, whose only response was to offer a humble nod of astonished gratitude.

Now awash in flickering light and shadow, the theater pulsed with tense excitement as all eyes turned to Columbine, who dangled high above the stage from the underside of a rotary ring.

A minute, then two passed before there was a slight metallic clank as the ring began a slow rotation. For a moment, Columbine remained still, allowing the slow spin of the ring to shift her body in momentum until she found her rhythm. After that it was a quick shift from splits to handstands to a dizzying spin connected to the ring by only the back of her neck. Breathless, the audience sat on the edge of their seats.

Often accused of heartlessness and of possessing a cold candor, both of which she would proudly acknowledge as true, Columbine had learned early that one cannot live with sentiment and expect to come through unscathed. Hardness had been her only defense against a world that would not accept her as anything other than a freak.

The rumor of an albino in Canning Town had drawn Dr. William Abbott to her family's door. The neighbors' whispers had already caught the ears of the grandsons of the Cape Colony and the sailors. Not more than a year out of Tanzania and Namibia, these men thirsted for safety on the seas and there was no better charm to carry than a talisman made from albino skin or bone, or from the ashes of a heart. When Dr. Abbott arrived, she could hardly blame her family for giving her up at his request to study her condition. In their own way, it had been the purest act of love that they had ever shown.

Columbine took hold of the ring continuing to spin as she stepped into her memory with Abbott, and into the world of learned men, by whom she was studied and exhibited. Too clinical to be thought cruel, this sort of display was more in line with what Dr. Joseph Kahn's Anatomical Museum encouraged. Both the medical professional and the curious visitor could observe and learn from his wax models, his Venuses and embalmed specimens. Dr. Abbott's stage was the Royal Society and open to physicians only, but there was no less showman-ship in her disrobing for an audience to enable the study of her body and skin. Others might have crumbled under such invasive conditions, but she took to wearing a stoic inner plate with the same purpose as a battle-tested knight to thwart the eyes from seeing all of her.

One afternoon a friend of the Society paid a visit. He was a man of clearly refined taste, well dressed with a thick thatch of hair and eyes so dark that the night sky would bleed with envy. That afternoon she walked away from the Society, away from Dr. Abbott, and into The Athenaeum. As she left the Society with Aurelius there were birds flying overhead with abandon. Aurelius noticed and he had asked: If she could have one wish, if she could do anything in the world, what it would be? In that moment, looking up at the sky, she could think of only one thing. She wished that she could fly as free as the birds above. That day Aurelius Ashe opened in her the few fleeting moments of kindness she had left. Tonight, she graced this kindness on Georgie, who loved nothing more than to watch her fly. Tonight, she flew for him.

Columbine's sylphid body streaked through a single column of light that glanced across her ghostly skin as she let go of the ring and spun on a single silk like a dervish. The silk unwound and she hurtled toward the stage, stopping a mere eight feet above before arcing back and regaining the swing until she ascended the heavens as Icarus himself had, cradled in the protective arms of the air itself.

The audience erupted in applause. It was a roar that was almost to be feared. Yet the only applause she basked in was the clapping from the wings. From her perch, she saw his small patched and swollen face looking up at her as he sat astride Luce's shoulders. Luce's eyes were elsewhere. They had drifted toward the audience, to the first row of the right loge where he had fixed his cold hard gaze on Pretorius, or more so on the two well-dressed men in the seats next to him.

With scrupulous courtesy following the performance, Pretorius brought the two men to Aurelius's office. Luce trailed behind. He had not bothered to return to his dressing room to change but rather rushed straight from the stage, still costumed in leather and smelling of brimstone.

"If you would please wait a moment, gentlemen. I will let Mr. Ashe know that you are here." Pretorius disappeared through the door, leaving the men in the dark narrow hallway.

In this close setting the small figure that passed from the wings, hugging the wall, did not go unnoticed despite her slippered feet.

"*Pardon, ma petite,* but you were exquisite this evening."

Angelique paused and looked up at the man who spoke. His silk top hat was in his hand and he had a pleasant enough face although there was something to his eyes, something in the cold, dark indigo that was ideal for hiding secrets, that raised the hairs on her arms. He was well dressed and well spoken but that did not alter her rule about engaging patrons. Too many wanted a chance to touch, to gain evidence beyond any doubt that she was in fact an adult and not a child or a miniature automaton. A less respectable show would not only allow such transgressions but rather encourage it for the right price. She slid her hand into the concealed pocket of her skirt and closed her fingers around the penknife's hilt.

"Thank you, monsieur."

"Angelique, allow me to introduce our guests, Mr. Odilon Rose and Mr. Josiah Emmett," Luce said.

"I had a good friend who had the opportunity to see you dance in Paris."

Her smile remained firm despite the color fading fast from her cheeks.

"He had said that you were the loveliest, lightest creature ever to grace the stage. He was not wrong in his estimation. Perhaps you might have met him, a youngish fellow by the name of Laurence Hawkins. A jovial chap, about as tall as Emmett here, ginger, his love of fine food and drink exhibited by his expanding waistcoat? He was a promising figure in the foreign office and he was an admirer of yours."

"You are too kind, sir, but I am afraid I've no recollection of having met anyone of that description. I have many admirers but as you can imagine, I could not possibly remember each one. But do pass along my regards."

"If only I could. I am afraid that he met a rather sticky end on one of his Parisian excursions. A robbery gone wrong as it was reported, his life ended with a small sharp blade and not far from one of his favorite establishments if I recall, La Pantoufle Bleu. Of course, I would not expect a young lady as yourself to have intimate knowledge of houses such as that."

He grinned. "I do like to think that he

had a last happy moment, perhaps to have seen you dance once more before his untimely and unfortunate passing."

A thousand icy thoughts went through her mind but only one showed on her face and it was a look not lost on Luce.

"Gentlemen, Mr. Ashe will see you now." Pretorius held the door open for them.

"Bon nuit, mademoiselle," Rose said with a nod of his head. "I do hope to see you dance again sometime."

As she passed, Luce grabbed her, encircling her small arm in his hand. "Angelique —"

She turned her wide eyes from him and without a word shook off his hand before hurrying down the hall to the shadows. He would have followed had it not been for Pretorius.

"Are you coming, Lucien?"

Drawn before Aurelius's desk were two chairs in which the man himself had directed them to sit. Mr. Emmett maintained the previous night's nervous energy, wincing at each pop and squeak of the chair as if he sat on a living thing. His demeanor was very different from the man seated next to him; the impetus of the night's meeting.

A sober, thin man, Odilon Rose did not demand attention so much as expect it.

Neither young nor old, he rather rested in that comfortable range between indiscretion and wisdom. He was dressed in perhaps the finest suit London had to offer, the crisp lines of his formal jacket and trousers fitting him as neatly as skin. Aurelius instantly disliked him.

"Brandy?"

"No, thank you," Mr. Rose said, removing his gloves and tossing them into his hat. "I prefer to conclude my business before partaking in spirits."

Aurelius nodded. He swirled the caramel liquid in the snifter. The slow soft slosh rounded the glass until the warm aroma of vanilla and sunlight pierced the room. On nearly every surface, a candle flickered, their open flames marrying with the gaslit globes that burnished the walls. The glow brought an immediate intimacy to the proceedings.

The desk tonight was clean. The clutter of notes and pictures of the night before had been reduced to a single letter on paper of the finest cut.

"I was disappointed that we were unable to meet at our prearranged time." Aurelius ran his hand across the letter as if he were wiping away crumbs.

Luce had seen his father use similar tactics before and it always amused him how the smallest gesture of dismissal, a mere tip of the hand, could upset the balance of the most dominant of men. It was not lost on Rose, who maintained a perfect composure aside from a slight shift in his eyes.

"Yes, it was most regrettable. I am of a rather punctilious nature so only the unavoidable would cause an interference in a business matter. Thankfully Mr. Emmett was kind enough to keep the appointment for me. I appreciate your being able to accommodate me this evening."

Aurelius regarded the two steadily for a moment with the quiet patience of a tiger who found himself before a wolf and a rat. Even Pretorius could not hold back a grin as Aurelius brought the snifter to his lips, allowing a second moment to pass before graciously bowing his head.

"So tell me, Mr. Rose, what is it that brings you to my door? Your Mr. Emmett here was less than forthcoming with details last night, and I must admit that my interest is piqued."

"I wish to offer you the opportunity to make history." Rose smiled with all the welcome warmth of a chained gate. "There is a woman — young, cultured, with a very bright future ahead of her."

"And I presume that a shadow has since

crossed this otherwise sunny forecast."

Rose shifted in his chair. "Your presumption is correct. Her health has taken an unfortunate turn."

"Then it is a physician you need, sir, not me."

"On the contrary, Mr. Ashe. The state of her condition makes you exactly the man I need."

CHAPTER SIXTEEN

"Your reputation is well known in circles fortunate enough to have benefited from your services, sir," said Mr. Rose. "And it has been reliably reported to me that you hold the key to a great many things. That you are in fact a man of true magic, the only true practitioner perhaps in the world, with an ability for, shall we say, unnatural influences."

Aurelius gave a brisk laugh, although directed less to the gentleman at hand and more to the proposal. It was a fact initially lost on Rose himself, who sat back in his chair like a child faced with his first reprimand.

"You flatter me with your expectations," remarked Aurelius. "However, I do think that Mr. Noanes and his compatriots might have exaggerated my talents. I certainly wouldn't take the word of drunkards and thieves as gospel."

"I might be of the same mind if I didn't know better. You see, Mr. Ashe, something that I neglected to inform Noanes of before setting about to track you down is the fact that you are not a stranger to me. If you were to think back far enough you might see that I am not to you."

Aurelius kept his eyes fixed on Rose. A gold pince-nez pincered the man's hawkish nose and a neatly trimmed beard made of his chin an inverted *A*, which gave him the strangely pleasant appearance of a Doré illustration.

Rose's indigo eyes grew bright as his lips tightened to a sharp hard line and there, in that moment, the pieces fell together.

"You inherited your father's brow and his high flat temples but your mother's eyes, they give you away." Aurelius's mind sped through the past, recollecting every person, every face, with whom he had dealt until *she* rose out of the dust. "Though I've never had the pleasure of meeting you."

"I was still a child when my mother sought out the witch after one of your shows. She had heard from a friend of a friend that to gain a meeting with Aurelius Ashe was a guarantee of your greatest desire being attained."

"Yes, she had fancied herself a maker of

men, if I recall," Aurelius drily replied. "Although when Catherine Rose came to me she was already the wife of a junior partner who was also the favored nephew of the then bank president. Not a bad life that your father, Milbrough, was providing. Certainly more than satisfying for any other woman, but not your mother. She hadn't the patience to wait for him to be fully groomed and measured for a role he was more than likely to inherit. Your great-uncle was not a young man. Another five, ten years, a prospect too long. You might not be the Rothschilds, but Catherine's aims were just as high. I've no doubt that she would have happily cleaved the head off her nearest rival and used the bloodied stump as a step if it raised her an inch closer to her goal. To be the wife of the president of T. Rose and Company and all that that would entail: the finest clothes, the powerful husband, a place in the best of society. And most important of all to have a name that would be remembered. A legacy."

"Wanting to better one's station is hardly a sin." Indignation balled in his gut at the casual disparaging of what he admired most in his mother.

He sipped his brandy, with every drop begrudged by Rose. "You will forgive me but ambition carried that woman with the fury of a storm's wind sucking up everything in sight. Want and determination fanned those flames to the point that she could not see what she already had. Pity . . . but she paved a pretty path for you, so obviously, she was happy with her sacrifice."

"Success is as much a series of sacrifices as it is of gains."

"Indeed it is."

"Three days. You had promised that in three days there would be a windfall that would set into action a series of events that would culminate in my father's rise at the bank within nine months' time. A seemingly impossible feat to leapfrog the ladder so quickly, but then came my uncle's unfortunate accident. Three days after my mother contacted you, a loose flagstone caused him to fall into the street. No time to avoid the oncoming omnibus . . ."

"Life is full of coincidence."

"On the last day of the ninth month, my father stepped into the position vacated by my uncle's death with the unanimous decision of the board. Now, a fool might take that to be a form of magic, of prophecy, but you and I know better than that."

"Do we?"

"Mr. Ashe, you've traveled quite far in this

world and what you have achieved with this company is tremendous. You have made a freak show into an exhibit of remarkable talents. These people seem almost normal in challenging the audience to see the ability and not the bodies, so it is not a stretch of the imagination to believe that you have also garnered powerful friends along the way. Admirers who also happen to have great influence in a variety of fields such as financial, legal, medical . . ."

A smile like smoke whirled across Aurelius's lips. "That is a presumptive leap. True, I have many acquaintances, and if you were here to ask for help in furthering your career or in a matter of money, I would have no qualm over offering . . . encouragement. But your hope that I might somehow pervert the course of nature is sadly misdirected. To all there must be an end," Aurelius said at length, "and we've no recourse but to accept that and move on."

"You've done so before to great aplomb and credit to your craftsman" — acknowledging Pretorius.

"Lucien was a singular exception."

"Your hesitation disappoints me, Mr. Ashe," Rose said, removing his thin glasses. "I would have thought that saving a young woman's life would be something of an easy challenge for a man like you. After all I'm not asking for a name. I've no issues with anonymity but you have wandered far and I've no doubt that you've crossed paths with medical men who may be better versed in certain disorders that have so far eluded our own local physicians."

Rose took out a handkerchief and began wiping his pince-nez. He was in no apparent hurry. "I am not a man who takes no for an answer. No one in my family ever has, as you are aware. Mr. Emmett, if you would."

Emmett, who had sat in silent observance as his master and Ashe played their game, reached into his inner jacket pocket to retrieve a thick envelope. He did not open the envelope but rather tossed it lightly across the desk. It landed with a soft thump.

Aurelius stared at it as if it were a sleeping snake that might bite if startled.

Luce stepped forward and grabbed the envelope. It had heft and bulged out slightly so it clearly contained more than a single folded sheet. Carefully he slid his finger under the seal and popped open the flap.

A deep, single crinkle formed from the unison furrowing of his brows as he looked at the contents.

"News clippings," he said, dumping the

yellowed and feathered slips onto the desk. "Old news clippings."

It was a seemingly innocuous pool of papers that Luce sifted through, turning them over one by one until a headline stilled his hand. Bold as you please glared a single word.

Fire

It was promptly followed by a detailed account of the Southwark stalls fire, complete with lurid illustrations of flames licking the heels of fleeing people. The etching of the man in the checked trousers engulfed in flames was particularly vivid. As was the drawing of the little boy who still held on to his arm.

Luce turned the clipping facedown. The hot fetid smell of burning flesh and wood to this day still coated the back of his throat, so thick that it would never entirely be washed away no matter how much whiskey he drank. If only that man had not grabbed her. He had to make him let go of her. It had only been a light touch . . .

Aurelius betrayed nothing. At least not to the naked eyes of his would-be clients. But those closest to him, Pretorius and Luce, both saw the slight tremor of his hand as he set the glass of brandy to his desk. They noticed the almost imperceptible dilation of his pupils as he read over the clippings and came to see whom this cold, arid man in the fine waistcoat was for him to be both this comfortable and this forward.

"Not every day that a man suddenly combusts in the middle of a crowded street. It must have been a shocking sight for those poor souls to see. Out for a day's market shopping, the stalls brimming with life, and then to have something like that happen. But I suppose to a man such as yourself, who has grown accustomed to the oddities in life, you would not be troubled by a strange and violent death." Rose lingered on the word, letting the *TH* slither before dropping from the tip of his tongue like a challenge.

"I feel that there is an accusation lurking somewhere in that statement." Aurelius smoothed the news clipping, his thumb tracing the blackest word. The tremor from before had completely stilled. "I can assure you that my hands are clean of that unfortunate event."

"Can the same be said of your name?" Rose grinned, fingers absently stroking the arm of the chair in a series of concentric circles. "Such a fragile currency, names.

Reputations. It takes a lifetime to build and yet one well-placed whisper, one wicked calumny, can send it crumbling. I have seen so many good men come to ruination often through no fault of their own. There have even been men who have chosen suicide rather than live with the shadow of a scandal — never once taking into account how this deplorable act would affect their families' futures by causing an even greater scandal. That is why we must take care with our actions, our associations, our kin."

It was as if the wick lifted into the lamp. Rose looked at Aurelius with the clearest, coldest gaze Luce had ever seen and he knew that *he* had left his father vulnerable. He need not look any further than to the two unspoken words that hung bloodless in the air between them.

I know.

"The thing about Southwark, Mr. Ashe, is that a beautiful woman will always be noticed. When she appears on the stage as the assistant in a popular act on a nightly basis she will be unforgettable. And I hear that the act was something to see. What was her name?" The light danced off the lens of his pince-nez.

"Isabel, wasn't it? What was it like watching night after night your mother bravely standing against the wheel while Emilian Kosh's knives narrowly missed her? I can hear it now, the audience collectively heaving a sigh with each thunk of the blade into the wood. Did you worry? That one slip, one miscalculation and —" Rose clucked his tongue against his teeth, a sharp hiss of air escaping his lips. "I couldn't think of risking the life of any wife of mine like that, even one who proved herself inconstant."

He leaned forward and turned the newspaper clipping toward himself and ran his finger over the bold black accusatory word. "I suppose if there could be a consolation for the poor man who lost his life in that horrible fire, it would be that he at least enjoyed a moment in her company."

Rose looked up at Luce with a predatory eye. "Was that when you first learned what you could do?"

The air had stifled in his lungs. Luce had never so despised a man as he did Odilon Rose in this moment.

"But that of course is conjecture," Rose resumed. "I suppose that could have been any child who was seen with her. Of course, this conjecture is based on the observation of the subsequent actions —"

Ashe's eyes narrowed. "Subsequent actions?"

"The way I understand it, from Mr. Noanes, was that the show quietly closed in less than a day following the tragedy with the whole of the company spirited away. It is animal nature to draw threats and danger away from the nest. The innate need to protect one's own. Were I a father, I would do the same. Of course, efforts were made, but they never did find the woman or the child."

"Mr. Rose, you're talking dust and bones."

"Yes, the dust and bones of a dead man whose friends have long memories. You see, this man had a younger brother, a young constable at the time who, through hard work and drive, came to join the detective force and is currently a ranking chief inspector. Imagine how much peace it would bring to him and to his family to finally know what happened."

"It would be Mr. Rose's civic duty to provide whatever information he might have gleaned on the man's death to the proper authorities," Mr. Emmett chimed. "And as an officer of the court, I am sworn to see that justice is served. Even after fifteen, sixteen-odd years, the case for murder can be made. It is sadly a hanging offense."

"You bast—"

"Lucien," Ashe said. "We do not insult

our guests." He leaned back in his chair, joining his fingertips together. "I suppose after handling so much money and all those secrets, convincing your victims into handing you the keys to their lives without so much as a thought as to what you might do to them in return, blackmail comes easy."

"Oh, Mr. Ashe, no, no, no that is a vulgar word. We prefer *persuasion,* do we not, Mr. Emmett? It has a nicer ring."

"An effective presentation extends beyond the bathing of ugly things in flattering lights, Mr. Rose. Call it what you will but it would take a finer magician than even I to make blackmail appealing."

"I have found what lacks in appeal, exceeds in effect. You are a man of means, Mr. Ashe, and I have been warned off you. I am aware that you might not be as susceptible to my methods as others have been. Still, I do not think that you would be overly eager to have your days intruded on by the police should we take our suspicions to them. All that prying into your life and business, that might give pause to your audience regarding attending your show. Or seeking any of your other services. And there would be no way to keep this out of the news, not to mention the scrutiny your son would face. Hounded in the press.

Labeled a murderer. Not an easy title to dismiss. So much needless attention."

With each word that Rose spoke, the temperature in the room fell by one degree. The cold crept over Luce the way it had the night he saw the shadow on the ship as they sailed on the Thames.

"And where do Messrs. Noanes, Kosh, and Skym fit into your scheme? If you come by your quarries in so genteel a fashion, what need have you of them?"

"I don't think you need to be told that foolishness is endemic among the upper echelons. When someone suffers an indiscretion that I only learn about once the request for monies come into play, my concern is raised and I take it unto myself, with the help of my legal attendant Mr. Emmett of course, to ensure that a second attempt would not be made. Our mutual friends are very good at driving the point home that such criminal actions will not be tolerated."

"Excluding your own."

"Secrets must still be kept, Mr. Ashe, even after the lesson has been learned."

The two of them looked at each other in silence before Aurelius laughed. It was a deep, jarring sound that in an instant threatened to dismantle the foundation Rose had built. "You intrigue me, Mr. Rose.

Although I do find your methods distasteful, they are nonetheless effective . . . to a lesser man. However, I do not like being bullied and I will not have anyone thinking for one moment that they have an advantage over me. That is not how *I* work. And yet you are not wrong. I do not wish to have people nosing about in my business nor any undue attention placed on Lucien."

Aurelius glanced at the orrery. A single planet turned one click that Luce felt in his chest. "I will meet your young lady, I'm sorry, her name?"

"Charlotte Bainbridge."

Luce noticed that the girl's name affected his father the way the revelation of the news clipping had, the tremor in his hand, the dilation of pupils.

"I do not feel that Charlotte," he recovered, "needs to be a victim of this business, but I make no promises or guarantees that I can or will help her."

"Perfectly fair," Rose said. "I of course will pay you for services regardless of the outcome. This —" He pointed at the news clippings. "This matter between us was simply insurance."

"Leverage."

"Semantics." Rose sharpened his grin. "Of course do keep those if you wish. I have duplicates."

It was clear to all that Rose was enjoying himself and Luce wanted nothing more than to burn the smugness from the man's face.

"If I may inquire as to the nature of her illness?"

"A disorder of the blood. A cancer. All of the doctors say it is hopeless."

Ashe looked at Pretorius, who offered little more than a shrug.

"And she is dear to you?"

Rose's eyes twinkled. "Mr. Ashe, I cannot begin to express her value to me."

Emmett shifted in his chair.

"It would be best if we could arrange this meeting as soon as possible. She worsens each day. Tomorrow afternoon perhaps?"

Aurelius nodded.

"Excellent. Then, gentlemen, I shall expect you at Regent's Park, Decimus House, at one o'clock."

"One last thing, Mr. Rose —"

He and Emmett were halfway to the door when Ashe called them back.

"I do not appreciate attacks against my family. What was done to our young Georgie was uncalled for. Do warn our mutual friends that it will not be tolerated."

"I'm sorry?"

"Do not prevaricate with me, Odilon

232

Rose. You've made it your business to know everything so let us not start pretending to be lacking in knowledge now."

Rose reddened at the familiar use of his Christian name. "If Mr. Noanes or his compatriots have caused you a personal grievance —"

"You speak freely of names and the fragility of reputation and yet you keep company with thieves and murderers. You profit off the frailties and misfortunes of the very people you claim to serve simply because you can. Because those who have the most in this world are the ones who have the most to lose. In your view, sir, you are a king who stands above this land's laws."

Ashe's black eyes burned like ice as he watched the deepening blush suffuse Rose from cheek to collar. "But do not think for one moment that you stand above mine."

A shadow crossed Rose's face and for the briefest second Luce saw the man's mantle of assurance droop.

"Good evening, Mr. Rose. Mr. Emmett. Until tomorrow."

CHAPTER SEVENTEEN

23 October, The Athenaeum

A thin line of sunlight glanced across his face in a manner best reserved for lazy Sunday mornings, not for days when appointments are to be kept no matter how loathsome the company is assured to be.

Luce sighed, shifted the pillow beneath his head, and stretched. The movement caused the modest weight at the foot of the bed to stir. They had not shared a room or a bed in years but he knew instantly who it was. Even through closed eyes, he felt the watchman's gaze.

"You know, it's rather bad form to crawl into bed with someone without their knowledge or permission."

"You never complained before."

"Was I that bad off?"

"Somewhere between mildly inebriated and completely rat-assed. I've seen you worse."

Harlequin sat cross-legged with his back pressed to the footboard. He barely made a dent in the blanket. "You had fair reason, though. That bastard was good. But I think that Aurelius proved who was the better man at the end, wouldn't you say?"

"Listening at doors again?" Luce said, slowly sitting up, keeping his head steady to assuage the resident thumping.

"Much closer than that." Harlequin winked.

The midmorning shadows dusted Harlequin's face like a Venetian dream, all bands and bars and sunken hollows. Luce blinked into the bleary light. God, how many times had he wanted to shake the grin from the hobgoblin's face?

"Then let me pose the question to you — why did he let Rose get that far? I've never seen anyone talk to him like that before."

"I think it's a case of Aurelius having for all these years dealt only with clients and adversaries whom he's found wanting. There is a challenge in Rose, a man of influence and power, albeit of a dubious nature. A perfect game of cat and mouse."

"After last night, I'm wondering who the cat is and who the mouse."

Luce kicked aside the twisted sheets and walked over to the washstand. He dipped his hands into the basin and doused his face and neck with cold water. Toweling his face dry, he sighted resting on top of the opened book of Keats, marking the place of the fated "Nightingale," a scrap of paper. Soft and aged and as inflammatory as the blackened word emblazoned at its heart.

The towel stilled in his grip. He had forgotten that he had taken the clipping from Aurelius's desk. Folded and slipped it into his pocket, quick as you please, with the intent of ripping it up and burning the scraps to ash.

I know.

Rose's threat rattled through Luce's whiskey-numb brain. So long, it had been evaded. No one ever spoke of that day and in a small shameful part of his brain resided the gratitude he felt for that kindness. He pressed the towel to his chest. The cloth was rough on the scar.

Harlequin watched him thoughtfully. "You don't have to worry. Nothing will come of it."

"Come of what?"

"Rose's threat."

"Reading minds now?" Luce tossed down the towel and walked over to the window. In the street below, Georgie and the twins were kicking a ball back and forth. A small

236

brown-and-white mongrel bounced and barked around them.

Concern furrowed his brow but once he saw Columbine step into the street the tension relaxed.

"I can be down there like" — Harlequin snapped his fingers — "but Columbine can handle any situation. Including those that are worrying you. You were a child, Luce. What's past is past."

"And that makes everything all right? Because the past is unalterable and being a child at the time, I am not culpable for a man's death. Do you find that an adequate excuse?"

"When you weren't even aware what you were capable of, then yes I do. Luce, you didn't set out that day with the intention of harming anyone."

"You weren't even there —"

"No, I was a day too late, but I doubt it would have changed the outcome had I been."

"I was younger then than they are now," Luce said, watching the boys at play. "I was helpless and afraid and all of those people, those men. The way they touched her, brushed against her as if they had the right because she was on stage — that somehow . . . cheapened her. They thought her no better than a whore."

Columbine caught up the ball and tossed it back to Georgie. He wore a grin as big as the sun that seemed to erase the glaring white bandage striping his cheek.

"If he had let go when she asked —"

Harlequin shook his head. "You were provoked and that unfortunately prompted an aspect of your nature that you, that everyone, was unaware of. It was an accident, not a murder. Besides, it's not happened since."

"Only because I've mastered the fire. But there are days, moments when —" His voice faltered. "Rose in the office last night, had we been alone and he started making those threats, I wouldn't have had a single compunction about burning him alive. He and that Emmett fellow. When I ran into Kosh at Crossbones, my fingertips —" He held up his hand. A faint blue-white glow limned the nails where the fire burned beneath. "I could burn this city to the ground if I wanted to, Tim, and that scares the hell out of me. It wouldn't take much."

"Now, we both know better than that." Harlequin's breath was hot against the back of his neck. He had not so much as heard the bed creak, but one rarely ever heard Harlequin. "We'd never allow you to run so grave a risk of losing yourself." He closed his hand over Luce's, folding his fingers down into a fist and extinguishing the fire within. "The gibbet's not for you."

Luce turned but Harlequin was already gone. Not simply faded from sight; in close quarters such as these Timothy did not need to be visible to be felt. He was gone. As was the accusatory clipping from the pages of Keats. Outside he heard Georgie shout and when he looked back out the window, he saw his friend's quicksilver figure, kicking the ball to the boys.

"Hoo, hoo!" Dita announced as she whirled into his room like a mad dervish, yesterday's unpleasantness a thing of the past. "Oh, you're up, good, good. I've brought you a coffee. Your father expects to leave within the hour. Michael has been sent for a cab so if you want something to eat best get yourself downstairs. Haven't got all day you know."

The heavy fog of yesterday had thinned to a pale-brown gauze, allowing a nearly forgotten sun to break through. Not that this slice of heavenly brightness aided the squalor. In fact, it merely spotlighted the blight.

In the fruit and vegetable stalls housewives bickered over prices while another band of women frequented the crockery stalls where teapots, caddies, and jumbles of pots sat haphazardly displayed. Similar bits of tat featured in the grimy storefront windows of the rag-and-bone shops. Even a covey of unfortunates had stepped out to enjoy this brief moment of natural light before the fog descended again.

Luce watched these small dramas unfold as the hansom cab rattled along the cobblestones. The driver was steady, keeping both hoof and wheel from trampling any of the children scavenging the stale and mucked gutters for salvageable refuse.

A brewer's wagon paused in the street, causing the traffic to slow. A busker took advantage of the moment to stand at the corner and recite in a grand manner Mercutio's tale of Queen Mab. He was in good voice; even Aurelius cocked an ear in his direction, though his eyes remained on his paper. Despite the performance, Luce could not overcome the distraction of the open-air cooking. The smell of fried fish and butter wafted from the carts and he immediately regretted not eating before leaving. Coffee had not been nearly enough.

"I suppose this sign of appetite is good in the face of last night's indulgence," Aurelius said. He turned the page, snapping the paper erect before folding to read the opposite side. "I do hope that you've not left your sense and your civility back in that bottle as well."

"I'm fine, thank you," Luce said, pressing his fist into his gut to stave off the grumbling.

"So you say —"

Luce's eyes narrowed as he combed his memory for what he might have said or done, sober or drunk.

"It wasn't anything that was specifically said, Lucien. It was the volumes spoken in your stance. You positively reeked disapproval."

"I'm sorry," Luce faltered. "It wasn't my intent —"

"Never show anything but confidence in the face of a tip. They can never doubt you, otherwise the game is up before it even begins. I know what last night looked like, that Rose was running the mark. He thought so too, but he overcompensated with his cleverness, to my favor." Aurelius's lip curved into a jester's grin. "So put it out of your mind. His threats are as empty as your gut."

He returned to his paper and Luce to the study of the street, trapped somewhere between reassurance and regret, as the

hansom jerked forward and the stink of
Southwark faded behind.

CHAPTER EIGHTEEN

23 October, Decimus House

A house can have many meanings. It might be a young woman's romantic conjuring of stability, family, a comfortable haven; a less fortunate lot might be racked with more bitter memories and conflate the idea of a house with the pain and the endless promise of pitiable work. A wealthy man will see a reflection of his status while a thief will see only an object to plunder. And for some, a house is simply a cruelty of what could be, as if you only had a shilling or two for a brief stay.

As the hansom rolled past the gates and walls of the fine houses lining Regent's Park, Luce could not help but think of one other institution that a house could be: a prison. Though of one's own making, as his father would be quick to state.

'Do you want a staid life? Something normal? Something permanent?'

The question had been posed when he was only a boy on one of the troupe's first trips into Venice. Aurelius had taken him down to the canals that were overlooked by three-, four-, and five-story palazzos that leaned precariously close to the water's edge.

'How many of these residents do you think have ever been outside their walls, Lucien, beyond these waters? How many do you think have actually lived? You're not more than seven years old and have already seen more wonders than most people will ever see in a lifetime, if at all, simply because they've grown fat with complacency and are afraid to dream.' Aurelius had smiled at this. *'I've always pitied the ones who stay, because permanence is a form of stagnation, which is only another way of dying. And what sort of man would I be to allow that to happen to you?'*

"You are a million miles away," Aurelius said, folding his newspaper and tucking it down into the footwell of the cab.

"Only as far as Venice."

Luce looked over the lip of the cab's door and noted the signs of permanence in the wheel ruts of the grooved street and in the common paths that the well-dressed ladies walked as they took their turns around the grounds. It was a vast distance from the brown and muck-ridden streets of South-wark to the green of Regent's Park, relatively quiet and exceedingly clean.

This disparity was not to be taken by halves and was not lost on Luce, who wondered what secrets were kept behind the facade. How many of these neighbors did Rose have under his thumb? How many wives greeted him with a pleasant nod at his tipped hat while their husbands squirmed with the fear of revelation? How many wives averted their eyes in his presence while their husbands gleefully shook the great man's hand? How many indeed.

Filthy as Southwark might be, it was nonetheless an honest filth.

The hansom pulled to a halt outside a gated wall behind which sat Decimus House. Opulent without being overwrought, the villa sat well detached from its neighbors on a parcel of land bordered by wall and gate. Bricked and gabled with color dripping from the stained-glass panes, the house was like Shalott, isolated on its patch of green. The house number was absent but the height and thickness of these walls, when compared with those of its neighbors, clearly indicated that the owner required privacy as much as protection.

From the yard scattered an unkindness of

ravens who inked the sky before returning to ground a good ten yards away. The large house, situated as it was on its parcel of land, currently enjoyed the rewards of the fleeting sunshine.

The gate stood open in expectation of their arrival and the two had barely disembarked from the cab before two people, a rather vociferous pair, pushed past them and started along the path to the front door where they were met by a dour-faced footman.

"You've no business here," he said, halting the lean-figured woman, her wasted face a mask of murderous rage as he held her back.

"I will not be dismissed! That *man* holds property of mine and I demand to meet with him."

She lunged like a dog baiting a bear and for a moment, the footman fell a step back before he gained control of her.

"Here now, there's no need to roughen the lady," Luce said, seeing her wince under the man's grip.

Her companion, a short, wizened, and equally wasted man, was about to add to the protest when the front door swung open and Mr. Josiah Emmett appeared on the porch.

"Mrs. Harcourt, you have chosen a most inconvenient time. I would advise you to make an appointment with my office, at which time I will be happy to sit down and sort this matter out with you. Until then, however, you are on private property and involving the police at this moment would only exacerbate the issue and shed an unfavorable light on you."

The anger swept from her shoulders only to be replaced by a burden of defeat as she allowed her companion to lead her back out the gate, with the assistance of the footman.

"You there, sirs, heed me. You enter the Devil's Den if you cross through that door. Don't let *him* fool you —" she cried back as the gate slammed shut, locking her out with the flip of a latch.

"I do apologize, Mr. Ashe, for that unseemly scene," Emmett said, coming down the steps to greet them. "Occasionally altercations among the undesirables occur."

Ashe smiled. "Considering Mr. Rose's line of work, I'm surprised there weren't more taking advantage of an open gate."

"Quite. Now, gentlemen, I welcome you to Decimus House. If you would be so kind as to follow me. Mr. Rose is waiting."

Much of the commotion she had heard had

passed by the time Charlotte managed her way to the second-floor window that overlooked the street. From where she stood, she saw only a man and woman hurrying away beyond the gate and Mr. Emmett who was greeting two men, both of whom were dressed far more suitably than Odilon's previous acquaintance. The older gentleman greeted Emmett with a degree of familiarity but it was the younger man to whom Charlotte's eye was drawn. He stood slightly back, unassuming and almost in deference to his companion, with his hands in his pockets. Quite tall and lean, surpassing both Odilon and Mr. Emmett, he was all sharp angles and length beneath a head of thick dark hair that curled past the collar of his coat. She was unsure how long she watched him, but when his head turned upward as if knowing that he was being observed, despite her care to duck back, she was certain he had seen her as clear as she had seen his flame-blue eyes.

With walls the color of blood, a well-tended fire, and the faint scent of good tobacco, Devil's Den was an apt description of Rose's office. The man himself was not yet present so it was to Emmett's discretion to act as host. Ashe took his seat at the round oak table.

Luce crossed over to the tall windows and looked out onto the gardens. The grounds were beautifully manicured, and when the flowers were in bloom it would most assuredly be a vision of paradise. However, in October, the flowers were nested and the grass, though still green, was already beginning to lose its luster. Seated below on a bench was a figure, whom at first Luce would have discounted had he not flicked a knife into the ground.

He turned to tell his father but stopped when his eyes lighted on the cephalopagus skeletons. Posed upright in a near embrace, their perfectly formed bones, thin as glass pipettes, looked barely sturdy enough to support the weight of the single fused skull. An abstraction of Janus, the two faces had merged as one to share a set of eyes, one nose, and a single elongated mouth that gashed the fragile skull in a grotesque grin.

Luce lingered over the case lost in the gaze of the hollow eye sockets, long devoid of life but not of humanity. It was a queer place to be trapped, between fascination and disgust.

"Can you imagine Danny and Davie like that? Coveted for their bodies, their bones on display like the trophy head of a beast."

"If it's any consolation I can assure you

that they did not live long past their first breath."

Rose closed the door firmly behind him and extended his hand to Aurelius. The pince-nez glistened from his top pocket. "Your reaction surprises me. I would have thought such a monstrous specimen would have been your purview."

"Not all of us in the business are interested in the undignified display of human remains for easy profit. And they are not monsters. They were children, and though their lives were short, I am sure that they were nevertheless mourned. Although why they were not buried —"

"Perhaps, or they might have been a great source of pain to the parents, a blight on their family that nature saw fit to excise. People grieve in different ways. Some will cling to their sorrow where others wish to forget. My own family did both following the loss of my youngest sister, Louisa." Rose watched in disappointment as Ashe remained blank as stone to her name. "Of course, we shall never know how these parents felt."

"Even the greatest houses are not immune to tragedy," Ashe said.

"No, they are not. But that is the past and we are in the present," Rose said. "So let us dispense with such grim talk and turn to the matter at hand. We are busy men, after all. So what is it that you have brought me?"

"A small idea," Aurelius said.

Rose nodded. "And this idea — is it ready to be shared?"

"You stated last night that the lady has been diagnosed with a cancer of the blood."

"That is what the physicians at the Royal College have said."

"If you have spoken to the College then you are no doubt familiar with the procedure of transfusion? The introduction of blood from one healthy donor to a patient suffering a deficiency?"

"I have heard that it has proven successful in some cases of hemophilia, but such a treatment was dismissed as a cure for Charlotte. It could provide a temporary resolution, perhaps for six maybe eight weeks, but futile in the end. Are you saying otherwise?"

Aurelius teased a grin of a secret he kept. "Be assured that since you left us last night, Mr. Pretorius and myself ended our evening with our own consultation, in which the practical applications of such a method in regard to the young lady's problem were discussed. It is not an easy task you have put before us. This is quite new territory. This is not putting together puzzle pieces

251

and replacing what has broken with an artificial piece. This is something far more delicate, far more invasive. And as I said last night, there is no guarantee of success."

"Of course," Rose said. "Though I do not think that you are a man who welcomes failure easily. So will you speak to the resolution you have in mind?"

"I'm afraid that the methods behind the magic are never spoken aloud."

The two sat across from each other, another estimation taking place as each studied the other with well-practiced eyes.

"We're not all that different, you and I," Rose finally said.

"Are we not?"

"We both deal in hope, in a fashion. I mean, when someone sinks to the lowest depths in their life, caused by love or lust, or from carelessness or by an untempered want, they turn to men like us to find a way out of their situation."

"Men like us?"

"Harbors of last resort." Rose grinned. "The gains of love and ignorance."

"If gain is your interest, that is. I, however, do not seek superficial profits."

Rose cocked a brow. "Do you not? Not even from the satisfaction of holding a debt? Under which you will soon have me once we begin this transaction proper. A rare position if I do say so myself."

Aurelius laughed, his tone almost cordial. "What is rarer still is when *I* am the lesser of two evils in a room. Oh, Rose, there is a difference between what profit is and what pleasure is; the latter of which I shall hold dearly over you. Now, might I meet the lady?"

CHAPTER NINETEEN

Mr. Emmett led Ashe out the door and for a moment Rose looked quick to follow but when the party exited, Rose remained.

"You're not going as well?"

"Mr. Emmett is more than capable of making the introductions and I'd rather not intrude on your father's methods." Rose turned to Luce. "He's a secretive sort isn't he?"

"Nature of our business."

"Yes, yes, yes, smoke and mirrors. Tell me, is that what this is? Has he a plan for helping Charlotte? I'd hate to think that my time is being wasted."

"We'd not be here if he didn't have something in mind. Whatever that is remains guarded between himself and Pretorius." Luce wished that he could be sympathetic and take Rose as sincere but there was little on the surface to trust in the man and even less within. "I hope you know what it means to involve yourself with my father."

"Young Mr. Ashe, in my line I deal with men like your father daily, and you learn in handling other men's money the finer points of discretion, confrontation, and how to smooth everything in between. Now I hear you speak almost disparagingly about your father, attempting to cast doubt when you are the best example of why I should place my trust in him. You benefited greatly. Do you wish to deny another that?"

"Point counterpoint," Luce said.

"I think you will find that I do not scare easily."

"Give us time, Mr. Rose." Luce leaned back in his chair. "We've only just met."

"You disapprove of this venture." It was not a question but rather a simple, straight statement.

"I do. But it is more your methods in bringing this matter to us that I don't like," Luce said. "That news clipping was low."

"But effective, as it brought your father to my door. I would imagine that by now you would understand that every man has his vulnerabilities, and that he must always be aware of them and how easily they can be discovered."

"You including yourself in that?"

The question rolled off Rose's back. He

walked over to his desk and removed a ring of keys from the drawer.

"An acquaintance of my father's acquired them," he said, acknowledging the skeleton twins. "The mother was saved but the boys, well, thank God for small mercies I suppose. I was six when I first saw them —" He waved at the bones, the keys jangling in his hand as he casually strolled the room, deliberate in his pace as he straightened a book on a shelf then palmed the dust from the base of statuette of a satyr.

He smiled as he sidled toward the twins' case. "Good old Dr. Knox. Even at that age I was fascinated by science, animal anatomy. I considered a career in medicine, anatomy specifically, but Father had other expectations. These twins came into Knox's care at his practice in Hackney, and he thought of keeping them for medical reference. But ever since the Edinburgh business and then falling afoul of the Royal College of Surgeons, he thought it best not to hold on to bodies. When he died, he stipulated in his will that they should go to me since I had shown an interest in the study, much to my father's chagrin."

Luce shifted uncomfortably in his chair.

"Certain stigmas remain around anatomists, and there are vulgar twits today who still condemn the study of anatomy as sacrilegious. But what they fail to see is the need for progress and understanding; that to find a cure for these anomalies the cause must first be found. I'm sure you'd agree, Lucien, if I may be informal, that it is the fault of ignorance and dare I say even superstition that keep people clinging to their crosses."

Rose's predatory circling of the room left Luce feeling as exposed as the twins. "Leaving them whole, fully preserved in a jar, would have been unfashionably clinical. There is a vulgarity in being able to still see their faces. Their bodies brined but recognizable as something close to human. Emoting their last tragedy of living before death removed their troubles." Assurance was failing in Rose's voice, a fact Luce noted in the softening of the edges.

"No, I find bones far more . . . elegant," Rose said after a moment's recovery.

"And far more suited to the Royal Society or a charnel house than a banker's parlor."

"And what of sideshows? You've interestingly omitted them."

"Believe me, Mr. Rose, when I say that I've seen worse in the penny gaffs and the ten-in-ones. Pickled punks that didn't meet your aesthetics have always been a cheap and easy draw. Both the real and the fake. But that doesn't mean that I have to like them."

"They disturb you as well. I find that surprising. I would have thought that somewhere lurking in the dark corners of that theater of yours, a body or two could be found."

"That's not the kind of show we run."

"What about the O'Kearne boys? Danny and Davie, isn't it?"

"They are performers, theatrical performers, who happen to have an unusual condition. They are not set up on a shelf to be gawked at but have a say as to whether or not they want to be on that stage. One word of discontent and they'll never need to perform again."

"Have you never wondered, though, what lies beneath the skin? I have seen their tumbling and whatever binds them is too flexible to be bone, so what is it? Muscle? An organ? I am sure queries have been made for the purchase of their bodies when they pass, just for a look inside. I know I'd pay top price even for the death cast."

"The girl, Charlotte is it? She will die?" Luce asked, hoping to change the talk from the twins' mortality to another's.

"Yes, most assuredly."

"What is it you think that my father can do?"

"Fix her," Rose said. "She is thought incurable. I wish to challenge that and your father, if the rumors are true, is the man who can make the impossible possible. Look what he has done for you."

Rose ran an appreciative eye over Luce. A fine specimen. Far taller than average, a bit scruffy, but his features reflected a certain refinement. A highly controlled man of intelligence and loyalty and yet palpably dangerous. It was an intoxicating mix that made his sister Florence's attraction easy to understand.

"That heart of yours? You're a walking wonder, Lucien Ashe," he said, his gaze practically boring through Luce's clothes to the scarred flesh beneath. "What I wouldn't give —"

"My heart will be at the bottom of the Thames before you or anyone else would get hold of it." Luce's response was harsh and quick. Too quick, and both men recognized it for what it was. Rose had gotten him to blink. "As for the twins, they'll be buried in a place you will never find. I assure you that. Aurelius would never allow it."

Rose lifted a self-satisfied eyebrow. "That

is a declaration of an intent to be admired. And I don't doubt for one moment your sincerity. Moreover, for your sake, your peace of mind and all, I hope it proves true. But might I first show you something? You might find it of interest."

Mr. Emmett led Aurelius up the grand staircase to the small bright room at the end of the hall. A ginger knock and the door swung open.

The room was tidy to the point of sterility. Not unexpected considering the lady's sickly state, but the nearly absolute lack of personality was striking. He had not made it a habit of inspecting ladies' chambers, but Aurelius knew that every person, even the most minimalist, left a mark and carried in their possessions who they'd been, who they were, and who they hoped to be. But this girl barely dented her surroundings.

"Miss Bainbridge, my dear, you've a visitor."

It took effort as Aurelius could see as the lady stood up from her chair. She cut a striking figure even in her illness. She had a feverish beauty, thinness and pallor with large green eyes that smiled in challenge to the pain that resided in the wince of her mouth.

"Miss Charlotte Bainbridge, I would like you to meet Mr. Aurelius Ashe."

"I am happy to make your acquaintance," she said with a slight bow of her head. She hoped this quick nod was enough to mask the fleeting moment of disappointment that had crossed her brow when she did not see the younger gentleman as well. "Odil — Mr. Rose told me that you might be able to help me. You're a physician?"

"You might call me a specialist of sorts," Ashe said. "Please, my dear child, do sit down." He rushed to her side and gently eased her back into the little chair before the fire.

Mr. Emmett remained by the door watching Ashe closely. His presence was not overlooked by his subject. "Mr. Emmett, if you would be so kind as to leave us. In this instance I am not seeking an audience."

"That would not be appropriate —"

"Your concern is taken but misplaced. I assure you, the young lady will not be harmed."

"It is all right, Mr. Emmett. I will be fine. Please."

"Then I shall leave you to your consultation, Mr. Ashe. Miss Bainbridge, I shall be right outside the door if you are in need of anything."

"Thank you," she said, settling herself back in her chair. She folded her hands in her lap and Ashe watched as the most serene recovery crossed her face. She was either exceedingly strong or exceedingly brave, or perhaps a bit of both, which made her a very good candidate for the procedure Pretorius had suggested.

The man seated across from her smiled and a look of absolute generosity passed over his face. It was an expression that immediately eased her mind, as if they were the most natural of old acquaintances rather than strangers meeting for the first time.

"I must thank you as well, Mr. Ashe," Charlotte began, "for taking the time to see me. I am sure that you are a busy man and considering what I have already been told concerning my . . . condition, the mere fact that you are here consoles me. That Mr. Rose wishes to confine me to your care is, in and of itself, a true test of faith. He is a particular man, as you have seen."

"Who has formed a rather high opinion of my abilities without any real benefit of proof. And while flattering, I hope that you have not yet followed in similar suit. You seem an intelligent girl whose opinions should be formed entirely of their own merit. I would hate to disappoint you."

"Mr. Ashe," she began with eyes raised and chin stiffened. "I am dying. That has not been kept secret from me. I know that you cannot promise me a cure and I have no expectations otherwise. However, that does not preclude my having hope. I've had more than my share of fortune but also of —" She paused, searching for the right word, but chose instead a small tight smile that to a man like Ashe, who knew what pains hid in the curve of lips, served more in answer than any single word ever could.

"You are brave to hope. I have seen men tremble and pale when Death neared and yet you keep quiet company with him. Are you not afraid?"

"Mr. Ashe, there are days when my head aches to the point of splitting. There are mornings when I wake to a stained pillow, the remnants crusted around my nose where I've bled in the night. On good days the aches are fleeting and I count that as a mercy. On the bad, I cannot make it down the stairs before noon. Even now I am winded from the exertion of speaking to you. So am I afraid of dying? No. But that should not be mistaken for my wanting to do so."

"And what do you want, Miss Bainbridge? What nestles in your heart?"

To be healed. To have a life, an escape. To love. To be loved. To belong. To be free. To matter. Ashe was staring at her as if he could hear this litany of wants that screamed in her mind before she uttered one aloud.

"To no longer hurt, Mr. Ashe. That would be the greatest kindness that God could bestow."

Aurelius nodded. "Then if you will allow me?"

The ruby on the third finger of her left hand sparked in the firelight as he gently took her hand in his. "Your fiancé is a good man?"

"Fiancé? Oh no, there is no, this is not . . . there is no meaning behind this," she muttered. "It no longer fits the finger I used to wear it on. An effect of my illness." She offered a tight grin.

Carefully he turned her hand over in his and unbuttoned the cuff of her blouse. It was an intimate gesture but Charlotte did not draw back. As the fabric fell open, he caught her pulse, which fluttered under his touch like a butterfly's wing.

"That surprises me that a young man has not yet made an offer. You are what, twenty-three?"

Charlotte watched his fingers deftly roll back her sleeve. "I've no connections nor means of my own that would have offered any opportunity of meeting —"

"The Roses did not present you?" Ashe said, his brow raised. "I would have thought that they would have taken pride in that pleasure."

"Were I blood perhaps, but as I am of no relation that was not deemed a duty of the family. And Madame Rose had quite tragically passed the year I turned eighteen. It would have been inappropriate for me to attend such an event when the house was in mourning."

"But to make you a match? I'm certain that your Mr. Rose would be concerned about your future. Had he no expectations? Have you?"

An ugly procession of purple bruises spread like a blight along the bend of her elbow.

"You ask a great many questions, Mr. Ashe, but as you are so curious, such pursuits are of little interest to me, especially . . ." She paused, fearing her face would reveal what her tongue could not. "It had been discussed that I might hire out as a governess. My piano skills are passable but I am more than qualified when it comes to reading and writing. Unfortunately my illness has . . ."

"That is Society's loss," he said, gently tracing the line along her arm. "I am more than certain that you are a lady of taste and sense and anyone would find any house would be made more worthy by your association. And that is an opinion made after only a few moments in your company."

The way he drew her wrist up she half expected a kiss and she steeled herself to call out for Mr. Emmett but instead Ashe leaned over and inhaled, his nose hovering barely an inch above her exposed skin.

There he caught the scent. Beneath the talc and the lavender, the sickness in her that lurked like a black whisper in the vein.

A quick flush of pink imbued her cheeks, bringing a delightful light to her pale skin before fading again to white. She tucked back a loose strand of hair behind her ear.

"I am curious, Miss Bainbridge," he said, cupping her chin as he looked into her eyes. "As you have confessed to not being blood, how did you come to Decimus House? Where is your own family?"

"My family?" Charlotte felt herself falling into the depths of his eyes.

"Yes, miss. Your family. Mother, father, siblings?"

Charlotte blinked. "My mother passed when I was very young."

266

"And your father?"

Ashe felt her jaw tighten and her urge to look away but he held her steady and watched closely.

"I never knew him," she said softly. "My mother's tragedy was going from bride to a widow with child in too short a time. I have no siblings aside from the Rose children, who have always treated me as a sister."

"Yes, the Rose family. What part do they play?"

"Part played? I don't . . . I . . . they were my guardians. Milbrough Rose, the elder Mr. Rose, I learned was acquainted with my mother. I am afraid that she kept much to herself in that regard. It was with restraint when she spoke of her past. Any declaration of a previous familiarity with this house could not have been guessed until his visit."

"I suppose so. There is quite a distance between Regent's Park and, where —" Ashe inhaled as if drawing the scent of her past. "— Spitalfields? The Devil's Acre? The Old Nichol?"

Charlotte stiffened in her chair. Ashe's eyes never left hers, but the darkness that had first enchanted her had engulfed the white until there was nothing but shining black pools.

"No, you have too fine bone, too clear an

eye to have come from so low a place. You have worked hard to overcome your past. Under the Roses' patronage you have learned how to dress, how to talk, how to blend into polite society and present yourself as a right and proper lady, and yet you are excluded. You have mastered the illusion, but strip away the finery and there remains the little girl from . . . Charing Cross in a charity school smock. An irregular choice of a ward for such a notable and genteel house. Tell me, your mother's acquaintance with the family, was she a char? A servant? A secret?"

'Kindness, Charlotte, everything begins with kindness.' Her mother's words were urgent in her ears. *'Do good to those around you and goodness will be visited on you. We might have much between us and the world, love, but what we have, we have because of a kindness given.'*

"My mother was in service to a great house, this house, before she married. Her sewing and occasional char work later ensured our rooms in Charing Cross, and while we may not have had much in the way of luxuries, I never wanted for the necessities. Needlework kept shoes on my feet and clothes on my back and plain as they might have been my frocks were sturdy, and never

268

once did bare skin show through. Our ends were met, Mr. Ashe."

"You say that almost with pride, Miss Bainbridge."

"And you have spoken with impertinence, sir," she said, withdrawing her hand sharply from his. "I may sit here in one of the finest homes in London, with dresses far better than any I had on my back, but never once since coming here has there been the fear of either hunger or the street. Beyond that glass pane is a world of towers and brick and filth that a less fortunate girl might have found herself. Scoff at my provenance, Mr. Ashe, but the circumstances by which I joined the Rose household has never been an issue, and a word has never been spoken in regret."

She was about to stand and call for Mr. Emmett when Ashe again touched her hand.

"And Catherine Rose? Was her welcome warm?"

"The Roses welcomed —"

"No, miss, it is Madame Rose who interests me."

"Madame Rose was a sober woman. Reserved, respectable to a fault, but not the most demonstrative. She had suffered a tragedy. Her youngest child, a girl, had not survived infancy. A loss such as that is bound to affect a person but she did encourage Odilon . . ."

Charlotte slowly sank back into her chair, remembering how often madame would excuse herself from the room to leave Odilon and herself alone. No sooner had the lady exited, the grating squeal of the chair legs pushed back still lingering, than his long, sure fingers would glance across Charlotte's first set of stays.

"She encouraged him to accept me as as . . . a particular friend. Him being the eldest, it would fall to him to see that I was . . ." She looked down, her lashes shading her cheeks.

Shame was an easy read. As was the cruelty of the privileged, and this implication of being a man's particular friend left no doubt that her illness was not the only hurt she wished to escape. Aurelius reached out and touched her face.

Her eyes dilated as quickly as the dyspnea attacked her lungs. Color flooded her face and her breath came in short hard hiccups as if in hunger for air.

"Now, now, calm yourself my dear." Ashe took her hands and lifted her from the chair and led her to the window seat. He opened one of the panes and a rush of cool air swept the room. Gently, he loosened the neck of her high collar, exposing her skin. The result was immediate. Her breathing steadied.

"Charlotte, listen to me, I did not ask these questions lightly and I do not mean any disrespect, not to yourself or to your mother, who was clearly a good woman who wanted nothing more than the best for her child. My inquisition was merely to find out your character and your strength in preparation for what you will need to endure."

She looked up into his eyes. The black had receded, and she saw again the gentleness that had first greeted her.

"My first instinct when your guardian approached was to refuse his query. But now, having met you and seeing for myself your condition, I can promise you that I will do everything in my power to help. However, you must understand that in my doing so nothing in your life will ever be the same. You will not be the same. This world" — he waved his hand outward toward the room — "will not be yours, not as it is now. If you choose to accept what I offer that choice is yours and yours alone. Your guardian might press my hand, but only you can force it."

Aurelius studied her face. Under this close scrutiny Charlotte felt the blood rise in her cheeks.

"Now, there may come a day, Charlotte,

when I will ask something of you and I expect you to act without question in return. I might ask of you something that goes against the very fabric of your being, of your conscience, of your faith, but you will acquiesce. There will be no refusals. I ask and you obey. But until that day, nothing will be expected or demanded of you."

'Stay diligent in your duties, Charlotte; observe obedience and charity and you will always be loved. That is what matters,' Mary Bainbridge would tell her. *'That is all that matters.'*

"Do you understand? The terms of this deal."

Charlotte impulsively wrapped her arms around Aurelius's neck and kissed his cheek. "There is nothing that you could ask of me that I would not do freely if you can help me."

Ashe could do little else but accept the familiarity of her embrace, yet her gentle touch and lavender scent did little to assuage the suspicions that clouded him.

From the window, he looked across Regent's Park to the distant towers of London, a second smaller idea beginning to burn in the back of his mind.

"Ah, Mr. Ashe," Emmett said. As promised

272

he had posted himself outside the door of Charlotte's room like a faithful hound. "How did you find our Charlotte?"

"A most charming creature." Ashe pulled the door closed behind him. "Considering what she is facing, she possesses great fortitude. It is plain to see why your Mr. Rose is so keen to save her and why he came to me."

"Yes, he is placing great faith in *you.* I am hoping that he will not be disappointed."

"I never guarantee an outcome, which I have been upfront and honest about," Aurelius said, Emmett's tone not lost on him. "You don't approve of this venture."

"I have advised my client against it, which he has chosen to ignore. Hence your being here. I hope that you have not given Charlotte false hope as well. She deserves better than to be deceived."

"Again, no guarantees, which she accepted with grace. I'm surprised, Mr. Emmett, that after having examined my son and seeing his scars — and as I understand feeling the mechanism in his chest — you are still questioning my skills. Was none of that enough to alleviate some doubt?"

"The opposite, Mr. Ashe. It has only raised more questions."

Aurelius slid his hands into his pockets,

hiding the tattoos of Fortune's Wheel and the Magician from Emmett's view. "Tell me, do you care for her?"

"I am concerned for her health."

"She is a pretty girl. Lovely eyes, pleasing face. Delicate hands. A fine form." With each feature listed, Aurelius watched the flush of Emmett's face. "Have you wondered what it would be like to have her? Imagined what it would be like to possess her? Her mouth? Her body? It's not too late. I could make it happen for you, if you wish —"

"That is an affront to that good woman! Miss Bainbridge is a ward of this family, which makes her no less deserving of my respect, and I will be damned before I allow anyone to besmirch her character or the reputation of the Roses with such baseness."

"Steady yourself, Mr. Emmett. I mean no disrespect. I merely wanted to see how deep your loyalty goes. But I wonder if that loyalty is to her or to *him*?"

Mr. Emmett took two deep breaths, smoothed back his hair, and allowed the calm to descend over him. "What did you do for this family? Who are you?"

Aurelius stepped close enough to feel Emmett's breath. "I am an illusionist, Mr. Emmett. One who conjures wishes into being, if one only has the courage to ask."

Emmett looked Ashe in the eye and for a moment he thought he saw them bleed to black before returning to their original state.

" 'While my father does possess greatness, it does not in any way mean he possesses goodness.' That is what *your* son said about you."

"Did he now?" Aurelius said. "Well, he has always been a bright boy." Ashe broke out into laughter that chilled the blood in Emmett's veins.

CHAPTER TWENTY

The corridor Rose led Luce down was
ordinary to the point of dull. Oak-paneled
with marble flooring where the only interest
was the Turkish runner with its mosaics of
red and gold. Luce had not expected Ver-
sailles but for Rose, a man who seemed to
pride himself on being remarkable, this
home was most unremarkable.

But as any good showman knows, appearances are often deceiving, as Rose soon
showed when he paused in front of a tall
wooden cabinet.

"It's not many that I allow in to see my
little collection," he said, his hand disappearing along the side of the cabinet.

It was a clever concealment. The false
cabinet swung forward on the door it was
affixed to. The hardware and hinges were so
well hidden a person could walk up and
down the corridor one hundred times and
not notice anything amiss.

Rose lit a candle and the pair entered a second shorter passage.

"This was once a priest hole, a relic in itself of a less enlightened time," he said, leading Luce down a staircase that opened onto a chamber at least twice the size of the anteroom upstairs and three times more cluttered, though in the most organized and orderly fashion.

The room itself was as ordinary as any other in shape and design, but what it housed within reached far beyond the extraordinary. It was like walking into a museum repository as there was not a shelf, case, or surface that did not hold an object or three. Books, vases, porcelains, classical marbles and terra-cotta; one entire étagère contained only ivory netsuke figurines of which each was rarer and more valuable than the last.

Rose moved about the room lighting candles, casting his shadow high on the walls. Each new spark revealed another item of the man's interest. Rose had not lied when he spoke of the elegance of bone.

Arrays of skeletons were displayed in cases. A range of animals posed singly or in embattled pairs; complete or by piece, it was an anatomy lesson in calcified detail.

Then there were the skulls.

All in a row on a single shelf, they looked on in mute observation. They were all human, and in various stages of development from child to adult, but none were as exotic as the twins upstairs. Luce preferred not to think about the manner of acquisition, knowing of at least three ways to come by a skull in London and none of them particularly pleasant. He turned his thoughts instead to what he had assumed to be a large table at the room's center. With the final candles lit though, he saw that it was anything but.

For what he had taken as a table was instead a large stone box, beautifully shaped into a near-human form.

"Is that?"

"He was a temple priest, Eighteenth Dynasty I believe," Rose said, leaning over the open sarcophagus.

The mummy was well preserved. The weave of the linen wrappings was still visible even over the thin dried fingers. Luce had seen mummies before. On occasion one would find its way into a gaff shop, though always much worse for wear than this exquisite example.

"For thousands of years he had lain in peace, buried in the sands on an undisturbed path to immortality. Yet somewhere along the way that path was discovered and his course diverted down an expensive road into my collection. A place I'm sure that he could never have foreseen himself."

Rose gently touched the mummy's arm, mindful of the delicacy of the linen bandages, brittled by time and resin. "This fellow might have been bound for an unwrapping party had he not crossed into my hands. But he remains safe. Pristine and intact, right down to the amulets nested between the layers of linen that still protect his journey. I even have his viscera. Heart, lungs, right over there preserved in their canopic jars if you'd care to see them."

It was uncomfortably clear that Rose was toying with him. He could see it in the curious mix of superiority and half-suppressed satisfaction that spread across his host's face.

"Makes the Thames seem less a challenge," Luce said.

"Congratulations, Mr. Ashe. I do believe that you're beginning to understand."

Rose ran his hand along the edge of the sarcophagus with tender care. "It has taken years to acquire my collection. A great deal of planning goes into each piece. It begins with the first whispers of existence and availability. On to the watching and the

279

verifying of authenticity, and then and only then comes the incandescent moment of success when the prize is sighted and then possessed.

"Of course there are times when something unexpected falls in your lap," he casually added. "Long before anyone else has had the time or the opportunity to recognize the value. They are rare events, but they are certainly among the sweetest."

The realization did not come all at once in a sudden crash, as is the habit of great thoughts, but rather lay before him in the supercilious grin that pierced Rose's eyes.

None of this talk, none of this show, concerned the inanimate at all.

Luce looked across the gallery. Rose had ceased his prowling and now stood with hand in pocket like a lord surveying his dominion. No, these precious items were rewards wrung from the real collection, the poor sods whose indiscretions Rose had bled on their behalf.

The wonder with which he had first greeted these treasures vanished as he thought of Mrs. Harcourt, the woman who had been dragged from the front gates with a warning to himself and Father not to be fooled. Which object here was bought with her desperation? Was it a porcelain vase? A piece of jewelry? Or perhaps it lay inside the small velvet-draped casket that resided on the shelf behind Rose's head. It was an unsettling thought and he had one desire: to flee the room, the house, the presence of this man.

"I have known many a wicked man in my life. Hell, I myself have been both author and subject of a few wicked acts, but never have I met anyone that harbored so deep a malignancy as you."

"That is a harsh estimation," Rose said, the humor never wavering from his eyes, "though I confess that in matters of business I've never found mercy to be much of an advantage."

"Well, when your business with Aurelius is over, you're not to darken our door again."

"From what I know of your father, once you enter into a bargain with him, there is no real conclusion."

"There is always an end."

Rose inclined his head. "It's a pity that you feel this way. I could use a man with your talents. Those in my current employ are satisfactory, but you would certainly add an impressive element."

"I'd sooner die than hitch my prospects to you."

Rose picked up one of the tiny netsuke figures. It was a delicate piece. It was that of a young woman beautifully wrought from a single piece of ivory.

"Oh, Mr. Ashe." He smiled. "Now, that would be a terrible waste."

He tossed the figure into the air and for a moment Luce's half heart skipped, the cog turning hard to maintain a steady beat. It would take only one false move, one slip of the hand for that rare beauty to shatter on the floor.

However, Rose's hand was quick and he caught her up with the gentle ease the wind does a feather. "A terrible waste indeed."

Charlotte remained in the spot where Aurelius had left her, on the window seat, the air blowing cool on her face where he had flung open the pane. It had been nearly twenty minutes and his presence remained as palpable in the room as his touch on her wrist. She looked at her hand, pulling back the cuff of her sleeve as he had. There was nothing visible but she could not dismiss the residue.

How did he know so much about me? Where I came from? Odilon would never have told him. He never spoke to anyone about my past. My God, what else does he know?

Her mind reeled as she looked down on the grounds that bled into Regent's Park. From where she was seated, she could just see the grounds below Odilon's office and the three men who lingered in the shadow of the balcony. A shabby trio, unkempt and suspect to her eye; she had the misfortune of having met Mr. Noanes but the others only at a passing distance. She did not understand their relevance to him, as they were not the sort to socialize with someone of Odilon's ilk, but she didn't ask. It was no matter, despite the instant dislike they caused in her. Especially toward the one who always carried a knife. There was a hostility in his eyes that frightened her whenever he looked her way.

Charlotte heard the floorboard creak in the hall before the door opened.

"I do hope that you did not greet our guest with such a face," Odilon said, watching a veil of disappointment fall across her eyes when she turned to him.

"Has Mr. Ashe left?"

"Yes, the hansom pulled away a moment ago. And I am pleased to say that he has fully agreed to help us in our little matter," Rose said, joining Charlotte at the window. "I take it the consultation went well?"

"He was very kind and patient if not a bit

—" She thought for minute. "— uncanny. He seemed to have a sense of me, of who I am, without any prompting. In three ticks of the clock he guessed that I was from Charing Cross. He was curious as to how I came to be here. It was an altogether extraordinary meeting."

Odilon grew quiet. "Why is the collar of your dress undone? And your cuff? You are in absolute disarray. I do hope that there were not any liberties taken in my absence."

"I suffered an attack," she said, trying to move, but she was pressed back into the corner of the window seat. "I couldn't breathe so . . . so Mr. Ashe brought me to the window and —"

"He was with you for nearly three-quarters of an hour and without a chaperone. You can see my concern —"

"Odilon, I swear to you, there was no impropriety. He was a perfectly courteous gentleman. And Mr. Emmett was just out-side the door. I would have shouted to him if I had felt threatened. Like I said before, Mr. Ashe's interest was about my health, how I came to be here, and my relationship to the family."

"And what did you tell him?"

"The truth. By the grace of your father

and mother taking me in after my mother
—"

"Your mother? He asked about her?"

Charlotte looked up at him, but the glower
on his face nearly silenced her. "I . . . I can
hardly speak of coming to this house without mentioning the circumstances that
brought me here. I've said nothing wrong."
She lowered her eyes. "I've said nothing
more."

"Nothing more?" He slid his hand under
her chin and forced her to look at him.
"And what more would you be inclined to
tell him?"

"Odilon, what reason would I have to
speak ill of you or your generosity?" she
said, attempting to quell his growing temper
with flattery. "Look at all that you are doing
for me." Each word was a small death but if
these half-truths spared her the worst of
him, then it was a simple price. "I owe you
everything."

"Everything, Charlotte. The clothes on
your back. The roof over your head. The
bed where you sleep. Which is why you need
to be careful. You cannot be careless in what
you say around a man like Ashe. He is
someone who can hear what it is you want
to hide. A thoughtless word is all that it
would take, Charlotte, for a name to be

ruined. And all of this" — he looked around the room — "would be gone. And we would not want that, would we?"

"No, Odilon."

He ran his fingers along her chin, drawing a line along her neck. "You know, I've wondered over the years, watching you grow up under our roof, if you are truly deserving of the honor of *our* association. Truly worthy of all our effort. I mean, you were one foot in the street with your charity school and a charwoman mother. Hardly a promising beginning but we took a chance, a mercy on you. We allowed you into our family, into our proverbial pack. And you have since become a reflection of us and so far I have been pleased."

He tilted her head toward the window, allowing the light to catch her profile. "I often think of the nature of packs, of the order, of the respect, and of how and whom wolves come to love within."

She braced herself, silently praying for his trailing fingers to stop.

"The close tactility," he continued, her discomfort igniting a perverse pleasure in him. "And the loyalty that it breeds. So, tell me, Charlotte, who does a wolf love? Who deserves his love?"

His caress stopped just above her clavicle.

"The lamb," she whispered. "He loves the lamb."

"Yes, he does." Odilon reached up and pulled the windowpane closed.

The clicking of the latch was like a two-pound stone plummeting in her gut. "Odilon, please, no," Charlotte said. "I'm tired and not feeling —"

"Shhh," he said, kneeling down in front of her. "Don't tire yourself further with needless resistance." He buried his mouth against the curve of her throat as his hands slid along the buttons of her bodice.

"Please," she said, trying to wrest herself free to no avail. The more she resisted, the harder he held her.

"After all these years, Charlotte, and you still haven't taken to heart," he said, pinning her arms down, "that I always get what I want."

What strength she had faded into a hot wash of shame as she forced herself numb, her eyes closed to his hands and mouth as she wished herself far away.

CHAPTER TWENTY-ONE

23 October, evening, The Athenaeum

Less than five minutes. That was all it took for Dita to sense that someone was there. On the nights when the theater was dark, sound traveled. Not that she relied on anything as pedestrian as footfalls or the creaking of a door or breathing in the night. She simply knew.

"Why do I go to the effort of making meals?" she said, setting aside her book. "No sooner does he get back than Aurelius disappears to the shop with Pretorius — and then you, I believe the cab had barely stopped before you bolted. Let me guess — drank down your dinner at the Elephant?"

Luce smiled sheepishly from the kitchen doorway. "A nip, that's all. I'd things to think about."

Dita looked at him. What was he now, twenty-five? He had an old blue scarf wrapped around his neck and oft-scarred leather gloves that had seen far better days. They were a significant contrast with the good black wool frock coat that was now draped over the chair.

"Sit yourself down. I'll get you a coffee, warm you up."

"Dita, I'm not in the mood to socialize. I'd rather go up to bed —"

"Sit you down! I swear, Lucien Ashe, I often wonder what your moth—"

Dita stopped herself from speaking further. She would not speak Isabel's name, not directly and not because she thought it for the best. She would have much preferred Luce to take her into his confidence completely. But to do so she would need to take him into hers, and if he were to know all that had happened that night — well, despite the niggling regret that gnawed at the nape of her neck, the thought of what could happen if he did come to remember, God help them all.

"You can say my mother's name. Isabel," Luce said, flipping through the pages of the book left on the table. The rich aroma of a fresh brew filled the room. Dita remained silent as she poured out a cup.

"Radcliffe?" He tossed the book down. "You'll be seeing ghosts in every corner."

"If I see any ghosts most would be of my

own creation and not sprung from a page."

"A seer who doesn't believe in spirits? Remind me not to put that on the marquee," Luce teased.

"Hush you. I've no need speaking to ghosts, thank you very much. And I make no denials that there are things out and about the veil, but all too often we invite our own hauntings because we've loved too hard or too fast, we have guilt and regret for what we may or may not have done, and while we bear those pains, we still run forward while looking back. Holding tight as we can when we should have long let go. That's what most ghosts are." Dita held out the cup. "Let go the past. Let go of guilt. Let go the ghosts and all would rest better."

"What about the living ones?" He took the offered cup and posited himself before the hearth.

"A guilt that is not yours to carry," she called over her shoulder as she prepared her cup.

Luce sank back in his chair and sipped his coffee. He was in no hurry to continue the discussion, because the answer would only come back the same. Ghosts, much like any demon, could be exorcised by the force of your own will. You simply had to take that first step.

"So what happened today? I took dinner down to the shop but barely got a word out before Aurelius shunted me out the door. He has had Pretorius holed up in conference for nearly the whole afternoon and evening doing God knows what. All that he told me is that we're expecting a lady tomorrow."

Luce put down his cup. "I don't know what happened between Aurelius and the lady other than he agreed to help. However —"

Slowly the comforts of The Athenaeum slipped away to the blood-red room, back to where Odilon Rose sat at his oaken desk, smug-faced as he made clear his authority by separating himself from the equality of the round table.

'I take that your meeting with Charlotte has convinced you that your time is not being wasted on a trifle. You do see that you are the best and only person who can help her?'

The hearth, despite being well tended, did little to elevate the chill that had settled into his bones. The ghost had seeped within.

'Of course you must understand that this is going to be a complicated procedure. This is not like pulling a tooth. Once she comes to us, she must remain until I see fit for her to return. Can you bear to be parted from her?'

'Her absence will not go unnoticed, but it is not a hardship that I will find difficult to manage.'

"I don't think I've met a more wicked man in my life than Odilon Rose."

"I had gathered he wasn't an altogether good man," Dita said. "Most who come to Aurelius's door are self-serving in one way or another. But not having met him, I can only go off the feelings I read from those who have. Is he really as bad as that?"

"He preys on the secrets and sins of others, sniffing out others' miseries like a damned vampire and contriving ways to line his own pockets with their misfortunes. I suspected as much going in but I didn't expect it to be such a flourishing business."

"And Aurelius agreed to help him?"

"He's agreed because of the girl. She is dying, Dita, and Aurelius knows that he may be the only one who can help her but —"

The hearth fire whipped at the logs like the pronged tongues of a cat o'nines on a flagellate's back.

"But?"

Luce sighed. "What is he going to do to her? I mean, look what he did to me. Is it fair to her? To condemn her to, I don't know —"

"Lucien, all that any of us have ever done

is to love and care for you. You are alive and there is no sin or shame in that. This girl is not Aurelius's blood so there are some things that she cannot possibly inherit. Yes, inheritance weighs on you. How much of my father is in me? What do I still not know about myself? I can't divine that but I can tell you that you can't live your life denying or regretting that part of yourself. If you ask me, that's not much of a life."

"But the cost, Dita. There is much at stake, on both sides."

"Lucien, what aren't you telling me? Has Rose threatened you? Has he something against Aurelius? Or . . . someone else?"

Luce met her eyes. Folded papers and glaring headlines swirled in his mind, and he prayed only that they swirled too fast for her to read.

"A man would have to be fairly well stupid, naive, or both to threaten Aurelius, especially if he wants something that no one else can provide. As for me" — a thin plume of fire waved from the tip of his finger — "a man like Odilon Rose would be quick enough to learn that threats would not get very far. There is nothing to worry about."

"Two halves of the same coin, you and your father," Dita said. "Both of you so intelligent, wills of iron and utterly mal-

293

adroit at intimacy. How very like the pair of you to remain blind to the fact that we all have our vulnerabilities, and that the best way to face them is to admit their existence. I can forgive Aurelius his secrets as part of his nature but *you,* after all these years, I would have thought that you would credit me with having sense enough to see under the mask to the scared little boy you still are. Hiding behind your fire when that is the very thing that terrifies you the most."

She sighed. "I suppose there is an ease to keeping a distance. It's best to be cautious in whom to place your trust, sound reasoning for any man and especially so for curiosities when even within family trust must sometimes be earned."

She walked over and cupped his face in her hand. "Leave the others in the dark if you will, but try leaving me in the dark and you will find it to be a dangerous game."

Through her fingers he felt a charge. It was not an unpleasant sensation like one would get from a sudden shock. This was more like the tingling numbness that follows the awakening of nerves. But the longer she held him, her eyes fixed on his, the deeper and harder the charge surged until it coursed through his body, from the rising hairs on his arms through his knees

294

to his toes like a bolt of lightning.

"It's not just your life, you know." She slid her hand from his cheek and through his hair. The electric charge receded once contact broke. "I'll trust you this time. I will trust Aurelius as I have before and I will believe that we are safe. But I promise you this, Lucien Ashe, I'll be watching."

CHAPTER TWENTY-TWO

24 October, Decimus House

It was perhaps the soundest sleep Charlotte had experienced in a long time.

At one point during the night there might have been footfalls that lingered in the hall, pausing outside her door, but she took less notice than she had on other nights. There wasn't a familiar knock and even if there had been and the door had opened, what did it matter now? He had taken what he had wanted that afternoon, what would have been giving one more night to him? She would soon be away from this house and, God willing, cured.

The soft glow of the morning sun broke through the window. Bands of light fell across her face, the warmth tickling her nose. She rolled onto her side without so much as a wince and buried her face against the pillow.

In the absence of pain she was reluctant

to give up this refuge of warm sheets and soft coverlet, but she could not stand the tickling sun any longer. She opened her eyes to see a figure standing at the foot of her bed.

"You finally slept." Florence smiled over her.

Charlotte sat up with a start. She tugged the sheets up, covering her embarrassment at being caught enjoying the slothful pleasure of the good night's rest that had been evading her.

"You were mumbling when I came in," she said, smoothing Charlotte's mussed hair. Faint at first, the perfume of cold orris and rose held in delicate counterbalance by the warmth of amber vanilla and the middle note of musk wafted from Florence's skin. It was a unique and unmistakable scent handcrafted for only one person. Charlotte loved the smell.

"Was I? I don't recall."

Florence strode back toward the window and sat down on the seat. The sunshine fell across her shoulders, setting to light her copper hair. She was the definition of enchanting. Charlotte had thought so the first time they met on her first day with the Roses. It was immediate that there had been a design in place that the two would and should become friends. It had taken less than a week for the pair to become inseparable, much to Milbrough Rose's pleasure.

"I admire you, Charlotte," she said, folding her hands in her lap.

For a moment Charlotte could not speak. This beautiful woman, so polished and refined, recognized and adored by the society she kept, was looking at her with that same admiration.

She tumbled out of bed. "You admire me?"

"I have been to the Carnivale of Curiosities, as you know, many, many times." She stroked the fading burn on her inner wrist. "And you're going behind the curtain."

"And what will I find?"

Florence smiled. "Magic. Real magic."

Charlotte took Florence's hand and allowed herself to be pulled onto the window seat beside her. There was nothing but warm affection in Florence's eyes. Everything about her pure sweet face exuded sisterly concern.

"I have never seen such spectacle. There is a boy who has the face of a dog. A dog, can you believe, Charlotte! And he plays the most sublime violin. If you closed your eyes, you would think that you were listening to Paganini himself. In addition, there is a man who vanishes in smoke and an aerialist, conjoined tumblers, an automaton, and a dancer. The smallest dancer you have ever seen. You'd think her a doll."

Charlotte felt Florence's hand tighten over hers and she knew there would be bruises when she let go but the woman seemed lost in her own reverie.

"Among the troupe, though, there is a man who is fueled by fire. I honestly believe that were he to be cut, he would bleed flame. And if that were not extraordinary enough he possesses a heart unlike any other."

She spoke with the sanguine adulation of a young girl.

"He claims to have a mechanical heart. Or at least partially so."

"That's not possible. Such things don't exist."

"I've seen the scar, but that could be from anything." Florence lowered her eyes. "Odilon doesn't know. I mean he knows I went to the show but . . ."

"Florence, I —"

"You needn't disapprove just yet, Charlotte. Unless you consider a kiss criminal. There hasn't been any further impropriety, despite his obvious flattery and attentions," Florence interjected. "I am a married woman after all, and he has acted the gentleman. Although the idea is not an unpleasant one."

Charlotte had tried for years to overlook Florence's impetuous nature, but there were times when she could not tell where the teasing ended and the truth began. At heart, she knew that her friend enjoyed shocking people. She had a wild nature and though adherent to the luxuries her privilege commanded, Charlotte wondered if Florence would not have been spiritually suited to a life on Brontë's moors.

"I overheard him speaking with Mr. Emmett. Neither knew that I was there, and Lucien showed him the scar."

"It was wrong of you to listen."

Florence leaned over to kiss Charlotte's cheek. "Always so obedient. Never a minute's trouble from you, our quiet little mouse. One day, though" — she tapped the ruby ring on Charlotte's finger — "you will see that once the cage door closes on you, you too will find a little mischief is the only distraction that brings any sense of relief."

She was wrong on one point, and that was that Charlotte understood cages well, perhaps better than anyone knew. Trapped in a body that was betraying her, in a house that she had rarely left and then always under

Odilon's watchful eye, the desire for distraction in whatever form was appealing. Who was she to judge Florence for wanting much the same as she herself wanted? But at what cost?

This was the debate that Charlotte put herself through as she sat beside Odilon in the carriage riding into Southwark. Should she inform him of his sister's confession, or at least make Mr. Emmett aware, or should she keep the confidence? Was it even her place to cast aspersions on Florence? Would Odilon even believe her? Florence was his sister and it was with her he would side. But an illicit attachment? Would she honestly risk the shame it would bring to the family, and more important to the Rose name?

She looked across to Florence, who was dressed in a daring shade of crimson silk and Valenciennes lace, striped and flounced in a far more daring cut to her own plain dress of soft primrose with its simple drapery and satin ribbon. Mr. Emmett sat beside her in lieu of her husband. The Honorable Judge Suskind preferred his evenings spent in the company of his club engrossed in a game of cards to a night at the theater.

There was an innocence to Florence, despite her being four years her senior, which only caused Charlotte to worry even more about the consequences of a late-night perambulation. She should know better, but as is often the case with those born of wealth and standing, fear and good sense have the unfortunate habit of being bred out of the stock.

Charlotte gazed out of the carriage window and saw Southwark for the first time.

The streetlamps were lit but the glowing globes only cast on the street and its inhabitants a sickly shade of sallow. Women strolled the pavement in a crude pantomime of Society ladies in their frilled frocks and lace while men observed with appreciative interest. A flash of skin, a drop of a shawl — so different were the signals of availability on the street from those of the modest parlor games of gloves and fans. Yet the purpose was the same. Catch the eye and capture the prey. One ends in shillings, the other in marriage.

There but for the grace of God . . . ran the familiar refrain through Charlotte's mind. They seemed to go on for ages, her mother's warnings, her admonitions.

'Those girls might be all smiles and laughter on parade in their frippery, without a seeming care in the world,' Mary Bainbridge would remark, seated in her cluttered kitchen fol-

lowing a trek through the Dials.

'Believing themselves free because they're not mopping tavern floors or sifting through filth or, God help 'em, making matches, but when the difference between eating or going hungry hinges on whoring yourself for the change found in a man's pocket, I wouldn't call that freedom.'

All of which made the sight of the well-dressed women and men in black coats and tall hats that much more incongruous, as the carriages lined up to deposit their custom to the Athenaeum doors. Settled amid its dilapidated and ramshackle neighbors, the panopticon theater was positively elegant. The gas lamps flickered along the street while red paper lanterns hovered above the steps and the entryway. No one expressed any concern about the danger of having a score of small fires hovering in the sky so close to the other buildings. One strong breeze could scatter the delicate inflamed vessels and engulf the street, but the lanterns defied the threat and hung steady, tethered in place by some unseen thread.

As their carriage circled, there appeared to be a show already in progress when they passed a group of men, women, and yes, much to Charlotte's surprise, children who had settled on the dank cobbles for a bit of free entertainment.

" 'Ere I might 'ave known. Out wit' it. You been at me 'usband again!"

"Oh, yer a fine one to talk."

"Don' yer lie to me. I can still smell 'im on you, slut!"

That was all it took before the two women were shrieking and brawling in the gutter to the cheers and calls of the gathered crowd.

Florence wandered out here on her own! Charlotte sank back into her cushion as if by watching she too was complicit. Three constables, truncheons raised, waded into the crowd.

"Are you all right?" Odilon asked.

Charlotte saw Odilon's eyes drift over her hands, which she wrung tight in her lap. "Nervous, I suppose." She offered a weak smile.

"You've nothing to fear, girl. I'd not leave you in the hands of anyone I didn't have confidence in." He folded his gloved hand over hers and squeezed firmly.

Charlotte smiled and returned her watch to the street outside until the carriage inched its way forward and the door swung open.

CHAPTER TWENTY-THREE

24 October, The Athenaeum

Violins hide their voices as people do their flesh. Shy of discovery, it is only the deliberate and determined hands of a maestro that are capable enough of stripping bare the clothed notes. With bow poised, the horsehair caresses the strings, increasing the tempo with each stroke until the moment of exalted release like a lover's cry and the instrument sings.

From maestros and virtuosos, this boldness and skill was expected, but from the boy on the stage brandishing the bow across the lower strings in unquestioned control, it made for a startling sight.

He played with a man's passion, yet not a passion derived of lust or love. Those were emotions that the boy's years had yet to lead him to discover. No, the passion on display tonight for the eyes and the ears of the audience was born from a child's pain.

It was Georgie's first night back on the stage and he held the stage alone. Sweat dampened the hair on his face and his cheek ached but he hammered the strings with the fury of the hands that had beaten him in the alley. In a series of strokes, the violin pleaded and cried, acting as a substitute tongue for all that Georgie himself had left unspoken; all that he could not bring himself to say he poured out in song.

Luce knew the defense of silence well. There was not a curiosity walking the earth who did not understand that after the bruising and the battering, when there was nothing left to feel but the isolation of silent stares and jeering points or worse, the turning of backs and hearts, there remained only one particular pain. Loneliness.

Georgie's small frame swayed in the spotlight. He had been the exception. Raised among them, he had never known what it was like to hurt until now . . .

Luce watched Georgie's thin arms shake, his wrist curved hard over the neck of the instrument as the stage hummed the audience out of submission and to their feet. Music would now be Georgie's salvation, as fire had become his.

Harlequin had joined him in the wings as had Dita, the two drawn to the stage like moths to light. Dita had been especially worried that the first night back would be too much for Georgie. Confronted by all those people, like the crowd in the street when he had been grabbed. But he sallied on.

Georgie had reached beyond the song and had become their voice. From the dampness of their eyes, Luce could see that they felt it too. Georgie now spoke for them all. He spoke of the desperation, of the sadness, of the pain. Of the lost.

The bow pierced the highest point of the strings and slowly the last note drawn before his hand stilled. At first, there was stunned silence and Georgie cautiously raised his head before the raucous applause pealed like church bells through The Athenaeum.

Charlotte had never attended the theater before, let alone the spectacle of the Carnivale of Curiosities. From Florence's description, it all seemed too fantastic. But sitting watching the boy on the stage, she understood the fervor.

How could this child, this strange child, play like this?

Her face felt hot and for the first time in her life, she felt awakened as the sound caressed like wings. She sighed, her breath deepening.

Then . . . tears. She tried to stifle the sob, having pressed her thumb tight to her lips, but it was too much. The music spoke to her. The sadness and all the familiar stings of fear and isolation that had been bound within her by grace and reserve were unlocked. She cried for the mother she had lost and for the father she never knew. She cried for herself, for the death that waited, and for the hope she had.

"Are you all right, miss?"

Charlotte looked at the man seated beside her. He had a kindly face and hair the color of dust. He offered her his handkerchief.

"You must think me terribly foolish," she said. "But he plays . . . so beautifully."

"Not at all, my dear. You are not the first lady to be overcome by tears during one of his performances."

Pretorius grinned as she took the kerchief, her hands shaking as she quickly dabbed her eyes. He ran a quick appraisal of her. She had good form. Slight, but there was an underlying strength; a fortitude of spirit that should respond well to the procedure he had in mind.

Yes, he thought. Aurelius had made a good decision.

There was barely a breath taken from the moment Georgie left the stage until the entire theater fell dark save for four gas mantles that burned above each of the four banks of seats. It was as the eyes adjusted that a single spark lit the center of the stage, and immediately a nervous titter rolled through the audience.

After the initial spark came a second, a third, until a thick flow of fire streaked along the stage with force enough to terrorize a fireman's heart. But the danger was part of the thrill. Would tonight be the night that the curtains caught fire, bleeding up to the silks above as the roof rained embers and dousing every man and woman in a glorious barrage of furious heat?

From the fury of the ridge of flame Lucien Ashe stepped in complete control over the element that spurred these primal fears. His leather coat swirled in the heat, bubbling and cracking, but the man himself remained unscathed as he embarked on what was nothing short of an unbridled show of power. The meeting with Rose, whose threats had been laced with the gentility of his status, had not left his mind; and knowing that the man himself was in the audience fueled the pitch in Luce's veins. Rose might be thought a god of commerce in London proper but in The Athenaeum, it was fire that reigned.

This night's act was an impressive display of rage and art. First from a small ball of white flame a lion, full-grown and maned, was coaxed, a roar of fire bellowing from its lungs. From its nape a goat's head rose and its tail a serpent spit, hissing sparks. It was a terrifying sight, and those in the front row who did not faint lurched back in their seats to avoid the lunging creature. Under Luce's control, the monstrous chimera followed and reared before it nearly bounded from the stage and into the audience until Luce pulled back on an invisible leash, dragging the beast back until it dissipated to ash with a wave of his hand.

He scooped up the fallen ash and blew it into the air, causing a scattering of embers like fireflies. But he was just beginning. He had become a Lucifer and beast after beast he conjured — three-headed Cerberus howled at his feet, a bull charged, and a wolf slavered in hunger before the dragon once again rose above its domain in flight then crashed into Luce until he stood alone in the dying embers, the only flames remaining being the wings that folded around him.

What tears she had for Georgie had dried in the fire and Charlotte could only watch the man on the stage, encased in the wings encircling him, in enthralled terror. As the flames licked at him, never burning but lingering like a lover's touch, her breath caught in her chest. The way his hair curled around the horns of his diavolo mask, he was *Le génie du mal* made flesh and the most beautiful man she had ever seen.

Impressive as the display Lucien Ashe had offered had been, it was not the fire on the stage but the admiration in Charlotte's eyes that had held Odilon's attention. When the curtain fell and the audience roared en masse to their feet, he remained seated. He long suffered his sister Florence's weaknesses, but Charlotte, always serene, always stoic — to see her now so easily swayed to passion with a light in her eyes denied to him gave him pause. Until he felt a tap on his arm and saw Pretorius at his side.

"It is time, Mr. Rose. If you, Mr. Emmett, and the ladies would follow me."

CHAPTER TWENTY-FOUR

By the time Luce had left the stage and waded through the straggling throng of well-wishers plaguing his steps for a moment of his attention, the party of his interest had gathered in Aurelius's office.

"Come, come now, and tell me what you thought."

It was the question Aurelius posed to every guest he had given the privilege of an audience. No matter how often a show was seen, whether you were friend or foe, Aurelius wanted, no he *needed,* to know that the performance was great.

Luce lingered near the door. His appearance had caused only a minute shift in the balance of the room. A slight turn of heads and sweep of eyes that one might see directed to a parishioner who had come late to the sermon. Except for Charlotte, whose gaze remained a second longer than the rest, breath fluttering in her throat.

"Mr. Ashe, if I may —"

In a rustle of crimson silk, Florence stepped forward as bold as any actress on the stage or harlot in the street. Her hennaed hair was bound in a neat chignon save for one stray tendril that slid with purpose along the nape of her white neck.

"I am not a stranger to this theater. I have had the distinct pleasure of attending previous shows, but I must confess that this evening's performance was nothing short of a triumph."

"And that is high praise indeed, as my sister is particular in her entertainments and is increasingly hard to please. However, when she does find something that fascinates her, she is drawn back to it repeatedly. A rather ardent devotion." Rose glanced at Luce.

It was the sort of a petty volley most siblings left behind in childhood, and one certainly better suited to closed doors than open forums. And its meaning was not lost on anyone.

A flash of color touched Florence's cheek that only a practiced eye trained in the reading of others could see was a shade more of anger than of embarrassment. She turned a hard eye to Odilon.

"We have many faithful followers, Mr.

Rose," Luce interceded. "Every performance we do we try to make a unique experience, which does promote a degree of loyalty. But I would certainly never single out any *one* person as greater than another in their devotion, as you call it."

"You must excuse my brother, Messrs. Ashe. I am afraid one of his frailties is his inability to appreciate artists and what their talents can evoke in an audience. I suppose that it stems from his distinct lack of empathy."

She lowered her eyes as she crossed back to the wing chair nearest Charlotte. As she reclined, the silk gown pulled tight across her legs, offering a clear outline to the knees where the fabric fanned out and pooled at her feet like blood.

"Of course he's not a complete philistine. He does have an eye for collectible pieces."

She pressed her fan to her breast, grazing the strands of onyx beads at her throat. Her eyes never dropped from Luce's.

"Florence!"

The shrillness of her own voice startled her. It was the first time Charlotte had ever spoken out of turn and it was not the impression she had wished to make, but she could not hold her tongue. Whatever mischief Florence had intended that brush of

314

the fan was dangerously close to crossing all boundaries of propriety for a married woman.

There was a slight if not uncomfortable shifting of feet, and Florence opened her mouth to respond but quickly closed it as she looked at Charlotte, whose face had become a portrait of distress. Anger furrowed her brow as caution tinged her eyes and her lips. Her lips, which were normally reserved for pleasantries, were now little more than a tucked, tight line of embarrassment that pulled all the way to her soft chin.

Charlotte averted her gaze, the bones of her corset pressing as hard into her as every eye in the room now did. Though she tried her best to ignore it, no gaze was felt harder than Luce's was. Her heart crashed against her ribs.

It became quite clear why he stared, why they all stared.

A small spot of red on her dress. At first it was merely a startling contrast to the primrose; this brilliant red against the palest yellow that only grew as one spot, then another expanded the stain. It was a perfect succession of droplets as the thin trickle of blood rolled from her nose to her lip and along her chin.

"Charlotte —" Rose moved toward her

but Aurelius was already at her side.

"Oh, my dear child," Aurelius said, kneeling down before her. He pulled his handkerchief from his breast pocket and offered it to her. "You've come to us not a moment too soon."

Charlotte looked at him and there behind the cracked powder and stage facade was the avuncular smile he had first greeted her with at Decimus House.

"Mr. Pretorius, please show our guest to her room and do be gentle. Lucien, fetch Dita. We will need her."

"I will help you," Florence said, taking Charlotte's arm.

"No."

"Excuse me?"

"No, madame. You will not help her."

Florence stared at him as if he had slapped her across the face with neither warrant nor provocation. The look in his dark eyes, though, suggested that it was best she not offer any further challenge.

Aurelius stood up and smoothed back his thick hair.

"Come, come, there is no need for a show of petulance, dear lady. I am sure that you have been struck down by harsher admonishments than any I can set before you. Please do return to your seat. Your friend is in our care now, and though your concern for her does not go unnoticed, it is unnecessary. Think no further on the matter."

An icy draft slithered through the room. Florence felt it grasp her shoulders and meek as a mouse allowed it to press her back down into the chair.

Pretorius carefully slipped his arms around Charlotte, gently encircling her waist as he helped her from her seat.

Charlotte quickly obliged and allowed herself to be guided from the room. It was a narrow pass and she clung to Pretorius's arm. The hem of her gown dusted Luce's leg in passing, the faint smell of lavender catching him as he held the door open for them before following them out.

"I would rather you not admonish my sister, Mr. Ashe. Are you forgetting that you are working for me? I will not stand for such treatment."

It was a meager attempt at reassurance. In part it was for his sister's honor but mainly to save face for himself. An insult to her was an insult to himself.

"Not at all," Aurelius said when patient and party were little more than footsteps in the passage. He pulled from his locked desk drawer a sheet of paper. "Apologies if you find my manner brusque, but as you are not unaware Miss Bainbridge's condition is rapidly deteriorating and I see no reason to dally."

"Then perhaps I was mistaken in my —"

"And as it was so eloquently put during our initial meeting — I am exactly the man you need."

Something in the pitch black of Aurelius's eyes caused Rose pause.

"Of course you are still free to walk away from this entire endeavor if you wish, but in doing so you have assured your ward's death."

"Perhaps we should reconsider the possibility of traditional methods," Mr. Emmett offered. "Miss Bainbridge's infirmity clearly speaks to the need of sound professionals." His voice lowered as he drew closer to Rose. "We do not even have the name of the physician that they have contacted, if one at all. There remains a strong possibility of fraud and we have only this man's word to the contrary. I am certain that we can find her a place in a reputable and esteemed hospital or sanatorium."

"That is out of the question."

"Sir, I mean no disrespect but I cannot reiterate my objec—"

"Did you not hear me? This is the only resource not yet tried. I cannot lose her."

There was a ferocity in Rose's determination. And with it something of a half memory in the lowering of voice and glower of eye that clearly stated that dissuasion was not going to be an option, no matter how loud the protestation for reason became. Emmett had encountered this doggedness before, many times and in many guises. It was a trait of the family.

"Do not speak too harshly to your man here. His concerns are genuine and well meaning without doubt," Aurelius said. "It is typical, this second-guessing. Nearly everyone who has stood before me has had a moment of doubt. A small flicker of apprehension, a questioning of *should I or should I not.*" He smiled. "Of course it's always short-lived."

"Mr. Ashe, I can assure you that it is not with any sort of pleasure that I have had to seek out your peculiar skills."

"It rarely is."

"Then you needn't question my fortitude."

Aurelius slid the sheet of paper across the desk to Rose. For all appearances, with its yellowed edges and antiqued scrawl, the page might have been ripped from a text that had not seen the light of day since the sixteenth century.

319

"I didn't question your mother's either."

With a wave of his hand, Aurelius plucked from the air a long black quill. "It is not enough anymore to simply do magic when so many expect miracles. Can you make my business profitable? Do you have a spell or potion that will make so-and-so fall in love with me? Can you promise me a child?"

He trailed off on a path unto himself, one that even Rose was hesitant to intrude upon. It was a brief worry only as Aurelius abruptly returned with a gleam in his hard eyes.

"If you would please sign," he said, handing the quill to Rose. "Bottom of the page. Mr. Emmett, Madame Suskind, you will stand as witness of this transaction. Do bear in mind that it is a binding contract. I don't believe that I need to spell out what that entails."

Rose adjusted his pince-nez and leaned over desk. He had hoped to have a moment to read over the contract but the writing was faded on the antique page.

"It is usually good business to read before signing any document but this doesn't even appear to be English. At least what I can make out of it. Latin?"

"Something much older," Aurelius said. "I can translate, but basically it states that you are entering an agreement of your own volition devoid of duress to which a debt will be held by me until the date of collection, which is to be determined. Collection may occur anytime between one month and ten years. Of course these terms can be revisited up to but not exceeding three times with the knowledge that doing so will accrue certain penalties. Additional time now will be borrowed from your future. Any attempt to break free of the contract, to trick, betray, or deceive me, will lead to automatic forfeiture of said deal and collection will be immediate. Do you understand?"

"Regarding collection, I'm afraid I'm not seeing any mention of monetary compensation for this endeavor," Rose said, looking up from the page. "What is the cost?"

Aurelius thought a moment, taken aback by the fact that Rose, for all of his seeming intelligence, had not quite caught the plot. "Money," he finally said. "All right. One hundred pounds to Pretorius, for the expenses he will need to take."

"So little." Rose raised a brow. "And for —" He waited, the air pregnant with anticipation for the revelation of the doctor behind the upcoming procedure, but was met instead with silent disappointment as Ashe did not take the bait. "And you, Mr.

Ashe? What is the cost of your time?"

"Your soul, Mr. Rose. My time will cost you your soul."

The two men stared at each other across the desk. Florence had retaken her seat disquieted by this turn yet not as unsettled as Mr. Emmett, whose blanched face clearly played to the thoughts that they were possibly dealing with a madman.

Rose let loose with a laugh, shattering the tension like glass. "Not all that different from my own policies," he said, regaining his composure.

"This is not a game, Odilon Rose. When you relinquish temporary guardianship over your ward to me, all decisions concerning her health and well-being will be made by myself and myself alone. She will be mine."

The look that fell across Rose's face would have been as at home on a feral dog protecting its own. "Yours, Mr. Ashe? Yours! She will be of no such thing. It is with great reluctance that I leave her with you, with only your word that she will be cared for and not abused. Our trading of hands, sir, as you said, is temporary. Do not step outside your bounds or I will see to your ruin. I am not without resources either. My mother left her to me. Charlotte is my responsibility and what I do for her or

322

where her future lies is of no one's concern but mine. That woman has grown more dear to me than anyone else in my life and she will see . . . she will see that all I have done is for her."

It was an almost imperceptible break in his voice but Florence heard it clearly. She snapped the fan closed, resolute in her brother's dismissal as nothing more than second best.

"Now, there is the fire that stokes the Roses. But you have come to me and as long as she remains within the walls of my house, there will be no interference from any outside party. I speak to you, Mrs. Suskind and Mr. Emmett, in this as well. No contact from this moment until I summon one or all of you back on the third day. You are in agreement and understanding that no guarantee of success has been made and neither I nor any in my association are culpable should the procedure fail or should she return to you in an altered state."

"Altered state?"

"She will not be the same, Mr. Rose. Her temperament, her personality, there are many unknown factors that could come into play. I will of course try to preserve her as she is but there is always the chance for an unforeseen circumstance. We cannot prepare for every eventuality. So for the last time, sign the contract and question no further or take the girl, walk away now, and never speak of this night."

Rose quickly scratched his name on the paper. A shiver rolled down his arm nearly blurring his signature. "As long as she comes back to me. That is all that matters."

"All that matters." Aurelius shook his head. "No real concerns over lasting effects so long as she returns. Is that all she is? A possession? A body devoid of any agency other than what you have bestowed in her? It hardly seems worth the effort to attempt saving a life if that is all that one has to look forward to."

Mr. Emmett shuffled his feet. He found it distasteful the intimate turn this conversation had taken. Odilon had a proprietary tendency in regard to Charlotte, something that bordered on the uncomfortable, but he was in no position to judge his employer. And he was genuinely seeking to help her. There was kindness in that, surely Ashe could see.

Odilon Rose settled back down in the chair. "You disapprove, Mr. Ashe."

"It is not my business one way or the other regarding anyone's actions, despite what my general feelings might be toward another's moral compass. It is of no matter to me. I will provide a service when asked and collect what is owed when the task is completed. No more, no less. The outcome will be what it will be, Mr. Rose, and you will have to live with whatever consequences come of it."

"I always do."

"Then we are in accord." Aurelius retrieved the contract and quickly folded it in three and returned it to the drawer.

No sooner was the lock turned than the brass orrery jerked and spun a half turn on its axis. It was a sudden but pleasing quirk of the device to see it in action and for a moment, in the presence of so innocent a toy, the burden of the business was forgotten. After all, only Aurelius knew to look for the shifting of the orbit.

"Three days, Mr. Rose. You may collect her then."

CHAPTER TWENTY-FIVE

Step by step, Pretorius carefully maneuvered
Charlotte up the stairs to a room at the top
of the theater. Pain burned deep in her
thigh, nested in the bone that threatened to
moor her several times to the stairs, but
cradled in Pretorius's strong arms she perse-
vered.

"We're almost there, miss," he said, feeling her lag. "Apologies but these storage
rooms are all we've got free. We've made it
up nice for you, though."

The room at the top of the stairs proved
his words true. It was small but serviceable,
and although there remained a touch of
staleness to the air, as would be expected of
any room left in vacancy, it was not to the
point of offense. Rather it was as warm and
dry as a memory.

The furniture was simple and plain. There
was a chair and a washstand, a small walnut
table, and a narrow single bed with fresh

linens. A lit lamp burnished the wood paneling to a golden glow. Heavy timber made up the floor where a thick runner of carpet lay and despite the scrubbing, a spider's web sagged from the corner of the lone windowpane.

Charlotte smiled. She liked this place very much.

Pretorius had not needed to duck but a taller man would need to mind his head about the aged black oak beams of the low ceiling.

"Do mind the pegs and hooks," he said, pointing out the bits of brass protruding from the walls. "They're up high enough but we still wouldn't want you catching yourself on any of them." He settled her down on the narrow bed. "We stored costumes up here."

Charlotte had not been able to settle an age on him. He was of an average height but of a solid frame. His clothes were well tailored but bore the signs of wear. His waistcoat in particular was a tad threadbare at the pocket, where the outline of his watch had indelibly scarred the fabric.

His face, however, held its secrets. She guessed him to be at least five years younger than Mr. Ashe, although his hair was already the color of dust. There was also something to his eyes that spoke of the wonders he had seen and those he constructed.

"Here now, don't bore the girl. A fine lady like herself, I'm sure that she couldn't care one whit for what this room was used for."

Dita swept into the room, tray in hand with cup, saucer, teapot and a plate of buttered bread. "Trust me, my lovely: He's better with his hands than he is with his conversation. Blessing for us all in that, eh?"

Her long skirts skimmed the floor as she nudged past him and set the tray down on the table.

"You'll have to excuse Dita, miss." Luce dropped Charlotte's case with a thump at the foot of the bedstead. "She never could help mothering. Always fussin' over us."

Charlotte looked up at him. Pain creased her brow but that did little to dissuade the fact that hers was the face he had glimpsed through the window of Decimus House.

"Hush now," she said. Gold earrings glittered against the loose curls of her dark hair. "I don't see how showing common concern has hurt you any."

It was an easy warmth that passed between the two, and relief flooded Charlotte when Dita gave her a wink that held nothing but affection. In a moment's divination, Dita leaned down and kissed her on the forehead.

"Now, my dear, I've a nice cuppa here for you. Need to keep your strength up."

Charlotte smiled but it was a lie. She winced and sweat beaded along her brow.

"Pain?" Dita said. "Here?" She laid her hand on Charlotte's leg. "And here as well." She traced her fingers gently along the girl's side. Dita found every point that ached.

"It's all right," Charlotte whispered. "It will pass —"

Before anything more could be said her head whirled and she wretched forward. She bit down hard, bruising her lips against the impending force rising up from her gut. Her throat burned like a knife being forced up and she choked against the blade.

Dita held her head, her hands cool against Charlotte's cheeks. She felt a strong arm encircle her, another hand holding her hair back from her face as she became violently ill in Dita's hands.

"Shhh, calm yourself now, child. Luce, fetch the basin from the washstand, and the towel, please."

"I'm sorry," Charlotte coughed. Her eyes prickled with tears and she wiped her mouth on the back of her hand.

"S'all right, love," Dita said.

She looked into Dita's dark eyes. She felt another ripple roll in her stomach but it quickly abated as did the stitch in her side. This was not what she wanted. She did not want to be seen as an invalid. She thought of Florence. Pretty, confident, bold; had it been she who had been struck down with illness, she would have found a way to remain elegant.

Her eye strayed to Luce who stood at the foot of the bed, concern in his eyes.

"When will I be transported to hospital?"

"Hush now, everything that you need is right here. That's why you've come to us." Dita dipped the towel in the basin and wiped her hands clean before rinsing and placing the cloth across Charlotte's brow. "Mr. Ashe and Mr. Pretorius are going to make it all better. Isn't that right?"

"We will do all that we can," Pretorius said, releasing her shoulders. He gently smoothed her hair back.

"You aren't a doctor?"

"Physicians aren't gods. Your faith should not be based solely in them." He winked. "You are frightened, but I assure you that houses of healing come in many surprising shapes."

A tear slid down Charlotte's cheek and she blinked hard to keep the others in.

"Here now, we need to get you out of these damp clothes." Dita stood and replaced the basin on the washstand. "Gentle-men, if you would be on your way. Give the girl some privacy."

Once the door closed, Dita slipped off Charlotte's boots and then the thick stockings she wore under her skirts.

"What is going to happen to me?" Charlotte asked as Dita unfastened the buttons on her dress.

"I'm afraid I'm not privy to Aurelius's dealings, my dear," Dita said as she slipped her out of the voluminous fabric. "All I can say is trust in them." The bracelets on her arm jingled as she unlaced Charlotte's stays.

"What did Mr. Ashe do for the Roses to make Odilon have such faith?"

"He made their name, child."

Charlotte listened to the ribbon hiss through the grommets, feeling the relief as the corset loosened. "But Mr. Ashe is a magician. He practices illusions, correct?"

"That he does." Dita's hands stilled. "So how can he make a man notable? Raise his status? Which leads to your next question, of how can he possibly provide for you what doctors so far have not been able to?" She smiled and returned to the laces. "My dear, you need only look at Lucien."

The mention of his name rippled her stomach in a manner unfamiliar. "I've heard mention of his heart."

"And I'm guessing that you thought it an act, maybe a lie, but little more than a ploy as good as an egress sign."

Charlotte felt a rising blush. "I . . . I . . . I only . . . I don't want you to think that . . ." She trembled, half furious at the implication that she suspected them of anything improper or false, and half shamed at leaving herself open to such thoughts.

"Charlotte," Dita said, laying her hands on her shoulders, the humor quickly passing from her mind. "There's no shame in having doubts. Half of our audience comes in with doubt, until they see it with their own eyes, and even then —"

She removed the corset and tossed it on the floor with the gown. Charlotte stood barefoot on the rug in her thin shift. The drafts raised gooseflesh over her arms and legs.

"I've seen a great deal in my life that would take another lifetime to explain, but I am not about to pretend to understand what that man is. There are some things that I am better off not knowing. Aurelius keeps his secrets close to his skin, which is all the better because it is not a burden I want. All that I know of Lucien and the business of that night are the wounds I dressed."

Dita's mouth twisted into a sad smile. "Our poor Lucien. He was but a wee nip and it was an ugly stitch running down his little chest, bare and raw as a hatchling's. And when that gear shifted under his skin, dear God I thought the teeth would tear through and he'd be ripped apart all over again. But the skin stretched, the stitches held, and he lived."

Charlotte looked into Dita's eyes that were as dark as the sky before the storm. "How did you know where the pain was?"

"I see things, sense them. It's what I do. The past, the future. I see the wants, the regrets, and those things you want to hide or want to deny. But only when asked. I do respect the privacy of those around me."

"You're a sensitive? A medium?"

"All of the above and much more."

"What do you see for me?" Charlotte glanced up, half afraid her thoughts would show on her face. "In light of what's to come."

"You've been through a great deal this evening." Dita let out a tired sigh. "It might be best to wait until another time. When you're stronger."

"Will I even have another night?"

She fixed her gaze on Charlotte. "Are you sure you want to know?"

333

"Please."

Dita took her hand palm upward. Gently she traced the lines of her palm but her eyes never left Charlotte's. "You weren't born into the circumstances you live in now, though you have every appearance and grace of the manor-born. You think yourself an imposter because of your modest beginnings, which could not be further from the truth. Gentility is not exclusive to those highborn much as money does not promise class. And though it has eluded you so far, despite that ring on your finger, you will know what it means to love and to be loved. In this you will be exceedingly fortunate."

Her touch was feather-light. "Though not without sacrifice." She cupped Charlotte's chin in her hand. "I'll be leaving the rest for Aurelius to tell."

Dita's eyes turned tender, the furrow of moments before relaxing from her brow. "Do you like where you are living? With your guardian, that is?"

"Decimus House is a beautiful place. I adored the walks in the park when I was able. I think I miss that the most. Being out in the green. I am grateful to the Roses for —"

"That wasn't what I asked." Dita brushed the hair back from Charlotte's cheek where the strands had stuck to her skin. "He hasn't a wife, has he?"

Charlotte pulled her hand from Dita's.

"My girl, it doesn't take a seer to see some things." Dita settled her down into bed. "When Mr. Pretorius held your shoulders and your hair when you were ill a moment ago, you made no attempt to draw away. Most ladies, out of instinct, will initially flinch or protest a stranger's touch, especially that of a man and in so intimate a way — even if he is only offering comfort. But you resigned yourself to him. And that glance at Lucien, the mixing of shame and curiosity, of wondering 'is it in every man' . . ."

Charlotte stared into Dita's eyes without saying a word. She hugged her arms around herself and offered only a shamed nod.

"It doesn't matter the class, doesn't matter the age, when that restlessness rises in some men's britches it defeats what sense they should have in their heads. Even the finest gentleman can be rendered a rutting fool looking to make a woman, any woman, into a moment's mattress. Of course if you're charging for the pleasure you have some say, but strays like us we hardly have a chance. But that doesn't make it right."

Charlotte nodded mutely, her tongue

wrung dry.

Dita pulled from a hidden pocket in her skirt a small brown bottle.

"Rest assured, though, as we're all strays of sorts here, you needn't fear. 'Tis not in all of them. The family here knows a thing or two about honor and respect. Even the master himself waited a proper year and a day before returning to my door following Luce's mother's —" She quieted with a shake of her head. "No matter. You should not feel shame. The fault is not yours. Now here, take a sip of this and then a sip of tea. It will get you off to sleep."

Charlotte did as she was told, although she feared her stomach's rejection. The liquid was a familiar, sweet tincture rooted in cinnamon and opium. She had grown accustomed to laudanum since becoming ill, and tonight more than any other night she welcomed its warmth.

"That's my girl," Dita whispered. She hummed a soft familiar cadence as she stroked Charlotte's hair. She had not thought of the song since the little rooms in Charing Cross.

"Please, the lamp," Charlotte mumbled through her drowsy thoughts.

Dita pressed her hand against Charlotte's cheek before gathering up the damp and stained gown. The girl's face was mottled with heat. "Of course, dear. Rest. This will all soon be a memory, and I'll be here when you're ready."

Charlotte heard the door close and she listened to Dita's footsteps fade down the stairs. She curled up under the blanket, rolled onto her side, and faced the wall. The lamp threw darting shadows over the wood panels.

In the near dark with her nose buried in the clean pillow, she was alone.

Alone. The word hit her harder than any fist could, because it was a blow that reached beyond the physical. It reached instead deep down into her and made of itself a hard knot.

Dita was right. She was a stray who had lost hold of her world the moment her mother passed and Milbrough Rose took her away. From that point on her life was not her own, but rather based on the charity of others, which Odilon never let her forget. Charity brought her here. It would always be charity.

She touched the ruby ring on her finger. It was given to her in lieu of a ball. It had been Florence's, a trinket that she had long lost interest in but a moment's pity was the closest she had ever felt to being accepted into their world. To be acknowledged as such.

She rolled onto her back, her eyes tracing the wood panels in the soft light. She twisted the ring around her finger.

Madame Rose had not been pleased when she saw it on her hand and had noted as much with cries of "Thief!" and "Ungrateful creature!" until Odilon stepped in to advocate the gift. Such a cold woman. She had never been kind, but after Mr. Rose's sudden death, she had become far meaner in her attitude. Positively cruel. What kindness was shown was never free. Repayment had to be made. Odilon always saw to that.

But she continued wearing the ring. Her small rebellion in the face of the woman who had hated her from the moment she had arrived. What had she ever done to deserve such outrage? To have not only the ire of the mother but the acts of the son. In tandem, the pair of them, set to dictate her life. She had not expected many freedoms in life but she had hoped to have some say, somewhere.

You will know what it means to love and to be loved.

Dita's voice echoed in her ears. She looked at her palm. The lines to her were insignificant but Dita had seen something or someone?

Lucien. His name had sprung to her mind with more force than expected, carried on the tail of what felt like hope, but it quickly shook free the more she thought on her situation. Odilon was paying them to save her, so of course kindness was to be expected and they were quick to take her in at his behest. He had left her to the care of strangers. Strangers! And not to those in a hospital but to a traveling troupe who sold miracles; who could easily steal away tonight, taking his money, taking her, and be gone before first light — or worse, leave her behind.

The laudanum tolled a bell in her brain and her eyes fluttered.

'Observe obedience, submission, charity, and duty.'

Her mother's words hummed like a gnat. Those words had been her religion for so long that they had become part and parcel to her sense of self; a tattoo of her existence.

'I learned long ago that it is best to follow this path of least resistance. It might not be the happiest or easiest, being forced to hold your tongue when you wish to scream the loudest, but keeping silent and smiling through often grants the greatest chance for security, which is better than the alternative.'

'The girls in the pretty skirts along the Dials.'

'Yes, the girls in the pretty skirts." Mary Bainbridge nodded, touching Charlotte's hair. "It could have all been so different for us if I hadn't shown gratitude. We wouldn't have what we have if I hadn't made that sacrifice.'

She spoke with resignation rather than regret. 'My darling girl, you should have had an easier lot. But it weren't yours to have or mine to give. You are too young to understand any of this but one day, you too may find that gratitude is the only weapon you have.'

A tear ran down Charlotte's cheek as her mother slipped away. She understood only too well what the holding of a tongue against the scream had kept her from. The streets and the skirts. It wasn't the easiest or happiest path but she was secure thanks to her sacrifice to Odilon's will. And yes, she would continue on by showing good faith and gratitude for whatever Ashe had planned for her. For better or worse, she had nothing to lose. She had never expected her life to be glittering, and if it was to be forfeit . . .

But Lucien lived, Charlotte.

Dita's reassuring voice whispered through the walls around her and in the half fog of the drug, she saw him. Standing as he had at the foot of the bed, a device lodged in his chest that kept him alive by whatever sorcery Ashe possessed. She saw his eyes. His brilliant eyes.

"Virgin blue," she whispered. She knew she had seen that color before. It was the rarest of outings, one that had taken her for the first time to the Continent, to Belgium. Odilon had business, so she and Florence had visited St. Paul's Cathedral in Liège, where Florence had giggled like a schoolgirl over the famous statue of the fallen angel, *Le génie du mal,* and then a museum whose name escaped her now. There had been in one gallery several religious works, many paintings of the Apostles, of the Child Jesus and his mother the Virgin. Though the artists and styles were different, they all shared one commonality in the shading of her mantle.

She sank fast under the weight of the opium, and when she resigned herself to the silk arms of the dragon she floated off into a sky of blue.

CHAPTER TWENTY-SIX

24 October, The Athenaeum workshop
It could be said that there was only one true
artist of the company. Although Pretorius,
himself, never once graced the stage, he
nightly played a supporting and to some a
leading role.

For there were those in the audience,
engineers and inventors, who attended
specifically to see what marvel of mechanics
had been added. Unfortunately, the stage
on which Pretorius now played was not for
public consumption. That stage was a
workshop kept well hidden behind closed
doors, and it did not welcome visitors. Not
that many, the fanatically curious aside,
would choose to come, as it was a dangerous place.

On entering the shop it was not uncommon to be assailed by a miasma of ash,
wood, sawdust, metal, and chemical fumes
that hung like draperies in the air. A thin

greasy film covered nearly everything, which brought a perilous challenge to touching any surface for fear of toxic repercussions. There was not a cabinet or shelf that did not hold a tool.

Spare parts of pipes, gears, and shards were piled on shelves alongside half-finished metal and wood torsos while the famed Automaton sat silently housed in a special framed case that resembled a hybrid marriage of coffin and gibbet. It was the gaudiest charnel house one would ever see. And it was here, amid the controlled chaos, that a figure was laid out on a table.

Two hours had passed since Charlotte had taken the laudanum and she remained firmly in the drug's hold.

On a standing desk, a large ledger was opened to a page covered in a thick but neat scrawl. Weights, measures, strange symbols and numbers littered the page that to novice eyes would be viewed as a foreign language — and they would not be in the wrong for holding such a view. The language on the page was in fact Science, its nativity was that of chemistry and mathematics, the languages essential for the endeavors under way this night. The ledger would be the only record as to what was planned and was not meant to ever be published in any other book.

"Are we set to begin?"

The hand over the page stilled. A tear of ink fell from the tip of the pen's nib.

"The laudanum has held well," Pretorius said. "And I dosed her with chloroform to be safe. I don't want her waking up in the middle."

Aurelius nodded and started rolling up his sleeves. In the corner of the room, a small bed was occupied by a smaller figure. Michael Mayhew slept soundly, more soundly than Pretorius ever had when that bed was his. Pretorius rarely seemed to sleep, choosing instead the role of Vulcan working tirelessly at his forge, so it was no hardship to give up his bed to his young apprentice.

"Not having him help?"

Pretorius shook his head. "No, too soon I think for such practices."

"You know best. So, walk me through."

Pretorius removed the white cloth that had been covering a tray on the workbench, revealing several syringes, rubber tubes, a scalpel, and a brass and wooden box connected to two very large glass basins. One basin sat empty but the other held a pale reddish liquid.

"I give you, sir, Aquae Mortem. A concoction of my own comprising mercury and arsenic, which make for an excellent base, to which I've added formalin, camphor, powdered resin, and a sprinkling of natron salts. This should preserve the body as well as prevent any venal collapse. God willing."

"Such a lovely, lovely girl." Aurelius brushed the hair back from Charlotte's forehead. She slept peacefully. There was not a wrinkle of worry or thought of pain anywhere on her sweet face.

"Do you believe in repercussions, Pretorius?"

"I'm sorry? In what?"

"Repercussions? For past actions. It's something that Lucien asked. People come to me looking for help, for solutions to their problems, to alleviate their circumstances, for a better life. All of which I supply and that is as far as I go. I have never really wondered about the aftermath, never cared. After all it is what they wanted, and in their beds they must lie. What matter is it to me? But this girl, she is a collateral piece to what I have done for the Roses."

He gently stroked her cheek. "What would your life have been like, my dear Charlotte, had you not crossed paths with that family? Might have been happier."

"Or worse off, just as sick but without any means of saving herself," Pretorius said. "For every action there is a reaction, but if you think she's been wronged in some form, then we make our amends tonight."

Aurelius looked at the scalpel in Pretorius's hand. The tip shone under the gas lamps. "At the master's word, of course."

"Go on then," Aurelius said. "Gently, though."

"I'll do what I can but I'll not make a promise. There will be pain." The scalpel slid into the carotid artery with ease. Charlotte lay still as the blood flowed from the wound. Pretorius lifted the sheet, careful to keep her as covered as possible to preserve her modesty, and made a second incision into the femoral artery.

Aurelius watched as the blood ran heavy and steady from the small incisions, soaking the sheet and table beneath as it dripped into a long trough under the table. "Keep her close, Pretorius. I need her to fight to stay alive a little longer. She is going to need that desire if she is to survive this work."

"Patience, Aurelius. I have this well in hand." Pretorius cleaned the incisions and inserted the rubber tubes that were attached to a large syringe neatly into the arteries. With a press of his thumb, Pretorius injected his concoction.

Within seconds, Charlotte felt the burning. Her veins and nerves on fire as the blood and interstitial fluids were displaced by the injection. A moan escaped her lips and her eyes rolled violently under their lids.

Her body seized and Pretorius quickly strapped down her thrashing arms and legs. Her eyes opened, revealing only the whites, and a thin stream of froth teased between her lips as her head jerked upward.

Aurelius quickly laid his hands over her eyes and placed the chloroform-soaked cloth over her mouth and nose until her moaning stopped and her body stilled.

A second, third, and fourth injection followed until the empty basin had filled with the remaining displaced blood from the tubes. Pretorius carefully massaged her arms and legs to ensure even distribution of the preservative and worked through her veins any persistent clots.

It took three hours to kill Charlotte Bainbridge. Three hours, two minutes, and forty-eight seconds to be exact.

Aurelius counted down the minutes, as precision was needed.

It was a delicate matter, the raising of the dead. It was not an act he liked to perform, nor was it one to be taken lightly. It took a great deal of strength and it went against everything in the natural world. Although he himself was not an adherent to such laws, there was the matter of respect and of burden, which he did take seriously. One could only go to Death's well so many times before someone or something took notice.

Aurelius traced the stitches on her neck. Her skin was cooling. The last time he had spoken the words, a time that he had sworn was to be the last, had been said for Lucien. It had pained him to the bone to see his boy laid out, his small body a puzzle of stitches and so much blood, on the floor, on scissors and knives, drenched into dressings and swabs. But Lucien lived, he had made sure of that, and so too would Charlotte.

He waited for Pretorius to draw back and the lights lowered. Darkness wasn't a guarantee, as reapers have a keener sense of smell and hearing than of sight so one whiff of life in the room could cause a great confusion in its search. But as long as he retained control, only a few moments' worth . . .

The lights dimmed and Aurelius leaned over Charlotte's prone form. Softly he whispered, with a kabbalist's tongue, a black chant born of a forgotten faith that ended with a lingering kiss on her lips.

This was the most dangerous part, the offering of himself as a vessel between life and death. Fortunately he had the strength and the confidence, but this act left him vulnerable; and despite the moment's brevity, it would be time enough to wreak hell should the reaper wish to do so. Even a demon can tether death for only so long.

From his bed Michael stirred, the cot creaking as he turned in his opium-enhanced sleep. It had been a light tincture slipped into his night's tea but it was more than enough to incapacitate the boy for the duration. There are some things that children should never see.

The temperature dropped as Aurelius entered the darkness of a twilight plane. It was an alternate Southwark he slipped into beyond the walls; a blue twin of shadows that his spirit walked as his body remained in Pretorius's shop. It would not take long to encounter a reaper. Cities, towns, villages no matter the size had their resident reapers. Every family had their own who waited in the corner of the front room or the kitchen, the back garden or at the bedside of the sick, to claim what was theirs when the final breath was taken either by accident, illness, or one of those conveniently unfortunate household tragedies. Judgment always withheld.

But here, along the rooks and the street, they lingered sometimes two and three deep waiting for their opportunity, no different from working misses, really. Death was as vital a commodity to the slums as sex, and Aurelius needed only to sink his claws into one who stopped to notice that there was life within *this* shade.

Back in the shop, Pretorius waited. He cursed the letter that started this venture, cursed the man and very nearly cursed the girl before turning eyes and ears to the grate above and to the Southwark he knew and the one that he didn't. This was one of the few moments he allowed himself to pray.

As predicted, a wraith came quick, drawn half by curiosity and more by will. Aurelius lured the creature to where he could just see into its half-blind eyes, glassed over and bluish white.

I need a moment of your time, he whispered, sinking his sharp nails into the unfortunate shade, *and a breath of your life.*

Aurelius's shoulders jerked and twitched as he pulled the wraith screaming into him until the two spirits held fast in one vessel. Reanimated, he clutched and cradled Charlotte's head in his hands, keeping his mouth pressed hard to hers. He only had a few moments as time was of the essence in tethering a reaper. Hold too short and the procedure would fail. Hold too long and his own life would be challenged. Necromancy was a fine art that needed careful balance.

He dug his fingers into her hair and exhaled, pushing the reaper's breath down into her until her lungs filled, heaving her chest.

One breath, two, three . . .

Lights burned late into the night on the first floor of The Athenaeum. From the street, the burning lights meant nothing more than the normal harmonious aftermath following a performance when the crowds thinned, the carriages and patrons slipped back over the bridge to London proper, and the streets were returned to the denizens of the rookeries and wharves.

However, to initiated eyes, those burning lights told quite a different story.

Skym watched from the street, hidden away in the thinnest of shadows. He, of all people, knew those stories well, had been a party to them. They had given him a bodily strength that he should never have physically had.

But what could they be doing for her? She was a sickly sort, as fragile as Kosh had said. It had to be something like what they did to the boy. That damned boy who should have stayed dead.

He felt his blood rise, thinking of everything that had changed because of Lucien Ashe.

"What is it you are up to, Aurelius? What have you promised Rose?" he muttered to himself. To find that out would be a feather in the cap, a truth to use against either man should it become necessary. It never hurt to add to the arsenal.

"I might have somethin' more of interest for you, love, than that building there."

He might have been able to hide in the shade of the doorway but to a whore's eye no man stood invisible. Not when there might be money to be made.

She stepped into the glare of the lamplight arrayed in sapphire satin and lace. Her dress was an ideal mimic of the expensive fashions that had graced The Athenaeum earlier, but the rough scar and even rougher accent clashed with the image she portrayed. A ribbon jauntily adorned her thick black hair.

Skym stepped from the shadows.

"Blimey, mate, if you wouldn't fit right in

them lot," Silvia said, staring at his skeletal frame. The veins in his hands and face ran under his skin like wine-colored ropes.

"You know them well?"

His putrid-yellow eyes bore into her and in her heart she knew that anything she said he would take for a lie. Still . . . "Only as far as the shillings will go."

"Anyone in particular? The boss or the bastard?"

"You ask a lot of questions, mister, but I'm not seein' you buyin' anything and I've a living to make. So my advice would be for you to move on and forget all about burgling the place. There'd be hell to pay to do so."

He reached out and pinched her cheek, grinding her scarred skin between his fingers.

"Hell is empty, darlin', because all the devils are here." The thin man released her and slipped away across the street.

CHAPTER TWENTY-SEVEN

The following day, Pretorius returned his shop to its former self while Aurelius retired to his room to recuperate, until the first of two meetings with prospective clients drew him to his office. By evening he would be recovered enough for the stage. For now though, the strain of the act was plain to see in the shadows of his eyes.

After the procedure, Charlotte was returned to the attic room. Since the initial stir, a twitch of the fingers of her right hand and a slight tremor of her lip, there had been little else. Not the best sign but Aurelius remained confident and entrusted her to Dita's care.

"Does she need to forget?" Dita asked seeing Charlotte laid out on the bed.

"Doubtful she will remember much, if any of it," Aurelius said. "Anything she does recall will do little harm. What is to come next is up to *her*. She will need to choose between the shade and the light, betwixt and between. Watch for any changes and report to me, good or bad."

He leaned down and touched her hair. Fortune's Wheel spun on the back of his hand.

"Transformation! Transfiguration! Metamorphosis!" Aurelius Ashe shouted to the eager audience. "To completely change form into something more beautiful and exalted —" He coolly stepped to the edge of the stage that tonight Pretorius had modified to thrust into the audience, whose members watched rapturously from three sides. "— has long been a state exclusive to the gods . . . and the insects. Take the butterfly. From lowly egg, to larva, to pupa, until it gloriously breaks through its dull gray shell in a flash of glory."

He cast his eye across the crowd as gaudy and glorified as money could make them. "Does that seem fair? That an insect can do what we cannot? Is there any among us who has not wished to metamorphose into something greater? Has the char not dreamed of being the lady? The thief a rich man and the dowager a girl?"

A woman in the second row shifted uncomfortably in her seat as if Aurelius was speaking to her deepest desire. Her steel-gray hair was swept up from a neck choked by three rows of pearls. Youth was a memory housed in the thin lines at her eyes.

"But what if *we* took that godly gift and made it exclusive no more? Do we dare to dream of such a thing?" Aurelius stepped back as Luce entered from behind the curtain.

No sooner had he reached center stage than the front-of-house doors burst open, driving nearly everyone in the audience to their feet. More than one woman screamed as framed in the doorway stood a massive black horse. Well muscled, withers shining, its mane flowed to its shoulders and tail swept its feathered fetlocks. An impressive creature but there was an otherness in its quicksilver eyes enhanced only by the strange juxtaposition of ram's horns on its head.

A white figure sat astride the animal. Before anyone had a chance to retake their seats, Columbine had snaked her fingers into the horse's mane and kicked her heels into its sides. The horse reared before taking off at a gallop down the aisle toward the stage. People cowered as the pair passed, kicking up an arctic breeze, but not a single set of eyes could look away as the animal charged the stage.

Luce remained standing as he was but as the animal raged forward, he raised his hands. Already aflame, he began to spin an ever-widening circle of fire. If the flames were to deter the beast they failed, as the harder the flames swirled the faster the horse ran until it launched itself full-bodied into the circle.

At the moment the animal leapt at the stage, Columbine jumped skyward from its back and to the astonishment of the crowd soared straight up until her hands reached the dangling silks, turning herself twice before swinging to the safety of her ring above the stage.

Luce dropped to one knee, maintaining the force of the circle as the horse began to pass through the ring above his ducked head. But what entered the ring as beast came out as something quite different. In place of hoof and leg came instead the well-formed hand and forearm of a man. As the head appeared, the audience was privileged to see a grotesque transformation that was sure to haunt their dreams as the horse's muzzle began to shrink back, the jaw and cheekbones condensing in a crush of bone and flesh into the shape of a man's face, his naked body a sheen of sweat as he fell from the circle to the stage. He was familiar to them all as the one constant remaining of the animal's nature were the ram's horns adorning either side of his head. And as he rose to his knees, transfigured from beast to man, he was once again Timothy Harlequin and the audience erupted in a roar of relief and awe.

Safely tucked away in a room well above the stage and the din, in the shadow and the dust, Charlotte's eyes fluttered like butterfly wings unsheathed from the chrysalis before the lids stilled again.

"Welcome back," Dita whispered, smiling into the dark as Charlotte slept on.

CHAPTER TWENTY-EIGHT

26 October, The Athenaeum

Charlotte woke to a world of pale yellow.

Her first thought was that the room was awash with morning light, but if memory served her from the day before the small window, thick-paned and dusty as it was, would at best diffuse only a modicum of natural sun even on the brightest London day.

The little attic.

Had she left this room? She had a vague sense of having been carried down the stairs and of the smell of wood and grime and burning.

She blinked once, then again, until her eyes convinced her that the swath of color running down the wall was not in fact a trick of light but was her gown from the night before, freshly laundered and hung from a peg on the back of the door.

The air was dry and still and she pulled

the thick wool blanket up to her chin, unable to feel any of its warmth. She turned her head against the pillow and heard a soft scratching against the fabric where the pillow met her neck.

Slowly she sat up. With the blanket bundled around her, she swung her legs to the floor. She stretched her arms over her head, cracking the tight muscles in her arms and back. Grasping the blanket tight around her shoulders, she stood up.

It was an overwhelming rush to her brain as in her eyes the floor spun away from her bare feet, from the thin piece of carpet, the pitted and splintered wood beneath; not in a swirl of stars but in sudden darkness. She sat back hard on the bed.

"You'll adjust, my dear."

Charlotte jumped. She had not expected anyone's intrusion, let alone that of himself.

Aurelius stood in the doorway. He wore checked trousers and a dark-blue waistcoat embroidered with silver thread in a series of starbursts. He was absent a tie and collar, which left the neck of his shirt split open; his sleeves were rolled to the elbow. It was a striking difference from the manner of men she was accustomed to seeing. Neither Odilon nor Mr. Emmett would ever chance such informality. But Mr. Ashe was proving himself a different animal altogether.

"Go ahead, try again."

Disoriented, Charlotte rose from the bed.

"You've done well," he said, leaning against the doorjamb. "A resounding success."

She stood up straight and looked at herself in the mirror. She did not notice any difference, aside from being a little paler. Other than that, she could see no perceptible change.

The bandage wrapped around her neck fell away with a light tug. There was a small incision on either side of her throat that had been neatly stitched along the jugular vein; a minor inconvenience that a high-necked collar would easily hide. That, to her eye, was the only evidence of any procedure having been done.

"After a single night —"

"Two nights. You came to us on Sunday. It is now Tuesday morning."

She hesitated before speaking, hoping to find in her jumbled mind something more elegant to say, but all that she could muster in her reflection was —

"Tuesday! I . . . . I have slept a full day? How could I — It was just —"

"Shhh," Aurelius said. "Your body has been through much and needed the rest."

"I have lost a day."

"You have gained a life in the loss of that day."

"Then I am cured?"

Always the meticulous observer, it took less than half a second for Aurelius to discern the trouble in her eyes. "My dear, these are not charms to be overthrown."

"But how? How can you make such assurances?"

Aurelius placed his finger to his lips. "A magician never reveals his secrets."

Charlotte watched him cross from the doorway to where she stood. He walked with slow authority and offered a half smile that reflected as much in his eyes as on his lips. Then he did something peculiar. He touched her shoulder. It was a glancing touch as if he were merely brushing away a stray hair. If it had been anyone else, Charlotte would have protested such an intimacy, especially as only a blanket, shift, and the air between separated her body from his. But with Aurelius, it was less being touched by a man and more by a god only without the arrogance of either.

"You've no need to worry, Charlotte."

He chastely pulled the blanket closer around her and she watched the tattoos on his hands move. She looked up into his eyes.

Inviting and dark, but tired, if the purple shadows bruising his otherwise pale skin were to be judged.

"Mr. Ashe," she said. "I cannot possibly express how grateful I am for everything that you, Mr. Pretorius, and everyone have done for me. I . . . I —"

"Your gown from the other night is a bit too formal for day," Aurelius said, noting the glisten of a tear in her eye with a nod. "And you'll find we are a less-than-formal bunch. Dita has aired the dresses you brought. I'm afraid that we could not salvage your gloves, though, what with the blood and all, but I hope that you will take these as recompense for their loss."

Charlotte looked at the offered pair in his hands. They were wrist-length with three bands that stretched along the main sheath and held in place by three small silver buttons, each of which was engraved with a delicate butterfly. But it was their color, a most extravagant shade of blue, that made her eyes light up. "Mr. Ashe, this is quite unnecessary —"

"Think nothing of it. Now, while you are with us I do not wish you to feel that you must remain confined to this room. Feel free to wander the theater, but do so with care. The Athenaeum is old and she has memories, many of which are unpleasant due to her past, although we are doing our part to leave a happier mark."

"Thank you, Mr. Ashe."

"Aurelius, please." He nodded. "I would escort you downstairs myself but I've an appointment to keep. I'll send Dita up to help you dress and then I hope to see you at tea this afternoon."

"Did you have to kick me so hard?" Harlequin asked. "I've got bruises."

"Best for the show," Columbine said. "I had to make the ride look authentic. It could have been worse, I could have worn spurs."

"Lucky night for me after all," he said, cracking the newspaper he was reading stiff. "Hoy, listen to this: 'The mutilated body of a woman was discovered Monday night on the Southwark side of London Bridge. A young man reported finding the body, however at this time no further details are being released.' The police have put an injunction on the press, 'from the highest authority.' Must be a right corker of a case to do something like that."

Harlequin laid aside the paper. "Of course it will do no good. Not when there are so many other sources to turn to."

"And what, I'm afraid to ask, have those sources told you?" Luce drained his cup and set it back on the table.

"A rather reliable flock of muddy little birds have been chirping away about how she was found butchered. Her throat slit, clothing half asunder and her face . . . well, let's say more than one copper lost his supper after one look. The whole street is talking about it. How it could have been any one of them."

"How awful." Angelique crinkled her pert little nose. "Was she a working miss? I wonder if it was anyone we've seen down on The Mint?"

"Dunno," Harlequin shrugged. "Safe assumption, I suppose, considering I don't know of any proper lady who would find herself on this side of the bridge at night and unaccompanied. Says here that it might have been the work of a High Rip gang moving down from Liverpool to stake a London claim or one of the local gangs. The Deckers, Fitzroy perhaps — any of them looking to extort her earnings in return for their protection. Killing her as warning to the other ladies. It won't be easy finding out who she is, though, considering how little of her face was left." He looked across the table to Luce. "She had lovely red hair, though."

"You would know that because —"

A bright light sparked in Harlequin's eyes as if he held within that gleam some great secret of the universe bursting to be set free.

"Oh God, you didn't!"

"She's laid out over in St. Saviour's Mortuary under the care of the estimable police surgeon Jonathan DeWitt. I was curious. I can get you in if you want to see."

"I wanna see!" Georgie piped. His wounded cheek had healed well thanks in large part to the poultice Dita had concocted: crushed bay leaf and steeped marjoram for the bruising, crushed sage seed and honey for the swelling, and a touch of chamomile for the pain.

"You will do no such thing," Dita said, sweeping back into the kitchen with her new ward following close behind.

Every eye but Dita's glanced her up and down, and under the scrutiny of these strangers, Charlotte was grateful for the high collar of her slate-striped serge. The wound was far too fresh for comfort and collars at least offered the pretense of perfection. Unconsciously her hand inched up and she twined a lock of hair around her finger.

"Timothy Harlequin, how can you talk so

lightly of such matters?" Dita scolded. "You should be showing some respect, after all that unfortunate girl is not a spectacle to be gawked at."

"Everything is a spectacle," Columbine said, in the same dull tone she might have used to announce the state of the weather. She hovered cross-legged an inch above her chair and arched her neck like a cat, stretching the muscles of her upper back and shoulders. "Why should the dead be excluded?"

"It's unseemly is what it is."

"All of Southwark and most of London is talking about it, Dita." Harlequin tapped the paper's garish headline. "Everyone is thinking the same thing, how it could have been any one of them."

Luce glanced at Charlotte who remained quite self-contained, her head tilted, eyes focused squarely on the paper's garish headline. He had not fully prepared himself for the delicacy of her features, the paleness of her skin, and the green of her eyes. Last night had been too brief a meeting but now —

"Can we have no more talk of murder? I don't think this is the most polite conversation to be having in front of our guest, especially after the ordeal she has undergone." He reached out and turned the paper over. "Please, Miss Bain —"

"Charlotte," she said, raising her eyes to meet his.

"You had us worried for a bit with, ah —" Luce stumbled. "Um, your not coming down yesterday. Aurelius and Dita both—"

"I am sorry to have been a bother to anyone," she said. "I . . . I —"

"No bother at all, child," Dita said.

"You look well anyway, miss," Harlequin said, tipping his hat with a slight nod of his head. "Glad to see the ghosts didn't keep you up, I hope."

"Ghosts?" Charlotte said, taking her seat at the table.

"This building was an old debtors' prison before Pretorius got his hands on it. No amount of paint or renovation can scrub all the memories and incidents from these walls."

"Timothy, you'll be scaring the girl out of her wits," Dita said. "Never you mind him, dear."

"Morning, miss," Michael said.

Charlotte nodded to the quiet boy at the end of the table who was curiously spinning three balls across the palm of his hand. The deft whirling of the juggling was a pleasant distraction and she almost complimented

368

his skill before the voice at her elbow sounded.

"Hullo."

Charlotte turned and found Georgie, who was sitting on his knees in the chair next to Harlequin. The talk of ghosts faded under the wave of shame she felt for staring at the child, but he was extraordinary. With the hair on his face and his expressive eyes, he was like an unusual shell or one of the pieces in Odilon's weird collection. She had never seen let alone been so close to a living oddity.

"Hello." She smiled. "You're the violinist, aren't you? You play beautifully."

Georgie beamed.

"Have you hurt yourself?" she asked, seeing the bandage on his cheek.

"I was grabbed in the fog."

"Grabbed?"

Harlequin tenderly patted Georgie's shoulder. "The streets are dangerous enough for everyday folk, Charlotte. What can you expect it to be for us? Georgie here would fetch a very pretty price for the enterprising sort."

It was a moment of clarity for Charlotte to see in the flesh how dangerous and unpredictable human beings could be. First the account in the paper and now to learn of this. At Decimus House she had been sheltered from such outward ugliness. It was appalling to think that this small child, different in look but not in sensibility to any other, could be so ill treated by strangers.

"What is true for the average man living in the slums is doubly so for those like Georgie or the twins, Angelique or myself for that matter, we who possess a particular talent or a deformity that make us seemingly less human but highly prized commodities on the sideshow circuit." Columbine flashed a humorless smile.

She had not wished to stare, but Charlotte was fascinated by Columbine's skin, as she was as pale as Pretorius was dark.

"Not all slavery has been abolished, miss. As an adult, an act can be sold, the contract passed from one manager to another. The ones like Georgie, why pay money when abduction is a viable option."

"It won't happen again, I promise you that," Luce said.

The fierceness of his voice forced in Charlotte a sense of immediate pity for the next person who dared to hurt this child.

"What do you do?" Georgie asked.

"I'm sorry? Do?"

"Are you an acrobat? A dancer? A singer?"

"I'm afraid I've no such talents as those."

"Miss Charlotte doesn't have an act, Georgie," Dita said. "She's here on business not at all related to our show. And before you ask, it is not your business either. No need haranguing the poor girl."

Dita rested her hands on Harlequin's shoulders. "Now my dear, have a cuppa?"

CHAPTER TWENTY-NINE

25 October, Decimus House

This was the time he liked best, the first moments of dawn when the house stood silent and the sun was little more than a bleary eye.

In less than one hour, the world would intrude with a knock on the door and Mrs. Adelaide would enter with his morning's coffee. In two hours, he would be in his coach en route to the financial district and his bustling suite of offices filled with clerks and the hum of voices, but for now there was stillness.

Odilon Rose sat at his desk and studied the room, whose floor had recorded the tread of countless feet that had found and wended their way to him, whether by legitimate business or absolute desperation.

Yet it was one pair of feet that disrupted his thoughts and made the stillness in which he normally found respite into a standing testament in violation. Because one visitor had gone unrecorded. One pair of feet had managed to slip through the gates and the heavily locked doors and sidled along the stairs to this room as if it were a common evening perambulation. He had dared to walk in right under the sightless eyes of the skeleton twins.

Nothing was amiss, as far as he could tell. There were no discernible signs of theft. The dutiful eyes of the servants would confirm that, although the fact that the silver candlesticks remained on the mantel and the cut crystal was where he had left it on the table, crusted with the remnants of last night's port, was proof enough that a cracksman was not behind the night's visitation. He ran his thumb along the edge of the desk drawer. It too remained locked and untampered with.

No, it was not a matter of thieving that prompted this visit, but rather that of delivery. And it was as much an act of showmanship as it was of power.

On the desk, centered squarely on the black leather desk pad, was a cream envelope. Of a superior quality, the thickness and texture almost equal to that of his own choice of correspondence.

Rose turned the envelope over in his hand,

unsure whether the anger he felt should be directed more to the man who was bold enough to deliver the missive or toward the arrogance of the man who had commanded him to do so.

From the envelope, he pulled a single sheet. A finger's width of light slid between the shutters and glanced off the elegant handwriting.

It is done.

It was a simple statement, strong and resolute. He laid the note down, his agitation dissipating slightly in the acknowledgment that he had indeed made the correct decision and for a relatively small price at that.

However pleasing the news, though, he could not possibly overlook the intrusion on his home. No, it would not do to allow Ashe or anyone in his company to think that such liberties would be acceptable. That was not part of the bargain. It would not do at all.

He opened up his desk drawer and withdrew a sheet of paper. A moment later came the expected knock and Mrs. Adelaide entered with a tray.

"I shall have a letter within fifteen minutes," Rose said, setting down his pen. He looked up at her. "Ensure its delivery and then organize the staff. We're going to have a little inventory."

CHAPTER THIRTY

26 October, borough of Hackney, London
Her best cups and saucers perched precariously on the small tray that she carefully set on the sitting room table. They were a fine green and rose floral against a white china surface. Florals were emblematic of her taste, as they made up much of the tidy house, a virtual garden in cushions and paper.

"I confess, Mr. Ashe, that I was taken aback when I received your letter." Mrs. Harcourt carefully poured out two cups of tea. "Our encounter outside of Decimus House was brief if not rather disgraceful on my part. And you say that neither Mr. Rose nor Mr. Emmett disclosed my name. Most extraordinary. And you found me how?"

"I have my ways." He smiled. "And I do apologize if you find my actions to be forward. But if you will excuse my mentioning that you seemed quite upset the other day and your warning regarding my appointment with Mr. Rose, well, you can understand my intrigue."

A rough shade of pink rose to her cheeks with the visible flinch at the mention of the man's name. "I should not have spoken so harshly of so . . . distinguished a gentleman, especially to an acquaintance of his. It was a fit of temper, nothing more."

The flush of color had softened her sharp features, and for a moment he could see the underlying girl beneath the surface of the woman. She had been handsome before whatever burden she carried etched itself in the lines around her pale-green eyes and resided in the deep furrows that straddled her pinched lips.

"You are kind to be concerned with my well-being, but it is quite misplaced and wholly unnecessary."

"And yet you accepted my offer to visit when it would have been perfectly agreeable to decline. It would have been of no offense to me if you had and absolutely within your right as we have no previous acquaintance and yet here we are. In your lovely sitting room."

She folded her hands in her lap and sat back. Aurelius sipped his tea and waited. She studied the tattoos on the backs of his hands. They were incongruous with the fine cut of his clothes. Such images would have been better suited to a carney or a sailor, not to the gentleman seated in her parlor.

"Your letter indicated that you might be of service to me. I gather that you are in some way involved in Mr. Rose's business, a client of his perhaps? Or an employee?" She had come to learn over the years that Rose was no stranger to utilizing the skills of particular men when a point needed hammering home or an example made.

"In a manner of speaking, however you need to reverse that relationship. I am not a client of Mr. Rose. *He* is a client of mine."

Her eyes widened. "I have never known a Rose to seek the help of anyone."

"Oh, my dear Mrs. Harcourt, you would be surprised the people who seek my custom." He set his cup back on the saucer on the table. "Now, you mentioned 'a Rose,' a statement I find curious as it leads me to believe that you have been previously acquainted with someone other than the son."

She stood and crossed the room toward the window. It was not the most pleasant view, as several laborers were hard at work in a quagmire of red clay and muck of a drainage ditch just beyond her lane.

"The infliction must run deep if you cannot even look your guest in the eye and acknowledge a truth."

Her back stiffened as if his voice physically hurt.

"Perhaps I did misunderstand the actions of the other day." He rose from the settee. "My apologies for my intrusion and if I have in any way upset you. Thank you again for your gracious hospitality but I shall take my leave and will disturb you no further."

"No, sir! Please!" When she turned back to him trouble streaked her face. "You were not mistaken. Please, do sit a moment longer," she implored.

"You must understand, Mr. Ashe, that it has never been my intent to speak ill of anyone. As you are a stranger to me, I do not know your intent, but if you are acquainted with the Roses, if he is indeed a client of yours, I must advise that you end whatever business you have with the man. For your own sake and good name."

"Mrs. Harcourt, I'm afraid that your attempt to dissuade me has only added to my interest." He resumed his seat on the settee. "I do appreciate your concern, and trust that I do not take what you have said lightly. But I am not blind. I have seen what Odilon Rose is and I am aware of his rather unsavory actions, which I presume you are all too well acquainted with."

She nodded.

"Then I ask you to place your trust in a stranger whose only interest is in helping a lady, if he can."

"I abhor gossip, sir, and I do not take any pleasure in this," she began, "but I shall trust you. Though if you are to understand what has led to present events . . ."

"In your own time, madame. I promise that I am a man of discretion."

Mrs. Harcourt slowly exhaled, her head bowed and hands as if in prayer. "I did not always live as an independent woman, Mr. Ashe. If you were to have told me that I would one day have my own home, I would have dismissed you as a lunatic. You see, I was once a nursery maid and when I was just eighteen, I entered into service for the Roses. I had previously worked for another family, the Crafts-Burtons, but they moved abroad to India when Mr. Crafts-Burton was assigned a foreign station. However, I was fortunate as they were acquainted with the Roses who had an open situation for a nursery maid. The family already employed a nanny who was seeing to the children's etiquette and education. I would handle the day-to-day, the cleaning, the washing, all that pertained to the son and daughter. Mr.

Rose, Milbrough Rose, had done well for himself in business. He was astute and much respected and Madame Rose, you could not look for a better foundation than what that woman provided her husband. It was a fortunate situation that suited us all."

"But?"

"A great unpleasantness found its way to them." She shrugged her shawl up around her shoulders. "As if a darkness had settled over the house."

Aurelius watched her fingers absently pluck the fringe, each thread twisted and slipped from her hand.

"Mr. Ashe, do you believe that for every success a due must be paid?"

"Now, that is a curious thing to ask. As a matter of fact, I do."

Mrs. Harcourt sat down and took a long draught of tea before beginning again. "By the time I came into the household Mrs. Rose already had two young children and was not having an easy time of her third confinement, which was unusual as she was known to have a strong and healthy constitution. She had an incredible stamina, which made the difficulties she experienced that much more worrying and led many in the house quietly to believe that she would not survive. It did come very close, and we had all prepared for the inevitable, but she rallied. Unfortunately, the child . . . Mr. Ashe, a mother should never have to be separated from her child, no matter the extremity of the circumstance, but in this instance —"

"Forgive me, madame, but I don't follow your meaning. The child was removed to avoid contracting an illness?"

"Were it only as simple a thing as that," she frowned. "The child was removed so as not to further stress the lady. You see she had been born early, by nearly a month and three weeks, and was —"

"Mrs. Harcourt?"

"I only glimpsed her, curiosity on my part I'm ashamed to say, but I've never forgotten. The pitiful mite had a twisted back and her rib cage curved so far inward that the left side of her chest was sunken. And her face." She shook her head. "It was the sort of thing you would expect to see in one of those horrid traveling shows or a circus or something."

"They are known as pickled punks, Madame. A deplorable name, I know, but easy moneymakers for sideshows. The greater the defect, the higher the entry fee."

Mrs. Harcourt's eyes widened. "It was rumored, belowstairs of course, that the lady and Mr. Rose attended one such show and that something had frightened her so deeply the child was affected. I had always thought maternal impression was simply a superstition but . . ."

"And what became of this extraordinary child?"

"That's just it, sir, I don't know. She was only in the house perhaps three days, maybe four, and one morning I woke early and she was gone. I vaguely recall seeing a carriage drive off in a hurry, which led me to assume that the child had died in the night and was taken away, which would have been no small mercy, God forgive me for saying, but what was odd was that there was no funeral, no service nor mention of the child ever again. It was as if Louisa had been erased."

She took a deep breath and for a moment contemplated the teacup that had cooled before her. "Mrs. Rose was understandably caught between grief and disbelief while Mr. Rose appeared unbothered by this loss, as if Louisa had never been born at all. It was a sentiment shared by the daughter, though Florence was quite young and perhaps did not understand. The boy, though, he seemed strangely affected."

"How so, and please, Mrs. Harcourt, do

not leave out any detail."

"Like I said, a darkness had settled over the house and it seemed to creep into the family itself after the child's birth and unfortunate death. Young Odilon had always been a quiet and studious child. He was very bright, almost too bright, but cold and distant with a penchant for selfishness that bordered on cruelty. Of a curious mind, he was encouraged in his studies by his tutors and mother, troubling as they sometimes were."

"Troubling?"

She lowered her eyes. "He liked to know how things worked, Mr. Ashe. At first, his curiosity was satisfied with taking apart and reassembling machinery, toys, and clocks, but as he got older, these trivialities bored him and his interests turned to other pursuits, anatomy becoming a great favorite. It began with mice, frogs, squirrels, birds . . . needless to say it was not a nice hobby for such a well-bred boy. But when he began to involve his sister —"

"And being of a curious mind, he would not be able to resist seeing the unfortunate child."

"Mr. Ashe, he had the strangest expression on his face when the nanny scurried him away. Thankfully Mrs. Rose did not see."

"And the lady? She recovered?"

"Bodily yes, emotionally . . . Mr. Ashe, I don't know if you have children, but when a mother loses a child, no matter the circumstances she will feel that loss like a limb lopped from the body."

"And is this a familiar loss?" he asked.

The surprise on her face was followed by a quick closing. He was stepping out of his bounds and were it anyone else they might have lost her, but Aurelius Ashe had many tricks to draw on.

It was a sudden move and she attempted to pull away as he took her hand. His touch was cold, hard, but soothing. His nails scraped against the tiny hairs as he swept across her wrist. He leaned closer and her nose filled with the sweet scent of fire-licked wood.

"Come now, madame, I know that you carry a pain within you well beyond the point of the cut."

She looked into his eyes that had pooled black as night, into which she could have dived headlong. He was well inside her head and her mind split open like an overripe fruit. "It was not my intent, any of it. Mrs. Rose in a moment of weakness confided

385

that she could not bear the thought of intimacy following her loss. Initially I was shocked by her confession but I soon pitied her, and I did not give her circumstances a great deal of thought beyond that. I was far too naive to understand what her decision would hold, but neither did I believe him capable of —" The passage of years had offered the kindness of distance since the day that Milbrough Rose assaulted her in his own son's bed, but the memory lingered close under the surface that Ashe had scraped through. "I had thought him to be such a good man."

He traced a circle with his thumb along the back of her hand.

"I never told a soul, not even after my dismissal. I wanted only to disappear. Mr. Rose, which I can only presume as an act of repentance, arranged a marriage for me so that I would not have to shoulder the shame. My husband was a man who did not ask questions but happily lined his pockets with what was offered. He would die before the year's end. Too fond of drink." A sigh escaped her and shook her head. "I suppose I should be grateful to have been saved from falling any further, but the idea of being indebted to the man who caused it in the first place was cruel. But that seems to be a trait of that family as I'm sure you have discovered."

Aurelius released her hand and she sank back in her chair. "Mr. Ashe, I don't know why I've told you any of this, but I am four stone lighter in doing so."

"Sometimes confessions come easier with strangers. But do now think of me as a friend." He offered his warmest smile. "You have neglected to tell me what brought you to Decimus House the other day when you tried to warn me off. You said that he held property of yours?"

Mrs. Harcourt licked at her paper-dry lips. "I have already told you, Mr. Ashe, that there is a cruelty that runs through that family. The son learned from the father and what debts the father collected, the son inherited. Milbrough Rose took something precious from me years ago for reasons I do not know. Considering how little I had in comparison, it was —" She shook her head. "After I heard of his passing, I had hoped that Odilon might recall our past acquaintance when I cared for him and his sister. I had hoped for mercy, but I have been shown none. And now that I have shared secrets with you, should you in return use what I have said against him, then it is guaranteed that I will never lay claim on what is mine."

She wiped her face, leaving only the glisten of the tears on her cheeks. "Perhaps it is for the best. So much time has passed. I should let go of what is lost."

"Mrs. Harcourt, I don't believe that anything is lost forever. Why, even the prodigal came home. And since I have a certain sway over Odilon Rose I might be able to convince him to return what is rightfully yours. If you would like me to try."

"Mr. Ashe, you cannot promise me such a thing but I would not refuse your offer if it is earnest. You should know that I cannot pay you —"

"My dear lady, I would not ask for a penny. But perhaps sometime in the future I might need to call on a service from you. Nothing egregious or improper of course. It might even be as simple as a friendly cup of tea. And perhaps your family could join us."

"Family?"

"Your husband? You have remarried, I presume. To a good man whose ring you wear with pride?"

"Yes, I was fortunate the second time, and I think that he would find your company fascinating."

"And children?"

"I've a daughter, grown and gone now. I'd prefer her not to know anything about this

388

matter, you understand." She picked up her cup, which rattled against the saucer. "I don't mean to be rude, Mr. Ashe, as you have listened kindly, but who are you to be making such offers? It is highly irregular."

"Have a little sympathy, Mrs. Harcourt, and a little faith. I have been known to do many things. Now tell me, have we a deal?"

CHAPTER THIRTY-ONE

26 October, The Athenaeum

Columbine threw her entire body over her shoulders again and again as she slid the length of the silks. It was a deliberate action so precise that the silks barely moved in her grip. Only the tension in her knuckles betrayed the strain.

"Too slow?" she called midway down.

"Not at all," Luce said. "Are you going to add a plange?"

"I don't know. I might do something —" She bobbled forward then released the silks. Her loose frock swirled around her as she fell. She glided over a dozen feet and landed safely in Luce's arms.

"— like that," she giggled. She pressed her hand to his chest. "That made your heart race."

"Fair warning next time, please." He spun her around before setting her to the stage. "I might have missed."

"We both know better than that."

Charlotte watched the easy exchange between the two from the front row, her own breath coming back to her once Columbine had firm earth beneath her feet. It was a spectacular act of courage, trust, and an intense intimacy that could only have been born from years spent in close companionship.

It did not escape her the way his hands fitted Columbine's waist as firmly as any set of stays and how her eyes never once dropped from his. Charlotte cleared her throat against the choking serge and collar.

"She wouldn't have fallen. Colly always lands on her feet."

Charlotte shifted in her seat, caught off guard by Angelique's sudden intrusion.

"I've seen your gent here before, and the red-haired woman, but I don't remember seeing you." Angelique climbed up into the seat beside Charlotte. "And I've a good memory when it comes to faces."

"The other night was my first attendance and if you are referring to Mr. Rose, I can assure you that there is not a romantic attachment between himself and I."

"Begging your pardon, but I thought that ring had a different meaning."

Charlotte's thumb rubbed against the

ruby as quickly as the lie that formed on her tongue.

"This, this is nothing." She spoke too eagerly. She had no idea what Ashe might have told them about her or why she chose to say what she did, but at that moment the truth was the last thing she wanted to admit.

"That's a pretty nice nothing," Angelique said.

"She's very talented," she said, turning her attention from talk of her to Columbine cantering and pirouetting across the stage. The silks were wrapped tight around her upper arms and the ends billowed like wings as she took to the air. A second man had joined them on the stage.

"Harlequin is playing Orion tonight. They are rehearsing a new act. A reinterpretation of the myth of the Pleiades. Do you know that story?"

"No, I'm afraid I don't," Charlotte said, shaking her head.

"They were the seven daughters of Atlas. As punishment for his banding with the Titans against the Olympians, Zeus forced Atlas to bear the burden of the heavens on his shoulders. It was after this that the great hunter Orion began to pursue the Seven Sisters. Seeing neither end nor escape of his pursuit, Zeus is said to have been moved to pity after hearing their prayers and cries for deliverance from the chase. He turned them into doves and later to stars as a comfort to their father."

Angelique shifted her eyes and saw that Charlotte was rapt on the stage. "But that is not where the story ends. For every kindness that Zeus was capable of showing there was also a cruelty. Orion, being a tireless hunter, continued his pursuit and on his death was placed in the sky himself. But even then, the sisters remained just beyond his reach, locked forever in an endless chase."

For several minutes Charlotte sat with Angelique's story. "How sad," she finally said.

"Is it?"

"Seven women have their physical selves willingly destroyed to escape an unwanted suitor, only to be pursued into the sky for time immemorial. Imagine being pressed into such a choice because you wished —" For a moment she felt herself making an eighth to the seven in the sky. "Because you wished for deliverance. Do you not agree that is a sad fate?"

"Myths aren't always meant to be optimistic," Angelique said. "Often they are as much lamentation as celebration, but they are always a good story and that's what matters in the end. The stories we tell of ourselves, the truths, the lies, the smoke and mirrors. You must have an extraordinary tale to tell, miss. Aurelius doesn't take to outsiders —"

Aurelius's name invoked Charlotte's attention and she turned her head to Angelique, who continued to talk, seemingly oblivious to her audience. "He doesn't usually have such a keen interest in those who seek his favor. He's always kept his distance and yet here you are. Practically given pride of place while we dance attendance to your needs. A rare privilege."

"I assure you that my invitation here, my stay, is thoroughly correct and proper. Any suggestions to the contrary are indecent."

"The world is an indecent place so you can climb down from your high horse," Angelique retorted. "And I mean nothing by it. I'm only saying that it is curious because it doesn't happen. We are a close sort and strangers aren't extended invitations, as you say, to stay with us. Which makes you appear special for the treatment. Aurelius is a lot of things but first and foremost a man and I just wanted you to know that there wasn't no shame in it should you and —"

"Please!" Charlotte said louder than intended. "It is nothing like that. My reasons for being here are mine and mine alone and are nothing of the sort that you . . . that you shouldn't even be thinking of."

"I'm not a child, despite what my size might suggest. I know what I'm talking about. I saw enough at La Pantoufle Bleu for a lifetime's worth of knowledge regarding the ways of men."

"And what is that?"

"A house in Paris that catered to various entertainments. Drinks, cabaret, and, for the right price, company." Angelique sank back into her seat, pulling her legs even further from the floor and onto the cushion.

"And before you ask, I was strictly on the stage. But I observed and being small I could do so without being intrusive. My appearance was a big draw and we girls made a fine amount of money, after the owners took their share. I lived well. In fact I became the face of the show, right down to the blue slippers I wore in honor of the house's name. And the way those men threw their money about and those who held tighter purses loosened right up once the wine got into them. I dressed in the finest silk, perfumed, cosseted like a proper little pet, and I had fun. Dancing and teasing and making promises I had no intention of ever filling. And the more I resisted the offers tossed my way, the more ardent the pleas of devotion came in the guise of gifts and treats. It was all so much fun," she said. "Until it wasn't."

The wistfulness that had graced her a moment before slipped and left in its place something more desolate, and Charlotte watched this gentle loss settle over the girl at her side. She noticed a quick glint of silver in Angelique's hand, her tiny fingers wrapped tight around something she could not quite see but suspected to be of comfort to the young woman.

"What happened to you?"

Angelique looked at Charlotte and for a moment saw an extension of the man from the night before who had greeted her outside Aurelius's office with far too much familiarity for her comfort. "No, Miss Charlotte, that is mine and mine alone," she parroted. "I found the Carnivale and the Carnivale found me and that is all there is to say."

"Of course, I wouldn't dream of pressing any further." It was a cautious but not unfriendly draw between the two.

"Tell me," Angelique said, leaning toward Charlotte. "Do you think that if the Seven

Sisters had had a bow or a knife instead of their beauty and wit, Orion might have left them alone?"

"Against the pursuit, the capture, and the cage?" Charlotte met Angelique's doll-like eyes. "Somehow I don't think that there is much that would dissuade an unwanted suitor from his hunt. Half the fun is in the cruelty of the persistent chase after all."

She looked back to the stage. Columbine's legs stretched and scissored like a prima ballerina as she tipped back then leapt up, higher and higher with each swing toward the star-painted silks above. She had never seen such elegance and freedom. It was only the touch of small fingertips at her neck that woke her from the spell. She cringed but the hand remained, probing and twisting against her collar.

"Charlotte, I think you're bleeding." Angelique held her hand out, her fingers stained a wet pale pink.

CHAPTER THIRTY-TWO

In the alchemy of memory, there is no more persuasive compound than that of smell. Although bodiless and colorless it is yet able to assail the mind with the first breath, imprinting in its wake a time, a place, or a person with pinpoint precision.

For Charlotte, it was the faint stink of oil. From the lamps and the train station, the smell was a permanent canopy over the street. Mix that with the close, hot smell of open-air cooking, coal, tallow, the must and the sweat of hundreds of people pressing and pushing themselves through Charing Cross to the Dials, and that was the scent of Charlotte's childhood.

Seated now on the workbench in Pretorius's shop, wood ash and grease would have come to burrow into her memory as deep as the stink of blood and rank fat into the hands of a Bermondsey tanner had she been able to catch the smell, which was oddly absent.

She pressed a handkerchief tight to the open wound on her neck, stanching as best she could the blood. Though already it had slowed.

Before she had met Angelique at rehearsal, she had spent the morning wandering the theater, taking care as Aurelius had told her. She had felt like Alice having once fallen down a rabbit hole into a world she could not have imagined. Young Georgie had been her guide with the twins following behind. Such strange children, but all three had quickly become dear to her. With each step Georgie grew more and more talkative in her company, pointing out items of interest, the nooks and crannies and the adjustments and designs that Pretorius had created. The twins occasionally piped up in their singsong way. Everyone had been welcoming. Everyone except for Lucien.

Following his initial attempt at concern, he had fallen quiet throughout breakfast. After Columbine had spoken of the perils the curiosities like her faced, Luce offered only the occasional glance in her direction. Glances that were quick, quiet, and extinguished by the return of her own. She had hoped his attention would linger enough that he might speak, and had they been alone that might have happened. For all his stage bravado, the distinct impression he left was that of shyness and at heart a bit of sadness. Even among his family, protective as he was of them, he remained closed off and slightly out of the moment. But that was only an impression of her making.

Perhaps, before she left The Athenaeum that moment would come. She held no illusion that their acquaintance would last beyond her stay. Odilon would be certain of that. So for now, however brief, feeling the hairs along her arms lift with each pass of his eyes was touch enough.

Her eyes darted everywhere around the workshop. The Automaton hung in his gibbet blind to her stare although she half expected at any moment that his head would lift in accusation.

"Now, my dear," Pretorius said, removing the cloth from her neck, "let us have a look."

Her collar flapped damp against her neck as he gently tilted her head. A dark stain on the floor lurked in the corner of her eye. It had been scrubbed recently as it seemed less grime-coated than the rest of the shop. But the attempt had not been enough to blanch it completely and it left a ghost in the wood.

Pretorius gently ran his finger along her

neck. "You've pulled the stitches but nothing serious, nothing that can't be fixed."

"I didn't feel anything at all," she said.

He looked at her thoughtfully. "I would be surprised if you had."

Charlotte locked eyes on him. "That is a rather curious thing to say. What do you mean?"

"Pretorius, I think it best if I explained your meaning." Aurelius greeted her with a smile. The informality of his morning's attire had been corrected with buttoned sleeves and a fine black jacket. His starched collar cut a sharp white line across his neck. "These conversations tend to be awkward."

He bowed his head, relief visible on his face. Pretorius was not a man of words. His work spoke for him and he preferred it that way. "I will ready the sutures while you two talk."

"Perhaps we should wait until you are fixed up and then we can talk somewhere more conducive for conversation. This is not a room meant for receiving, let alone for polite company."

"No." She spoke sharply, far more so than she intended, but at this point she cared little for Ashe's coddling manner. "Please, Mr. Ashe, changing the venue is not going to change what it is you have to say."

Aurelius did not take offense as she had half expected; to the contrary, his grin broadened. "You are spirited. That is good."

He appropriated a nearby chair and sat down in front of Charlotte. The chair was much lower than the table, which forced Aurelius to look up at her.

"Where to begin, my dear, where to begin?" He took her hand. "Tell me, are you familiar with the term *revenir*?"

Charlotte shook her head.

"It is a French term. It means 'to come back.' " He squeezed her hand but she remained stone-faced, as if his touch hadn't registered.

"Come back? Back from what?"

"When your Mr. Rose came to me with his proposal, he had only one desire: that you were to be cured by whatever means necessary. He had not a care or given a thought as to what might ensue. I let it be known that there were dangers, and that I could make no promises as to the outcome. It was the same as when I spoke to you. And from you both the order remained the same. Yours was an extraordinary case to which there was only ever one means to the end."

He turned her hand over and centered squarely in the middle of her palm was an

402

innocuous dot of dull silver.

Curious, she thought as she touched the metal ball. It did not roll under her probing as she expected but was instead seemingly adhered to her skin. She gave a quick tug but it did not move. Another pull, harder this time, and the bearing shifted.

She had not seen the pin in Aurelius's hand and she had certainly not felt the piercing, which made the viscous pink bead marking the pinhole that much more re-markable.

"Pliable skin. No venal collapse. Good color." Aurelius swept his thumb across her palm, smearing the wet bead across her skin. "The perfect illusion of life."

He looked over to Pretorius. "I feel I don't give you nearly enough credit for what you do. A stroke of pure genius. This work might even surpass what you did for Lucien."

Pretorius dismissed the praise with a wave of his hand.

This exchange of pleasantries and praise was lost on Charlotte. They were a string of random and empty words that were of no consequence save for a riddling three: *illusion of life*. Those three words chased one another around her brain like a dog his tail.

"I don't understand. Illusion of life, what does that mean?"

"What do you think it means? Sound it out." His voice had the cadence of a teacher instructing his pupil, and Charlotte felt very much the stumbling student.

"An illusion is a deception, a trick, so I know that what you are suggesting is not possible. It can't be and begging your pardon, sir, but it is cruel if all that you have offered is just a hoax, a game."

"You question possibilities? After meeting Lucien?" Aurelius shook his head. "I do not trade in hoaxes, Miss Bainbridge. You came to us a challenge and though your Mr. Rose believes that I have some sort of arrangement with a medical wunderkind, the only skills ever utilized are Mr. Pretorius's and mine. As I mentioned to Rose, we had to look at all possibilities and there was only one in the end that was feasible: transfusion. This is a procedure that has had successes for hemophiliacs but remains a loss for your particular condition. So we had to make certain alterations to the process.

"Following a total exsanguination, Pretorius, to his genius, performed an infusion crafted from a synthetic substance of similar consistency to blood that would prevent a total venal collapse and preserve your body, completing the illusion that you are as anyone else. That is why that 'blood' seeping from the torn stitch is pink and not red. For my part, it was a matter of resurrecting you. Although I cannot tell you how as it is an act that is both profane and frowned upon. Those of us who have the ability to perform it do solely on personal judgment, and it is not to be done often and never to be abused." Aurelius slapped his hands on his thighs. "So to put it in the plainest of terms, my dear, you had to die in order to live."

The scream was building deep within but Charlotte's throat refused release. She could only sit and stare at her hands and her veins, now pumping with some foreign concoction.

As she sat mouth agape like a haddock in a fish stall, Aurelius couldn't help but recall the many times he had sat with a client following the completion of a job to help them understand what they had experienced and what to expect. At least one avenue of expectation. After all, what has been set in motion by default cannot be set in stone.

"But death is not always the end, my dear. If it helps, you are now what we call betwixt and between, walking the fine line between the living and the dead but neither fish nor fowl. Properly, you are a Revenant. Now, do not mistake that with one of those bloodthirsty creatures that haunt the penny dreadfuls. Various appetites drive vampires whereas a Revenant exists for a purpose, most often to right a perceived wrong. The drive is vengeance."

He reached for her hand but she pulled away. "Please, don't."

"I assure you, Charlotte, that I am the same man as this morning. I am the same man who sat with you in your room in Decimus House."

"No. You have his face, his eyes, but I don't know who or what you are."

"That depends on where in the world you stand. To some I am a path of salvation, to others one of destruction. I have seen the rise of empires and their inevitable fall. I've aided in both. I have been around since the world was young and man first started to ask questions in the dark without thinking who might be listening. Most of the time those questions are easy to ignore, but sometimes the temptation is too great to resist, especially if said at the right time and the right place. Preferably at a crossroads."

Sheltered as her life had been, even she understood the insinuation of what he was saying. "You are — you —" She could not get the accusation out. For some reason *the devil* never rolled easily off the tongue.

Aurelius laughed, his eyes a flash of black at her hesitation. "Oh my, nothing as grand as that! I may have fallen with the Lucifer but I did not land on the throne. Although I have been compensated, as any good soldier would be, with possession of the gateways, of the liminal places. So there is no lie when I say that I am an illusionist. As to whether I'm seen as an angel or a demon, though, is entirely up to the one who summons me."

He rested his hand gently on her knee, but Charlotte did not notice his touch. "Now my dear girl, considering the circumstances and if you'll excuse my noting your current discomposure, perhaps we should allow Pretorius to mend your wound and leave this talk for another time. I would offer you a brandy if I thought it would help but —"

"You presume to make light of this matter, Mr. Ashe, by speaking to me as if I were little more than a child!"

She looked down into his face and found courage in the spirit he had remarked on. "No, no no, this is all part of a trick. Is Odilon behind this? He is cruel enough to do so, to hire you to tell me these lies and . . . and the illusion with the pin —"

"What would I gain from playing a trick

on you?" Aurelius said. "Do you think that I have the time or the inclination to entertain such fancies? That I hire myself for a rich man's amusement?"

"I don't know what your game is but your humor is sorely misplaced. Now I wish to go home."

"I can assure you, Charlotte, that this is no game. I never make light of my work, so if there are any presumptions being made they are markedly your own. As to your going home, I would not be so quick to do so." Aurelius stood up, which changed the balance of the room as Charlotte now looked up to him. "You speak of game and folly, well, let me assure you that this is all quite real. And that ring that you so inelegantly twist around your finger is as good as a shackle."

She had not noticed that she had even touched the ruby. "I don't know what you mean."

"No? How often are you allowed out of Decimus House? Do you ever go anywhere alone? Or are you always under someone's eye?" A shade passed across Aurelius's face. "In your room you spoke of becoming a governess, but there was no determination in your demeanor of ever doing so. Because you know, deep within, that Odilon Rose would never allow it. He is not a man who lets go of what he deems his, and for that you may thank Catherine Rose." His voice softened. "Clever in cruelty, she found another way."

"Catherine?"

"Odilon is not the first Rose to seek my service. You should be grateful that I denied her a wish. But then —" He shook his head. "Your being here is merely a reprieve, Charlotte. You know what is waiting for you."

It was a dawning horror to think that this man knew what was happening within Decimus House. Her deepest shame at what Rose had forced her into. His nights coming to her room despite her locked door. Once she had wedged a chair beneath the doorknob, which had kept him at bay. The next day the chair had been removed from her room.

Aurelius passed his hand over her brow and this time she did not draw back.

"I ca . . . can't feel you. Your hand." She grabbed at her dress, at the worsted serge, twisting the sturdy fabric in her fingers. "I can't feel this. I can't feel anything!"

Aurelius ran his thumb along the collar of her dress. "This is serge of a fine weave, thick, woolen. Silk, however, is smooth and fur soft and satin is as cold as a widow's heart. Now this should conclude our brief tutorial on things that you already know. These sensations are ingrained in your skin and in your mind so there is no need to feel them. Have you not had enough practice in your life so far pretending to know things that you were not born to? To be panicked over something so trivial."

He brushed his hand along her sleeve. "At the start of all of this, I specifically asked what it was that you wanted. Do you recall what you said?"

Charlotte shook her head.

"Not to hurt. So in the course of Sunday night's action, I took away your pain or should I say your ability to feel pain. In the process, touch fell aside, and I'm sure that you will find taste and smell possibly inhibited as well. Your eyes and ears remain unaltered as you will need them. But as a small consolation, the ability to feel pleasure was left intact. I thought of all the sensations to remain, *that* was the one you might be most thankful for."

Charlotte lowered her eyes as his hand glanced across her wrist and down her hand and for half a second she thought she felt him though she quickly dismissed it as nothing more than a phantom of what she had known.

410

"Perhaps given time," he said, "we might be able to restore a few more of those senses. After all a butterfly cannot feel pain but they know when they are touched. You must understand, Charlotte, that when I concede to entering a venture with someone I've no more idea the final outcome than they have. I merely offer a key, but as to which lock it fits and which door it opens, well, that is left to pure chance. It is a fifty-fifty chance that it will open onto the room wished for. And even when it does, you should always check for cracks in the ceiling."

"It is action and reaction," Pretorius said, rejoining the two. He set a tray laden with thread and needles of various sizes on the bench. "Every achievement, every desire, requires its sacrifice. Sometimes it is the life we have known. Sometimes it is life itself."

Charlotte's face grayed as she looked at the large angry needles in the tray.

"This cannot be what Odilon imagined," she said, shaking her head. "What am I to do, Mr. Ashe, now that I have been made into . . . into one of your —" The word *freaks* clung to her tongue. "What sort of monster am I now?"

"You are nothing of the sort. You are the product of the deal I made with Odilon

411

Rose. A consequence of what he enacted."

"Why would he make such a deal? Why would he seek you out? He is not a man of faith. I have never heard him whisper a word of prayer in my life."

"In a time of need, a man of faith will turn to God. In a case of want, a man without faith will turn to me."

"There was no other way?"

Aurelius sighed. "I suppose I could have snapped my fingers and restored you to health, but I would have hated to read in the papers how a year after Charlotte Bainbridge miraculously overcame leukemia, she passed from a battle with tuberculosis or cholera or any of the myriad afflictions you mortals are prone to. Curing you of one would not make you impervious to the rest. The only way to cure you of all was to kill you outright, which has the additional benefit of devaluing you in his eyes. Perhaps the idea of a living dead woman might be enough for him to let you go. And before you bring up the question of choice, that was yours and yours alone. Odilon Rose might have made the proposal and signed the contract, but it was you who thanked me with the full knowledge that the life you would return to would not be the same. I am sorry that you find this now such a calamity."

"I didn't think . . . how could I possibly know what you'd planned for me?"

"Few ever do." Aurelius looked at her sharply.

Charlotte sat for a moment in silence. Ashe spoke with honest conviction but it was nonsensical. All that he said defied nature, defied truth, defied God. "It is absurd. People do not die and then return. People do not sell their souls. It is not possible."

"Oh, but it is and they do," Aurelius said. "Odilon Rose sold his soul even though, like yourself, he doesn't believe it to be real either. Which is going to make collecting on him a pleasure. To see his face —"

"Even in jest I cannot fathom him signing his soul away on the belief that you could save me. It is absurd to even be saying this but if true, when his time comes, what will happen to him? What is done to souls collected?"

Aurelius leaned back on the stool, his hands propped on his knees. The tattoos on his hands seemed to shimmer in the gaslight. "Since the time of the fall, the first war of heaven, a second war has been brewing. One of hard feelings, long memories, and injustice. Though millennia away, all

413

wars need soldiers. That is where I and my brethren come in. Collecting souls to fight for us when the time comes. It is a win either way for them. Should heaven fall, they gain their freedom as hell will no longer exist. Should we fall again, these same souls can seek absolution and thereby gain their freedom. It is the only way out. Until that time, though, they are sent to hell where the punishment for their pride, their greed, their lust, is servitude. As to how long they remain on this earthly ground — it depends upon the terms of the contract they enter. Usually ten years, a good round number, but that is always open to negotiation. Of course, for those who sell their souls for altruistic purposes such as for the life of another, a case can be made for appeasement toward freedom. But only if they have lived an otherwise spotless life."

The thought of Odilon Rose languishing in hell was disturbing but also deserved. All of those years spent at his mercy and she was going to be the reason he burned. "What is to become of me?"

"That is not for me to decide, Charlotte," Ashe said. "But I can assure you that war will not be your fate."

She looked at him, at Pretorius as well, waiting thread in hand, with so much more to say, to ask. She wanted to argue, to scream. A million and one thoughts tumbled in her brain and yet not one dared leap from her tongue.

"I'm sorry but I can't . . ." she sputtered, slipping off the bench.

"Miss, please sit back down. I've not fixed you up," Pretorius said as she pressed past him. "Oh dear . . . Aurelius, we really should —"

"Let her go," Aurelius said. "She will return when she is ready and has had a moment."

Charlotte rushed blindly for the door, narrowly knocking into Luce as she raced out of the shop.

"Is she all right?"

"A bit out of sorts."

"Did something happen with the procedure? She seemed fine this morning. Is she —"

Aurelius shook his head. "She will adjust in time. When she comes to see what she has gained."

"I suppose you can't expect everyone to go gently."

"Is there something you need, Lucien?"

Luce blinked like a man suddenly coming into a bright light. "I thought that you should know that Skym was seen skulking

415

around last night. Sil saw him —"

"Who?"

"Silvia Marquette. Remember, seven years ago? The woman I brought to Pretorius? Her face had been slashed and he stitched her up."

"Ah, I do, yes," Aurelius said, nodding. "A terrible wound. And such a pretty girl she was."

"She still is," Luce said, the ugly reminder of his own scars itching beneath his shirt. "Anyway, Sunday night, she saw Skym on her stroll and did not like the look he had in his eye. She said he was across the street hiding in the shadows and he seemed to her a bit too interested in the theater, especially the lights on the first floor. She put a right flea in his ear but not before he gave her an equally good scare."

"Was he now?" Aurelius's face betrayed nothing despite what slithered behind his eyes. "Interesting."

"Noanes. Skym. Kosh. After all these years, why now?" Luce asked.

"As you said before," Pretorius chimed. "They're emboldened by Rose's status and presumed protection."

"Or it could be opportunity," Aurelius added. "With Charlotte here, they see a reason to be as well. A perfect confluence of

416

events. It is not for me to say, Lucien. I have not yet had words with any of them, but I do believe that will soon need to be rectified. And I will again remind Rose to keep his hounds chained if he does not wish me to loosen mine. Until then, this business is not yours."

"No." Luce shook his head. "This business became mine the first time Kosh knocked me to the floor. So don't be thinking for one second that I plan to stand by while —"

Aurelius silenced him with a wave of his hand.

"It does no one any good keeping secrets." Luce looked from his father to Pretorius, who absently fumbled with his watch fob, an anxious tic indicative of his desperation to avoid unpleasant confrontations. "I am trusted with everything else. Why is this the exception?"

"Pretorius, hadn't you mentioned needing to check the hydraulics on the music box?" Aurelius said.

"Yes, yes, I did." Pretorius nodded, the watch fob stilling in his hand.

Aurelius's easy dismissal gave rise to a small, resentful voice that niggled in Luce's head.

Aurelius should have as much faith in me as

he has in Pretorius. I am his son and yet he prefers to share his confidences —

Luce watched as Pretorius carefully gathered his tools as if they were priceless gems — *while I am left in the cold. Blood should be thicker than water.*

The refrain tempted him like a pocket to a thief, but Luce knew better than to speak out. He had beaten both heart and head against this particular wall before and had gotten no nearer to the secrets that Aurelius kept.

"I should have expected no less." Luce shook his head and turned to leave when he felt Aurelius's breath on his neck, his mouth close to his ear.

"Do thank your friend for the information, Lucien. It is appreciated," Aurelius said. "But advise her to keep her distance. It would be to her own benefit if she did not involve herself regardless of her concern."

Luce turned fast, expecting to see his father behind him only to see him standing as he was, at the bench across the room, hands firmly in pockets.

CHAPTER THIRTY-THREE

26 October, T. Rose & Co. Bank, London
"This is quite extraordinary. Is he expecting you?"

Noanes held up the crisp white letter he had received that morning. Mr. Emmett immediately recognized the handwriting.

"I was unaware that a meeting had been arranged for today," he said. "Let alone here and during business hours."

"I don't know what to tell you," Noanes said, shrugging, "but you see the letter."

"Very well."

The unlikely pair proceeded along the imposing staircase to the second floor and Mr. Rose's suite of offices. Politic as Emmett attempted to be, it did not pass without the stares of the bank patrons, clerks, and associates. The sight of the man in his company, with his shabby suit and dust-coated shoes, was unprecedented. His face darkened with the prospect of the discussion he would need to have with his employer. The risk of such sudden intrusions of private matters on the public world would not do.

Odilon Rose was seated at his large oak desk. There was a precision in the floor plan of the room, a Grecian symmetry to the office with the twin banks of cabinets and bookcases. It was a plan reminiscent of the office in the house at Decimus House, or so Noanes had remembered from the map in his head.

The blinds were nearly drawn despite the hour only being a quarter past one. It seemed to Noanes that daylight or any light save for that which was controlled and artificial was to be discouraged. Two chairs sat before the desk.

"You do prove a difficult man to find," Rose said, peering over the thin gold rims of his pince-nez. He lowered the paper he was reading. "Mrs. Adelaide was quite distressed at having to send her boy to visit more than one public house including the rather —" He paused, looking for the choicest word. "— insalubrious one that you were finally found in."

"Beg pardon for the inconvenience but we all don't keep office hours," Noanes said.

"Not that I was expectin' a summons from you."

"Quite." Rose folded his paper neatly. "But as you are now here, please." He waved to the chair.

Noanes took his seat. "You must have yourself somethin' urgent to discuss to warrant a command visit."

"Mr. Noanes, I am at something of an impasse at the moment. An unusual place to find myself, I confess, but —" Rose removed his spectacles and laid them on top of the paper. He opened his desk drawer and withdrew a sheet of paper.

From where he sat, Noanes could read the words:

It is done

"What do you have for me, Mr. Noanes?" The two looked at each other in silence a moment before Noanes shrugged, hands thrown up in defeat. "Nothing useful. I'm afraid Mr. Skym was unable to access the theater. There were too many eyes about."

"There was an altercation?"

"No, not quite. He was seen by that black-haired whore who is always strolling outside the theater. He was warned off."

"That is disappointing," Rose said. He

stood up from his desk and walked over to the sideboard. "I was hoping for some information regarding the procedure they had planned for Charlotte. Or more so the benefactor of the procedure. I'm afraid Ashe was less than forthcoming, and I confess their methods . . . intrigue me."

Noanes had noticed the carafe of wine and the glasses when he had come in. Impossible to miss as they were seated eye level and for a man like Noanes, who was moved more by the promise of a drink than by any word or sentiment, it was nearly more than he could stand.

Rose took up the carafe and filled his glass. "I was certain that you would have had no difficulties getting a man inside considering your past acquaintance and familiarity with the area."

The clear crystal turned burgundy, bubbles swirling as the wine slowed to droplets of shimmering circles across the still surface. Noanes could nearly taste each tortuous drop that hit the glass.

"Which draws into question whether or not you are as suited for this endeavor as I first thought after seeing the ease at which one of Ashe's own was able to access my home."

"Someone broke into Decimus House?"

Emmett said. "Why was I not informed immediately?"

"Calm yourself, Emmett, nothing was stolen. To the contrary, something was left. That note on my desk in my securely locked office."

Rose returned to his desk with a single glass. "What are your thoughts on that, Mr. Noanes? I would sincerely like to know. Do I need to warn my neighbors of potential prowlers? Or should I perhaps retain the man's services, as he is a damn sight more suitable to the job."

Noanes shifted uncomfortably in his chair. "Not a lock opened or a window broken. Absolutely no indication of tampering whatsoever and yet in he walked as if he were a ghost. Which of course we both know cannot be true."

Noanes's breath grated in his chest, the only sound in the otherwise silent room.

"I will not have such easy liberties taken against my home."

"Well, there's always going to be consequences when you go looking for miracles and magic."

A hard, humorless smile crossed Rose's lips. "You find this amusing?"

"No, sir. I find it neither amusing nor surprising. He's been doing that ever since

423

he showed up at our door at nine years old. The cheap little crook popped up out of thin air like a spirit."

Rose continued to look at him a long and steady moment, as if weighing the merit of Noanes's words before slowly nodding for him to continue.

"The Harlequin," Noanes said. "He's the only one of them that can do what you're saying. But you're wrong in thinking that it is anything but a trick. You've attended a performance, seen his disappearing act. It is all real. A bit too real for my tastes I don't mind saying."

"You've not been entirely forthright, have you, Mr. Noanes, in your association with Ashe. I believe you've been holding many things back. You spoke before of your hatred of him. That it ran as deep as your Mr. Kosh's. *Hate* is a strong word, born of strong feeling. Kosh's hate is understandable. But yours is unclear. So now is the time to speak, sir. Tell the truth and shame the devil." Rose sat back in his chair and drew the glass to his lips.

Noanes had grown flush. He ran his hand across his mouth, lips and tongue dry. "We've a code among kinkers in that we take care of our own."

"As do I. This is why it would pain me to

have to contact the constabulary with the information that I've acquired about some of the rather more unsavory activities of a few in my employ." He leveled his gaze at Noanes. "I've overlooked much, however—"

"A'right now, there's no need for that. What is it you want?"

"I want full disclosure on everything that you know about Ashe and his company, including how you became acquainted. Mr. Emmett, if you would please, transcribe what is said for the record."

"How'd I meet Ashe?" Noanes shook his head. There was little point in dissimulation now. Rose would smell the lie. So the truth it would be. "Would you believe I wished him?"

"You wished him?" Emmett said.

"Knew you wouldn't believe me."

"Go on, Mr. Noanes."

Noanes sank back in his chair. "There was a time that you could exhibit anything. An empty table for trained fleas. An oversize bloater for a baby whale. String together a few bones from a butcher, half a hide from Bermondsey, and you've the remains of the Beast of Borneo."

He sighed. "You see, it didn't matter what it was you displayed as long as you had a story to tell. Having a penny gaff or a ten-in-one could earn you a living, but soon you had folks like Tom Norman —"

"The Silver King," Rose said. "He's done very well. Advised him on a small financial matter once. Unfortunate about the Merrick business."

"Yeah, well, live acts draw the crowds." Noanes lowered his eyes. "But they're not always enough. Even with Kosh and Skym on the bill, it wasn't enough. Not with Norman and his ilk putting on bigger and better shows. One night I even saw him, the man himself, down the pub, waving that silver Albert chain about like the king he was. I left soon after and got no further than Newington Cross when I said it."

"What exactly did you say?"

"I asked God for one brilliant act. That I'd give anything, anything at all for one brilliant act." Noanes looked rueful. "Three days later I was down at the same pub and there he was. Aurelius Ashe performing the most amazing feats I had ever seen at the time. He levitated an entire table, occupants and all, as if it were nothing. And then he asked if anyone had a wish. A desire. A longing and if they dared speak it aloud, he would give them what they wanted. After much tittering, a young woman spoke. A single word."

Noanes fell silent as if he were living the events again.

"What did she say?" Rose asked.

"*Diamonds.* Ever the showman, Aurelius leaned against the bar and started blathering something about the pleasure of having a throat cut with diamonds before waving his hand. The woman clutched at her neck and, damned if you know it, there was the perfect line of a diamond choker cutting cold against her skin. Well, I don't need to tell you the reaction of every person in that house."

"How do you know she wasn't part of the act?" Mr. Emmett asked.

"I knew that she wasn't," Noanes growled. "After this display, he approached me. Said he could smell a fellow kinker a mile off. We got talking, he said he'd been offered spots, star billing, in some of the biggest and best shows, including that of Norman, but he wanted to be boss. Being new to London he had no way of establishing himself. He was looking for a partner. We were on terms easy enough, and here I thought my prayers had been answered."

Noanes sighed and shook his head. Sweat leached from his scalp into his already greasy, thin hair. " 'Course I was soon to learn that God isn't the only one listening in the dark. And he'd produced that contract. Turns out I'd not found myself a miracle but a damned Master of the Crossroads."

"A Master of the Crossroads?"

"Are you a religious man, Mr. Rose?"

It was an improper question to come from an underling and Rose weighed answering, but if he were to learn all that Noanes knew about Ashe then he had little choice.

"I have never had reason to doubt," he said, sitting up taller in his seat.

"Well, I have. I've never known much decency living in Southwark being that it's not the sort of place that promotes clean feelings. Wickedness, though? Yeah, saw it and lived it every day. But then came Aurelius Ashe and his impossible offer. You see, that's what devils like him do, linger at crossroads waiting for fools like me to stumble through. Sell myself for his bidding in this life and my soul to him for soldiering in the someday 'war' and he'd give me what I want. I thought he was a talented nutter, talented being the key. So I signed his bloody contract as you did, thinkin' nothing of it. A business deal. But if what he was saying was true and being as I was hellbound already, I had nothin' to lose so why not take what I could get? I bet you can still hear the pen scratching on the paper. Couldn't read a word of it, could you?"

'Your soul, Mr. Rose. My time will cost you your soul.'

A chill rippled the room and Rose felt the hairs on his arms rise against his sleeves. "If you are referring to *the* contract, it was written in Latin," Rose lied, ashamed at his own ignorance in not being able to read it either.

Noanes fell silent. He tugged at the loose threads dangling from the cuff of his broadcloth coat.

Rose watched him, head bowed, tugging at those infernal strings, a thoroughly broken man, and wondered for a moment if he wasn't looking at his future. Two nights had passed but he still heard the scratching of the pen.

"With a draw like Ashe, money was good. It came in fast," Noanes finally said. "Too fast and all too good, I suppose, to take notice of the subtle improvements to the other acts in the show."

"Improvements? What sort of improvements did you note? And please be as detailed as possible."

"It started with Skym, who was always a thin man, but after Ashe showed up something changed. He grew strong, stronger than his feeble body could have ever been. Same goes for Kosh, who'd always had a good arm. But he started throwing knives as if they were bolts from Zeus's own hand."

Rose looked at him with concentrated attentiveness. "Yes, yes, that is all well and good, but to the present purpose of inquiry. If these changes in your compatriots are to be attributed to Ashe then what was the method? Was there anyone else involved? A doctor? An alienist versed in mesmerism? You have to understand how remarkable your accusations sound. And if they prove true, what this would mean? So I demand full disclosure, Mr. Noanes. I am the one who is paying you now and paying you well."

"Then you'd best be asking them now, shouldn't you?" Noanes eyes darkened. "I don't know what you're expecting to hear. I could tell you that there was some sort of show, some ritual, but the truth is there weren't nothin'. That is why when I started noticing changes it was too late. It was the ordinariness of it. There were times I thought I was going mad. Sometimes I think we are nothing but experiments to the man." He shook his head. "Believe me, don't believe me, it's no skin off my back. But mark my words: You will see it in that girl of yours. Maybe not at once, but gradually the changes will come out."

"And what of you, Mr. Noanes? You do not seem to be an entirely unsullied man, yet I have not seen anything particularly extraordinary about you. Since he benefited our mutual friends, what did you gain? You spent a great deal of time in his company, he considered you a partner, and yet what have you to show?"

"No, nothing extraordinary about me, that you have right. All I wanted was the money, a bit of prestige maybe, and to never fear a workhouse or jail again. I might not have much now but —" He shrugged.

"Then what soured so promising a career?" Emmett asked. "Ashe insinuated that your unreliability led to unpleasant yet unspecified consequences."

"He would say that, wouldn't he?" Noanes said, reinforcing his words with a shake of his head. "Unspecified consequences, eh? He ought to know well about that."

"What does that mean?"

"Let's just say there are some wants it's best not to toy with."

Rose caught Emmett's eye. To the trained ear, Noanes's words carried the sort of conspiratorial intonation that ofttimes prefaced a valuable revelation. Having been privy to many such moments, Rose courteously waited for Noanes's own time.

"Meaning you no disrespect, sir, but you went into this venture blind as a beetle."

"Then enlighten me," Rose said, his patience thinning.

"Ashe can sniff out the broken pieces in your life, whether you know of them or not, and fix them. Whatever you lacked, whatever you wanted, for better or worse."

Noanes cleared his throat. "The heart is a singular thing, 'specially when it has its wants and needs. There is no depth or distance some won't go to satisfy that need, like a starved dog looking for food. You'll take the first scrap offered without looking at the hand, and once on that path there's no coming back. And Ashe, he's waiting with welcoming arms to guide you on. It's what his kind do."

All of his confidence and earlier bluster evaporated with the fire in his eyes. "There was a woman who had had herself a certain want, a longing that became to her a derangement she never recovered from."

"Someone close to you, I presume, to know such intimacies."

Noanes nodded. "Aye, she was part of an act. Kosh, the wife, and the knife."

"Kosh's wife —"

"Ashe's convenience and my daughter."

432

Rose blinked at the dawning of the realization of how entwined these men were. A smile that carried all the warmth of barren ashes crossed Rose's lips. "Lucien Ashe. Your grandson. It was a child she wanted."

Noanes stared at him, wishing he had nerve enough to break that crystal glass and grind the shards into his smug face. Instead, he dug his fingers into the arm of the chair.

"If Ashe is what you claim him to be, you did nothing to warn your daughter off? Your own daughter?"

"I tried my best to warn her off that path as I tried to warn you. Before you throw that in my face, all three of us warned you. He ain't human, I said that to her same as I said to you, but she, like yourself, was driven by one purpose and once the promise was within reach she gripped it like a blind man does the dark; wanting only something, someone, to call her own."

His momentary weakness passed and his voice regained a fraction of its former bluster. "She sure as hell deserved better than what she got. I only hope that for the sake of that girl of yours that she fares better."

"Tell me, Mr. Noanes, do you know of a way to break a deal once it's made? Have you seen anyone succeed in doing so, considering how long you were in his company? The fact that you are still walking free leads me to believe that you found a way around his rules."

"He hasn't collected on me because he wants me to live with my decision. He killed my daughter because I encouraged her to . . ." He trailed off. "He's been punishing me ever since. That's what he does to those who cross him. There have been those who tried to break their deals, not many and none successfully. I remember there was one chap, a rich businessman whom I think you would've liked. I think he was called James Ackroyd . . . or Atherton. Yea, Atherton. James Atherton, something like that —"

"Atherton?" Rose sitting up straighter in his chair. "I know that name. I've heard it before. James Atherton . . ." His voice tapered off with his thoughts.

"Doesn't surprise. Cut from the same cloth as you as I recall," Noanes said. "Good schooling, good family, good standing in the world. But it wasn't enough. He wanted more. More money, more success, so he turned to Ashe. He got what he wanted but he lost more than he bargained for. First his mother. Then his father and a sister and then his wife. And he started to see that for every gain there followed —"

"Soon after a loss," Rose said.

"That's right. That was the way his deal went. He was so afraid of losing his two sons that he visited a priest and some scholar and it was from the latter that he got hold of a devil's trap."

"A devil's trap?" Rose asked.

"Yeah, he lured Aurelius to his house with something about wanting to renegotiate his original deal. Well, he had a little surprise waiting. On the floor of the foyer, he had drawn out a design that he was assured could trap something like Ashe. He had hoped to catch him and keep him bound until he freed him from his contract."

"How do you know this?"

Noanes's fingers tapped nervously on the arm of his chair. "I was there. Aurelius had me go with him. When he goes to meet a client, he usually has someone accompany him. But I waited outside in the street with the cab while he went into Atherton's house alone. Two hours later he limped out bloodied and in an absolute state."

"Two hours, Mr. Noanes?" Emmett asked. "That is a long time to wait. Weren't you concerned?"

"Wasn't any of my business. I might have heard some shouts," Noanes said with a shrug, "or it might have been a dog howl-

435

ing. But it wasn't worth investigating."

"And what came of Atherton?"

"Dunno. I understand that the contract did end that day, just not how that unfortunate sod thought it would. Aurelius sent me and Kosh around later that night to tie up any loose ends and we found the house empty and in shambles. Windows broken, a huge crack in the floor where the trap was drawn, but not a trace of Atherton. Up and left his business, his sons, everything gone. He disappeared from the world. I can tell you that Aurelius wasn't happy when we came back —" Noanes sighed, drawing his hand through his thinning hair. "There are rumors that Atherton's still somewhere here in London. Gone to ground, taken to the street, or worse. For his sake, I'm hoping the poor bastard's dead."

"Very good, Mr. Noanes, thank you. This has been very informative. Have yourself a drink, please."

Noanes eagerly crossed to the sideboard and took the carafe in hand. He was grateful to have this interrogation over so he could once again drown the memories.

"And Mr. Noanes, about that other matter, the failure to gain access to the theater. Do be sure that in the future we are not met by any other interferences." Rose

436

returned his glass to the desk. "We do understand each other?"

"Yeah, completely," Noanes said, before he quickly downed his wine.

"You are not taking a single word of what that man has said as truth," Emmett said as soon as Noanes had gone. "He is talking absolute twaddle."

"Maybe," Rose said. "But there might be substance in what he said." He jumped up from his desk. "Come with me, Emmett, I want to show you something."

The two men hurried down the stairs to the first floor of the bank, rushing past customers who glanced at them casually and clerks who stood up straighter, as they proceeded toward a set of locked doors.

"For the most, Noanes is a drunk and a fantasist whose word is not usually worth a sheet of paper, but —" The keys jangled in Rose's hand as he unlocked the door and led Emmett down a narrow hall to another locked door. "— the man he mentioned, James Atherton, was known to my father."

Rose opened the door to a secured storage room. Here nestled a second trove, though less personal museum and more personal archive. There were files and locked boxes and ledgers brimming with information that had been collected over the years, starting with what Milbrough Rose had accumulated.

Here were the sins of London. Cataloged and compiled by name and date, the Roses had documented the transgressions of many of the best houses in the city. If there had been an illicit affair, a spate of robberies, the odd murder, or suspicions unleashed by a vengeful tongue, they could be found amid the news clippings, personal correspondence, legal papers, and photographs, when the occasion allowed such evidence.

And it had all started by accident. One day a customer had come to Milbrough Rose, in desperate need of a large sum of money. A young man, without much fortune of his own but with a father of impressive means and a notorious temper, it took little to gain his confidence and even less to guarantee a loan but at an exorbitant return; for keeping the transaction from his father and a scandal out of the papers, the young man would pay him to make the problem go away. This young man would pay until the first gray hairs entered his beard. In this way an empire was built and Odilon Rose was now its head and heart.

"Atherton showed up one night at Decimus House. I only recall him because of the state he was in." Odilon walked over to one of the shelves and pulled down a lockbox. "Disheveled and panicked, he looked no better than Noanes and his compatriots. Certainly not the sort who would dare knock on our door, yet my father let him in and took him directly into the downstairs study." A conspiratorial smile teased the corner of his mouth. "I knew I shouldn't have done so but I was a boy and curious as to who this was. I hung back at the door, far enough not to be seen but close enough to hear."

Emmett watched Rose unlock the box. Neatly stacked inside were three books, a crucifix, and a stack of paper, which Rose shuffled through. "And how did this man know your father? Was he —" Emmett thought a moment how best to phrase it. "— indebted?"

"Surprisingly, no. I've never found any trace of the man or his name outside of this box. He apparently held accounts with our bank to the amount of two hundred thousand pounds."

"Two hundred thousand . . . my God, that . . . that's a king's ransom," Emmett said.

"And my father never wrangled a single shilling out of it. If there were indiscretions,

Atherton kept them well hidden, until that night." Rose shuffled through the papers. "I could only hear snippets of conversation. 'A deal.' 'Payments exceeding gains.' 'Mutual acquaintance.' 'Our Mr. Ashe.' 'I found a way out.' Ah, here it is."

From what Emmett could see it was an ordinary sheet, not particularly fine, but the hand that had drawn the strange image on the page was skilled. At its center was a sigil comprising two circles, two heptagons, a heptagram, and at its heart a single pentagram. Circling the image was a string of archaic lettering that resembled nothing remotely English, Latin, or Arabic. "What is that?" he asked, the specter of his near-forgotten catechism rising up like the hairs on his neck.

"A Sigillum Dei," Rose said. "That is according to the note Atherton left. My father later confirmed it with the Bodleian by comparing this image against an Italian manuscript in their archives. He gained a second confirmation from the British Museum, whose collection includes a copy of the *Liber Juratus* that was once owned by John Dee."

"John Dee. Queen Elizabeth's adviser —"

"And teacher, mathematician, astronomer, astrologer, renowned occultist," Rose said.

"But what is it? What is it for?"

"Well, according to Atherton, the holder of this sigil will have power over all creatures, save for archangels."

"Archangels? Power over all creatures? Odilon, are you listening to yourself?" Emmett asked, using his employer's Christian name in the hope of snapping him back to sense. "What you are saying is nonsense. This" — pointing at the sigil — "is the scribbling of a madman. Aurelius Ashe is a man, no more and no less than you and I."

"I know, I know, but Atherton's belief begs notice, and questionable as he is, so does Noanes. Something drove Atherton to my father's door to warn him. Something made him give up everything he had and forced him to disappear. Noanes swings from rage to terror when Ashe's name is mentioned. I'm not saying that Ashe is anything more than a man of influence. But he wields a power that —" Rose's hands shook over the sigil. "Maybe, just maybe, he is a real magician, an authentic practitioner who has tapped into something greater than anything previously imagined. To be able to harness the gifts of a man with that sort of power. What I could achieve —"

"You cannot possibly believe —"

"Atherton had this for a reason —"

"And whatever that reason was, it obviously failed," Emmett said. "Seeing as he is nowhere to be found and Ashe is going about his daily life without a bother."

"Ashe bled. Noanes saw it after he left Atherton's house so something happened and this" — Rose tapped the sigil — "was used."

"Noanes lies. You know that as well as anyone."

"Emmett, there are some things I neglected to tell you. As you know my parents had contact with Ashe. What I never mentioned was his responsibility in my sister's death."

"Louisa? She unfortunately passed in infancy —"

"She was born a monster. Malformations that I cannot even begin to describe. My father took her to Ashe looking for a way fix her. Ashe refused, claiming that there was nothing he could do even though he was the source of our misfortune."

"The source . . . are you suggesting that your mother —"

"I don't wish to think that either but if ever there was the face of a demon, that child was it. If that were not enough, years later I stumbled across a decrepit ten-in-one that some college friends and I went to

442

on a lark. Imagine my horror at seeing her again, when she was long presumed buried, on display in a jar with our name emblazoned on the placard."

"My God," Emmett said. It wasn't often that Rose displayed such passion, and there was something unseemly in his current state.

"It took time but I was able to retrieve her. Yet she was only the beginning of the fall. Father's death, Mother —"

"Odilon, as your counsel, as your friend, I advise you to not pursue such folly any further. Tomorrow you will collect Charlotte and she will either be well or there will be no change in status. Remember reason. Aurelius Ashe is simply a man, gifted at tricks and tales but nothing more. The business with Louisa is complete. Now please take a moment and compose yourself and you will see I'm right."

Emmett patted Rose on the shoulder and left the secure room.

Rose heard the door close and felt the room deflate. Of course everything that Emmett had said made sense. He was right in every challenge. Reason far outweighed faith, and Noanes was an unreliable drunk with a fanciful imagination as well as being a noted liar. And though his father had known Atherton, it was not a great friendship, or so he suspected. Atherton could very well have been a troubled soul faced with something so dark that he thought it better to disappear than to be shamed.

Yet there was something greater than reason that clawed at the back of his neck. Rose picked up the paper and carefully folded it, first in half then by quarter, and slipped it in his jacket's inner pocket before locking Atherton's box and replacing it on the shelf.

He ran a hand through his hair and straightened his waistcoat and tie. He took a deep breath, feeling his stoic calm return before returning to his office.

444

CHAPTER THIRTY-FOUR

The clarence was chosen not for its comfort but for its inconspicuousness. Dull, square-bodied, and appropriately road-worn, it did not look at all out of place in the street across from The Athenaeum. As for the driver, he had thought nothing of being summoned to the terraced house in Mayfair, as transport was often needed by traveling parties to and from the train station. However, when he had arrived to find only one elegant woman, absent of luggage and with a request to go into Southwark instead of to the station, he found that odd. Especially as there was a brightly polished brougham far more suitable to a lady's taste not more than two carriage lengths down from her door. But the generous payment he was given for both his time and his silence more than allayed any lingering questions; after all, what matter was it to him the quirks of the rich.

Now situated with a clean line of sight on the theater's doors, the coach waited with its lone occupant fixed at the window. Outside, the street buzzed like bluebottles and Florence Suskind dropped the thin-netted veil over her eyes, not because she feared recognition, as who would know of her here, but rather as a precaution against remembrance. Were her presence to be noticed, all that anyone would recall would be a veiled woman in a coach, nothing of the face and the name.

In the street, the people milled their day-to-day, hawking their wares and driving carts back and forth oblivious to the observation they were under. There was a delicious pleasure in knowing that Odilon would be positively apoplectic were he to learn of her trek into Southwark unaccompanied. For a man so obsessed with the currency to be had in the reputations of others, he guarded his own with the ruthlessness of a Borgia. And though she was a married woman no longer under his roof and his watch, by blood she was still a Rose. And here she was defying not only her brother but also the very directive of Ashe himself that no one was to interfere with Charlotte's treatment, no visitations until three days following whatever procedure was planned. Though she did not intend on entering the theater for that direct purpose, her presence nonetheless remained an act of rebellion.

Florence's smirk had barely settled in satisfaction before the theater doors opened. She had hoped to see Lucien. Since the night he left his mark on her wrist she had thought of nothing other than stealing one moment alone with him. Had last night been about anything but Charlotte she might have had that chance.

Charlotte.

Ever since she came into her family, it had become all about Charlotte. Now she was here in The Athenaeum, with *him,* for three days.

She leaned forward and lifted her veil to better see the man himself, though it was alarmingly apparent that it was not Charlotte who followed him out as she had half expected, nor was it any one member of the troupe. No, the woman who so casually hung off his arm wore a harlot's skirt in a gaudy blue. A matching blue ribbon twined through the loose knots of her long black hair, tendrils of which dusted her shoulders.

A whore in daylight! It was an affront to the eye and a brazen act against the very nature of such women. Yet . . .

Florence was not some naive virgin. She knew well how to navigate the intricacies of the parlor, and though the actions were more refined in a gracious setting they were nevertheless recognizable cousins to those of the street.

Yes, she understood men's appetites, so it made sense that Lucien, dear Lucien, absent of a wife and in possession of such unusual gifts, might find a whore's company more than amenable. But genuine feelings for such a woman? The thought galled her to the bone. If that was what he wanted, all he had to do was ask and she would cast off her marriage and her name. He had to realize that after the many shows she had attended, and the many times she had purposely caught his eye, her lips catching his. He knew her name and cared not one whit about the ring on her finger.

She sank back into the clarence's bench seat as Luce parted with the woman on the street, sending her off with a quick peck on the cheek that Florence could feel on her own. She was not accustomed to being an outsider looking into the world. Her station, her name was entrée enough into the highest echelons of society where *she* commanded the eye of everyone in her circle. And yet at this moment none of that mattered, because she was here, and Lucien was there — a world away.

As her rival sauntered down the crowded street, Florence wondered how pale a shadow she would cast if this woman, suitably dressed and half mannered, were to gain entry to the houses she frequented. Clothes after all were only a costume for the actor, where even a pauper could pass for a prince as long as his tongue was silent and eyes watchful. Would men's eyes follow her as they did now, coveting and imagining what lay beneath her skirts? Would they too look at her the way Luce had?

Florence wrapped her fingers tight around the purse beside her. In matters such as these, there was always someone in the way, but then again, half the fun was in the challenge. She knocked on the clarence's front window, signaling the driver that it was time to move. The carriage lurched forward, the wheels growling on the cobblestones gaining speed.

As Southwark fell away, Florence rested her head against the cushion, gently thumbing the purse's onyx beads as her mind turned.

Black. She would wear black this evening. Yes, black would indeed be best.

CHAPTER THIRTY-FIVE

If she ran hard enough and fast enough perhaps she could outrun the mouthful of vagaries and contradictions that Aurelius and Pretorius had spewed. If she kept running, the horror could not settle.

'In the plainest of terms, my dear, you had to die in order to live.'

Die to live! Die to live? It was nonsense. How could it possibly be?

Charlotte slowed, hugging the corridor wall, her cheek pressed against the grit of the plastered brick.

She ran her finger along the lip of the wound in her neck. The skin flapped loose as curiosity forced the nail between the folds. There was no blood when she withdrew, only a pale-pink substitute that coated her fingertip. This was what was giving her a semblance of life.

She ventured further from the shop, away from the underpinnings of the stage, behind the plaster and the beams. Pretorius had worked hard to strip away the panopticon's shameful past as a debtors' prison and present the glittering face of the theater. However, here in the labyrinthine halls that led to his underworld where so many men, women, and children had passed their days picking oakum, he had merely grafted a subdued facade. This area was not for public consumption, so it did not need adornment, not for Pretorius nor for the myriad strays that had taken up house. It remained in exquisite dilapidation.

"Are you a'right there, miss? You lost? It's easy to do down here."

Charlotte jumped and saw in the shadows the young man who breakfasted earlier with her. "No, no, I'm fine . . . um . . . ah."

"Michael Mayhew," he said. "We weren't properly introduced this morning."

"Yes, of course, forgive me," she said.

"Beggin' your pardon, but why are you down here? It's not really, well, a place for a proper lady —"

"Mr. Pretorius," she stumbled out. "I required his assistance." Her hand wandered to her damp collar. "I don't recall seeing you on the stage last night, Mr. Mayhew."

"*Mr.* Mayhew?" Michael laughed, stepping forward. "Not heard that before. No, I wouldn't be on the stage. I assist Mr. Pretorius with fixin' up whatever needs doing."

"Oh, I assumed with the juggling —"

"That's something Mr. Timothy has been teaching me."

Charlotte folded her arms across her chest. There was a pleasant affability to Michael, guileless and inquisitive; opposite to what she had felt in some of the others. "You have been with the company long?"

"Oh, I've about four, five days on you. Mr. Luce found me down on the river — well, I might have made myself known — and he offered me a place as long as I was willing to work and didn't ask too many questions."

"What were you doing on the river?"

"Larkin'," he said. "It takes money to eat and there is always somethin' the rag-and-bone man is willing to take."

"But you're so young. Where is your family?"

"Ain't seen hide nor hair of home in some five, six years now. Not since Mam took up with her new fella. We didn't get on well, so choices were made."

There was a plainness, a matter-of-fact way in which he spoke of his lack of home and abandonment that chilled her more than if he had raged. Anger would have been

452

understandable. She understood anger, had felt it in those first nights when her own mother was gone and the fear palpable.

"The river offered me a living. Though it is a life not meant for the squeamish, not when everything from false money to false teeth pass through one's hands on the whim of the tide. 'Course animal carcasses are the most frequent, though often enough, there would come bobbing along the body of a tosher who had sunk into the slime of the sewers before being flushed out into the Thames, all gnawed and nipped by the rats. The bairns, though, that can get to you."

"Bairns?"

"Poppin' up like bobbins in the water. Usually cholera, pox, or inconvenience, the poor mites drifted in the murk like any other bit of trash. White-faced as fish, floatin' along till someone scoops them out or they wash up somewhere or sink back down into the muck."

A shudder rocked through Charlotte's shoulders. The thought of dead infants and bodies and God knew what else drifting through the Thames sickened her. And that Michael, little more than a child himself, lived amid that filth. Everything was so far removed from her previous life and nothing was as it seemed. Not the theater, not Aurelius, and certainly not herself any longer. All this stardust made her head swim.

"Oh my, miss." Michael reached out and held her elbow, steadying her on her feet. "I didn't mean to upset you. Me, running off at the mouth about things no lady should or would want to hear about. Suppose I'm not very good at nice talk, 'specially to pretty ladies."

Charlotte looked into his dark round eyes and thin face. She couldn't help but notice how his collarbone jutted out above the loose neck of his shirt. "No, Michael, it is not you or anything you said. I — " *'Betwixt and between.'* Aurelius's voice echoed in her ear.

She stepped back but stopped short when she bumped against something solidly pliable.

"Careful there."

Turning her head, she found herself pressed against Lucien Ashe. He must have followed her from Pretorius's shop. His hands gripped her elbows, gently lingering longer than propriety would have allowed between two unmarried and unbetrothed people.

"Forgive me, I didn't hear you." The heel of her shoe bumped his foot in her clumsy attempt to step away, which resulted in her not moving forward but stumbling back further against him.

"No harm done," Luce said. He slid his hands away from her arms, a reluctance he admitted only to himself but he allowed a moment for his fingers to grace her waist before releasing her completely. "These boots have seen worse."

No sense. Nothing of this day made sense. What was she doing? Dear God, she needed someone, anyone to take her hand and say it would all be well, even if it were a lie. She needed . . . She looked up at Luce and into eyes that did not shy from hers. A rebellious curl graced his brow above his right eye, tempting her to brush it away. Only Odilon had ever stood this close before, but with him it was a threat. With Luce, though . . .

'I will be here when you are ready.'

"Dita. I need to see Dita," she said, finding her footing.

"Mind how you go," Michael called after as she darted away. Luce watched as she disappeared out of the belly of the understage, leaving in her wake a slight grin on his lip.

Here he comes with flaming bowl,
Don't he mean to take his toll,

455

Snip! Snap! Dragon!
Take care you don't take too much,
Be not greedy in your clutch,
Snip! Snap! Dragon!
With his blue and lapping tongue
Many of you will be stung,
Snip! Snap! Dragon!

"Careful now there, Georgie." Dita watched as his fingers danced over the wide, shallow bowl of burning brandy. "You'll singe yourself stem-to-stern and then where will you be?"

"A hairless dog boy is what you'll be," Angelique said, nimbly snatching a currant from the low blue flame that played across the liquor. "Who'd pay to see that? Hardly worth the bother."

Georgie stuck his tongue out, provoking a squeal of delight from the twins before they continued in their song as each took their chance at grabbing raisins and currants from the fire. In the shadow of the doorway where Charlotte stood, it was a picturesque study of domestic bliss. Columbine reposed near the stove, hovering above her chair as a hummingbird does a flower, a well-thumbed book in her hand. Harlequin was seated where Michael had been that morning. She noticed that he had the sticks she

456

had seen him perform with the night before, which he twirled with ease, click-clacking as they bounced and balanced against the center stick.

In the drawing room at Decimus House, a painting reminded her much of this moment. Of a similar theme, familial and friendly, it was so vividly rendered that it never ceased to evoke in her the desire to leap into the canvas and join the gathering. Anyone else outside of these theater walls would witness this scene and dismiss them all as deviant and outcast. She might have done so herself. But now, she saw only a family and a home. Yet she remained at the edge of the threshold, pinned in place and not as ready as she had thought to intrude on their company.

"There's no call for your standing in the shadows, now, is there?"

Charlotte started, as she had thought herself hidden enough from the company's sight.

"I don't need to have eyes on you to know that you are there." Dita sat aside her teacup. "May as well come in, girl, no need to stand about like bump on a toad," she beckoned. "Can't very well be answering your questions if you're three paces out the room."

Dita's ability was unsettling and Charlotte wished that she could speak to her alone as the room was a bit crowded.

"Sit yourself down here. I take it that Aurelius has explained the procedure?"

"Did you see this? Did you see what was going to happen to me?"

Dita traced the lip of her cup with her finger. "I told you that you would survive. You never asked me how, though, so your anger is misplaced. Aurelius has given you a gift. He has handed you back your life, girl."

"A gift! You do not reconcile yourself to being told that your blood has been drained and replaced and that you are no longer living but you're not dead —" Charlotte shook with frustration. "It is ludicrous to even be saying such a thing. I cannot believe for one moment that any of this is true and yet I cannot discount what I have seen. And I am to accept this!"

Charlotte was near to hysterics before Dita laid her palm flat across her brow. "Calm yourself, girl," she said. "Calm yourself and you might begin to see reason in the unbelievable."

Dita's hand pulsed an ease that broke over her mind like water.

"How might I do so?" she asked.

"By letting it be." She had not noticed

that Columbine had set aside her book and was now watching her.

"Letting it be? That is fine and easy talk for someone who can be flippant of another's misfortune."

"Misfortune? Misfortune! God, you are all the same, every last pathetic one of you who come to Aurelius's door seeking miracles, making your pockets deeper or your name bigger and then crying in the street when it's not all that it seems." Columbine strode across the room like a Roman marble come to life. She sat down across from Charlotte and Dita, propping her crossed arms on the table.

"Walk a day in my skin, miss. Or in Georgie's or the twins' and then talk to me about misfortunes. Live your days under a veil because if you fail to it might be your last." Columbine sucked on her lower lip, before breaking into a mischievous grin. "Of course, now I understand what a gift I have. My skin. My hair. What I'm able to do with the silks, contorting and flying. My misfortunes have become my strength, and the greatest power you can possess is the ability to instill fear in the very ones who would hope to break you. So darling, I do not care one whit about the *how* of all this. All that matters is that I *can*. And should Aurelius ever come to me one day needing my help, then I will do whatever it is he asks of me. Even if it were to cost me my life. Seeing as I wouldn't have one without him."

"But I *was* to have a life," Charlotte said.

"Were you?"

She stared at Dita, wondering how she knew about her life at Decimus House.

"Don't try to take it all in in one day, pet." Dita laid her hand over Charlotte's. "No one's expectin' you to come to these changes lightly. There is going to be unease and fear, and yes sadness too, but we are here and we always look after our own."

Charlotte sank back against the chair, still feeling hopeless but a little less alone. Georgie, the twins, and Angelique had not stopped in their game, and she watched their fingers tease and escape the flames as they stole sultanas and currants from the dragon's mouth with no other care in the world than to keep from burning their hands.

The disturbance came with Luce, who walked into the kitchen and stuck his hand into the flaming bowl, much to the disapproving squeals of the twins.

"That's cheating!" Georgie said as Luce popped a handful of raisins in his mouth, a dusting of blue flame still around their edges.

"I can't help that I'm immune." Luce grinned and wiped the brandy residue on his leg. "That's why I don't play."

He leaned against the counter. His tie and collar were absent, so his shirt hung loose at the neck almost to his collarbone, and his waistcoat was unbuttoned. It had been too brief in the understage, too dark as well, and her spinning mind had not been able to fully see him. Whatever nerves he had expressed earlier in reference to Charlotte had long passed. This was a man who could take center stage and command a room as few others. The transformation was night and day.

"Now you've found Dita. Are you feeling better?"

"She'll be fine once she's had time to sit with it," Dita said. "Like anything else, it's a matter of adjusting, isn't that right?"

Charlotte gave an anesthetized nod that lacked both energy and enthusiasm.

"Right, I think that the lady here could use a bit of air." Luce clapped his hands. "Get your wrap, I'll get the cab and meet you on the steps outside in five minutes."

461

CHAPTER THIRTY-SIX

26 October, Ports of London, Southwark
Charlotte had never ridden in a hansom cab. Due to its compact size and raciness, it was not deemed the proper vehicle for a woman to ride in. So it had surprised her then when she walked down The Athenaeum's steps to see that Lucien had chosen that very mode of transport for them.

Once settled, though, she was struck by the lightness of the vehicle, with its single horse and only two wheels. The driver's maneuverability was impressive as they turned on a sixpence around the cluttered streets of Southwark. The intimacy of the ride did not go unnoticed by her either, as only two people could fit the seat in something of comfort and even then closely quartered. Across each bump and rut, Luce's leg pressed against hers. It was all an incredible rush, Charlotte marveled, speeding through the streets.

Within a matter of minutes, she was staring up at the star-speckled black hull of *Manannan* moored in her berth. The giant wrought wheels stood tall and still in their paddle boxes but the paddles' copper sheathing reflected the moving water beneath. The tall black funnel with the fluted metal lotus pierced the haze above. The dock brimmed with life, fishermen and sailors, keeps and porters moving goods from ship to shop, scraping down barnacles from hulls while chasing off the young Mud Larks who sought to profit off the scraps. She had never been this close to the river, and following young Michael's story she was careful not to look down into the water.

"She was an old packet set for scrapping, believe it or not, when Aurelius came across her. Bought her for a pittance and set Pretorius to restore her. He gutted her, added the paddles, steam engine, and funnel. Kept the masts for auxiliary power, completely refurbished the quarters and kitchen, and added the salons."

"She is a beautiful vessel."

"There is nothing that Pretorius can't fix if Aurelius sets him to the task."

That quick, her mind spun back to the workshop. Seated as she had been on the table with Aurelius holding her hand. He had been as gentle as a priest guiding a penitent through a crisis of faith in his explanation of what had been done to her, as Pretorius waited patiently with his tray of needles and thread.

"Are you coming?" Luce called, already halfway up the gangplank. "You'll not see anything from down there."

She hurried up to join him.

"It's not going to be moving, is it?" she said, crossing the polished deck.

"She won't move unless Aurelius gives the go-ahead."

"I'm sure that not much happens without his permission." She turned back to him. There was much more that she wished to say, to ask, but looking into his eyes and at the way he stood with a graceful ease, hands in his pockets and hair a thick mass of loose curls beneath a hat that tilted back from his brow, she was disarmed. This ease was a trait shared with Aurelius, and while her anger had managed to overcome his charms, it was not so easy with his son.

Several slow minutes passed and the air chilled between them before he spoke again.

"You should know," he began, "that no offense was taken, if that is your worry. Your reaction cannot be questioned or blamed considering how suddenly these changes have happened. You have had less than a day and that's hardly any time at all to adjust. Aurelius knows that, although I will warn you that Dita will be fretting. I can tell her that there is no need and that you will come to terms, but that's a bit like telling the wind not to blow."

Charlotte forced a smile, but even under the pale river haze the falsity was clear.

Luce studied her as much as the light would allow. She had a pretty face, damned pretty; and bright eyes that even death had not been able to snuff.

"Pretorius did a good job on your stitches. He's greatly improved since working on me. As to scars, consider them a proof of a life lived. We all have them, and whether we share them with the world or hide them under our clothes or under our skin, their existence remains."

"I do not concern myself with scars, sir."

"Then what do you concern yourself with, miss?"

Charlotte paused before clearing the breath from her throat. "Do you do this often, Mr. Ashe? Come out here on your own?"

"Often enough. It takes time to relax the nerves and settle the mind again after a performance. It is also a necessary respite

465

from the family. Don't get me wrong, I love them dearly, but they can be a boisterous bunch, especially the little ones, and sometimes you take the peace where you can get it."

Charlotte wrapped her arms around herself, snugging her jacket close.

"Perhaps we should move to the deckhouse? I think you'll find it a bit more private, more comfortable, and far more suitable to a lady's taste. I mean, imagine how tongues would wag if any of your posh set were to learn of your slumming about Southwark with the likes of me."

"Quite to the contrary, sir. I have been in the audience and seen the reaction to your performance and I'm certain there are many ladies who would be more than happy to find themselves in a similar situation."

"And are you among them?" He smiled seeing the fluster cross her face. "You needn't worry, love, I don't bite. And I don't creep about late at night scaring ladies like the fictions that Dita enjoys reading."

Charlotte lowered her eyes and allowed him to lead her into the deckhouse, where it was immediately apparent that Luce's talk of comfort was an understatement, as soon as her shoe sank into the lush rug that covered the hardwood floor. With the polished rosewood panels, the elegant glass globes of the lamps, and the large handsome desk, this parlor was equal to any to be found in England's finest homes.

"Please, sit yourself down," Luce gestured to the red leather chaise. "I'd offer you tea but Dita's probably left nothing on board. Though if you'd like something a bit stronger, Aurelius usually has something stashed away in his desk."

"Thank you but no," Charlotte said, settling herself down on the chaise. "Mr. Ashe, excuse my curiosity but why do you call your father by his Christian name?"

"Christian name?" Luce laughed in the exclusionary way one did when the truthful knowledge of a matter is at the expense of another's misunderstanding. "I don't know. I guess because until I was ten I only knew him as Aurelius. That was when I was thought old enough to know the truth."

"The truth?"

"Not to be crude, but my mother was available for everything but marrying."

It was an unexpected confession of bastardy as unadorned and raw as naked skin.

"And by the look on your face, I should add that despite her faults, she was at heart a good and gentle woman who happened to draw a bad lot in life long before my father ever came into it."

"She *was* a good woman?"

"Like I said, she drew a bad lot."

Charlotte noted the tightness in his jaw as she knew it well. The need to control the grief from spilling out. "Mr. Ashe, I am sorry. I too know that particular pain and how fresh the wound can be despite the years. I would never have —"

"I killed her, you know," Luce said, dismissing her apology. "I'm only telling you this because I thought you should know what sort of man you are here with. It was an accident. I swear to that but it doesn't negate the fact that I'm the one who did it."

It wasn't the weight of his unprompted confession that took her off guard but rather the rawness of the words and the odd wash of comfort that seemed to come over him after sharing this with her.

"If what your father says is true of me now, then I have little to fear."

Luce nodded, pleased that she did have an adverse reaction. She would have had every right to leave and he would not have blamed her if she had. But she remained seated, stoic.

"You said that you know that pain, losing a mother. Is that how you came to live at Decimus House?"

"Yes. My father passed before I was born and after my mother fell ill, went into hospital, and never returned. I was warded off and she was not spoken of again. I've never been to her grave, I'm ashamed to say."

"Mine was weeks in the ground before I was able to visit." He tapped his chest.

"Oh yes, your injury. Dita spoke of it. She was worried that you wouldn't survive." Her eye could not help but drift toward his chest, where she could just see the tip of the scar stretching above his open collar.

"She always worries."

"Mr. Ashe, please do not take what I am about to ask as an offense but rather as a compliment because I feel that you will be the most honest. What manner of man is your father? And please do not say he is an illusionist when it is plain to see that he is much more than that. He made some strange comments that alluded to —" She paused, mulling her words. "I have faith but what he told me, what he says that he is pushes those boundaries."

"But an illusionist is what he is." Luce leaned back on to the lip of Aurelius's desk. "That's not the answer that you want to hear. I can see it in your eyes, but you have to understand that when people come to him with their hopes and dreams, these things are illusions to begin with. Aurelius only expands on those. Thin air and high hopes that he makes real, which is a pleasure to his clients. But as with any dream, the luster is lost when the price is paid."

"I accused him of being the devil, which he denied."

"Of course he's not *the* devil." Luce shook his head, a broad grin on his face. "Oh, you asked the wrong question. Had you said *a* devil, his answer might have been different."

The subject of his father was not something that he comfortably addressed as the suggestion of the supernatural often stirred more questions and unease.

"I am sorry. My intent is not to insult you, but you have as much as said that your father is . . . not of —" She shook her head. "As incomprehensible as that sounds you can understand the implications regarding yourself and trust when I say that it is taking every ounce of reserve on my part to not run for my life."

"And where are you going to run to, Charlotte? As of last night you're a changed woman, which you might find difficult to explain without Aurelius's help. I'm sorry to be blunt but —"

"It's all lost. My God, what am I going to do?" Charlotte leaned heavily against the arm of the chaise. "What am I going to say to Odilon? He's going to —" She shook her head.

"Charlotte —"

"This is my fault. I should have pressed your father for details of what he had planned. I could have spoken up and told him no or insisted on another way. Oh God, why didn't I say something?"

"Charlotte, please," Luce said. He reached for her hand but hesitated, letting his hand come to rest on the cushion near her instead. He wished he had the calming manner that Dita possessed as Charlotte was deteriorating by the second. "What can I do?"

"Do? What is there to do? This cannot be undone!" She drew herself away from him. "It has been all for naught. And when I was so close."

"To what? I don't understand —"

Charlotte looked into his eyes, and seeing his ignorance roiled resentments she had held her entire life. Always the good girl, she had never spoken a cross word, never made a demand or resisted one. Compliance had been her failure while her ability to remain silent was her grace.

"Of course you wouldn't understand. We are after all sitting in what is likely to be part of *your* inheritance."

"I'm sorry?" Luce said, sitting back as if struck.

The thorn removed, the poisons she had held in her whole life poured free. "You have never needed to contend for a place in the world. Your status is assured as your father saw fit. But not everyone has a guarantee of such reliability, and women even less. So unless you have been truly afraid, and I do not speak of childhood terrors such as the dark or thunder or some such nonsense, but actual to-the-bone fear of what lies ahead, then you cannot begin to speak of understanding what I have lost."

Luce rubbed his thumb into his palm. He could feel the heat itching beneath his skin. "So with what you have undergone, that reliability of comfort and security is now in question? An uncertain future?"

"That is precisely what I mean. I was never promised much; nor did I expect to leave a mark on the world in any way. But I did have some hope that I might be able to carve out a small piece that would be mine. Reliant on no one but myself." She drew her hand to her mouth. Her fingers trembled against her lips. This is what she had

472

wanted to tell Aurelius, what she wanted to let him know had been taken from her because he thought it best to cure all ills by death rather than the remedy that would allow her to live.

"I think that your worry is misplaced —"

"Do you consider the loss of an assured constancy not something to be fretted?"

"No, but I find your reliance on the expectations of polite society and the asinine rules of manners that you think you must live by tiresome. What is it that you wanted? A provident marriage? Or —"

"I do not concern myself with such a folly but —" She thought of Odilon. Would he even allow her do that? "As I told your father, I might have found a posting as a governess. Florence has not had a child yet but someday she might. Possibly a lady's companion —"

"Or perhaps a shop clerk?" Luce shook his head. "You know your guardian far better than I. But from the impression I have of him, his pride and snobbery is not going to be satisfied with seeing you cast in a service role. Not that any of that should matter, it is all worthy work, but you are associated with the Rose name. It is games, Charlotte. Only games."

"Scoff if you must, but the conventions

that you find tiresome and useless are all that I know. They are all that I have. You can be dismissive of them because *you* can afford to be. But my future hangs on what Odilon Rose sets into motion. For me to fail now —" she shook her head. "I don't know what he will do."

'Odilon Rose will never let you go.' Aurelius's warning echoed in her ear, which she dismissed with a shake of her head.

"We take care of our own —"

"But I am not one of you! I wasn't born a freak, but I have been made into one." Charlotte clasped her hand over her mouth. For the second time this day, she had spoken thoughtlessly.

"Poor Charlotte, how the world has wronged you."

She could almost hear the clicking of the cog in his chest but his face, when she dared look, was unsmiling. She did not know why, but that lack of a smile pained her more than anything. It carried more than admonishment or anger, both of which would fairly be expected. No, what was couched in its absence was disappointment.

"I've sat here listening to you cry and fuss over what? That you might not be a governess? Or a lady's companion? *That* is your great worry? Christ, there are people starving in the street, fighting for a space in a rook so they don't have to sleep outdoors. Women using whatever currency they have to keep body and mind together for one more day and you are afraid that you won't secure a position in this world before you're, what, twenty-five? When you are already assured a room in one of the finest houses in London? You have no idea of what the world is truly like."

He held his hand out and, in his palm, a small glow quickly erupted into a flame. "The problem with living an insulated life is that it tethers you to a path of complacency. More's the pity if you ask me. I can't imagine being burdened with such tedious normalcy."

Charlotte was mesmerized watching the flame ripple and elongate. Slowly it stretched into segments, each rounding and curling until one by one they became a perfect petal. It was a replication of a rose in fire.

This was far more delicate than the beasts she had seen conjured on stage. She drew closer than propriety would normally allow, but there was an undeniable lure to the flame, and she knew that this was no magic; at least no magic she had ever heard of. There was only the open flame itself that bled from the center of his palm.

"How?"

He closed his fist and extinguished the flower. The sparks of the petals drifted down from between his fingers to the carpet, diminishing to ash on impact.

"There are some gifts that we are born with and there are others" — he tapped his chest — "that we are given. As Aurelius's son, I suppose I've been twice blessed. Or twice cursed depending on your view. You see, my inheritance, which you blithely dismiss, on the surface looks grand. Hell, I would be envious too. But look deeper and you will see that the ship, the theater belong to Pretorius. Only fair, for how much of himself he has put into both. His wish for something permanent. A home in exchange for his skilled hands and creator's vision. The land, however, the crossroads and what lies below, are my father's purview. So, what awaits me? As Aurelius's blood, I bear the fire. What else that entails, yet to be seen. We have much in common, Charlotte. Uncertain futures. The only real difference is that I am not afraid of mine."

She ran a quick eye over his face where the light from the gas lamps cast a drama of shadow. With each flicker a new line spoke, accentuating the line of his lips, the slope of his cheek. Kindness had once again settled into the slight crinkles around his golden-blue eyes, which she did not wish to scare away again.

"According to your father I am a Revenant, dead but not —" She bit back on the anger that was rising again. "And yet here I am sitting next to you as if it were a normal afternoon with the only things missing being a cup of tea and cake. And everyone around me thinks that this is perfectly fine. I attracted no notice, no shocked glances from anyone on the way here because to the world I appear to be a normal girl. Yesterday, I was just that, normal. Today, I am anything but."

"Charlotte, when you have seen the things I've seen nothing comes as a surprise anymore. There are all sorts in the world and *we* are hardly alone in it. But we don't all choose to make ourselves known."

"I don't know what any of this means and none of you question any of it. Look what your father has done to you." Her eyes trailed to his chest and the scars that lay beneath his shirt and waistcoat.

"What he has done to *us*," Luce corrected. "Like I said, we have much in common. Your blood. My heart. Both recipients of my father's 'kindness' or as near to kindness as he is capable. And I am sorry for what he has done to you, made of you. I know you are looking at me and thinking *How can he understand what I'm going through when he was born a freak?* But that's not entirely true." He held his hands up and stared at his fingers as if they were alien to himself, controlled by a sentience of their own. "None of this was easy, Charlotte. I might have been born with this gift of flame but I was unaware of it until —"

Charlotte could see the struggle behind his eyes as he seemed to want to say something that refused to be spoken. A soft blue glow slowly erupted around his hands, low flames that traced each finger until his skin shimmered under a translucent armor.

"It was terrifying that day when it first manifested. No one knew what to do with me. Well, that's not exactly true," he said with the cock of his head. "Emilian Kosh thought it best to beat the hell out of me. You know him, don't you? I know your guardian does."

Charlotte's eyes dropped from his. She knew the name and pictured the man whom she had seen lurking at Decimus House, and the knife that never seemed to be far from his hand.

"That's when Aurelius stepped forward.

And that day I learned who he was and *what* he is. He started to work with me, testing to see if there was a specific trigger but more important if I could control the fire at will. The hours that I spent staring into these flames all while he whispered on about what power is."

Luce sat up like a schoolboy and spoke by rote. "Power is strength and it is fear. Above all else power is something to be wielded with mindful care. This" — the flames leapt from his right hand to be nimbly caught by the left — "is power. So you see, I do know the fear that you spoke of, Charlotte. But unlike you, I ended up running to it. I embraced it. And I conquered it."

"But do you enjoy it? Having *that* within you? Are you comforted by the fact that you are not like" — she pointed toward the window that looked out on the river — "everyone else?"

Balling his fists, he crushed out the flames. "You are essentially asking me if I enjoy living. Charlotte, the fire does not exist without me and I do not exist without it. It begins with me and it dies with me."

"Whereas I cannot die. Although I have and yet haven't. What gift is that?"

Luce shook his head. "I can't give you an answer other than you should give yourself more than a day or so to see what awakens in you."

Charlotte looked down at her hands, at the blue gloves that fitted like a second skin. By the way her shoulders slumped, Luce could feel her wavering. He pressed his hand over hers and for a moment any thought of Odilon or her future disappeared.

"One thing I do know is that you are going to have to choose if you are more Charing Cross or Regent's Park. There is much to be discovered about you, Charlotte, and personally, I think that you are too spirited to waste your days locked away in a rich man's tomb."

Charlotte raised her eyes to his with the candor of a woman with nothing more to lose but rather something terrible yet deliciously exciting to gain. Yes, he had been flattering and dismissive, but there had not been any sense of the guile that she often found underlying her relationship with Odilon, whom she half suspected spoke with crossed fingers in his pocket.

"You dislike him. Odilon. It is all right to say so. Offense will not be taken on my part, as you would not be the first to make such an admittance."

"That's not my place —"

"He is not my friend, Mr. —" She paused

but held his eyes longer than intended, "Lucien. If I'm to be honest, I haven't any friends. Only Florence, whom I suspect has only shown me kindness because she was told to do so. As for Odilon —" She shook her head. "I find him repulsive. But I am nevertheless indebted to him. Please know, though, that those comforts have had their cost. Hateful as it is, I can't imagine where I would be now if it weren't for his charity."

"Friends can be few and far between. Haven't made many myself save for Silvia."

"Silvia?" Charlotte asked, a sinking churn of jealousy in the pit of her stomach.

"A working lass and the only person outside of the troupe who has treated me with any kindness and knows a thing or two about being alone." Luce's voice softened as did his eyes, like the melting of ice. "It might not be charity but when I said that we look after our own I meant it, Charlotte. And while it's not clear now, I hope you'll have a little faith in what Aurelius has done for you."

"I will try," she said, resting her free hand over his. "I've no other choice."

Luce broke from her gaze and looked down at her hand and the soft blue glove that denied him the touch of her skin. And so it passed, this intimacy best suited to strangers; the sudden recognition that at this moment, within this city, there existed two individuals so alike and yet so different who nonetheless teetered toward each other out of the pure fear of falling apart.

It was a most unusual enchantment.

CHAPTER THIRTY-SEVEN

26 October, The Athenaeum
Danny and Davie O'Kearne had worked hard to choreograph their movements. Aurelius trained with them nearly every day and when Aurelius wasn't free, Columbine stepped in. It did not take long until the ligament binding them had lengthened to nearly seven inches, which allowed them freer movement to walk, run, and tumble. With a little angling, the pair could stand almost shoulder-to-shoulder.

This mobility had not come without a degree of pain but now, years into their tumbling, such pain had lessened thankfully to the enjoyment of the audience who delighted in watching them in their harlequinade costumes. Danny wore loose black, white, and black-diamond-checked trousers, a white peasant's shirt, and a loose Elizabethan collar while Davie, the opposite mirror, alternated with black, white, and purple diamond checks. The pair wore matching red leather short boots with diamond-patterned socks and with their faces painted white, they looked like miniature Grimaldis, save for the bare band of skin that linked them.

Between their tumbles, pinwheels, and cantering, the pair offered comic panto-mimes of Babes in the Wood and Mother Goose. The lights would dim to a double spot and the anticipation of the audience rippled with the tension of a woman's overstrained stay. This was the moment that the twins truly shined.

As they stood together, one arm wrapped loose around the other's shoulder, the band of skin between them relaxed with the distribution of breath as in unison they sang the first note.

"It was many and many a year ago, in a kingdom by the sea —"

Their youth allowed them to reach the height of crystalline soprano so perfectly pitched with measured authority that it was often said the angel choir above would have stood in awed silence. Much like Georgie's violin prowess, the twins' gracious gift exceeded the severity of their physical afflic-tion. As the twin diaphragms rose and fell, the skin band vibrated with the lift of their lungs.

"And this maiden she lived with no other thought than to love and be loved by me —"

From her favorite seat in The Athenaeum, Florence Suskind's mood soared on the back of the boys' voices. Despite Aurelius's directive to keep away from the theater, she now relished the idea that one, or better both, of the Ashes would see her. A bullying word from her brother Odilon was one thing, but she would be damned to heed the order of a traveler. No matter how gifted and admired. Or in Lucien's case, how much she longed for his favor. She had greater aspirations than another deplorably dull night at home with her bore of a husband. Her small rebellion earlier now nested comfortably in the smirk of her red lips.

She scanned the rows of seats, half expecting to see Charlotte, but it became clear that she was not in attendance. Her absence prickled the hairs on Florence's neck. She did not care to think herself jealous but her inner voice screamed a testament to that truth.

"The angels, not half so happy in heaven, went envying her and me —"

If there had been one reluctance regarding Aurelius Ashe's involvement with Charlotte's health it was the fact that she would be welcomed into the private quarters of The Athenaeum, and into the very heart of the troupe for the course of the treatment. And much could happen over the course of a three-day internment.

She herself had fallen under Lucien Ashe's spell on that first sight not quite four years ago. So there was every possibility that Charlotte, with her desperate need to follow every propriety along the gated path of virtue, could also be susceptible to a man like Lucien. Even that blue-skirted, black-haired whore had shown a measured favor toward him that went beyond what the rules of her profession suggested. A whore does not fall in love, so how could she possibly be loved in return.

"Nor the demons down under the sea, can ever dissever my soul from the soul —"

The memory of his lips burned against hers as hot as his fingers had burned her wrist. It was an unbearable pull on her flesh, and Florence shifted in her seat, bumping the elbow of her neighbor.

"And so, all the night tide, I lie down by the side of my darling — my darling —"

The twins' voices soared into the silks above. Florence wrapped her gloved fingers

486

around her onyx-beaded purse and held it tight to her breast.

around her onyx-beaded purse and held it tight to her breast.

CHAPTER THIRTY-EIGHT

26 October, High Street, Southwark
There was no other city quite like London. In all of his travels, Luce had yet to encounter another whose noises and odors were so pervasive that they became a second skin on every soul who had the fortitude to call its dust home. And as often as he railed against her, England and Southwark were in his blood and bones.

Luce wended his way along The Mint on the High Street under the haze and hiss of gas lamps. Even at this late an hour, when only the most intrepid street vendor and public houses were open, the traffic of men and women continued. It had not been his intent to leave The Athenaeum after the show, but the afternoon's encounter with Charlotte had disturbed him far more than he cared to admit and had left him in no mood to be fawned over, or to mingle with any of the eager fans who tended to linger

488

at the doors.

It was not any particular thing she had said; in fact, she had said very little that was not expected. However, it was the silences in between her protest and her tepid acquiescence that struck him; the look she wore on her face that was of someone suddenly burdened by an extraordinary circumstance.

It was a look he could never forget, as it had only taken a single lick of flame to indelibly etch in another's eyes what she refused to understand.

You are not God's design.

The foot traffic had slowed to a bottleneck ahead as a raucous group of laborers, a mix of dockers and tanners, if the smell of the Thames and Bermondsey emanating from their clothes was any indication, continued a disagreement that had begun at The George.

He edged his way into the crowd. A ripple of aggression rolled through the mob fueling the men at the center of the throng. It was tempting to toss out a quick flash of fire and watch them all scatter for home. How quickly sobriety can fall when fear takes over but to do so, even for humor's sake, would lead only to questions he had no desire to answer; especially as he could hear police whistles over the din.

Luce pressed on, keeping close to the furthest edge of the crowd, mindful of any hands seeking an unguarded pocket. Crowds such as this made easy marks of one and all for the enterprising fingersmith. It was what he looked for when he and Harlequin ran the streets, and if the crowds were not accommodating it was quite easy to create a diversion when one had talent.

Twenty yards, only twenty yards to The George's doors, he thought, easing his way along.

A street stall was doing brisk business among those like himself, those who kept to the furthest edge of the mass who enjoyed the show but wished to keep out of the danger.

Sometimes the best seat in the house was the one nearest the exit, as Aurelius was fond of saying.

The woman behind the stall ladled out eel jelly from a large white basin. Cups filled with gray lumps of gelatinous flesh in an even grayer soup of fish stock were being gobbled down as quickly as the ladle allowed.

Luce ducked past the stall and dashed through The George's doors as the police arrived. Eight men in blue tunics and hard corked helmets made brave by their number descended into the crowd with truncheons raised. The unmistakable squelching crack of wood hitting bone followed as the doors closed behind him.

The crowd within was nearly as dingy and suspect as those outside had been. The length of The George and its three interconnected bars bustled with life. From travelers taking a night's shelter in the upstairs gallery to the usual clientele of laborers ending their day and the women just beginning theirs, there was not a snug nor table that did not have an inhabitant or three.

Luce pressed his way to the bar. The air was thick with stale beer and staler bodies. The shoulder of his coat collected the dust from the arm of a bricklayer who had stationed himself beside the dark maudlin face of a coal whipper; each of them had spent a considerable amount of time at their current posts as the one relied on the other for balance.

Two women behind the bar dispensed drinks as a wiry man with tobacco-stained whiskers and a nasal whine wrought from a nose twice broken weaved his way between the barmaids to haul out crates of empty bottles and replenish the shelves with fresh spirits from the cellar.

"Hello darlin', didn't expect to see you

out tonight."

Silvia's voice rang in his ear as warm as brandy on a winter's night. She smiled up at him. The scar on her cheek stretched with the curve of her full red lips.

"I hadn't planned on coming out."

"I'm glad you did," she said, leaning against him.

Luce ordered two whiskeys. At least a dozen different conversations swirled around him but the noise was a welcome diversion; welcome as the softness of Silvia's eyes that took away the need to think.

An affable-looking man sat near the fire engrossed in a card game with two equally affable companions. He had a ruddy face and was dressed well for the area, in striped trousers and a mustard waistcoat. The frock coat draped on the back of the chair was of fair quality, although the cuffs of the sleeves showed a good bit of distress. He leaned back in his chair. His watch chain was strained tight across the expanse of his round belly and threatened to break at any moment.

"Gentlemen, would you like to see a trick?"

Luce's ears perked up, his attention drawn as the seated man turned the top card over for all to see before turning it facedown and

492

returning the card to the middle of the deck. With a grand gesture, he snapped his fingers twice and then turned the top card over to reveal to his companion's amazement the original card that had magically elevated back to the top of the deck.

"Double lift," Luce said under his breath. "I did better sleight of hand when I was five."

"Not everyone has had your training," Silvia said, nudging him in the ribs.

"If only there were money in the little tricks," a man said.

The man's presence at The George should not have come as any surprise. He had long made such establishments second homes. Nevertheless, hearing that voice again after so many years sank down into the very coils of Luce's heart.

"Luce? Are you all right?" Silvia said, noticing his rigid grip on the lip of the bar.

"But to make it in the business," the man continued to the fellows nearest him, "to turn a real profit, you need to think bigger and better. You have to go beyond parlor tricks and turn to curiosities, to the freaks. And that, my friend, is when things have a way of turning to shit and you end up losing everythin' you ever thought you had."

Luce had dreamed about what he would

do when this moment came. After what had been done to Georgie he was going to enjoy this.

He took a deep breath and looked at the crowd of men huddled at the end of the bar.

Silvia couldn't see who had drawn his attention but she felt pity for whomever it was. Luce was a careful man and rarely expressed anger outwardly because of what he could do. His ability was of great concern to him, and she was acutely aware that anyone or anything that could draw this sort of focus out of him in a crowded bar was cause enough to worry.

"Luce —" She felt the heat before her hand touched his arm.

"Silvia, you may want to step outside for a moment."

The night's performance had ended an hour ago. An hour since the last vibration of Columbine's swinging reverberated through the attic room floor. An hour since the applause died and the music hushed. An hour since the last carriage pulled away.

Charlotte had half wanted to watch the show, but she could not bring herself to face Ashe and the others, despite Lucien's assurances that offense had not been taken. Thinking back, she felt herself a fool for having stormed out of the workshop without even allowing Pretorius to stitch the wound. It was not his fault, after all. He was only doing as he was bid. As for Aurelius, he was not wrong. She had not questioned the methods planned. She had not asked many questions at all.

Then there was Odilon. What if he had attended? He would be curious to know if the procedure had been a success. What if he had accompanied Florence? It was all too much and far too soon to contemplate what to say to any of them or what they would say to her.

She wanted to see Lucien. No, she needed to see him. To speak to him. To be near him was to find a comfort that she had not found in anyone else. It was like stumbling across a mirror thought lost. Their time on the *Manannan* was too brief. She wanted one more moment.

It was this restlessness of thoughts that had driven Charlotte out onto The Mint. It had come over her like a fever, which was the only reasonable explanation for why she had followed Luce when she heard from Angelique that he had left. Now she stood in the street trying to decide the direction back, while trying to avoid as many pairs of questionable eyes and equally questionable hands as she could.

She walked quickly, attempting to keep up a steady pace with the crowd. She had only caught glimpses of Luce ahead. His tall form and hatless head at first made it easy for her to follow but the speed in which he weaved through the crowd pulled him further away until she found herself completely turned around and lost amid the mass.

Noanes shouted over the roar of laughter from the raucous group of young men leaning on the bar.

" 'Course it weren't without effort, dealing with freaks that is. Nobody wants 'em, not their families, no one, and so you offer 'em an alternative and a chance to get out of the workhouse or off the street 'cause there isn't much else for them but their being the novelties that they are. So they come to us, to men like me and Sam Torr and Tom Norman, to earn themselves a living as human exhibitions and what thanks do we get for offerin' them that? Not so much as a word of gratitude. The miserable bleeders."

"If what you offered was your idea of helping, of managing a career, then by God the workhouse would have been the better alternative." Luce's voice carried across the bar, drawing several pairs of eyes to fall on him.

Noanes joined the quizzical stares, blinking through the gin-laden haze at the interloper at the end of the bar.

"Well, as I live and breathe if it ain't the devil himself, or should I say the devil's bastard?" Noanes's gaze had steadied as pointed determination replaced idle curiosity. The heat ran under Luce's skin.

"Come now, don't you folks recognize him?" Noanes stepped away from the bar and stood with arms outstretched as if he were again the showman urging the crowd in. "Well 'tis best to brace yourselves, for you stand in the presence of one of the most remarkable beings to ever draw a breath of life. He's the pride of Ashe and Pretorius's Carnivale of Curiosities. A freak extraordinaire."

"He looks normal enough to me," one of the men at the bar said, rolling an appraising eye over Luce.

"Never trust your eyes, good sir. When you've been around 'em as long as I have, you soon learn the best and most dangerous freaks hide in plain sight, with nary a hint to what they are. Now you get yourself a Thin Man or bearded lady, a joined-up twin or a dog-face and you'll find compla-cency because they're desperate to please and to belong and not lose their place. But the ones like him, well, they ain't got the same need because they got that look of normalcy."

"You always did have a silver tongue, I'll grant you that. I suppose that was the sole saving grace in Aurelius's eyes for keeping you around as long as he did."

"Luce, don't."

"It's all right, Sil," he said, slipping his arm from her hand. "Mr. Noanes and I are well acquainted, much to my misfortune. Actually that goes for anyone who's ever worked for or with him."

He kept his tone neutral, almost friendly, but there was no mistaking the intent. Luce looked him square in the eye. "Don't think for one moment that Rose's name and money are any kind of protection. I've already warned Kosh and now I'm warning you. Stay away from my family. What you did to Georgie will not be forgotten, and the only reason that you're still standing is because I don't want witnesses."

"Family!" Noanes snorted. "What do you know of family? Christ Almighty, if only your mam had finished what she had started twenty years ago . . ."

The question was in Luce's eyes and Noanes realized at once his advantage. "My God, the son of a bitch never told you."

"Told me? Told me what?"

"About that" — he pointed at Luce's chest — "that was all your mam's doing, bless her unfortunate soul."

The cog turned and it felt as if the pointed teeth were tearing their way through blood and bone.

"You don't remember?" Glee filled Noanes's eyes. "Guess when Aurelius worked his wizardry on you he erased that little fact. Make it easier to live with a lie than the truth that your own mother wanted you dead."

"You've always been a liar, Noanes, and a fuckin' bad one at that —"

"After you killed that man in the stalls, she couldn't take lookin' at you anymore; always reminding her what she'd done, what she'd brought into the world. Not of God's design, you remember that? Took to sayin' it every time she saw you. Took that guilt to her grave."

There was a nervous shuffling of feet as patrons eager for distraction circled the two.

"You weren't even there," Luce said. His arms itched from the fire building in him. "How would you —"

"I handed her the knife, lad. The only right thing to do to a rabid animal is to put 'em down. Like I told her, she'd blood on her hands already. It was one of Kosh's knives, poetic I thought, considering the way she whored herself from her marriage bed to your father's."

The blow came too fast to defend, a quick, hard right to the mouth. Noanes staggered and slumped to the floor. Luce hovered over him, his breath hard in his chest.

"That's right, show 'em all what you are," Noanes said. He spat a stream of blood and a couple of teeth onto the floor. "See! Witness to the devil's own."

The curious crowd that had once ringed them had started to move in a crush toward the door when the fire licked across Luce's shoulders to his hands, though he barely noticed. It would take one stray spark to a piece of clothing or the floor to burn The George and a block's worth of Southwark to ash.

"You destroyed her, you and Aurelius." Noanes wiped his mouth across the back of his hand, smearing blood across his chin. "Took my girl, all that I had left in the world of her mam, and ruined her body and soul."

He winced. The skin around his mouth was raw. Luce had landed not only a blow but a burn as well. "Planted alone as she was in Crossbones when the one that deserved planting was you."

"Gents, take it outside," the landlord shouted, waving a cudgel. "I don't want any trouble and I don't want to get anyone into trouble, but I'll call in the constables if needs be." He looked at Luce. "And you, we don't serve your kind!" he sneered. "Out with you!"

"Luce," Silvia said. "He's not worth it. Please."

The flames died but the eyes of every patron remained on him, and on the woman who ushered him toward the door.

"What's to happen to that poor soul you've got now? What's Aurelius done to her that I should be warnin' Rose about?" Noanes shouted.

"Keep going, don't listen," Silvia said, pushing Luce out the door before turning back on Noanes. "Was any of this necessary? Feelin' the big man now?" Her mouth turned into an ugly snarl. "Maybe I should drag you out and let him burn you anyway."

"I'd be mindin' that pretty little nose of yours, miss, if I were you," Noanes said, slowly getting to his feet.

"You can bloody well go to hell!" She turned and followed Luce out to the street.

Lost in the throng, Charlotte was bumped and jostled and once she felt a hand in search of a purse reach under her shawl. She could barely think in the madness. There was none of this at Regent's Park. There it was cool and green and the sidewalks were clean and a lady could walk unaccosted even when unattended. The Rose name and their closed gates were all the protection she needed.

The cold licked at her legs like a dog, but she took no notice and stumbled into an alleyway. Why had she not changed her thin house shoes for sturdy boots? Every stone and pebble rolled into the soles of her feet, unbalancing her gait. Even her evening shoes would have offered steadiness.

She leaned up against the wall. *How could you have been so foolish? If you had caught up to him what would you have said? What would he have thought, trailing after him like a lost soul?*

She heard a noise and saw that she was not alone. Two figures huddled close together, pressed up against the brick wall at the farthest end of the alley. Two distinct breaths, one heavy and impatient, the other more shallow and reserved to the point of indifference. As Charlotte's eyes adjusted, she noticed the smaller figure wore a dress, the skirt of which was bunched up in the man's hands. The pair moved to a distinct rhythm.

Charlotte held her breath, careful not to make a noise even as the sharp shards of brick poked at her cloak as she slid back toward the mouth of the alley. Her stomach churned and she thought she might choke as she listened to the grate of the woman's dress against the wall and the thin slap of flesh as the man thrust into her again and again.

The woman's petticoat was a froth of white around her arcing hips. The man's breath kept the measure of his pace.

Hush. Odilon's voice was in her ear, her skirts in his hands as they always were when he pressed her into the bed.

Charlotte stumbled. This time she was unable to catch herself and fell to her knees. Stones tore into her palms, but this was minor compared with the injury to her pride. God, would Florence ever be caught scrambling about in the dark in the street?

At the rate she was going, she would be a mess of scrapes and scars by the time she returned to Decimus House. She kicked back at the offending obstacle, her soft shoe connecting with the tip of another.

CHAPTER THIRTY-NINE

The fog was descending. The cold gasped in his lungs, a relief after the stifling atmosphere of The George, but it did little to cool the fire raging in Luce's blood. Noanes was a liar. He always had been and he had never shown one whit of concern or care for Isabel. For calling her his girl now, after barely acknowledging her as his daughter when she was alive! It was an affront to her memory to consider her his blood and yet —

The whiskey roiled in his gut. In the primitive part of his brain resided a nest of nascent memories. They had slept, nestled together under a thick knitted blanket, a terrible knot of blood and knives, of loss and survival and spinning brass. But every web, even those spun from the strongest strands, had its breaking point, and tonight they strained.

If what Noanes had said was true then they all knew. And they all lied. Dita. Timothy. Pretorius. Aurelius. All of them.

A stack of wooden crates standing in the alley beside The George, laden with empty bottles, was sent flying with a single kick.

Silvia heard the glass shatter before she saw him nearly five yards ahead unleashing his rage on the crates. At least it wasn't fire.

"Luce, darlin', come along. That old bastard was baitin' you. Your mother wasn't a monster and even if she were, what of it? She wouldn't be the first to ill treat her child."

"I knew she wasn't happy and I knew after . . . she never looked at me quite the same but I never doubted that she loved me. I've blamed myself for that rift even though I had no control over what happened." He looked down at Silvia, who had linked her arm through his. "But if it is true then I've grieved my whole life over a woman who tried to kill me; grieved over someone who wanted me dead."

"That's enough of that thinkin'. You are a good man, Lucien Ashe, and that is all that matters. Why don't we go back to the Row? I have a bottle of gin and you know I can make you forget everything that happened tonight." She nuzzled his neck, one hand sliding into his, as the other gently slid along his trousers.

God bless her but it was tempting. His breathing steadied as the rage washed out of him like the stale beer from the shattered bottles. Left in its place was a hole as black and deep as the one made in his chest years ago.

"Another time, darling," he said, cupping her cheek in his hand. "I'm not good company tonight."

Silvia stood alone on the street watching as he slipped off into the fog. The thick heavy cloud had softened the hard, rough edges of the buildings, and the hazy glow of the gas lamps made High Street into an almost pretty dream.

She shrugged her shawl up around her shoulders, pinching it tight across her neck as she made the walk home. Her heels clattered on the cobblestones, easily muffling the softer tread following behind.

Charlotte did not know how she had missed the girl seated on the ground when she had first entered the alley.

The night breeze fluttered the hem of the woman's pink overskirt, rustling the gauze around her thin outstretched legs. She had her back to the wall, propped as if she had stopped only for a moment's rest but had instead nodded off for a longer slumber. A damned fool thing to do for certain, sleeping in the rough on the cold stones in so flimsy a frock.

The woman looked quite young. Even under the heavy rouge and powder that covered her pox scars, youth bubbled under the surface. Fifteen? Sixteen? Her blond hair had come askew from her ribbon and the strands danced down along her neck.

Charlotte tapped the woman's foot. "Excuse me, miss?"

Nothing. Not a single stirring. She shrank back, her heart sinking.

"Dead drunk or plain dead?"

Charlotte looked up to see one-half of the rutting pair walking toward her, straightening her skirt.

"I . . . I don't know."

The other woman leaned over the prone figure and shook her shoulder. "Oi there, dearie, you a'ight?"

The blond head bobbed then rolled to an unnatural angle. "Poor mite, she had a good many more miles left to her. Ah well, it's the potters for you."

Charlotte stared at the girl, all quite disbelieving. How long had she been here? Had anyone looked for her? Any friend? Family? Or had she truly not a single soul in the world who gave her half a care?

"Wait, what are you doing?"

"She ain't no more use for this," the other woman said as she pulled the shawl from the dead body.

"Can you not leave her some dignity?" Charlotte said, looking at the thin waxen shoulders bared to the night.

"Dignity?" snorted the other woman. "Honey, that was given the ghost with her virtue the first time she spread 'em for a cull."

"Then perhaps she deserves it now."

The other woman gave her a hard cold stare. She had large wary eyes and her mousy curls peeked out from under her bonnet. She had the drawn, hungry look of a wolf in winter. "I never seen you around here before. What's your name, hussy?"

A wave of fear ran through Charlotte as the woman's predatory eye raced over her. Her skin stretched so thin that there were no secrets to the bones of her as she crept closer.

"Damned lot of cheek you have trying to begrudge someone a bit of tat when you're trussed up in that fine piece of cloth. Makes me wonder what else you've hidden under there."

Charlotte wished she had thought to leave

the ruby ring back in her rooms.

"Now I don't think this little one's any of your concern. Not when there is pickings right there for the having. Best get back to her before another does."

His voice was as firm as the hands that he wrapped around Charlotte's arms. He lifted her to her feet.

"Sir, I'm not —" she squeaked.

"What are you doing here, Charlotte?"

She did not know whether to cry or collapse, so grateful was she to turn and find the man standing behind her was not a stranger seeking a tuppence of pleasure but was instead Timothy Harlequin.

"Come along, girl, let's get you home."

"To Decimus House?"

"The Athenaeum. Word has it your Mr. Rose will be coming for you tomorrow morning."

Charlotte looked back at the dead girl left alone to the scavenger who, thread by thread, stripped her stiffened body bare.

CHAPTER FORTY

*27 October, early hours, Wretched Row,
rookery of Southwark*

It was not much, her room on Wretched
Row. But it was home. Silvia had managed
a small table and a mirror along with the
straw mattress, luxuries she had worked
hard for, although the mirror had come
from an admirer long before she had received the scar. Since then, the gifts did not
come as freely.

Her dresses and stays hung neatly on
hooks and served a twofold purpose. The
garments carefully layered atop one another
aided in keeping out drafts from the thin
walls while adding a spot of bright color to
an otherwise dreary environment.

Number Twelve was nothing special but it
was home and Silvia took pride in making
it presentable. Not for any man, though,
she kept her business to the streets like the
other whores. When you spent your days

and nights sharing your body with others you needed a place to keep yourself to yourself. Besides, there was danger in letting cullies know where you lived. You couldn't have them turning up whenever *they* pleased, like they owned you.

She had been warned years ago about girls who had gone sweet on a man; opening themselves, heart and legs, and for what? Was there any point to the deed if there were not a payment? Some of the lasses dared to go so far as to give up the life along with their liberty on a promise and a prayer only to find themselves burdened with a lover or worse a husband who pimped them out as he pleased, with over half their earnings taken leaving them tuppence or less to scrape from the dirt. *No thank you, sir,* she could say with clear agency if she didn't like the looks of the offer. It was always her choice.

Love had not touched her. She could have a hundred men over the course of a hundred nights and feel nothing more than the coins in her palm. But then one night she met a man who asked only for a kiss; beautiful beyond words but brutally scarred and bearing a heart like no other, who could thrill and terrify with the flick of a flame.

You'll burn the whole Row down!

So she had lain back down beside him, her head on his chest listening to the ticking mechanism as he created images of fire with his hands. It was as strange and simple as that. Though she dared not call Lucien Ashe hers any more than she considered herself his. It was an understanding, a convenience. But one she cherished. He was the one good thing about Southwark, the only good thing.

She smiled and reached for the bottle on the table and took a long swallow. The gin burned her throat and set her chest on fire. It was the warmest she had felt all day.

The sound of steps outside drew her back to the moment. They were quick and light and at first she took them for another miss returning home after a long night's stroll. But there was something about them that did not quite carry the assurance of a resident. They were hesitant as they stopped outside her door.

It was common for people to get lost in the Row. A ramshackle honeycomb of multistoried galleries and houses, Wretched Row backed up onto blind alleys and courts known to be havens of poverty, thievery, and prostitution. Any time of the day or night children could be found wandering barefoot through the squalor in coats three sizes too big, as men and women, when not lounging drunk, bided their time squabbling and scolding.

It was not a place you wished to lose yourself unless lost is what you wanted. But the knocking at her door begged familiarity. She ran a quick lick of rouge across her lips and rubbed a dot on each cheekbone before giving herself a once-over in the mirror.

She crossed to the door and turned the knob.

"Changed your mind have you, lover?"

Chapter Forty-One

26 October, early hours, The Athenaeum

"High Street is no place for the nocturnal wanderings of a lady." Harlequin frog-marched Charlotte into the kitchen and sat her down at the table. "It is barely suitable during the day." He pulled down a bottle of Powers whiskey, poured out two glasses, and held one out to her. "What were you doing out there?"

Charlotte took the offered glass of amber courage, although her nerves had steadied the moment he had taken her from the alley.

"I was curious."

"Curious? Damned foolish if you ask me. Just because you've been delivered up and reborn doesn't make you any less vulnerable to the world out there."

She set the glass aside and held up her palms. Her skin looked like wax shavings where it had torn from the fall, but otherwise they remained perfectly white from the absence of blood.

"I cannot feel pain, Mr. Harlequin. I've become quite impervious to it, so whatever vulnerabilities you think I am susceptible to, I counter you with this."

He took her hands and rubbed his thumbs across the rough patches of skin. She did not flinch.

"No, you don't feel pain. But I'm afraid you'll find that you don't heal either. Not in the usual sense, that is," he said, dropping her hands. "Pretorius won't be happy, but he should be able to clean you up. You best start minding yourself better otherwise you'll end up looking like a patchwork doll by month's end."

The momentary boldness that had driven her to thrust her hands in his face had passed with his release. She looked at her hands now limp in her lap. Already the heat was fading from where he had held them. It was the same as when she was in the street. She had barely blinked at the cold while others stood blue to the bone, shivering around what warmth they could siphon from the coal stoves of the food stalls. It was as if she were seeing herself for the first time.

Harlequin watched her over the lip of his

glass. He cared little for fools, even less for those whose weakness and want brought them to Aurelius's door. It was his opinion that whatever was received was deserved and being but a servant to a cunning man, it was not his place to question his decisions. Besides, to an old Púca like himself, he found the enthusiastic admiration that poured in from the Carnivale's ardent audiences entertaining. Aurelius did know how to draw and dazzle a crowd with deep pockets ripe for the picking.

To be fair, there was a difference to Charlotte. How much say could she have had against Odilon Rose's wishes? He almost pitied her.

"Ceux qui reviennent," he said, raising his glass. "To those who come back to altered lives.

"No need to look so stricken," he added, seeing the shadow on her face. "Nothing is as painful to the human mind as a great and sudden change."

"I'm sorry?"

"Mary Shelley," he said. "A young woman with wisdom far beyond her years. She had a most singular insight into the complexities of the human condition."

"Am I as monstrously changed as that?" she said, the soft curve of her face tightening. She was scared and overwhelmed, as raw and naked as that creature of Frankenstein's.

"You are dead flesh made live. You tell me."

It was a coarse statement that stilled Charlotte's tongue.

Harlequin sat forward. "Has Aurelius really told you nothing?"

"I didn't want to hear what he had to say."

"Typical." Harlequin took off his hat and ran his hands through his hair. "Eager to gain fleeting desires and wishes but blind to what it entails to possess them."

Charlotte sat dumbstruck. It had not passed her notice that Timothy Harlequin was terribly handsome. Classically featured with strong bones and brow, he was in possession of a profile that would have brought Michelangelo to his knees. But as the ram's horns that she had taken to be affectations for the stage poked through his hair, she thought him something quite different and startlingly profane.

Tucked close to the sides of his head, the horns' tips grazed his sharp Puckish ears. And though she knew it was rude to stare, she could not tear her eyes away. There was something in the way that the man and animal met that unsettled her to the core.

This was nothing like Georgie, about whose humanity there was no question, despite his unfortunate abnormality. Harlequin, however, was sublime; an example of perfectly natural aspects of an unnatural being.

When you have seen the things I've seen . . . Luce's words echoed.

"You've grown quiet, Charlotte. Cat got your tongue?"

It was the first time that she had noticed his soft brogue.

"Do you want to touch them? The horns? Quell any doubts to their validity?" he said, his head cocked slightly to the left, a smile on his lips like those of the devil she had accused Aurelius and Pretorius of being.

"No!" she said quicker than she intended. Drawing her reserve, she stood up and turned her back to him. She supported herself against the table. "Nothing should surprise me anymore," she whispered.

"I'd be careful." He leaned forward, stretching his hand out toward her. "I've never been able to resist a challenge."

The chair squeaked and she turned her head only enough to see his hand. His skin was turning from pale flesh to beech gray as his fingers, once graceful now gnarled, grated along the table. Whether it was a test of her own fortitude or simple weariness at this revelation, she did not shrink away, not even as she watched his clawed nails scrape against her wrist. "You were never a child, were you?"

"No, darling, I never was."

"You're not even human. Only the lie of one."

"Illusions are the lies that become our canon. I am whatever I need to be." He traced the bones of her wrist and even though she didn't react to his touch, he knew her eyes were on him.

"It just so happens that it was easier and kinder to Luce if he had someone to grow up with. Easier to gain confidence if the field is even. Which is what Aurelius wanted when he summoned me to look after his son, following the beating he got at the hands of one your guardian's current thugs. The same bastards who attacked Georgie the other day. I'd have thought they'd learned their lesson after the last time, but new ownership I suppose emboldened them."

It was Charlotte's turn to look gray.

"Oh, is that a look of surprise?"

"Surprise? No —" She shook her head. "Regret. Disgust but not surprise. I know that Odilon is capable of . . . many cruelties. Yet the beating of a child. I suppose nothing is beyond him."

"You needn't look any further than the company that a man keeps to know the character of the man himself. I think you need to start seeing that everyone is an illusionist in some form or another, projecting only what they want the world to see."

She looked down at his hand, which had returned to its former state of elegance. His long fingers gently wrapped around hers.

"When did Lucien learn that you weren't what you claimed?"

"It didn't take too awfully long for him to figure that out. The horns always give the game away in the end." Harlequin winked.

"You care for him."

Harlequin's silver-gray eyes softened. In his many incarnations over the course of his life so far, no other had been as enjoyable as or dear to his heart as his role as watchman over Lucien Ashe. "More than you can possibly imagine."

"I've much to learn, haven't I?" she asked. "Lucien said earlier that there are all sorts in the world and that we are hardly alone." She sat back down but allowed him to continue holding her hand. "I didn't understand what he meant exactly, but he wasn't referring to curiosities, was he?"

"He was talking about *us*. Aurelius, Pretorius, himself."

"And you."

"Aye," he nodded. "And you as well, now." He leaned over her, his mouth pressed close to her ear. "Tomorrow you go back to a world that will not accept you, no matter how much faith you have in your guardian. You said that you have much to learn. Then let your first lesson be that of instinct. Listen to it. That little voice that niggles at the back of your neck when you hear footsteps in the hallway late at night or the ripple in your gut when you find a door that should be locked —"

Charlotte's eyes widened. It was as if he was reading her nights at Decimus House and the footfalls that always stopped outside her door.

Harlequin ran his finger along her cheek, gently tracing the line of her jaw. "Instinct knows what sense doesn't."

She looked at his hand holding hers, as if the two fitted together like gloves. "Tell me, are you responsible for all of this? For Mr. Ashe's abilities?"

"Am I the man behind the myth? Don't let these horns fool you." Harlequin laughed. "I am but a humble servant. The old man, however —"

"Here, what's all this now? Does no one

522

sleep anymore?"

Dita stood in the doorway. Her dark curls had been tamed into a single long thick plait. She belted her dressing gown tight around her waist.

"Dear Lord, Charlotte, look at the state of your clothes. What on earth have you been up to?"

"I . . . I —"

"I found her wandering the street," Harlequin said, releasing his hold. "I'd say spurred by an ill-advised attempt at catching up to a certain fellow and perhaps continuing a conversation begun on a ship."

Had she an ounce of blood in her veins, her face would have colored the deepest shade of rouge. She looked back to Harlequin.

"My dear, a whisper can be heard through stone if one only knows how to listen. Imagine what you hear through a deckhouse door." His grin reached all the way to his sly wink. "Better to learn that now than never learn it at all."

"Never you mind him . . . Timothy here has always been a troublesome hob." Dita picked up the kettle from the stove and looped the handle over the faucet. "So, my dear, ready to let Pretorius fix up that neck

and those hands of yours now or would you
like some tea first?"

524

CHAPTER FORTY-TWO

27 October, The Athenaeum

Much like Pretorius's workshop, the suite of rooms on the second floor of The Athenaeum was off limits unless one was purposely invited. Whether it was on the ship, in a hotel, or anywhere he chose to lay his head, Aurelius declared his private quarters exactly that, private.

Luce knew that he should not be there. However, tonight was not about order or rules. Tonight was about a truth that not even the devil himself would dare deny.

The room was quiet and the air dusted with the perfume of herbs ground a hundred times over by marble pestles. There was an Alhambresque elegance in the dark wood and inlays that reflected Ashe's taste for the exotic. Luce sat in the hard spindle-back chair feeling very much like a small boy again. It was virtually unchanged from when Aurelius had invited him in and taken him up on his knee at the round walnut table at the center of the room to show him his first card tricks. It was on this very same spindle-back that his mother would sit, watching them, father and son, while she sewed. It was one of the few times he remembered her happy.

The table now stood littered with thumb-worn books and papers. In the far corner a tall apothecary cabinet housed vials and jars of crushed powders, herbs and oils, and — if he recalled correctly — in the deepest drawers a collection of knives, daggers, and chalices wrapped in velvet cloth. Along the same wall was a set of handsome shelves that strained under the burden of books and journals. There were several leather-bound volumes of literature and histories far nicer and older than any he had in his own meager collection. Some of the texts and manuscripts were priceless and written in the author's original hand.

On the wall opposite hung a large frame draped in black cloth that hid a solid square sheet of obsidian rumored to be able to show a person the past, the present, and the future. The scrying glass.

The glass had been a prop from the penny gaff days when Aurelius was first starting out. Luce always wondered if there was not something more to it. Knowing his father and the way he kept it housed always in his private rooms and had never allowed anyone save for Dita to use it, well, maybe, just maybe —

"Lucien? What are you doing in here?" Aurelius stood in the doorway. "This is highly unusual," he said, "but judging from the deplorable condition you are in you must have obvious reason to have intruded. Is that blood?"

Luce stirred. He followed where Aurelius's eyes led, to a large spot of red on his sleeve. Blood. He was certain he had not touched her body. He had not even left the doorway of Number Twelve, not after he saw the dark pool of shadow stretching like fingers from under the bed toward him. He heard the slow *plink, plink* of the blood that dripped through the straw mattress where Silvia lay brutally obliterated with all semblance of humanity, of personality and self, lost in the bloody wake of flesh and bone. Posed on her back, one leg stretched out on the bed, the other hanging limp off the edge. A deep gash crossed her throat like a scarlet ribbon and he hoped that that had been a killing blow and that she had not felt the gaping wound that stretched the length of her torso. The injuries to her face he could not register as there was not enough left to warrant calling the raw and bloodied flesh a face. There was nothing left from the hairline down. Her eyes, her nose, her lips, her scar . . .

The night's whiskey burned in his throat. "Lucien?"

"Silvia." Saying her name brought a lurch to his stomach and he quickly unspooled a full résumé of the night from his run-in with Noanes to his ultimately finding Silvia butchered in the Row.

Aurelius sat down and listened, carefully noting all that his son said. He did not ask any questions.

Luce rested his head in his hands. "She never hurt anyone. What would drive a man to do this to her?"

At length Aurelius sat back, stretching his legs out before him. "I am not an alienist, Lucien, nor am I in any way an expert on the depravity of others, but I do know that there are those who are filled with an unfathomable darkness of which we will never know or understand the reasoning behind."

"Like my mother."

"Lucien —"

"I saw Noanes tonight. He had much to say about her."

528

"Did he now?" Aurelius said. "Bound to come out eventually."

"Is it true? What he said about her, about what she . . ." He half choked on the thought. "Is it true?"

Aurelius felt Luce's eyes on him, laced with the questions and accusations he had long been waiting for. "Linus Noanes is a liar . . . but in this instance . . ."

It was a devastating acknowledgment. He had hoped for a lie. He had hoped that the hard turn of her face the day of the stalls fire had not also set in her heart. He had hoped that she had loved him despite what he had done.

"Your mother showed her ignorance following the . . . incident. Her making you swear to never cast another fire when doing so appeared as natural in you as breathing. How were you to learn to control it if you didn't practice? Lucien, she never understood what you are and she never tried. Denying you your gifts because she couldn't bear to think of it, yet alone see it. She was a bloody coward afraid of her own son. But I never imagined for a minute that she would go to such an extreme."

His rage turned to the man seated across from him. "I had a right to know! I grieved for *that* woman."

"So you should, she was still your mother —"

"You lied to me! You let me believe that this" — he slapped his chest — "was an accident. That it was my fault and that I killed her, when all this time it was her doing."

"I would think that you would be grateful to forget such a thing."

Fire erupted through him until he focused it into a ball. He had not used fire in pure rage since that terrible day, but Aurelius's disclosure and his careless attitude drove the flames from his hands directly at his father's head.

"I should have been told everything!"

Aurelius leapt up from his chair and caught the fireball with ease before it so much as touched a hair on his head, and threw it back at Luce with unexpected force, striking his son dead-center in the chest, knocking him off his feet and into the apothecary cabinet in a wash of flames.

"What have I always told you? Take care not to get too attached. Not to places, not to things, and especially not to people outside of family. And even then, you tread with caution. Because places fade if they don't run you out and possessions get lost along the way. As for people, you'll come to find that caring is a messy thing."

Luce looked up from the floor in time to see the black receding from the whites of his father's eyes. He did not have a hair out of place.

"Are you ready to be civil?" Ashe said, calmly shooting his cuffs before smoothing the lines from his waistcoat. Luce was stunned silent.

"Your mother was a troubled soul long before I ever met her. Between her father and Emilian Kosh, she did not have an easy time of it. Noanes mourns her now, but the only time he looked at her was when she handed him his gin. As for Mr. Kosh . . ." Aurelius shook his head.

"I needn't remind you of her scars. So I offered her kindness. I listened to her. I talked to her. I paid attention. And it is surprising how these simple acts are received in the heart of one who has never known it. In many ways she was a true innocent. Unguarded." He cleared his throat. "And even I am susceptible to personal weakness."

Aurelius closed his eyes. "Despite all she made me feel, there was to be no absolution for her in the end. Nor do I seek any redemption for what I did. Outcomes are not always the way we expect them to be, Lucien. No one knew what strange gifts you would come to possess. Of course, the poisonous influence of her father did not help her any. Filling her head with nonsense about it being an affront to her husband and a sin against God."

He spat the name as if having it on his tongue pained him. "Kosh was never careful with his knives. Never kept them locked away. By the time I reached her, she had flayed your back and was tearing away at your heart."

"Why can't I remember any of this?"

"Dita placed a memory barrier on you so nothing of that day would be remembered. We thought it best."

Luce thought of her ghost, of the rasping breath from her damaged throat. "What happened to her?"

Aurelius fell silent. He looked down into his son's eyes, *her* eyes. "I suppose in a moment of clarity she realized what she had done and . . . There was so much blood. I could only save one of you. I made my choice."

He reached down and pulled Luce to his feet and into his arms.

"I will not speak any more of her sins. Lucien, in time skin heals. Flesh scars over, leaving only a phantom of the pain. But the wounds to the mind, to the self, to the heart, well, I am not sure that any amount of time will fully mend them. We wanted to spare you that, whether you think it wrong or not. The one thing I could give you from that horrid night was the ability to forget. But only because the rest of us have suffered the memory for you."

"Aurelius!"

Harlequin stood in the doorway. He looked with surprise at seeing Luce in the room. "When did you —"

"What is it, Timothy?"

"I'm sorry but I had been looking for Luce earlier."

"Wonderful, and as you can see I have found him," Aurelius said, turning on Timothy.

"Forgive me; I would not normally intrude on father and son time unless it was impor—"

"Timothy! Out with it, man!"

"I saw smoke coming from the Row. It is burning. Half the block is alight. I thought that you might like to know."

For the first time in his life he saw his father pale. And when Aurelius fixed his gaze back on him, one didn't have to be a mind reader to see what was running through his thoughts.

"Lucien, what have you done?"

CHAPTER FORTY-THREE

Sounds traveled far in The Athenaeum, even at this late hour.

In a building this large and old, renovated or not, noises were to be expected. She was certain these walls, if they could talk, would spin tales better told by daylight. But even Decimus House, seated as it was on its neat patch of green, was known to moan and breathe on a quiet night, and in attic rooms that was especially so. Birds, bats, rats, all manner of vermin had ways of winnowing their way inside.

Charlotte dropped her hand back to her side and stretched out on the bed. She had heard a disturbance coming from a floor or two below, muffled voices followed by a thump like something falling. Ever since she had arrived, there was a constant hum of women's voices, children's laughter, and all manner of hammering and tinkering from the workshop four floors down. Outside there was a commotion of bells, shouts, and horses. Southwark was proving to be a noisy place and she took joy in every moment of it.

She rolled onto her side and drew her knees up. The bandage on her neck rubbed against the fresh stitches but she was careful not to tug at the cotton. She did not wish to see Pretorius for a third time that day, no matter how kind he had been regarding her earlier behavior and the additional attendance to her hands this evening.

The primrose gown still hung on the back of the door. Simple to the point of plain, it was not a style a more fashionable woman would have chosen for an evening at the theater. It was certainly not what Florence would wear.

It was not even a color a whore would choose. Being neither a bright jonquil nor even a vibrant chartreuse, it was instead a terribly pale yellow, soft and muted as a ghost.

Charlotte stared at the gauzy folds that streamed down the wood like daylight.

A ghost of a dress; a ghost of herself, which seemed to suit her terribly well.

She tried closing her eyes but doing so only brought her back to the alley and the dead girl, and to Timothy Harlequin. And to Lucien.

'But death is not always the end, my dear. If it helps at all, you are now what we call betwixt and between.' 'You are dead flesh made live, miss. You tell me.' 'Properly, you are a Revenant.' 'But an illusionist is what he is, miss.' 'Had you said a devil, his answer might have been different.' 'And I am his son, so what does that make me?'

'You have no idea what the world can now offer you if it is your wish to enter it.'

The hard, fast thumping feet on the stairs below roused her. She slipped from the bed and, taking a candle, was out the door and into the dark hall when she stopped suddenly. Whatever bravado had first stirred her had now melted away in the face of the venture.

Shading the flame with her palm, she listened, wondering what best to do. Concern quickly gave over to curiosity when a large marmalade cat raced past. Being creatures of high instinct, cats will go with caution into any situation. With his eager jaunt, she reassessed her fears with the swish of his fluffy tail disappearing down the stairs to the third-floor landing.

Charlotte cautiously made her way down, hesitating only when the candle started to gutter in the draft. She reached the landing in time to see the cat slip through the half-opened door at the end of the hall. As quiet as she could, she crept along, carefully approaching the room.

Luce stood before the washstand, stripped to the waist. He dipped a flannel into the basin and ran it across his face and neck. His hair was damp at his nape and the curls stuck to his wet skin. The light was dim, with a single lantern lit but she could see his form was exquisite, from neck to back; trim waist to hip was an ideal line.

She had not expected to walk into such an intimate moment and she knew she should slip quietly away and leave him alone, or at least avert her eyes until he was dressed. But somehow she reasoned that to do so would have been equally intrusive and embarrassing to both.

And it was not as if she had not seen a man before, shameful a truth as that was, but she had never seen one, nor anyone for that matter, who was as completely unadorned as Luce was now. There was no artifice being projected, no stage persona. Just a man as he was, fragile and terribly scarred.

Her eyes traced the vertical scars that branched across his shoulder blades like the limbs of a great tree, rigid and precise, almost too precise to have been accidental. His entire back was a canvas of stippled lines any one of which taken singly would have tested the hardest heart to think of its infliction on such tender flesh. *'. . . he summoned me to look after him following the beating he got at the hands of one your guardian's current thugs.'*

My God, she thought, before the quiet shattered in an explosion of busted ceramic and water as Luce sent the washstand basin flying with a string of swears. Charlotte cowered back to avoid the debris, the shards narrowly missing her as the bowl smashed into the wall.

"Now is not a good time —" He paused, seeing the figure cowering in the doorway.

He met her eyes.

"Charlotte? I didn't . . . I thought you were someone else. My apologies."

She noticed his shirt crumpled on the floor where he had dropped it. She stooped and picked it up. The stain immediately caught her eye, as did the broken chain from the crucifix that now lay discarded in the pooling water as lost as a man's faith.

"I couldn't sleep and I heard a noise. I didn't mean to . . . to intrude on you."

She held his shirt out. The scar on his chest nearly divided him in half. The skin was two shades of pale. To Pretorius's credit he had tried to make the two halves meet in the cleanest possible way, but there is only so much artistry a man can do with the materials given. For a boy, *only a boy,* there could not have been much to work with.

"Charlotte . . ."

Tonight the greatest, the most astounding aggregation of marvels and miracles have been gathered under a single roof.

"Dear God, what are you?" she whispered.

It was an impertinent thing to say but he knew she was not being purposely hurtful. "Not an easy answer," Luce said, closing the gap between them. "As I don't know myself anymore. I'm sure that there is a word for it but I can only think of the one that is most often applied. I'm certainly nothing of God's design."

She made no effort to move but remained firm where she stood as he approached. He took his bloodied shirt from her but never took his eyes off her. For a moment coherency slipped away from her. It wasn't so much a simple rendering of speechlessness but rather a nervous regard for the man standing before her and briefly she held the hope that he might chance a kiss but when he stepped back, so too did that expectation. She wasn't sure what to feel under his close scrutiny. Embarrassment? Regret? Pity? A bit of all three? Or was it perhaps that she saw in his damaged body a reflection of herself as she was now, simply another intriguing curiosity.

Luce knew she was uncomfortable. The tell was in her eyes but he couldn't help but stare. Her skin was unmarred, a soft unblemished plain. Full and intact. Unlike Silvia and yet . . . His eye glanced over the bandage on her neck.

"You went back to Pretorius."

"Yes." She touched the dressing. "He has been most understanding. I can see why your father holds him in such esteem."

"What happened to your hands?"

Charlotte had hoped that he would not notice the plasters covering each palm. Pretorius had managed to smooth out the scraped skin and to rub an oily balm across the raw surfaces to soften the torn edges. Fortunately, the scrapes were not deep. They would not require any grafts.

"An act of my own foolishness, I'm afraid. I must learn to take more care, all things considered."

"Yes, we should all take more care." Luce pulled away and walked back toward his bed.

She could not think clearly. Not as she

watched the scars on his back breathe and writhe in the half-light of the lamp before he turned back to her.

"Do you smell that?"

She inhaled deep but caught nothing. "No," she said. "I can't."

"Smoke. The Row is burning."

Charlotte's eyes darted around his room. It was a small space, as were all the quarters of The Athenaeum, and more than suitable for his meager needs. Two cases' worth of books stood stacked to overflow. There were books of maps, of charts, of fiction, histories, and poems. On a pair of two uneven shelves larger volumes sloped like melted candles while a smaller pile was home to a battered top hat. She was standing in the midst of a tinderbox. Outside the shouts and clatter of the fire brigade grew louder and nearer.

"You needn't look so worried. We are all safe, I assure you. Pretorius took great precautions when fitting out the theater. He had fire in mind so you see stone, brick, pig iron. It is more of a prison now than it ever was before."

Brick. Of all that she had seen of the theater, Luce's room was the only one whose walls were of brick. She noticed scorch marks blackening some and she had the sinking feeling that this was less of a

541

bedchamber and more of a kiln. It wasn't only exterior fires that were a threat.

"You know, when Timothy told my father about the fire his first thought didn't go to a mishap but to me. And not out of concern for my safety. No, for half a second his eyes held an accusation against me. *Me!* He thought that I could —" He shook his head.

"I'm sure that he did not seriously consider that," she said.

"I am certain of it." Charlotte nearly jumped three feet out of her skin when Timothy Harlequin stepped through the wall. The candle fell from her hand and guttered out on the floor.

" *'What have you done?'* That is what he said to me, Timothy." Luce turned on him, not in the least surprised by his intrusion. " *'What have you done?'* "

"Words, Luce. That's all. He knows damned well I —"

"Right, because you, the ever-faithful servant, would never let me lose control. Always watching just in case. That's a hell of a lot of trust he has there."

"If I can calm a situation before it escalates, then yes, I will step in. It is not a lack of trust in you, Luce, but a lack of trust in others. Outsiders will always push their way until the point tips and then cry foul when they have to face deserved repercussions. I don't have sympathy for them but for you —"

"I don't understand, why must they watch you?" Charlotte asked.

"Because I am a danger. I can do serious damage," Luce spat. "I can burn entire cities to the ground and leave nothing but a swath of ash that could make the remnants of Sodom look like a green oasis. And everyone knows that the only thing stopping me is —" He looked into Charlotte's eyes, wide and green and laced with an innocence he had lost when his mother plunged the blade into his heart.

"What stops you?"

"The fear of what I might lose in the fire." Luce shook his head. "I could have used you tonight, Timothy. I saw Noanes and I was tempted." He balled his fist but it did not keep the flames at bay and Charlotte saw the white-blue flicker rise from his skin. She took two steps back.

"But you didn't," Harlequin said.

"Only because of —" Luce dropped his hand, fingers loose as the flames dropped to ash on the floor. "Why weren't you there?"

"I wasn't far behind you but I got distracted." He side-eyed Charlotte, who returned his look with one of gentle pleading.

Please, she mouthed, afraid that she would die on the spot if Luce knew that she had recklessly followed him down The Mint.

"Distracted?" Luce asked.

"You know me, I can't resist picking up pretty things."

Luce did not respond but there was a discernible stoop to his shoulders as he sank down onto the bed.

"Lucien, is there something more? Has something else happened?"

He looked up at Charlotte. In his eyes there was a sadness that hitched her heart. "I lost someone today. Two people, actually."

"Who?" Harlequin asked.

"Silvia. She's dead."

"Silvia! What happened?"

Charlotte's mind raced back to the girl in the alley, frozen to the ground and stripped near bare.

"I don't know. She was killed at the Row, in her room, and from what I could see things were done. Her face had been cut, body . . . Tim, her heart . . . She's in the fire now —"

Charlotte rushed forward but stopped just short of sitting herself beside him. She was suddenly quite aware of her state of undress. She had left her room in her thin shift only, neglecting her dressing gown or even house shoes.

"Lucien, I'm so sorry." Her hand hesitated half an inch above his shoulder before falling back to her side.

"She returned home, to a place she felt safe. She's dead and burning because I made a mistake in letting her go alone."

"No, no, don't do that. Don't lay blame on yourself. You couldn't have known."

"She asked me to go with her and if I had she would still be alive."

This intimation of the nature of their relationship caused a sting in her heart that she hoped was not visible in her face.

"Or you could be dead as well."

Luce rolled his eyes over her as one does to an obstinate child. "You know what I can do. I could have gotten her out of the fire. And then one spark." His voice dropped low with as fine an edge as any knife in Emilian Kosh's arsenal. "And I would have been justified in doing so." He threw a look at Harlequin, who averted his eyes.

"It doesn't make you capable, though, as you said. To consciously hurt another, to kill another." Charlotte settled herself on the edge of the bed beside him. "I don't see

545

that in you, Lucien Ashe."

"You have no idea what I could or would do in the defense of those I love. Begging your pardon, but those are bounds to which you have never been pushed. And I pray that you never are. But I swear I intend to find who did this."

"How?" Harlequin asked. He leaned back against the washstand.

"There are ways, and I have a strong suspicion where to start. I'm not pleased about where it might take me, as it concerns you in a small way, Charlotte."

Charlotte smiled against the tightness in her throat. "Me? I don't understand. What does any of this have to do with me?"

"You're supposed to be going back to *that* house tomorrow. I would like to ask that you delay doing so by a few days."

"Delay my return? I couldn't possibly do that. Odilon is coming for me and unless your father has seen some reason for me to stay, I don't see how I can."

"You do have a choice, Charlotte, about where you wish to go and when you wish to leave. More so now than ever before."

"Why are you asking me to do this? Decimus House is hardly the most dangerous area in London."

"It might just be the most dangerous place."

It was a viciously suspect statement that struck Charlotte deeply. The idea that it would be perilous to return to the only family she had known was insulting. But seeing the concern in his eyes, it was plain that his words, his state of mind, stemmed from a place born not of malice but of sorrow.

"I know that you are speaking from grief, but do credit me with having some sense, Lucien Ashe. While I am not privy to the exact nature of his business dealings, I am not blind to the fact that powerful men make enemies and are often pressed into unpleasant situations as a means to an end. I don't pretend to believe that he is a good man. I know that he isn't. I have lived under his roof and I —"

She could not bring herself to admit the full nature of her relationship with Odilon, as that was a shame she preferred to keep buried, especially to Lucien. And in his current state that would have been unnecessary fuel to a fire she wished to keep doused.

"I can attest to the ugliest part of his nature, but murder? That is an extreme that even at his worst I do not think he would act on. A sin too great. Especially toward a woman with whom he held no association.

No, I see that no more in him than I do in you."

"No association that you know of," Harlequin said. He was crouched on the floor, his elbows resting on his knees as he balanced on the balls of his feet like an elegant cat. "Silvia knew a lot of men, and you'd be surprised just how many of your set spend evenings slumming down here. Men. Women. All sorts lookin' for a bit of rough. Lookin' for a distraction from their tedious little lives."

"And he associates with men who would think nothing of killing," Luce said.

'— the beating he got at the hands of one your guardian's current thugs.'

"Why do you think *me* endangered?" she asked, shooing away the thought like a fly. "I am their employer's ward. I am in Odilon Rose's keep and care."

"The night you came to us, Silvia saw the thin man lurking outside in the street."

"Skym was nosing around here?" Harlequin asked.

"I mentioned it to Aurelius earlier," Luce said. "Silvia was certain he intended to break in, undoubtedly to find out what it was that you were undergoing so he could report back to his master. She warned him off. They had to know that she would tell me and I would tell Aurelius, who would in turn confront Rose. The three of them have a comfortable situation. If that were jeopardized —"

"You believe that anyone would murder another over the loss of a position?"

Harlequin laughed. "Charlotte, in Southwark, a person would kill over the loss of a glove, an imagined slight, or for no damned reason at all."

Charlotte grew quiet and seemed to be studiously watching her limp hands in her lap. Her run-in with Mr. Noanes was fresh on her mind. "What of the other woman in the paper? The one that Mr. Harlequin spoke of. She was killed in a similar fashion. Are they responsible for that murder as well?"

Luce had not placed a great deal of thought on that first killing. The methods were similar if the paper's reporting was correct, and from what Harlequin had said after sneaking a peek at the body, the two deaths were grossly alike.

"I know it had to be the same hand because there are no two minds that could have conceived what was done. But there is one person who is capable of cutting someone up without a second thought and to whom your guardian has acquainted himself. I'm sorry, Charlotte. I just . . . things have changed for you and no matter how much Rose thinks he has prepared himself —" He took a deep breath. "— I doubt that he is going to look kindly on what has been done. Your fears will be proven true in this instance, I'm afraid. He is not going to understand, not immediately and perhaps not ever. I'm only asking that you be careful and be aware."

Charlotte swallowed back the tremor in her throat that extended all through her body.

"I'm sorry, you must be cold." Luce's eyes slid across the shadows that ran down her shift. "Here." He turned and pulled down a dark sapphire-blue robe that was hung on a hook next to the bed.

She accepted his gentle courtesy and slipped her arms into the sleeves, wrapping herself in the folds of the fabric. For a brief moment, she believed she felt the heat of his hands before he pulled away.

"I'm inclined to think that Luce might be right about you not returning to Decimus House tomorrow. Perhaps give it another day or two," Harlequin said, watching a gap closing between the two. "Rose is going to need time to digest all of this and you, yourself, have hardly adjusted. You say that you know your guardian. You know him enough to believe him incapable of instigating murder. Well, as Luce said, we know the men who work for him."

"But what benefit is there in harming me? Odilon has invested too much in this endeavor, and if these men have secured so comfortable a situation, why risk it all by angering the man who has provided it? As for Odilon, he is the man whose gates are taller and walls thicker than any of his neighbors. I've seen the way people look at him. I feel that it is a lonely life he has, though he never speaks of such things."

For half a second this admission made her feel something close to pity, although that was the last thing that he deserved.

"While I don't know exactly why or what he has done to them," she said, "I do know he has it in his nature to destroy a person's will. So you see, he has no reason to take a life when he can break a spirit." She hung her head, as it was easier if neither Lucien or Harlequin saw her face and possibly the deepest sin of Odilon's nature reflecting in her eyes. "No, my remaining here is not an option," she continued. "I am expected to leave with him. I haven't the choice."

"This afternoon, you were afraid to face Rose because you didn't know how he would react to what you have undergone. You were afraid of all that you had lost, yet you are running straight to him. If he takes the news badly, if he rejects you —"

"He will do so behind closed doors. That is when he is at his worst. His pride will not allow him to do so in front of you or your father. And I cannot run from the inevitable."

"What changed?" Luce asked.

"I have little doubt that I will not fit comfortably into Odilon's future plans and I no longer care if I do. But I need to return to Regent's Park to put those matters to an end," she said.

She looked into Luce's eyes and pressed her hand to his cheek. Stubble pricked her palm. There was no denial this time, as her fingers glanced across his skin from his cheekbone to where her thumb rested at the soft edge of his lip. Had Harlequin not been present, she would have welcomed a kiss. Would he taste of whiskey, warm and sweet, perhaps with the faintest hint of charred cedar, she wondered. Or would it be tobacco? Or simply the pitch that stoked his veins? *'The ability to feel pleasure was left intact.'* Aurelius was true to his word.

Luce reached to take her hand but she slowly drew it back.

"You don't understand, Lucien. Neither of you do. With Odilon, it doesn't end with no. He has a way of cajoling and manipulating his way to yes. And if you try to refuse —" she shrugged. "You won't win against him. But if you still entertain the idea that he is somehow involved with or aware of the unfortunate happenings at the Row, perhaps I can get you the proof you need."

"I'm not sure that you should involve yourself in this situation," Harlequin said.

"Mr. Harlequin, I am already involved. If it were not for me, he would never have come to your door." She looked at Luce. "And if he has anything at all to do with what has happened tonight, with Silvia's misfortune, then I share in that burden."

"No, no, I don't want you to speak to him of this. I won't risk —"

"There is little that he can do to me, Lucien. Not anymore and if *those* men are guilty, I can enlist Odilon in getting them prosecuted. He has no need to protect them from the law. And then it would be in the courts' hands. His word alone is practically conviction enough."

"The courts?" Luce laughed. "Charlotte, there will be no courts. We take care of our own. In all matters."

"As simple as that? You plan to confront

these men and then what? Kill them?"

"He can't," Harlequin said. "Guilty or not, Noanes, Rose, they are under contracts that only Aurelius can break. Until he sees fit, they cannot be touched, Luce. You know that. No matter how much we all liked Silvia, you ca—"

"I don't give a damn what Aurelius says or thinks! He should have taken that son of a bitch Noanes years ago. As for Odilon Rose, if he is responsible, even in the slightest way, I will burn that house down with him in it."

"Lucien, no!" Charlotte's hand flew to his chest before she was even aware of what she was doing. "You mustn't risk yourself, please. I couldn't —" Her fingers pressed the rigid scar and for a moment she feared the cog's teeth that ran beneath her palm. The strangeness of the metal pieces and flesh had still not married completely in her mind as being possible.

"She's right. You can't do anything," Harlequin said. "But perhaps I can. Aurelius will be vexed but it wouldn't be the first time and certainly not the last. Although I don't favor the idea of being banished back to an Irish bog. But it would be a worthy sacrifice to be sure and you would be protected."

Luce met Harlequin's eye and Charlotte saw something pass between them: unspoken and sacred and born of shared years spent as boys and men.

"Silvia would want it to be me, Timothy."

Charlotte's hand fell back to her lap. "Two. You said that you lost *two* people today. Who was the other?"

Luce's jaw tensed. His eyes, filled with a profound sadness, dropped from hers as his gaze swept over the silver cross on the floor. "The memory of someone I thought I knew."

"I think that you should return to your room, Charlotte," Harlequin said. "Please."

This sudden dismissal took her by surprise but she acquiesced to the request. At the door, she stopped and looked back.

"You knew," she heard Lucien say. "All of these years and you've known what my mother —" Three heavy breaths. "— and you didn't say a word. You kept that from me when I deserved the truth. I deserved that much."

Before Harlequin could answer, Luce had fallen back on the bed and turned on his side toward the wall, prone and vulnerable.

The desire to run back in and comfort him burned in her but Harlequin had moved and was sitting cross-legged at the foot of the bed, watching over his charge. The oil lamp cast his shadow long on the wall, horns and all, flickering in the light like Cernunnos.

CHAPTER FORTY-FOUR

27 October, Wretched Row, Southwark

Soot and ash spun through the air like a black blizzard over Southwark. Soft, slow flakes dusted everything from windowpanes, to roofs, to the clothes of the men, women, and children bustling along the street.

Fifteen dead were found in the burned-out husks of the Row fire, and more were expected in the rubble of three houses.

The police had cordoned off as much of the area as possible to allow the firemen to sift through the detritus, and to keep the curious safely at bay. Overseeing the excavation was a ruddy-faced man of middle height who hid his thinning hair beneath a black bowler hat. At first glance, he could be mistaken for any passing onlooker, but there was something in the cold hard stare he cast over the rubble that was Number Twelve that indicated his interest was more than just simple curiosity.

The whore had been the first body found and a deplorable sight it was. It took but a single glance, burned though she was, to see that there was nothing natural about her death. It was not some accident, some haphazard tipping of a candle. This fire was arson but the whore — there was not a fire or a crumbling wall that can peel the face from a woman. Inspector Joseph Grainger frowned.

"We've got two more 'ere, sir," called one of his officers, who carefully scrambled across the smoldering ruins. It was unsteady work as the remaining flooring and walls could give way at any moment.

"Found 'em down in a leeway. Two women. Must have thought it a good place to shelter for the night."

"What's that bring the total to? Seventeen?" Grainger removed his hat, silt falling from the brim, and wiped his forehead. "Christ Almighty, it gets worse and worse. All right, show 'em to me," he said, following the narrow path the firemen had made.

Keeping his focus on his feet and on the crumbling death trap beneath them, Grainger took no notice of the big black carriage that rolled past the Row along the High Street to slow before the doors of The Athenaeum. He took no notice of the well-dressed man who emerged and walked up the theater steps. He took no notice as this man paused on the step and looked back up the street in the direction of the Row before slipping out of sight into the theater.

"You must be counting your blessings, Mr. Ashe," Odilon Rose said, seating himself before Ashe's desk. "I've just driven by the Row and it is absolutely devastating. It makes one think that had the wind been with it, the fire could easily have spread across the whole of High Street. It would have been a tragedy if this theater had been lost. The grace of God, I suppose."

"I don't believe that such grace has ever shined on Southwark. Of course that does not mitigate the severity of the lives affected and of those lost."

Rose nodded but remained woodenly resigned in his chair, his legs crossed and hands loosely folded in his lap.

"But you did not come here to ruminate on the perils of rookery living." Aurelius stood up and walked around his desk. Dita had left a pot and service for four on the credenza. As he passed, the orrery clicked and one brass planet revolved in its orbit. "Coffee?"

"Thank you, no," Rose said. "And you are

559

quite right. My interest does not extend to those of the rookery, unfortunate as their circumstances currently are. My priority is on the task that I set you to. You stated in your letter that it was done but you neglected to say exactly what 'it' was."

"And you stated that all that mattered was that she be alive."

"Without knowing at least some of the means by which this miracle has been accomplished, where then is the assurance that anything at all was done? I have heard of your abilities, Mr. Ashe, and your son is an impressive example. However, you reside in a world of smoke and mirrors where disbelief must be suspended. So I do not believe that my doubts are misplaced, suspended or otherwise."

"Even after what your family has achieved?"

"Sometimes one needs only confidence and to have confidence placed in them. Persuasion can go a long way toward promoting achievement."

Aurelius laughed. "You began this endeavor with such faith, and now you express doubt. It makes a man wonder what has brought on this sudden change. If you will not believe my word perhaps you will believe your eyes. Mr. Pretorius, if you would be so kind as to escort the lady in."

At the sound of the summons, the door opened and Charlotte entered with Pretorius in tow. She was dressed as she had been on the night he left her behind, in the pale-primrose gown.

Rose crossed to her and took her hand, drawing her forward. He noted the stitches on her neck and the plasters on her palms, but little else seemed out of place.

"I see no marked difference in her," Rose said.

"It is a pleasure to see you as well, Odilon."

"Forgive me, Charlotte. Where are my manners?" he said before kissing her cheek. "You are well? All is well?"

"I am better than well, thank you. Since coming here, I feel positively . . . reborn."

"You certainly look in the pink. Perhaps a little pale." He touched her hair, running his hand down her neck to her shoulder. "But altogether very near to the Charlotte of old."

"That was precisely our goal, Mr. Rose. To restore her. However, to do so required an extreme method." Ashe walked over and took Charlotte's other hand. "If I may demonstrate."

From thin air, he produced a pin, which

he quickly inserted into the center of Charlotte's palm.

Odilon watched wincing as the sharp tip broke through her skin. However, Charlotte showed no reaction. Not a flicker of her eye or intake of breath. She did not even pull her hand away as the pin pressed deep into her.

"The greatest illusion of all is when the dead pass for the living."

Aurelius touched Charlotte's cheek. "You presented us with a thorny problem and at first I wasn't sure how to approach it. But then I —"

"Had a small idea."

"A small idea." He brushed her hair back behind her ear.

Whatever he felt at this moment, Rose was careful not to betray it.

"They have many names. Draugr. Dybbuk. Nachzehrer. Revenant —"

It was only a quick dart of the eyes on the word *Revenant,* but it did not pass Aurelius's notice.

"They are essentially the same in theory as they share one commonality. Transcending death to return to the world. Betwixt and between."

Odilon's eyes narrowed. "Mr. Ashe, you talk of improbabilities and do weave a pretty tale. What is once dead remains dead, and this woman is as alive as I am."

"In a manner of speaking."

"Odilon, please stop and listen. Mr. Ashe is telling you the truth," Charlotte said. "I didn't believe it possible either, but look." She held her hand out and pulled the pin from her palm. A tiny pink bead remained in the track. "No blood. No pain."

"It is a trick, that's all. Charlotte, it is what he does, what they all do. He's convinced you of this but —"

"Mr. Rose, I would advise you to listen to the lady. After a few days you will see."

"Then how was it done? You've had an answer for everything else."

"Tch, tch, Mr. Rose," Aurelius clucked. "That is not the protocol of magicians. If I were to reveal —"

"All that you would reveal is yourself as the fraud that you are!"

"Odilon!"

"Now, now, Mr. Rose. No need exciting yourself," Pretorius said. "You have to understand that there are strange things in this world, stranger than you can imagine. But sometimes you need a little faith and lot of trust to see them. That is what magic is. It's having faith in the things that shouldn't be."

Rose reflexively placed his hand over his pocket where the paper with Atherton's sigil burned. "What you are saying is not magic. No mort —" His mind raced and he was too aware of the unconcealed attention that the loss of his control was allowing. "Is it not enough that there are natural-born monsters? Must you pervert what is normal?"

Ashe looked him deep in the eye. "Still haunts you, doesn't it? You have never been able to let go. Is that what has driven you to save Charlotte? Too young to help the other?"

The color drained like water from Rose's face "What did you say to me?"

"You know very well what I've said." The speed by which he clamped his hand on Rose's neck startled everyone in the room, though no one more than Rose himself, who found Ashe's mouth at his ear.

"Quite familiar with natural-born monsters, are we?" he whispered. "I know about your sister Louisa. I know all about the poor creature."

Rose drew back as if bit by a snake and for a hair's breadth of a second Aurelius thought he saw a shift in the man; a fleeting expression of the strangeness that Mrs. Harcourt could neither describe nor forget.

"As you should," he said. "I want out of the contract. This is nothing like what I wanted."

"Out?" Ashe grinned. "Are you hearing this, Pretorius? He asks to be released from our deal. Tell me, Mr. Rose, what am I to say to such a novel idea? *Oh jolly good, I'll burn your contract while you put the kettle on? No harm, no foul?* My goodness, if you are as forgiving of debts as you expect me to be, I may have to consider banking with you."

Ashe shook his head. "No, Mr. Rose, it does not work that way. We can renegotiate terms, even modify the request, but it changes nothing. You can make a new deal that cancels out the former. Of course, doing so means that this lovely young woman dies. Perhaps today, tomorrow, a month from now, but she will die. And whatever your plans are die with her."

Charlotte closed her eyes. This was a turn she had not expected.

"It is of no matter to me, Odilon Rose, but whichever path you choose, the outcome remains the same. I will be compensated for what I am owed. *That* is non-negotiable."

"Odilon, please, this is my life."

"Seeing as Miss Bainbridge's current state has affected you adversely" — Ashe's tone softened at her direct plea — "I would be more than happy to offer her sanctuary here with us. It would be only fair since the goods delivered did not meet your expectation. I can be moved to extend our contract by five additional years in exchange. Five additional years, Mr. Rose. Trust me when I say that is a most generous offer."

"Most generous," Pretorius echoed.

"Oh no, Mr. Ashe. It's not as easy as that. I've invested far too much time, effort, and money on this venture, and my responsibility for this woman remains intact. Our contract will stand, for now. But this discussion is far from over."

Charlotte tensed as Rose gripped the back of her neck. It was a gesture she knew all too well, as it usually preceded the twisting of her hair and the cruel pressing of her face into a pillow.

"Now bid goodbye to Mr. Ashe and to Mr. Pretorius, Charlotte. We are leaving."

"No! You can't take him!" Georgie wriggled in Dita's arms.

"Georgie, hush, this is all a mistake. I'm not going anywhere because this man's business is not with me." Luce stepped closer, his eyes darkening. "I wasn't even there."

566

"Now then, Mr. Ashe, that's contradictory to what we've heard," Inspector Grainger said. He maintained an affable tone to prevent further provocation. "We've heard several witnesses firmly put a man matching your description at the Row, and what's more the landlord of The George remembers you very well. He and at least twenty patrons who were present for your little altercation."

"Fuckin' Noanes. This is all his doing, isn't it?" Luce muttered, turning away.

The inspector grabbed hold of his arm. "Not so fast, laddie. You're in my custody now."

"Custody!" he said, wrenching his arm free. He could measure his temper by the heat in his hands. "What for?"

"For one, suspicion of arson —"

"Because of my act I must have been the one to set fire to the rookery?"

"There has also been a murder. A woman, a known prostitute. Found in the rubble of what was Number Twelve. Are you beginning to understand my interest?"

Luce stared at him.

"I know that you were at The George and that you didn't leave alone."

"I knew a woman who lived in the Row. We parted ways outside The George."

"Well you're a smart lad, so you won't mind telling me what time that was and where you went afterward. Remember, we know roughly when the fire was started and why it was started, which is why I'm obligated to caution you that anything you say from this point forward can be held against you. So you might want to choose your words carefully, or wait for a solicitor to talk for you."

"Gentlemen!" Aurelius walked into the front of the theater house. "To what do we owe this unexpected visit?"

"Mr. Ashe senior, is it? Well, it is my duty to inform you that your son is under arrest on suspicion of murder and arson."

"Is that a fact, Officer? I'm sorry, I've missed your name."

"Grainger. Detective Inspector Grainger."

"Well then, Detective Inspector Grainger, before you commit a gross injustice, it is only fair to inform you that you indeed have the wrong man. I can attest that my son had nothing to do with this crime."

"Sir, meaning no disrespect, but I would not doubt your saying just about anything to help him."

"Would you believe me, Inspector?"

All eyes turned to Charlotte, who calmly stepped forward. "Both of these gentlemen

568

are true to their word. Lucien Ashe could not have possibly had anything to do with what he is accused of."

"And why is that, Miss . . . ?"

"Charlotte Bainbridge."

"Well now, Miss Bainbridge, why are you so certain of Mr. Ashe's innocence?"

"Because he was in my company at the time."

"Charlotte —" Luce said. "Please —"

"There was a performance last night," she continued, "after which there was a small gathering that ran rather late, and I'm afraid that I left my purse behind. Which is what brings me back this morning."

"Miss, you are aware of what you are saying? Think of your future and what testifying on record will do for your reputation."

"Inspector, perhaps you would care to take my reputation into consideration."

It was the first time that Grainger noticed Odilon Rose in the company. Quickly his hat was off and in his hand. "Mr. Rose, I . . . was . . . I didn't see you there, sir . . ."

"I'm afraid that you must disregard Miss Bainbridge's claim. There was a performance but young Mr. Ashe did not linger. And Miss Bainbridge is a good-willed girl and thinks that she is helping. I do hope that her excitement to help will not be used to cast an aspersion against her reputation or mine."

Grainger would have liked nothing more than to lift the man off his feet if only to see the smugness drop from his face, but he swallowed hard on the desire. "I don't believe it will be necessary to bother yourself or the lady in this matter at this time, but we may need to speak again in the near future."

"Of course," Rose said, replacing his hat and taking Charlotte's arm firmly in his hand. "Miss Bainbridge and I will be more than willing to assist in any way that we can."

"That is good of you, sir, miss. But as for you, Mr. Ashe," he said, turning back to Luce. "I have a few questions. You were the last to see the . . . lady, and I'm sure you can understand that any light that can be shed on her last hours would be of great help."

Luce thought for a moment, weighing options that were growing fewer and thinner.

"Fine, let's be done with it."

In the heart of London, in a large third-floor office in a dreary old bank, Mr. Josiah Emmett's thoughts drifted toward a fire. In a close-quartered city like this, such events were more expectations and less exception. Yet this one caused Emmett pause, spurring animation in his normally dry, reserved features.

"You are certain?" he said, turning from the window.

"As sure as the crow flies," Emilian Kosh said, leaning back in his chair. "Skym here saw enough to remove any doubts. Which is why we stepped in and did our part, which has since sent the police in a specific direction. The question now is what's to be done."

Emmett wearily glanced at the discarded newspaper on his desk. Based on the headline alone, he knew the value of what lay in those pages right down to the last farthing were the connections made, which only made the subject of this meeting even more tedious.

But so it was and here they were. Emmett looked at Kosh, at this insignificant little man in a shabby waistcoat, and his partner Skym, whose drooping yellow eyes returned an unwavering gaze.

"Well, gentlemen, I suppose that if the information proves valid, and that is a very big *if,* we can come to an amenable arrangement."

CHAPTER FORTY-FIVE

The carriage ride was subdued as the two occupants were both lost in thoughts better kept to themselves. Charlotte had tried to read Odilon. A difficult task. Even at his most sociable, there remained in him a stoic distance. Now that she was alone with him, the series of furrowed lines making up his brow spoke to his displeasure. But the rest of his face remained as stone. She abandoned the exercise.

In her own heart, she knew she should not have spoken as she had, boldly putting herself into a lie, or at least a half-truth. She had spent part of the evening with Lucien, but only part. It had sounded bad, quite suggestive, and the inspector was not wrong in the fact that her actions could come to draw inferences of impropriety that would cast a shadow not only on her, but on the Rose name, and onto Odilon, a man to whom reputation was everything. The consequences would not be pleasant. Odilon was capable of many things, but . . .

She looked out the window as they passed the remains of the Row. The fire had been far worse than the bells and shouts last night had indicated. The air was still hot and smelled of burnt wood and grief. Three of the buildings had been reduced to skeletons on whose rubble firemen sifted across like beetles at a feast. As the recovery proceeded, body after body was brought out into the street. Mercifully, cloths were draped over them, offering small comfort to those who watched and wailed.

"That inspector is a fool to think that Lucien Ashe could have anything to do with this horror. If anyone on this earth knows the destructive force that fire is, it would be the one person who can create it from his own hands. He would not be careless."

Odilon reached over and jerked the drape across the carriage window and shut out the vision of a woman, soot-stained and cradling a child's shoe to her breast, falling to her knees when a small bundled figure was retrieved from the ruins and laid out next to the other bodies.

"Don't defend people you do not know, Charlotte. Three days might inform an opinion but it does not show you the truth.

573

You have no idea what they may or may not have done and it is not *your* concern. That inspector is doing his job. And if his suspicions brought him to the Ashes, so be it."

"There was a woman murdered there last night." She looked to see a reaction but met only indifference. "I heard that her throat had been slashed —"

"And I am supposed to care about what happened to some Southwark slattern?" Odilon settled himself back into his seat. "If there has been a murder then the guilty will pay. The guilty always pay."

Charlotte turned her face away, no wiser to Odilon's actions, as the chill between them returned and the stone once again set in his face.

He had fully expected being tossed into the cells as soon as he passed through the station doors at Stone's End, which made it something of a pleasant surprise to be directed instead to Grainger's office.

"I didn't expect you to have friends in such high places, Mr. Ashe," Grainger said, taking a seat at his desk.

"Rose? I would hardly consider him a friend."

"I was referring to the young lady, Charlotte Bainbridge."

574

The office was cold, but it did little to lessen the sweat beading across Luce's scalp. "What has she to do with any of this?" Luce asked, settling under Grainger's gaze.

"Mr. Ashe, when an upstanding woman blatantly lies to my face I find it curious as to why."

"That is a big presumption, Inspector. As well as an insult to the lady."

"She was too quick in her defense. She didn't know that you had already admitted to being at The George with the victim and that witnesses placed you there. And then Odilon Rose —"

The shift in his eyes was minute but Grainger was accustomed to catching such changes, even in the most self-possessed.

"Leaving her purse behind after a late-night engagement and then coming to retrieve it the next morning. A story to almost be believed if I didn't have two daughters of my own and a clear under-standing of how easily the most levelheaded girl can be turned a fool when infatuated," he said, softening his tone. "A good-looking fellow like yourself, mustn't be too hard —"

"Inspector, I'm a performer. That is it. I am not a criminal. I'm not out to hurt anyone, so when I'm offstage I am on my own time and what I do on that off time is of no one's concern but mine. I frankly do not need to define any moral ground with you or anyone else. As to the behavior of Miss Bainbridge —" He paused. So much of his life was under his absolute control with little to no expectation of relying on others for anything, yet Charlotte's sudden kindness — "Is there any reason to draw her into this?"

"Mr. Ashe, to borrow your parlance, I am merely positioning my players, and when Miss Bainbridge inserted herself into this investigation by offering you, a relative stranger, with a false alibi, I have to ask why."

"She didn't lie, Inspector, not entirely. She was at the theater last night, but not for an after-show engagement. If anyone lied it was Rose." Luce shrugged. "Following the performance I did go to The George. I often go for a drink to unwind. I ran into Silvia and then Noanes, of which you already know. I then returned to the theater and as to any further details, I prefer to keep those to myself."

"And Rose?"

"He came for her this morning."

The tip of Grainger's pencil tapped the desk. "She's his ward, isn't she?"

"Yes."

"That is a dangerous game to play, Mr. Ashe, and yet Rose appears to be tolerant of her behavior. Which is unusual considering who he is."

"The best way to save face is to not react, especially in front of you, sir. Which is why he had tried to throw me into this mess."

"It would have been a ripe opportunity to bring charges against you, though. Abduction. Rape. No matter what the girl would have said he could counter with the ugliest accusations, and he has the clout to make them stick."

Luce smiled. "And risk angering my father? Rose is too smart a man for that." *Besides, we both know what kind of man he is and we both know that making a scene is not his style, not when he can easily use that information for his own gains at a suitable time.*

Grainger sat up in his chair. "Your father? Now, that is interesting. Why should Rose worry about angering him?"

"Odilon Rose isn't the only man of influence in London. My father too knows his way around a bargaining table."

"Does he now? And what sort of bargains might he be making that would be of interest to Rose?"

He had come to a moment when he would

need to tread carefully. Not that Grainger, or anyone, would believe what Aurelius was capable of or the service he had performed for Rose and Charlotte, but no one wanted or needed outsiders sniffing about.

"Investment. We are a profitable show and we have encountered many who have expressed interest in supporting us as patrons. Of course, I'm not privy to those dealings."

A smirk tugged at the corner of Grainger's lips. "Mr. Ashe, did you know that a man can purchase a child for less than ten pounds? There are houses that specialize in such procurements. Opium, gambling, fights be it dog, man, or woman for that matter, prostitution, pornography, baby farming; there is not a perversity that cannot be bought and sated in this city if you've the connections and more important the money. I do not think it a coincidence that two of the most prominent gambling houses have leases held by the very bank run by our mutual acquaintance. So when I hear that that same notable citizen now has cause for business with a traveling sideshow, I have to wonder —"

"He wouldn't need to come to us, Inspector. I'm well aware of what can be purchased —"

"Yes, Silvia Marquette for example."

The trod worm turned at the drop of her name.

"I wouldn't have hurt her, Inspector. I had no reason to."

"Someone did, Mr. Ashe. Someone had a reason to hurt her very badly, and then went to an extreme length to hide that fact. At least sixteen other people were killed and we are still sifting through the ashes."

"The fire, how was it started? Were there any accelerants used?"

"There are indications that something was used."

Luce held his hand up. A thin blue flame limned his fingers before engulfing his whole hand.

Grainger shrank back in his chair.

"I don't need accelerants, Inspector." He shook his hand and the flames dimmed until only a few sparks dissolved on the floor.

Pure will and several deep breaths calmed Grainger back to a speaking state.

"Sorry," Luce said. "It was the only way to show you. It startles people the first time they see it up close, but I assure you that I can control it."

"When I was a boy I went to my share of magic and freak shows. They didn't travel out as much then so I'd end up down at one of the shops and I can tell you I've seen some things, things that didn't seem able to exist." He cleared his throat. "But that, that beats all."

"You should come to our show some night if you want to see the impossible. Now, if you don't have anything more to ask I should be getting back."

"Sit yourself back down there, lad, I do have one or two more things I need clearing up. The George. What exactly happened there last night?"

"Disagreements happen in pubs, Inspector."

"Would you care to expand on that?"

There was a cardinal rule among kinkers and that was you took care of your own. It did not matter what the issue was or what the trouble a fellow might be in, you helped where you could; you did as expected and could expect the same in return.

"This Linus Noanes has lobbed some serious accusations against you according to those present."

"The man's a drunkard. I'd sooner trust the word of the devil himself."

"There must be some reliability to him considering his employer."

"He was quick to tell you that, I'm sure," Luce said.

"Yes, Mr. Rose does appear to be keeping

interesting company of late. Hearing a bit more of his name than I care to."

It was a tell that even an amateur could read. "You don't care for Rose," Luce said, leaning forward.

"Witnesses reported that after you'd left The George, Miss Marquette was seen having words with this Noanes," Grainger said, skirting the question. "Do you happen to know if the two had had prior contact? Any previous quarrels?"

"Silvia knows . . . knew a lot of men and her business was her business. I wasn't her pimp —"

"No, but even prostitutes have their confidants."

Luce sighed away the heat below his collar. It was not from any sense of shame, Grainger's knowing about his relationship with Silvia or Silvia's profession and the connotations of payment for services rendered, despite her never once taking so much as a shilling from him.

The flush he felt was from the presumption of an intimacy that did not exist. Were he to tell the truth, he knew very little of Silvia, only what she wanted him to know. A fault of which he was equally guilty with her. Give the world your body but keep your soul for yourself.

He shared that philosophy. It was one that all curiosities shared if they were to survive. The moments when he and Silvia had come together only happened when they chose; not from some purely romantic notion, though he was fond of her, but rather from the need to escape their solitary selves and if only for a moment believe that they mattered to another and that another mattered to them.

"It's possible, but I didn't get the impression that she knew him."

"Do you think, knowing him as you do, that he is capable of this?"

"Too soon to dismiss the idea, I suppose." *I handed her the knife.* Noanes's face twisted into his mind. "I doubt he's your man. He can be mean, but he is too much a coward to dirty his own hands." Kosh, though? Luce shook his head. "Noanes hasn't the skills to do what was done to her. And I doubt the stomach."

"And how do you know what was done?"

Caught as he was, Luce's gut plummeted and for a moment his veins ran cold, a sensation he had not felt since childhood.

"Mr. Ashe? You stated that you parted company with Miss Marquette at The George. So how do you know what was done unless you were there?"

Luce's tongue flicked over his dry lips as he watched the minute shift in Grainger's eyes.

"You see, Mr. Ashe, you're not giving me much of a defense. You were known to the victim. Seen with her earlier in the evening. And that little fire thing you can do, none of these factors are helping you, my lad. I've got bodies coming out of the Row by the hour, add to that Silvia Marquette's murder and there was a killing of another prostitute not more than two nights ago which I'm fairly certain we could tie to you as well with little effort on our part. The higher-ups are going to be looking for closure on this and you're the only one I've got with opportunity."

"But no motive. Why would I kill her, and then knowingly set a fire of all things?" Luce said. "I didn't do this!"

"So you say. But it's your word against the evidence. Perhaps we should keep you for the night. Let you think on things and then in the morning have you up before Judge Suskind. And let me tell you, he's a great adherent of swift justice."

Suskind. It was as if the noose was already around his neck and Odilon Rose was at the lever. The bastard was out for blood. And Charlotte was going back to him.

"If you could give me anything to support —"

"She was dead when I got there," Luce said. "She was on the bed, gutted out like a fish, and I couldn't get out of there fast enough. But I was back at the theater long before that fire started. Ask anyone over there. Ask my father."

"What time did you discover Miss Marquette's body?"

"I don't know. After midnight, maybe."

"After midnight? That leaves a bit of time unaccounted. Why did you go at so late an hour?"

"She had invited me earlier. I had declined. It was right after the fight with Noanes and I wanted to be alone. She left for the Row and I went out to the docks."

"And with Miss Bainbridge patiently waiting for you. You're a busy man."

"I went back to see Silvia to apologize for the incident with Noanes."

Grainger leaned back in his chair, as comfortable as a man before the fire in his own home. "Did you see anyone lingering about?"

"Lingering? At the Row? When has there not been people about at all hours? You're talking about a place where there can be five to a bed in any one room and the only thing lower than the company housed there is the street itself. You're asking me if I saw anyone lingering —"

"Mr. Ashe, there is a gap of time between Miss Marquette's death and the start of the fire. A time that allowed you to enter and leave her room, which lends itself to two conclusions: Either you killed her and started the fire, which you have claimed not to have done, or the killer committed his act, left, and came back, which only magnifies his depravity. You could have very well passed this person in the hall, or on the stairs, or on the street. So I ask again, did you see anyone that you might now think questionable?"

His memory of the night before was in tatters. There was a hallway, a door, and Silvia. And blood. So much blood that try as he might, he could not recall much beyond that. He couldn't recall seeing Noanes or Kosh or Skym. Any of the three he would have noted, but there had been no one in the hall, no one on the stairs, and the tenement was a blur among the human hive that was the rook. The street was no better. Women, children even at that hour. Other prostitutes, one of whom had passed by close to him, black-clad from hat to foot, but nothing more of note on the dark street.

To think for one moment that Silvia's killer could have brushed his shoulder in passing galled him to the bone.

"I don't . . . I don't remember anyone. I just wanted to get away. . ."

"Now I want you to think hard. Did she ever mention having had trouble with anyone? Anyone at all?"

"Seven years ago, a man cut her, across her face and neck. She couldn't identify him wrapped as he was in a scarf, hat tipped low. She only saw the knife."

Grainger nodded. "We'll check and see if a report was made."

"Inspector, you have asked a lot of questions about me, about Noanes, and about Rose. That is a very tight circle of interest."

"As I said, merely arranging my players, Mr. Ashe."

"There is another name to check on," Luce said. "Emilian Kosh. He's good with knives."

"I think that's all that I need for now, thank you, but do keep yourself available in case we need to talk further."

"You're letting me go?" Luce asked.

"For now," Grainger said.

Luce stood to leave, perplexed but relieved to be seeing what he hoped would be the last of Bow Street.

586

"And, Mr. Ashe, it seems that someone has gone to great lengths to incriminate you in this, and I'd like to know why. But if you will take a friendly word, it would be a grave mistake to allow your business with Odilon Rose to linger any longer than it needs to. It could wind up costing you dearly."

CHAPTER FORTY-SIX

When the carriage pulled to a halt outside Decimus House, there were no furtive glances from either occupant as they descended to the walk. Anyone watching that morning would not have thought anything out of the ordinary as the pair made their way, one in hurried determination up the steps and through the door as the other crossed the threshold in a stumbling tangle of feet.

"Odilon, please, you can ask the man himself, he will tell you —"

"You don't understand, do you?" He turned back on Charlotte in as near to panic as he had ever felt. "You stupid, stupid girl. Because of your pathetic infatuation my association with Ashe and his creatures is now known. And to a detective inspector of all people. After I have been so careful to protect my business interests . . ."

Charlotte had never seen Odilon in such a

state. He was always a man of self-containment, no matter what mischief arose; he of all people could be counted on to maintain a calm and logical head. It was what made his clients respect him. But now to see him unraveling as a pulled thread shook her.

"Lucien is an innocent man, Odilon. I could not stand by and see him arrested on what constitutes a hanging offense. That inspector had him guilted to the gallows for no other reason than his . . . abilities. And then you add fuel to the fire by saying he wasn't at the theater."

"Do you enjoy making me look the fool?" Odilon spun on her. "After all that I have done for you, that *we* have done for you? Taking you in like a mongrel, clothing you, educating you, treating you as one of the family, only to be repaid by your being made a freak's convenience."

"Best to be at his convenience than yours —"

A vicious blow knocked her to her knees. Charlotte fell back onto her hip and stared up at Odilon, who stood over her, his fist still clenched and face flushed a shade of red she had only seen in a harlot's skirt.

"Slattern!" he hissed. "Bainbridge bitch. I should have known better than to attempt to pass a mutt off for a show hound."

"Then let me go, Odilon. Please, I want to go back to The Athenaeum. I swear to you that I'll not say a word about anything that has happened in this house. I'll never speak your name or darken your door. If you will let me go, I won't tell and I won't return."

"You think that you are leaving me? You aren't going anywhere." He lifted her from the floor by her throat. She clung helpless to his arms. "You are mine! You have always been mine from the day Father brought you to our house. He thought he was doing a good thing, bringing you home. He thought you would ease the wound that Louisa left. But Mother was not pleased with the idea that he thought her child could be replaced with one so perfect."

He pulled her close until his lips burned at her ear. "Father brought you to us. But Mother gave you to me. So it is you and I, Charlotte. It will always be us because we are what is left and I will see you in the ground, dead or alive, before I allow you in Ashe's company again!"

He threw her back against the wall. "As for that." He tore the ruby ring from her finger. The band cut into her skin, stripping the surface layer like the flesh from a well-cooked bone.

"Now look what you've done," she cried.

If Rose was listening, he gave no indication. He merely stared at her injured hand, at the pinkish liquid oozing through the torn skin. And then a strange half smile twitched his cheek.

"Why did he take Luce away? He didn't do anything."

"He didn't take him away, Georgie. Luce went with him of his own accord to help." Angelique put her arm around his shoulder and pulled him into a hug. "He's coming home, don't you worry about that."

Angelique understood Georgie's fears. There was not one among them, not a kinker or a Roma, who wholeheartedly trusted the police. Too many times, performers and troupes found themselves run out of town or scapegoated for every petty crime within proximity.

"It's convenient," Columbine said. "The fire. Silvia. Someone does not like our dear Luce."

"Shhh, not in front of the boy," Harlequin said, pulling her out of earshot of the others.

"You must admit, though, it's all a bit suspect," she continued.

"I don't disagree but why? Who would be so depraved? And to what purpose?"

"I'm not sure that knowing the purpose would make the actions any more understandable," Aurelius said.

Both Angelique's and Harlequin's tongues fell silent as he swept into the hallway. "I for one will find no comfort treading the waters of another's insanity."

"But why Luce, out of all of us?" Harlequin said. "Meaning no disrespect, but if there is one person who has made enemies it is you."

"The sins of the father are visited on the son," Aurelius said. A faint bitter smile graced Aurelius's lips but did nothing to warm his eyes or to be of cheer to anyone. "Do you believe that I've not already thought of that?"

Passing the two, he continued along the hall back to his office.

He was not a man who disliked darkness. Today, however, there was something about the shadows of The Athenaeum that made him wish for more candles. Anything that would add just a hint of light. The hall was also not as empty as he first presumed. He knew they were there without needing to see.

"Davie, Danny? What is it?"

592

The twins stepped out of the shadows into the hallway cautious as ever. Their white-blond heads bobbed up at him.

"Did he leave? The bad man?" Danny said.

"Leave, the bad man did he?" Davie said.

"Boys, Inspector Grainger is not a bad man. He was doing his job and Luce is not in trouble."

"Not the policeman," the boys said in unison. "The other man. The one who took Charlotte away. Is he bringing her back?"

Aurelius knelt down, gently putting a hand on Danny's shoulder. "Now, why would you call Mr. Rose a bad man?"

The answer resided in their staring blue eyes. Within he saw the memory of an old and unhealed pain. These boys were versed in the obscenity of evil, even after all these years; they could sense in their blood the wickedness of others.

The twins leaned against each other. They shifted their bodies to accommodate the thick band of flesh binding them. Four superficial scars marred the skin, narrowly missing the vein that throbbed between them, measuring the rhythm of their beating hearts. The scars were an old promise from their "Auntie" O'Kearne of what might have been had they not done as they were told. It was a particularly cruel terror that left Aurelius cold.

I know what men can do when the evil within takes them. It is in you. It is in me. It is in us all. And sometimes it is only an angel's thread that keeps it bound inside.

"My trade has frequently involved the forced acquaintance with the unsavory and the gentleman alike."

The newspaper landed with a thump on the desk. Rose looked up from the sheet of paper on his desk to cast a disapproving glance over the offending object before casting a second glance over the man who threw it.

"However, I am not accustomed to being waylaid in my office by your ruffians," Emmett said. "I would have expected greater courtesy considering that I have prostituted my entire career in the name of your family."

Emmett's eyes darkened. "I have watched over the secrets, all of them, beginning with those of your father. And I'll be damned if I'll allow your carelessness to topple what I've worked so hard to protect."

"Mr. Emmett, please calm yourself. You are excited over —" Rose waved a dismissive hand over the newspaper's blazing black headline. "— nothing. Fires happen all the time, and I am more than certain that our friends can be pacified. You seem to forget that they are hardly innocent of questionable deeds."

"Between the tedious reiteration and the records I have there is little that I do not know of their past, which makes your blatant disregard for your own actions all the more frustrating. I credited you with having sense enough to shield yourself from such vulnerabilities."

"If you believe that I could be intimidated by whatever imagined threat you think them capable of, then you know less of me than I thought. That is disappointing."

"You've not considered, then," Emmett said, seating himself in the chair before Rose's desk, "what would happen if it were to become known who was present at the Row. Before the fire. There is only so much protection I can offer before questions are asked. If connections are made . . . No man is completely immune, a fact that you have profited on."

"That *we* have profited on, Mr. Emmett." Rose lifted his chin in defiance. "Besides, you are far too skilled and smart a man to ever allow the truth to come out. One stroke of your pen could put any one of them in chains before they can utter one accusation."

Emmett looked warily at Rose.

"Perhaps, though, your concerns are not completely without cause. I have been a bit free with them, freer than in the past, and I do not care for their clumsy attempt at blackmail. It might indeed be time to clean house."

"Or at least issue a reminder of their position."

"Oh yes, though that must be a pleasure delayed. We've other business to conclude."

Rose leaned back in his chair. He steepled his fingers under his chin.

"Charlotte? Did the —"

"Nothing like that."

He had spoken sharply, quickly; too much so as his voice carried a particular note that did not go unnoticed by Emmett's ear.

"I have another use for her. However, there remain loose ends. I am afraid an unforeseen circumstance has come into play. We will need to find another way to rectify that matter."

"I see. So what has been done so far has been for naught?" Emmett said.

"Not entirely." The inscrutability that Rose was renowned for had returned. "I'm afraid that a misstep has been made by the

596

Ashes. Not only the father but the son as well, which is unfortunate. Terribly, terribly unfortunate."

Rose picked up the sheet of paper from his desk. Emmett recognized the page by the sigil emblazoned across it.

"That again? I thought that you had tossed that back in the box where it belongs with the rest of Atherton's useless trash."

"Emmett, Emmett, Emmett." Rose shook his head. "I think that you are being too quick to judge on this matter. If you had been with me this morning you might understand the potential that this little paper holds."

"You have gained some leverage over Ashe?"

"Hmmm, leverage," Rose said. "I'm simply saying that perhaps it's time that we have a little faith."

CHAPTER FORTY-SEVEN

27 October, Decimus House

Charlotte lay on her bed. She had lain there for a long time, half sick with the idea of Odilon's hands imprinted on her cheek and arms. She had already experienced far worse, but the look on his face and twitch of his cheek had carried more threat than his tearing the ring from her finger.

She held up her hand. Two thin strips of skin flapped along the knuckle. Lucien had been right to worry. Taking up a thin piece of linen ribbon, she wound it around her finger. It was a makeshift bandage, but it would hold the skin in place until she could make her way back to the theater.

Dear God, The Athenaeum. It felt a million miles away.

Staring up at the cold white ceiling, she ached for the old theater like a lover. The building had imprinted on her so much that if she thought hard enough she could recall the smell of the wood and oil that had been in her clothes, talc and lavender in her hair, and sweat and brimstone on her skin. If she were to lie still enough she would feel the vibration of Columbine's swing and hear the rapturous play of Georgie's violin. Or perhaps Timothy Harlequin popping out of a wall to surprise her in the half darkness of Lucien's bedchamber.

She dropped her hand back to the bed and closed her eyes. She wished she could have felt Luce's touch. She hoped that perhaps one day feeling would be restored and she would know his hands, his mouth. Gentle but assured in tenderness, everything that Odilon was not and would never be.

She rolled off the bed and crossed the room to the window. It was beginning to rain and droplets pelted the glass but she could still see the grounds and the park. Yet as pleasing as this view was it held far less wonder, less warmth that what Aurelius and Lucien and the troupe could offer.

It was the difference between what made a house and what made a home. In one she lived as a permanent guest while in the latter she had been embraced with the ease of a long-lost child. It was the first time that she had never felt any doubt or fear about where she belonged. Even before she went to Luce's room, when they were on *Manannan,* she had wavered toward the idea of staying with him, with them. Yes, she had protested and had held tight to the expectations held for herself, but she was slipping toward a different possibility, one that did not require her to be anything but who she was.

'The choice is yours and yours alone. You will never be asked or expected to do anything in return. Do you understand? Nothing is expected of you.'

It was a beautiful offer, but there was one expectation that she had pressed on herself. A promise she had made. A promise to return.

Charlotte ran her hand along her neck. Odilon would not be letting her go easily. She looked down at the grounds below. Her window was on the second floor. How far could the drop be? It certainly wouldn't hurt but could she make it back to Southwark? Back to The Athenaeum and to —

"Family," she whispered.

She rolled her shoulders and stretched her arms when she sensed a disquieting presence. "I usually hear the floorboard, the squeaky one, two steps past the threshold," she said to her visitor.

CHAPTER FORTY-EIGHT

27 October, Decimus House

It was not any one particular thing about the man in the fine coat that twitched the curtains in the windows across the street from Odilon Rose's gates. After all, it was not the first and would be far from the last time that someone waited for access outside of those gates. Often seen were nervous pacing men, and the occasional woman, whose desperation sheened like the sweat on a racehorse's wither.

Yet there was something in the bearing of this man, whose boots were dusted in a thin film of a London that rarely saw the green of Regent's Park, that drew prying eyes. He stood at the gate without the hurried determination of pacing feet or the slight stooped quiver of regret in his shoulders that usually marked Rose's visitors. No, in the absence of nervous energy resided instead a decided serenity; the sort of calm that a man who had found salvation in the loop of a noose might have in the final moments before the trap fell.

Do you believe that Odilon is somehow associated with the death of this woman?

In Luce's mind, Charlotte's question wrapped around Silvia's bloody torn body, stirring up the dust and ash of the Row in his mind.

Luce was not sure what to believe, other than that Rose was a man who had his hands in a lot of pies and if Silvia had been an inconvenience, though his own hands might not be dirtied, he had at his disposal men who had no such qualms. Grainger obviously disliked the man. Whether that was a personal distaste or professional, when even monarchs bowed their heads to bankers what hope had a simple police inspector in confronting his suspicions, let alone bringing to light any of Rose's questionable dealings.

It would have been simpler to tell Grainger more about Noanes, and to have told him about Kosh and Skym to cover them all. Although he doubted any charge would stick, not with Mr. Emmett as solicitor, it would certainly cause a great deal of aggravation and perhaps, if lucky, a taint on his precious reputation. That would have been the just thing to do. But there was Charlotte.

Luce stared up at Decimus House. All the roads wended their way back here, and seeing the house again now only reinforced his hatred. Even without the unfortunate association with Rose, there remained something about the elegant building that left him cold. Perhaps it was the walls that were a little too thick, or the gates that were a little too tall, or that Charlotte could look at this pile of lifeless brick and hard edges and see a home.

"So what do you think it is? Naïveté or misplaced devotion that's keeping her in his sway?" Luce asked.

"Oh now, she's a lass who knows what's best for her. Better than one that I could name."

Luce had smelled the gin before Linus Noanes had spoken a word.

"You're a bit far from Southwark," Noanes said, tottering closer. "I'm surprised the filth let you go so quick."

"What would you know about that?" Luce replied.

"Saw them hauling you off, and I have to admit, I've not wiped the smile off my face yet. Though I'd have rather seen Aurelius's face when they did so. Not feelin' so clever now, are you —"

It was a fraction of a moment between Luce's turning to face Noanes and the press of the small steel barrel into his gut.

"Not a wise move, my lad. There are eyes on you. Too many witnesses if you're planning on using that," Noanes said.

"And you won't be using *that* for the same reasons, I suspect," Luce said, closing his fist until the flame in his palm diminished.

"Couldn't let matters be, could you? Not you, no, you have always been a little nuisance. Sniffing around where you've no business, when it ain't time for Aurelius to be collecting." Noanes's eyes were nearly as clouded as his voice. "Maybe I ought to do Rose a favor and put a stop to you once and for all. Be for the best. One less freak —"

"Is that what Silvia was? A nuisance?"

"Now, why would a man like Odilon Rose want to bother himself with a whore like her? Not when he's got that girl of his. She is a bit too fragile for my taste, but still a very pretty thing." Noanes grinned, the gin rolling off his breath. "And now she's home."

"How much longer do you think she'll be able to stay? We look after our own —"

"She ain't one of yours. She never was

and never will be. No matter what Aurelius has done to her, she can pass for normal. You destroyed my own girl but there's no need to be destroyin' this one." Noanes leaned close. The gun barrel slid against Luce's ribs.

"Golden lads and girls all must, as chimney-sweepers, come to dust," he breathed into Luce's ear. "I think it best we take this inside."

The day turned as quick as the weather and it began to rain slow, hard drops on the pavement and on the green, as the odd pair passed through the gate.

"Not the homecoming you were expecting, I suppose." Florence quietly shut the door of Charlotte's room behind her. "I was hoping for something happier, all things considered. But you know how our Odilon can be when his plans are tested."

If she had expected a warm embrace, Charlotte was quick to see that it would not be the case. Florence remained posted at the door, like a palace guard with her thin fine hands folded before her, her chignoned head held high, and an impassivity of expression better attributed to stone.

"He should not have gotten so angry."

She moved toward the window. Charlotte

noted Florence's slow deliberate approach. With a straightness of back came the impression of greater height, and with the long fishtail hem of her black dress swallowing the floor in her wake, Florence did not sidle so much as slither. She looked at Charlotte's hand. "He was much worse before you came to us. But then a lot of things were different before you came to us."

"I can't bear to think about what might have become of me had your parents not —"

"Father," Florence quickly corrected. "It was Father's decision to bring you here. And now you've decided to leave us, after all that we have done for you."

"You've spoken with Odilon."

"Yes, I've spoken with Odilon and what he has told me . . ." There was no warmth in the smirk that crossed Florence's lips. "To think you of all people had the audacity to condemn me for a harmless flirtation. So is it true? That Lucien Ashe hasn't a heart. He would not share that when I asked him. Another intimacy denied me."

"I don't know exactly what Odilon has told you but I've done nothing improper, Florence. But if I had, I'd not make excuses for my actions nor would I apologize for them. What transpired at the theater is of no concern or consequence to you or to Odilon."

"Concern? Consequence? My dear, there are always consequences."

Charlotte lowered her eyes, her thumb tracing the edge of the linen wrapped around her finger.

"I thought of visiting you. I traveled to the theater, but remembered Mr. Ashe's request that no one see you until three days after, when he would summon us. I waited in a clarence, hoping for a glimpse of you, because I was so concerned for your well-being. One glance would have alleviated my fears, but you were nowhere. Still recovering, I suppose. I did see Lucien, though he was not alone. He was in the company of that harlot he keeps. Did he mention her to you? Before —"

"Florence, you are grievously mistaken if you believe that I —" Charlotte paused, hoping that her face would not betray her words. She did have her wishes and desires, and though unrequited, they remained hers alone. "As for Lucien Ashe, he owes me no justification of his past actions or those that might come along. He is free to do as he pleases, as am I. I would however ask you not to be so flippant in your assessment of that woman. If you have not heard, she was killed last night."

"I am well aware of the tragedy that has befallen *that* woman." She waved Silvia's death away like a fly. "I don't believe that you have thought any of this through." Florence leaned forward and held Charlotte's gaze. "We are family, Charlotte."

Charlotte touched the lace at her throat. "And I appreciate your inclusion of me as such, but how can I make you understand —"

"I'm afraid that you are the one who does not understand. Have you really no idea why you were brought here? As if a man of Father's stature would take the slightest interest in a servant's child unless . . . she was his."

Malice had always run through Florence. In the way that she parried and challenged Odilon over the years, it was a force that simmered just below the surface. However, what she was saying now, what she was suggesting, bore horrific implications.

"Oh, my dear, you never put it together? They thought that they were being so clever. Your mother, our father. It was easy what with Mother having retired to her own rooms following Louisa's unfortunate birth, monstrous little thing that she was. She was never quite the same afterward and Father of course still needed his distractions. Your mother proved an ideal convenience."

"No, I'll not listen to this, Florence. My father . . . he was —" Charlotte tried to push past her but Florence grasped her shoulder and pressed her down onto the window seat.

"Oh, but you will. After all that Mother had done to make him the man he became. She was the one who went to Ashe, and quite the profitable meeting that proved to be. Father's star ascended and his name became one of respect, a name that men wanted to be associated with, a name some came to fear. Mother set that groundwork" — her fingers dug into Charlotte's shoulder — "only to have Father's little betrayal show up at the door. It was cruel of him."

"No, your mother —" Charlotte's thoughts stammered on. *The chair. Mrs. Rose's chair. The scrape of the legs when she left the room, left her to —*

Shame trailed up through her chest until it reached in her throat. She swallowed hard against the swell.

"Tolerated you, until Father's little accident. Did you know that when he landed at the base of the stairs, his head was almost backward. I think he hit every step until he was a twisted pile. He looked so much like

Louisa. All crooked. And Mother at the top of the stairs. I think that she might have surprised herself. But still, the authorities dismissed it as one those unquestioned domestic tragedies. Of course Odilon missed all the excitement and Mother swore me to secrecy." Florence pressed her to her lips. "But she still had you, though she couldn't bring herself to kill you too. I suppose your being a child was a bridge too far and so soon after Father, that would have been more difficult to explain. Fortunately, there was Odilon's curiosity, his need for exploration. And Odilon never wanted to disappoint Mummy."

Charlotte not only felt ill but had the desire to rip her skin from her body and scrub to her bones. What Florence was saying, admitting, enjoying. "Why are you telling me this? After all this time? After what he . . . You knew. You could have told . . . it has gone on for years. You should have told *me*!"

"I could have, but where would the fun have been in that? I could not hope to compete with Odilon, the only son. The one true heir to Mother's dreams and Father's aspirations. So I accepted my place. And then you came along, and Father's favor shifted. Do you know what that feels like?

To look into the eyes of a man you love and see that you have been replaced? *You* were to be the substitute for Louisa, a spare girl to be a comfort to my mother as Father first claimed, distraught as she was over losing her child. I would remain the rightful daughter. His only little girl. But soon you had his attention. Wrapped him around your little finger. Always first to praise you. *'How quick you are on the piano, why, soon you will outpace Florence. Why, Charlotte, is that one of Florence's dresses? How much better it suits you. That shade of green compliments your eyes. Pretty little Charlotte.'* Mother and I had to listen to his fawning on and on. Oh, how we hated you."

The veins throbbed in her neck above the line of her sharp black collar. "*I* followed the rules. *I* played my role and accepted my place in the bargain! Odilon traded me off to gain a magistrate and you, after swanning about here like the lady of the manor, you think that you can just run away as you please? That you can leave me like this?"

She could not have struck harder if she had used her fist. Charlotte had known that hers was not a marriage of hearts but of convenience, and the stories of flirtations and infatuations, while entertaining, had been to Florence all she had of romance;

611

flimsy as gossamer without any hope of real substance. And Lucien Ashe was one more imagined love that was now slipping from her grasp.

"Florence —"

"What makes you think that you deserve happiness? That you —"

"It's not that I think that," Charlotte said. "I thought my path fated. That these walls were all that I would ever know. That Odilon . . . but things have changed. I changed in a way that I can never explain because I don't understand it myself. But Mr. Ashe has assured me that I would have a home and I would have a choice and I'm making it."

"Lucien has made you an offer then?"

"This doesn't hinge upon Lucien's will! *I* am welcomed if I want. For myself alone, with no expectations of a duty that must be fulfilled for a place earned. Do you understand what that means? Oh, Florence, you could leave your situation as well. I could speak with Mr. Ashe. I am sure he could find you a place. You've played your part in Odilon's schemes long enough. Come with me."

Florence shook her head, a curling tendril of red hair falling loose from her chignon. "It's too late for follies, little sister." She cupped Charlotte's cheek in her palm. "You know, I warned that other little bitch, but she wouldn't listen. I was quite surprised to see her outside the theater the other day."

"Florence, what are you saying? Who do you mean? Are you speaking of Silvia? Lucien's friend?"

"A dead little friend now."

"No, you didn't . . . you couldn't. You would have been seen!"

"On such a dark and crowded street a woman in black can pass by quite unnoticed." Florence's eyes shone with a fever. "I even passed our dear Lucien on his way to her. It was hard not to call to him or reach out and take his hand. Of course he took no notice of me but I do half wish that I could have seen his face when he saw what I left behind. It was about time that a mark was burned into him for a change."

Charlotte drew her head back but Florence's grip tightened. "This pains me a great deal, Charlotte, seeing as you're family. But darling, I do hope you will be a better listener."

It was a fluid move. Florence's right hand deftly flew from her pocket a quicksilver flash of the blade she had secreted there. Its edge sliced cleanly into Charlotte's cheek, cutting a deep rut from her mouth to her ear. It was a twin to the scar Silvia had worn.

"Florence, no! This has to stop!"

Charlotte did not know how long Mr. Emmett had been present, but he was quick to fall into a slow waltz with Florence. His arm stretched to grab hold of her as she turned to face him, her own arm held out to bring the knife toward him in a swinging arc —

Blood stained Florence's cheek, spraying her dress as the knife sliced across Emmett's throat, opening the artery. His collar and tie spilled red; a thick flow seeped between his slick fingers as he tried to hold back the blood before dropping to his knees.

Florence turned back on Charlotte and in a moment of disconnection saw the face of a stranger.

What little color she had possessed had drained while the ends of the skin around the cut hung loose and open, as smooth and clean as any to be found amid the freshly stripped skins of the tanners' pools of Bermondsey. Charlotte did not make a sound, not a whimper of pain or a scream of terror, but remained in a state of stoic silence on the edge of the window seat.

Florence gripped the knife in her wet hand as she stared into Charlotte's empty eyes.

"Why aren't you bleeding?"

CHAPTER FORTY-NINE

27 October, Odilon Rose's private office,
 Decimus House

The room was as painfully exact as he had remembered, with the ordered cabinets and the skeleton twins looking out from their case. But the demeanor of the man behind the desk had changed. The cool commanding regard exhibited at the theater that morning had slipped into an agitated sheen. He returned the velvet cover to the small casket that he had brought up from his collection and pushed it to the center of his desk.

"Beggin' your pardon, Mr. Rose, but I found *this* sniffing around your gate just now." Noanes could barely suppress the grin from spreading across his face as he dug the barrel of his gun into Luce's back.

"Why, Mr. Ashe, you've strayed a bit far from home haven't you? The police decided not to keep you after all."

"They'd no reason to. No matter how hard you try to make me out to be, I'm not an arsonist, nor am I a murderer."

"Oh, come now, we both know better than that. After all, men rarely set themselves on fire."

The open carafe of whiskey at his elbow had loosened both his tongue and his judgment. "You've come to collect her, I presume." Rose's eyes narrowed.

"We both know that it would be for the best. She's not yours anymore, Rose. Circumstances have changed. Take my father's offer. Let her come back to us and we will not meet again. I will even speak to my father about the terms you and he set. I might be able to persuade him to void the agreement. In exchange —"

"Ever the knight-errant." Rose smiled. "Although I have to say that I am less than pleased with how matters have turned. Certainly not what I imagined when I handed Charlotte over to your father's care. She was sent to be cured not seduced."

Luce felt his face redden. "I did not —"

"It will not do, Mr. Ashe. When word gets out that she is associating with a man such as yourself — a suspected murderer and arsonist — her reputation will be ruined beyond repair, and as her guardian, mine too may hold a taint."

"I was under the impression that reputations were things to be bought and sold on easy terms. I'm sure that you will more than survive this minor blight."

"Here now, you show some respect."

"That's quite all right, Mr. Noanes," Rose said. "Mr. Ashe is entitled to his opinions. Please continue."

"You signed my father's contract. That was a bargain you freely entered, risks and all. Charlotte is cured. For better or worse, I would say that fulfills our obligation. As for your precious name, you may rest assured that we do keep civil and quiet tongues, but that doesn't mean we won't relish the knowledge we hold."

"And I can see by the look in your eyes that you've come to embrace this pleasure. You are not the only one capable of reading people. So what did your father do to Charlotte? Don't mistake me, I find a woman who cannot experience pain to hold many possibilities, but how? Is he really a demon as Noanes here believes? Or is he something else entirely?"

The thought of Charlotte at this man's mercy forced the black pitch to flow in Luce's veins and into his hands until the tips of his fingers tingled. *One touch is all that it would take,* he thought before curbing his tongue.

"I'm not privy to his methods, Mr. Rose. I know what you know. She is not sick anymore. I cannot say as much about others in this room."

"Should I believe him, Mr. Noanes?"

Noanes clucked his tongue. "Lucien here is a better liar than that. His father is secretive, so I'm not doubting his word on this."

"So where does this leave us now? Charlotte says she wants to go with you."

"Then let her."

"You are making an offer?"

"She will have a home. She will be secure. We look after our own. We always have."

"Have you? Is that the case for all freaks or just those of particular interest to you?" Rose stood up and started around his desk but paused at the glass-encased twins. "You see, Mr. Ashe, it is bad enough that nature allows such things into the world when they've no place and no purpose. What is it that you say, Mr. Noanes? Not God's design. However, when we start creating our own monsters that is truly an abomination. You are the exemplar, Lucien Ashe, with that clockwork heart and the fire in your blood. Why are you even alive?"

Rose traced the edges of the glass case

618

with his finger. "I can tell you. You are alive because of Aurelius Ashe, the man who can fix what is impossibly broken. Save for one."

He looked over to Lucien. "She was brought to him in good faith because my parents, my father, trusted his abilities. After all he had already done for us, why doubt his claims? Our poor Louisa."

The steadiness of Rose's voice belied the fevered restlessness in his eyes.

"She was a strange and deformed little thing, a curse on our otherwise good fortune. It was inconceivable that such a creature be delivered on our house, under *our* name. It would have been easier to take her for a changeling child. She was taken to your father to be fixed, to be made normal; after all, if anyone could do it, he could. But he refused. Looking back, with an adult's eyes, I've wondered if Mother went to your father and if he seduced her as well. She said once that Louisa bore his mark. What could that mean, Lucien? Her appearance, was that his mark? Of course after Louisa, that is when it all fell apart. Mother never recovered, Father took refuge with his whore, and then came Charlotte."

"Charlotte?"

"My father's daughter. And the enjoyment that I have had with her, I shall, thanks to

619

your father, have forever. She will never be yours, Lucien Ashe."

Luce felt the gun barrel slide down against his back as Noanes loosened his guard.

"But then of course Father died. And then Mother took ill and her last thoughts were consumed by Louisa and your father. Now why would he be on her mind? Louisa, yes, but why your father?"

"I don't know."

"Aurelius Ashe has been the source of our greatest success and the cause of our decline. And I have to ask: How many other lives has he ruined? He has taken my father, mother, sister, and he is trying to take Charlotte. Tell me, has your father ever lost anyone? Has he ever suffered?"

There was not time enough to register the click of the hammer to the ensuing shot but the shatter of glass and twisting of copper that exploded against Luce's ribs could not be ignored as the bullet exited his chest from the wound in his back. The teeth of the cog were finally free and protruded from the torn skin and bone as Luce fell to the floor.

Rose looked down at the prone body at his feet. "Oh, my dear Mr. Ashe, you did say that I would never have that heart. Pity, that."

"I'm sorry to leave it like this, Mr. Rose," Noanes said, wiping the blood from the barrel of the gun on his trouser leg. "But I think it best I leave before the questions start."

"Of course, Mr. Noanes. You had no choice after all. We both saw the sparks at his fingers. He threatened us. He would have burned the house down. You will be handsomely paid for your services but you will understand that we mustn't meet again."

Dita stepped lightly in the back hall of The Athenaeum, mindful of the small motorized car that raced between her feet to the delight of Danny and Davie O'Kearne.

"Careful there, boys," she said, keeping the tails of Aurelius's freshly laundered coat from hitting the floor. "No need to be causing me an injury."

She walked into the office with the twins in tow. It was a rare enough treat for them to enter Aurelius's office but rarer still to do so when the master was out.

"Mind yourselves, boys, and don't be messing about with anything in here. If something is out of place, he'll have my head, though I doubt he'd notice much if you did touch something judging by how he keeps things." Dita shook her head looking at the cluttered desk. "I swear, that man."

"We'll be careful."

"Careful we'll be," the boys said, eyes fixed on the Aurelius's precious orrery that quietly spun on the edge of the desk. It was a mesmerizing dance fixed in brass and the boys crept as close as they dared, breath held as if one exhalation would upset the miniature galaxy. Careful as they were, though, when the loud click emitted from the model, the twins fell back with understandable fear.

"It's broken, Dita!"

"Dita! Broken it is!"

"What is this fuss now?" she said, walking over to the desk.

"One of the planets has stopped spinning."

"The spinning has stopped for one of the planets," repeated Davie.

Dita leaned over the orrery and saw nothing unusual. Only the planets moving blithely in their orbits. Soon her eye fixed on one of the little brass spheres, and sure enough, as the twins had said it had stopped spinning. Her heart beat against her ribs like a breaker hitting a ship.

She closed her eyes and in the dark she searched for them. It was a difficult task to focus her mind on so many at once. Attuning to one at a time was better, but slowly the images came flickering in. Angelique and Columbine in the kitchen, Georgie in his room. Pretorius was in the shop. Aurelius surveying the stage. Harlequin . . . her brow furrowed but after half a minute she found him on the street.

Lucien. She closed her mind on everything but him, sifting her way through the noise, but found only darkness. Cold and black as lifeless as night. Her stomach sank and she wavered on her feet.

"We didn't do it," the boys said in unison.

"No, you didn't," she said as Aurelius's coat slipped from her hand to the floor.

CHAPTER FIFTY

Rose leaned back on the edge of his desk downing first one dram of whiskey and then a second as he coolly observed Luce's body.

A shot to the back was not the fairest but it was effective. Having landed half on his hip and half on his back, Luce's legs were inelegantly crossed one over the other at the knee, like those of an unstrung puppet, while his arms were outspread, hands loose and palms upward.

Rose stepped gingerly around him. Although he saw no light in his open blue eyes, death could not be a trusted absolute, not where Aurelius Ashe was concerned.

Carefully he knelt down beside Luce's body. The bullet had cut a ragged path. The exit wound was large and uneven where the metal, glass, and bone had torn through. For a moment, Rose considered retrieving one of the medical instruments from the cabinet, but decided instead to use his fingers, which he slid into the wound to better inspect the remains of the heart.

He folded the flesh away and exposed the mechanism. He had not known what to expect from Emmett's description, but what he now saw exceeded imagination and known artisanship. The original heart lay halved; over the years, the muscle had not only healed around the brass valves and glass bowl but had in fact fused to the foreign pieces into something nearly organic.

The glass bowl was shattered and the brass cogs that had worked the small clockwork motor were loose and bent where the bullet had passed.

"Extraordinary," Rose said. It took several back-and-forth wiggles of the central cog wheel before it finally broke free from its thin shaft. He plucked the piece from Luce's chest and held it up to the light where the sharp brass teeth winked through the residue of blood and tissue.

Outside in the street, clattered hooves and the spin of hurried wheels stopped short in a growl like a feral cat on the cobbles.

Rose closed his fingers around the cog. Slowly he stood up and stepped out into the hall.

"Do you not think we should have gone to Borough High Street first?" Harlequin said, swinging down from the cab to the street.

Aurelius turned back and paid the driver. "If you would please wait for us at the end of the street."

"There is nothing there for us, as you well know," he said as the hansom pulled away. "It's become a right mess, this business."

Harlequin did not like seeing his master in this state. Aurelius might project a calm collectedness but under the surface, in places where only a knowing eye could reach, the concern was clear.

"I should have gone with him, followed when the police took him. I'm sorry, Aurelius, I've failed you both."

"What good would that have done but prolong the inevitable. Lucien is his own man and he came here on his own volition. No one was going to stop him." Ashe rested his hand on Harlequin's shoulder. "No, I have burdened you more than enough, Timothy. I set you first to watch over him, but you have exceeded your duties and by rights have long earned your release from my service. I am afraid Prospero was a far kinder master than I. At least he kept his promise in the end."

"It's a kind offer," Harlequin said, shaking off Aurelius's hand, "but I can never return to the shadows after living so long in the light. Besides, I rather like this form." He shot the cuffs of his sleeves until a fair inch reached his wrist from the extended smooth, pale length of his hands. "It suits me too well to give up."

Aurelius smiled as they mounted the steps.

"Do you wish me to go in ahead?"

"No, Timothy. I am tired of this game and I feel it is time that Rose knows it."

Odilon flinched as the front doors flew open, splintering on their hinges as they struck the walls with enough force to rattle the foundation and set every piece of glass and metal in the house to shudder.

"Mr. Ashe, please do come in," he said. "I suppose at this stage of our relationship we do not stand on such formalities as announcing ourselves. Come on your own, have you?"

Ashe looked to the second-floor landing where Rose stood at the top of the stairs. "Where is he? Where is Lucien?"

"Lucien, yes. He did drop by, although I am sorry to say that his visit prompted a rather unpleasant incident."

"Where is my son?"

"I must commend your craftsman, Pretorius." Rose held up the bent brass cog, still dripping with blood. "He is a remarkable artisan."

Aurelius took a step forward and froze, his feet chained and weighted by an invisible force. He looked down at the long rectangular red-and-gold Turkish rug that had been absent on his first visit to Decimus House. It looked wholly out of place in the entryway, too narrow and thin for so open a space. But it was suitable enough to almost hide the ancient lines of a sigil he felt down to the bone.

"My God, it works," Rose said, leaning over the banister, eyes sparking with glee. "And to be so elegant in its simplicity. I couldn't get it out of Lucien, to say what you are rumored to be. But here you are. Can you really not move beyond that rug?"

"Clever man," Aurelius said, the black pooling in his eyes. "I never would have taken you as a scholar of Hermeticism, let alone of John Dee. Tell me, how did you learn about a Sigillum Dei?"

"Sigillum Dei Aemeth, Mr. Ashe. Do show some respect to the master Dee and refer to its full and proper name. After all,

James Atherton was very precise in what he copied from the original manuscript. Do you remember him? Atherton? The one that got away."

"So you presume —"

"So I know. It was Atherton who left this in my father's care after his last meeting with you. He came here as he was familiar with my family and following his own misfortune, he was concerned for our safety. I was far too young at the time and when my father passed, he left no explanation. It was my own search that led me to where he kept the sigil's design in case it was ever needed. And all this time, this gift remained locked in a box, forgotten until a comment from Noanes, of all people, jarred my memory."

"And what do you intend to do?" Aurelius asked, inching closer to the rug's edge. The tip of his shoe touched the outer ring of the circle but allowed no further movement. "Is this how I'm to be repaid after what I've done for you? For what I've done for your family? To be kept a prisoner?"

"I think the option is mine. I can think of many uses you could serve. First of all, I think we need to consider our contract void."

"No, Odilon Rose, it's not that easy. There

have been those who have attempted to break their contracts, none of whom met with happy endings, including your dear Mr. Atherton. I will not be made your cat's paw! *You* owe me! Charlotte was sent for a cure and while you might not be entirely satisfied with the results —"

"I didn't send her to you to be seduced by your company. *That* was not part of the contract. Her head has been filled with promises and ideas that somehow she is going to leave here for the Carnivale. Thinking that I will stand aside and let her go. No, Mr. Ashe. She remains mine to do with as I please —"

"And we cannot have another dog pissing on our property, can we?" Ashe's lips tightened over his teeth, as if trying to suppress a great rage. "All of this *mine, yours.* Charlotte is not a plaything to be bickered over like a doll in a nursery. I know her true relation to you and what you have done. Your own half sister. Does your depravity have no limit?"

"My depravity! Oh now that is rich considering —"

"Do you care to know how many lives were needlessly lost in that fire that you hoped would send my son to the gallows?"

"We both know that you are far too clever

to allow that to happen. Besides, while a few of the socially conscious will raise the hue and cry, I don't believe many others will lose sleep over the loss. The denizens of rookeries are hardly models of exemplary behavior. They will not be without a nest for long. They will rebuild and repopulate. Vermin are remarkably resilient."

"Vermin! You think so little of those unfortunates? They did nothing to warrant losing what little they had. Silvia Marquette butchered and now my son. Lucien did nothing to you and I served you honorably. I gave you what you wanted and still you killed without a care. A damned despot would blush in your presence," Ashe said.

"And what about a Master of the Crossroads, Mr. Ashe? Does he blush?" Rose looked down from his perch on the landing. "Or does he kneel?"

"Set me free and find out."

Rose laughed. "All the bluster with none of the substance. Honor? You see yourself as honorable? How many lives have you destroyed, Mr. Ashe? How many souls are waiting for you? *You seek my confession when you forced the sin!* My mother said that in her last moments. It was to you that she spoke. *Look at what you made of me, Mr. Ashe!* Well —" Rose held his arms outstretched over the banister like Christ on the cross. "Look at what you made of *me.*"

"You have tossed accusation after accusation without turning the mirror upon yourself when you, Odilon Rose, are a murderer, a blackmailer, and a rapist. Am I forgetting anything?"

Ashe looked up at the man on the landing. Even at this distance he could see the delirium in his eyes.

"She said your name. She spoke of Louisa in the same breath —"

"Am I to know the mutterings of a disordered mind at the moment of death? I'm not sure how many deathbeds you have sat by but I assure, in those moments people ramble —"

"My father brought Louisa to you. Best that she go back to the man responsible."

"What are you insinuating? That I am to blame for that child's misfortune?"

"Considering your son's unusual gifts I'd say that abnormality runs through your line."

"Your mother came to me for many things, but a child was not —"

"The Roses do not breed monsters!"

"No?" Ashe asked. "Where you saw a monster, I saw a child born of an unfortunate circumstance. Mr. Rose, the mark of a monster is not in his appearance but in his actions. I've come to find that the real monsters hide in plain sight and some wear the finest suits in London."

"You have a keen eye. Do you dare turn it on yourself? What sort of man takes dead children and displays them for profit, or sells them on to other shows? Have you any idea what it feels like to have to buy back the body of your own sister? Or not knowing the hands she had passed through or the eyes that have stared at her?"

Ashe shook his head. "My dear boy, you've gotten it all wrong. I ordered the child, your precious Louisa, be given a proper burial once your father unceremoniously dropped her at my feet, without so much as a look back. I have not, nor ever would, display any human curiosity unless it is by their choice. Unfortunately, I delegated the burial to a most unreliable man, one of great greed and greater want, who had no compunction about such entertainments. What was a pickled punk to him if not a shilling in his purse or drink down his throat. I am accountable for, I suppose, trusting him to do the noble thing; however, the man who deserves your wrath has been in your pocket. Tell me, how much did you pay Linus Noanes to kill my son?"

What Ashe had said had not had time to settle before the ground began to shake and walls of Decimus House trembled. Odilon held tight to the banister as he looked down at the foyer. Along the edge of the rug, where the sigil extended, four distinct lines clawed across the outer ring, effectively breaking the seal from which Aurelius Ashe lightly stepped.

"Obviously Atherton neglected to tell you how a trap can be broken." His walking stick click-clacked like a metronome on the hard wood as he began his ascent to the landing. "Although this time it was far less painful. Always best to travel with a companion, I've since learned. One you can rely on. Noanes has burned us all."

"Have no fear." The hairs lifted on Rose's neck at the feel of Harlequin's mouth suddenly at his ear. "I will set about finding Lucien myself. I know my way around your house quite well."

Rose turned in time to see the Púca fade away, his horns the last to disappear.

Aurelius drew even with Rose on the landing, who took note of the red spark that burned in the center of Ashe's black eyes. "When Milbrough brought her to me, dead in his arms, he swore to me that he would have one good child yet. I didn't quite understand what he meant at the time but the intimations were that he was dissatisfied with his existing children. You. Florence. Louisa."

"You know nothing about —"

"He saw a rot creeping in. Your mother did come to me with a desire, with a want for something more in her life, but she did so at the expense of what she already had. Milbrough would have risen in title and promotion in time, Catherine only had to wait, but she was entitled and wanted what she thought she deserved. But what she didn't consider, what none of those who seek me out consider, is that you cannot expect to change your world without the world around you changing in response."

"And is that not the devil's work? To give a taste of paradise before bringing the fall?"

"That has nothing to do with me. It is cause and effect where proximity breeds influence and with each of your mother's gains, so were those around her changed. Your disturbing curiosity. Your sister's dangerous need for attention. Louisa. None of this escaped your father. He was observant and what he saw scared him. But I never thought he would —" Aurelius squeezed the handle of his walking stick until the blood left his knuckles. "Poor

Charlotte. Milbrough was so blind to what was happening to his family that he neglected to see what had crept into him, and that poor girl has reaped the worst of all that he sowed."

Rose looked out over the banister to the broken sigil on the foyer floor. A deep crack ran the length from door to hall.

" *'You seek my confession when you forced the sin.'* You want to know what she meant?"

Rose nodded, never losing sight of the crack on the floor.

"At the time of collection, I always ask if there are any sins they wish to confess. My time to play the father confessor. After facing Milbrough's betrayal in the flesh, Catherine came to me one last time with a request that I chose not to honor. But my rejection did not stop her. When she pushed your father down the stairs, do take some comfort that by the fifth step he was beyond feeling. But I think in your heart you already knew."

"And Louisa?"

"An act of God. Not of me. I warned you, Odilon, at the onset of this endeavor that my family was to be left unharmed and yet you sought to punish me by attacking Lucien. You have betrayed me, which nullifies the terms of your contract. For that, the collection of your soul will be immediate. Have you any confessions you wish to make?"

Rose turned and met Aurelius, eye-to-eye.

"You spoke of the fall," Aurelius said, "and I suppose there is some truth to that. You see, once there was a time when it was thought that Man would not, could not, be corrupted by temptation. So he was loosed upon the earth, with the absolute trust that he would not stray. But temptation has its way."

Aurelius leaned back against the banister. "We all fall, Mr. Rose. Some fall hard and fast, some slow, and some merely stumble. But eventually you all fall." His eyes fixed on a figure walking swiftly along the hall toward them. "Oh, I see that our Mr. Kosh has yet to learn to take care of his knives."

It was only a quick shimmer that Rose saw as a slip of a hand seized his collar. The pain was a lightning shock. Blood ran hot down his neck and chest and he dropped heavy to the floor. He rolled over and through the blurred edges of his vision, before the last seize of breath escaped through the bubbling red of his gashed throat, he looked into a face that was only half familiar. He knew the hair by the color and the mouth half twisted in an exaggerated grin bore a memory but the eyes, large and green and lit with fire, were those of a stranger.

"You should have let me go, Odilon."

The knife fell from Charlotte's wet, trembling hand.

Chapter Fifty-One

"His mother had wanted the Rose name to be remembered. Pity that she didn't specify as to the manner."

Ashe knelt down. He dipped his finger into Rose's pooling blood and drew it to his lips. He winced at the taste. "Bitter to the bone."

"I had to do it. You know what he did, what he did to me. I had to stop him. My brother —"

"So you know."

"Florence told me. It pleased her to do so. She enjoyed it, knowing what he was doing to me —"

"The less you think about what has been done the sooner you will distance yourself, and if you find forgetting doesn't come easy, Dita can help." He looked up at Charlotte and for the first time noticed the slash across her cheek. "Oh, my dear child, whatever has happened to you? Did he —"

"Florence attacked me."

He shook his head. "We will get you back to Pretorius. He'll stitch that up."

"She killed Mr. Emmett and Silvia and probably that other woman."

"Shhhh, it's all over now," he said, wrapping his arms around her. "Where is she?"

"I left her upstairs. After she killed Mr. Emmett, I was able to push past her. She fell back and struck her head on the hearthstone. I took up the knife so she wouldn't hurt anyone else and ran from my room, closing the door, locking her in. When I came down the stairs and saw you" — she glanced over Odilon's body — "Mr. Ashe, I heard a gunshot."

The pair entered Rose's office and had Ashe not had his hand braced on Charlotte's back she would have collapsed. Harlequin was knelt over Luce's body. The floor was as red as the walls.

"I've packed the wound as best I could," Harlequin said. "It should hold for the trip back. Aurelius, you might want to have a look at that box on the desk."

"We'll need to work quickly then. I will oversee his transport home." Aurelius crossed over to the desk and lifted the velvet cover on the casket and closed his eyes in disgust. The tiny desiccated figure within was a pitiful reminder of a mercifully brief life. Her back was twisted and the inward curve of the rib cage had concaved the left side of her chest almost to her spine. "Poor little mite. What has your brother done? Timothy, if you would tidy up matters here including —"

Harlequin looked to Ashe but the sight of Charlotte froze his tongue.

"Lucien." She dropped to her knees and touched his face. Harlequin had done well in covering the wound but the damage was told in the state of his bloody torn shirt, bloodied waistcoat, and bloodier floor.

She had never asked him what lay beneath the scar on his chest but now she shifted the cloth and saw the remnants of his heart. While most of the blood had escaped with the shattering of the glass, there was still a shallow pool in the open cavity. A thick chunk of muscle hung limp from a shard of brass. She dropped the cloth back over the wound.

"There's no light," she said, staring into his open eyes. "Odilon did this because of me." Tears fell pink along her cheek. Her fingers twined through his curls. "This house. This family. My family . . ." she said, voice thickening with grief. "Everything that they have ever touched has come to rot and ruin. My God, Mr. Ashe, I've killed him. I've killed him . . ."

"No, no, this was not your doing. If anything you are a casualty of something started long before you were born. And for that I am sorry," Aurelius knelt beside her at Luce's side. "This isn't his death, Charlotte. He, like yourself, was betwixt and between. For those in that state, all that is needed is a name, a face, or a purpose to stay alive. The first time he died, family brought him back. Family." He touched Luce's cheek. "No, my dear, my son did not die today. His death was from wounds inflicted long ago."

"The scars on his back." She looked over to Harlequin. "You said that he had been beaten as a child. Beaten badly by the same men who attacked Georgie. But those scars weren't made by fists and I don't believe that they were made by the broken glass from a gas explosion either."

"No, Charlotte, they weren't." Harlequin lowered his eyes.

"His mother was not a well woman," Ashe said. "She had too many voices floating around in her head, and a few too many on the outside who encouraged her to do very bad things. I tried to help her, to be kind to her. I gave her what she wanted, but unfortunately it wasn't enough."

Charlotte looked at him. There was a softness to his face, in the lines around his eyes that spoke to a part of him that she felt would be alien to his nature. "You loved her."

Aurelius closed his eyes. "As much as she would let me. And much against my better judgment."

"What happened to her?"

"The night that she attacked Lucien, while Pretorius attended to his wounds, Isabel was visited by one other voice. One who induced her to atone for what she had done." Aurelius frowned. "She listened, and if I must say, there was no small satisfaction in having her father, Linus Noanes, watch as she slit her own throat."

"*'Once he cut my throat with diamonds,'*" Harlequin said. "Those were her last words."

Charlotte did not want to think how Harlequin knew what she said in her final moment. "Could you not have changed her? You can do so much —"

"I cannot make any deal for myself. No matter how much I might wish to do so. I could not even have someone do so on my behest because it would be an act of influence for my benefit and not one acted upon

643

the free will and choice of the one asking. Were I to try a method, I would lose my station, my status, and become indebted to one of three, God or an archangel, which would involve absolution for my original defiance and eternal servitude as a lesser angel. Or I could go to Lucifer, confess my weakness, and reveal to him how close I had grown to mortals. I would lose everything that matters to me. And I do have my pride." He smiled.

"I did love her, Charlotte, but she was surprisingly easy to sacrifice. And Luce's resurrection was my reprisal to Noanes and my apology to his mother and what I helped to cause." Aurelius held Luce's hand. "He is all that is left of her. All that I still have."

Charlotte sank back on her heels. She was certain that Aurelius had more to say. Grief glimmered in the corner of his eye, but it was not her place to press further. Part of her wished that she could feel pity for Noanes and for Luce's mother, but a greater part felt that vengeance had been best served. This latter feeling she enjoyed almost as much as drawing the knife across Odilon's throat.

"Mr. Ashe, he doesn't deserve to end this way."

"No, no he doesn't. He deserved something more noble than to be a pawn in a petty game of revenge," Ashe said. "And Rose played you as the queen in his gambit against me. Tell me, have you given thought as to what you want to do?"

"When I left The Athenaeum this morning, it was with regret. Not for what was to happen to me once I got here but the fear that I might not make it back to you." She looked at him with the clearest eyes. "What life I have I owe to you, as I had no life before. You told me that it was my choice to do with it as I wish. I believed that for the longest time that I was nothing. Odilon and Florence reminded me of that often enough how unworthy I was of sharing their world. I was a commodity of class until Lucien showed me otherwise. Until *you* showed me." She took his hand. "But without him, you, the others, I have little want to go on as I am. As you said, without one face or one purpose I'm already in my grave."

"Charlotte —"

"Mr. Ashe, you said that none of this" — she gestured to Luce — "has been my fault but you are wrong. As I told Lucien and Mr. Harlequin, I did bring Odilon to your door. In my own way I brought Mr. Noanes and the others and Georgie suffered. Because of my circumstances, an innocent

645

woman was killed and countless others displaced from the rook —"

"I do not hold you accountable. Odilon Rose would have found his way to me sooner or later and Noanes, well, his return was not unexpected. We would have met up again, eventually. If there are any apologies to be made, it is me to you."

Charlotte looked at him and saw in his eyes something she had never expected. Remorse.

"As you know the truth of your paternity, I suspect you may also know about Milbrough's death."

"Florence was all too eager to share."

"What you don't know, what I did not even reveal to Odilon, was that his mother, Catherine, came to me after Milbrough had brought you home, here to Decimus House. She knew immediately the truth. By your age, she knew that his infidelity had to have been shortly after her own child's death — which he barely addressed from what I understand. And here he was, his own child, a daughter of all things. Perhaps if it had been a son." Aurelius shook his head. "She came to me and asked if I would rid her of you. Kill you, in other words. It did not matter the method or means, as long as it resulted with your death and Milbrough's pain. I refused because it was wrong. Your only sin had been in being born, which was no concern of mine. But I did know the woman's determination so I warned her that if grave harm came to you by her hand, I would know. So in lieu of a second deal, I allowed her eight more years on her contract. She accepted but chose to enact her revenge by another route."

Charlotte closed her eyes. "Odilon."

"I am sorry, Charlotte. Lucien spoke to me of repercussions. You are the first that I have faced."

"Is that why you helped me?"

"I did not know that it was you when Odilon engaged me. But when I learned your name it was the least I could do. Knowing fully what has gone on in this house, I had to do what I could for you."

A brief, sad smile crossed Charlotte's injured face. "In the end she got her wish."

"Perhaps, but not on her terms," Aurelius said.

"But it enrages me to think that I am helpless to make amends to the lives I have shattered. Please, Mr. Ashe, what can I do? Do you need my heart to repair his? I will rip it out myself. I will help rebuild the rook. I will bury the dead. Tell me what I can do?"

"Remember, my dear Miss Bainbridge,

when we first met, I told you that I might ask something of you one day?" Ashe leaned over and with a gentle hand touched Charlotte's cut face. "Something that might go against the very fabric of your being?"

Charlotte nodded.

"Then I ask you to cling to what you are feeling now. The hate, the resentment, the animus that has brewed in you for all of these years, your grief, your guilt, hold it all close —" She looked down to find the knife handle back in her hand. It was still wet with Odilon's blood and perhaps remnants of Mr. Emmett's as well but that did not diminish how perfectly the hilt fit the soft curve of her palm.

"I think that you will find rage makes the best whetstone."

She looked into his black eyes and within them found the spark of a purpose after a life lost in the dark.

Chapter Fifty-Two

Less than a week following the Row fire, Southwark had returned to its normal day-to-day. The shops were open and the street vendors, hawkers, and peddlers offered their wares from tables and carts. Nevertheless, it was a cold day and the wind carried the first breath of winter. Many of the Row's inhabitants remained displaced, and in absence of a roof and four thin walls sought comfort around the nearest fire or warm food cart. Few had the leisure or the care to be watching the river or to listen to the sound of the Mud Larks' voices floating up from the ebbed banks of the Thames as the barges and lug-boats floated slowly along. However, there were one or two exceptions among the young and hungry, who watched with interest the man in the dark overcoat coursing up the gangway of the ship with the elaborate lotus funnel and the glistening copper paddles.

"Pulling up stakes I see."

Aurelius looked up from his desk. "Detective Inspector Grainger, what an unexpected pleasure. What brings you here?"

Grainger removed his hat, pinching the brim between his thumb and forefinger. "I had stopped by the theater but was told that you were here and I wanted to say my good-byes before you sailed. Surprised to see you leaving so soon."

"Considering recent events, Inspector, I felt that it was for the best," Aurelius said.

"Have you heard the news about Odilon Rose?"

"Yes, I read about it in the paper. Murdered in his own home and then a fire set to cover it. Not unlike the Row. I do hope that my son is not a suspect this time."

"No, quite the opposite, we have the culprit. The sister, Florence Suskind."

"Mrs. Suskind?" Aurelius raised a brow. "I knew the man had enemies but not so close to home."

"Killed not only her brother but Josiah Emmett as well, and then tried to set fire to the house. That was her mistake. Neighbors saw smoke coming from an upper floor and alerted the fire brigade. When they arrived, Rose was dead on the second-floor landing

650

and Florence Suskind locked in a bedroom with Mr. Emmett, who was also deceased. Florence set the fire herself, I suppose she thought it easier to end the matter. It was a clumsy attempt and she succeeded only in burning herself. The fire was contained to the one room and covered nothing of the crime. Of course, she will never see the inside of a courtroom. Her husband, his right honor, has had her committed to a private asylum. Best place for her really."

"How tragic," Ashe said. The orrery on the desk clicked, all nine brass spheres spinning. "Though I have a feeling that it wasn't easy growing up in that house."

"Of course now we will never know what was running through her head. I hear that no one can reach her anymore. Mind completely gone.

"As to her brother —" Grainger heaved a deep breath. "— I don't like to speak ill of the dead, Mr. Ashe, no matter who they are or what they've done in this world, but there will be few who mourn the man. We found his files kept secure at his bank. He was meticulous in his record keeping, I will credit him that, and all confirm a good many long-held suspicions. I am afraid the man's depravity was limitless."

Grainger shook his head. "I know he's

651

standing before a higher court now than I could have ever placed him in, and somehow I don't see mercy coming down in his favor."

"The price to be paid for favors given. What of the Row fire and the murder of Silvia Marquette? Any progress there?"

"I fear we may never know with certainty. But as long as I have breath, I'll be keeping my eye on Southwark. Twenty-two lost souls in the fire and then Miss Marquette. No, sir, whoever he is the moment he stirs, if there is even a whiff of malevolence in the air, you can rest assured I will be there waiting. I will say that if I never see another prostitute ripped like her in the East End again it will be far too soon."

Outside the gulls whirled upward in a shrieking spiral of white wings before diving back to skim across the oil-slicked waters.

Grainger was silent a moment before returning to Ashe. "Actually there was one question I had for you. We have not been able to locate Miss Charlotte Bainbridge. We've searched the house and the grounds and have fortunately not come across a body, so that gives us hope that she is alive. But as she was a ward of the Roses, we've not been able to establish any other family for her. The few far-flung members of the

Rose family have never heard of her. She's simply disappeared."

"Perhaps she's staying with a friend. She must have been frightened out of her mind when Madame Suskind —"

"My thoughts exactly. But we've not any name to check on except for yourself, sir, and your son. It had come to my attention that the two of them had become rather close, so she may have turned to him for help."

"Had she come to us, she would of course have been helped in any way that we possibly could have. If she had wanted transport to a foreign shore, we would have welcomed her. However, she is not among us, I regret to say."

Grainger rose from his chair. "You know, Mr. Ashe, there were secrets in that house. Behind a false wall, we found a cache of treasures, priceless pieces of art. We presumed at first they were stolen; however, as we looked into the files, we discovered that they were payment."

"Frailties and failings, Inspector. Never discount what people are willing to pay or the acts they are willing to commit to keep them hidden."

"We'll be looking into some of the more criminal offenses, but compared with what they've already been through, I don't think there is much that the courts can do to them." Grainger reached into his pocket, pulled out a news clipping, and laid it on Ashe's desk.

It was a familiar piece of paper, yellowed, not as creased as the one the Rose had presented him, the one he had allowed him to keep. This was the duplicate but the bold black letters still burned.

FIRE

"My brother was not a good man, Mr. Ashe. Sooner rather than later, he was going to meet his end. And it wasn't ever going to be a quiet passing in his sleep at a well-earned age. Still, it was a horrible way to die."

"Yes, and I'm sorry that happened to him. A great and terrible misfortune. I presume that the case is still open?"

Grainger shook his head. "Spontaneous human combustion. That sounds like something better suited to science to figure out, not the courts."

"Inspector," Ashe said as Grainger turned toward the door. "When we come back, and we will be back in the New Year, do come to the show. Bring your family as my personal guests. I have a feeling that 1888 is going to be a memorable year for London."

"That is generous, sir, thank you. I might just take you up on that."

"You are a good man, Joseph Grainger. You have the potential to go far. Perhaps one day we will see you as superintendent."

"Me, superintendent?" Grainger brushed off the compliment.

"Never scoff at the possibility. One never knows what the future might hold." Ashe walked over and shook his hand. "Goodbye, Inspector. If there is ever anything that I can do for you, please don't hesitate to ask."

At the opposite end of London, miles from the grime of Southwark and the green of Regent's Park, a woman sat in her tidy house, in Hackney, secluded in a parlor of flower prints and soft cushions. Two cups sat empty on the coffee table while a single cup sat untouched on the small table beside her chair; the tea had gone tepid as the morning's extraordinary events replayed in her mind.

She had not known what to make of the pair who had come to her door that morning. The man was tall, young, and dressed in neat charcoal-gray trousers, waistcoat, and jacket, miles above any of the rag-and-bone men who frequented the street at that time of day. He wore a broad-brimmed hat, a Wide Awake bowler, that was better suited to the country squire or Quaker than any city dweller. As for the woman, she had made every attempt to appear a proper sort of lady but fell slightly short in her black skirts and visible red underpinning. And the hat, black and emblazoned with red roses, was rather ostentatious for a midmorning visiting.

"Mrs. Mary Harcourt? Pardon my intrusion on your time but Mr. Ashe sent us. My name is Dita du Reve and this is Timothy Harlequin. He asked us to deliver this to you as he didn't want to leave it to the post."

She held out a letter, the paper of which was of a very fine weight and twin to the first letter she received from the man not more than a week past.

"From Mr. Ashe?"

"He would have come himself but he had another obligation that requires his full attention. But he hopes that you recall your previous conversation and his offer to help you with a long-standing matter regarding the Rose family and an item in their possession."

"An item?" Her stomach fluttered. "I don't —"

"Madame, open the letter, if you please."

Mary slid her finger under the seal. The first line of the letter buckled her knees and it was only Harlequin's speed and steady hands that kept her from falling to the floor.

"How?" Her voice wavered. She looked up into his quicksilver eyes. "I told Ashe nothing of —"

"He recognized in you the wild ache that only a great want or a great loss can produce. He has seen it before." Harlequin pulled her close, his mouth to her ear. "She has your eyes," he whispered, his breath warm on her skin.

When Mary Harcourt had recovered, she was in her parlor and Dita du Reve was seated across from her. Timothy Harlequin sat on the settee between them. A pot of tea and three cups sat untouched on the table.

"I hope you don't mind my taking the liberty of your kitchen but I thought you could use some sweet tea," Dita said. "You've had a shock."

Glancing at the letter again, she still had not quite been able to reason what the words were saying. She tried to find the child's scrawl in the refined hand but it was no more.

My dearest Mother,

I could not have imagined only a week ago that I would be addressing a letter to you. Not a day has passed that I have not thought of you and I can only hope that I, too, am remembered as fondly. The pen shakes in my hand from a joy I can barely contain in knowing that you are still alive. But it is rage that drives my thoughts at having been denied your company these last thirteen years because of the lies that I have been forced to live. And what pains me most is that what was deceit to me was an unimaginable cruelty to you. I know who Milbrough Rose is. I know what he did and why I was taken and I am sorry. I am sorry for believing their lies and for not having enough sense to doubt them. I can only thank our mutual friend, Mr. Aurelius Ashe, for letting me know the truth. He has done more than you can imagine, and I am forever indebted to him.

I am afraid that we must be apart a little longer, but please accept this small gift and keep me in your heart. Until we meet again.

Your own Charlotte

Harlequin watched as Mary blinked back the shimmer in her eyes. His continued silence was the courtesy she needed to compose herself.

"After I read in the paper about the tragedy at Decimus House, I was elated," she finally said. "To think that vipers' nest was finally routed by their own misdeeds. There is no finer justice than that."

"As I understand, there are a good many who would agree with you," Dita said, nodding.

"Charlotte?"

"Especially Charlotte," she said.

"She speaks of rage and lies. I cannot imagine what she was told about me. My death! Thirteen years, Miss . . . Miss du Reve, she thought me dead when all that time I was outside the gate. From the moment I was out of Guy's and found her gone —"

"Begging your pardon, but that has been something of a thorn to me this business around your going to Guy's Hospital instead of Charing Cross," Dita said. "Thinkin' back, do you remember what day you went in?"

"What day?" Mary asked. "I don't . . . I . . . I think it might have been a Tuesday?"

"You took ill on a Tuesday."

"No, I was ill the day before. I probably should have gone then to hospital but my landlady, Mrs. Rausch, said that if I could keep one day more then she would take me herself and see that I was admitted. She offered a letter of sponsorship that would assure my care."

"And there is your answer, missus. Charing Cross accepted general admission patients on Mondays not Tuesdays, which was Guy's Hospital's general admission day."

It was a moment of burgeoning horror as Mary Harcourt realized what her guest was implying. "I fell sick on the wrong day?"

"The wrong hospital's admissions day. Which is why you were encouraged to wait. As for the letter of sponsorship, I don't doubt that your landlady was a respectable enough woman but it would take a name a bit more respectable to gain entry to the hospital, especially with the threat of something like consumption . . ." Dita left the trail for Mary follow.

"Milbrough Rose. No one would say no to that name. My God, he planned it. He waited for the opportunity and enlisted Mrs. Rausch." Mary closed her eyes, her hand balling into a fist. "I had long suspected that the two of them . . ."

"That's the sort of deviousness that the devil himself would envy," Dita said.

"He never expected me to get out. If it

had been Charing Cross, Charlotte would have tried to see me, but Guy's." Mary swallowed back her tears. "I spent years after confronting, haranguing, and hounding that man, in word and letter. I made myself a plague on his step begging to have her back. If he wished to give her a better life, to own up to her, I would have borne that shame. But to steal her outright! He owed me at least the opportunity to see her as a mother. When he denied me so small a request I threatened to go to the police, to make a scandal, but —"

"But the Roses do not threaten easily," Harlequin said.

Mary shook her head. "Not the father nor the son to whom I pleaded my case, which makes it all the more remarkable that your Mr. Ashe was able to accomplish in less than a week what I could not do in all those years."

"Oh, my dear lady, you would be surprised by what he is capable of. Why, he can persuade the soul right out of your body and you would find yourself thanking him for doing so." Dita laughed.

Harlequin leaned forward and held up his right hand. On his little finger was a small ring. A single ruby was nestled in a delicate gold setting. "She wants you to have this.

Her gift."

It was all too extraordinary and was a happiness almost too great to bear. Mary Harcourt clutched Charlotte's ring to her chest.

"Thank you," she whispered, half to the God she prayed to every day and twice on Sundays and half to the man who had visited her three days before and had told her to have sympathy and a little faith.

CHAPTER FIFTY-THREE

1 November, The Athenaeum

"If Dita finds you up here I doubt that I'll be able to save you."

"It's worth risking her wrath to be outside for a bit."

Aurelius joined Luce on the bench. "How are you feeling? Much pain?"

Luce's body ached. The violence wrought by Noanes's bullet had been amplified by Pretorius's repairs. Despite the great care he had used it had been a painful violation on already tender flesh.

The remnants of the shattered mechanical heart had been extracted with some difficulty. Some of the deeply embedded pieces took nearly five hours to fully excise before the new mechanism could be placed and the remaining bits of old heart muscle that had been patchworked with new could be fused to the brass and glass. Skin flayed from a fresh corpse had been grafted and stitched to his already bruised and raw existing flesh, which left the whole of his back, where the entry wound had been, tight and tender. A bandage was wound tight around his torso, slightly crusted brown and scarlet where he had bled.

He sighed and pulled his coat closer. Under the clouded dusk sky, the bull lantern flickered at his feet. "No worse than the first time."

"And the fire? Let me see."

Luce pulled his hand from his pocket and held it out, palm upward. A small flicker formed in the center before fanning along the length of his fingers.

"Weak, but improving," Aurelius said. He took Luce's hand and for a moment studied the flames. "Good color. I'd say in three weeks to month's end you'll be back to form." He blew out the flames like candles.

Aurelius looked out over the city. From The Athenaeum's roof, the lines of Tower Bridge cut a silhouette in the evening haze. From up here it was easy to forget the mud in the streets and the nearly two million souls who mucked their way through it day in and day out in the ordinary business of living, while another quarter million barely kept their heads above unbearable destitution.

It was easy to forget the desperate souls as well as the greedy who had come to him time and again for a respite from the lives they led, or to gain an advantage on the ones they wished to hurt. It was easy to forget the wickedness of recent days past because here in the twilight, with the shop lights twinkling and the rare spark of a star, life was not only bearable but held a promise.

"I don't care what anyone says, despite its faults, London is the greatest city in the world. No other like it. Nevertheless, time away is needed after this unpleasantness. We will come back again in the spring, stronger than before. I have sent Michael ahead to the Continent to scout some potential acquisitions. He is a clever lad with a good eye and a scent for finding things. You did well there with him."

Aurelius looked back to Luce, who met him with a bleak eye.

"Any word of Noanes?"

"I'm afraid not. Gone to ground I suspect, taking Skym and Kosh with him."

"He enjoyed pulling the trigger."

"As he would." Aurelius nodded.

"What did I ever do to him?"

"You reminded him of how unpredictable

wants and wishes can be. That and you lived."

In the silence that fell between them the faint click of the cog moving in Luce's chest could almost be heard.

"It has long been my experience that those who have called on me do so for selfish needs rather than out of a selfless act. Not that there is any real harm in having a desire for wealth or well-being, a betterment of some kind. And for most the ends are met and the benefit usually stems beyond the one who asks. I make no apologies for the small part I play as it is of no consequence to me. That is how it had always been until —" Aurelius turned his eyes again to the city-scape.

"Until I took the life of Noanes's daughter and Noanes decided that he needed to take yours. Funny that he had no qualms about profiting off curiosities but when it came to having a curiosity as a grandchild, that proved an unbearable sin. It was much the same with Odilon Rose and his misguided theories about everything."

"He had a little casket in his trove room. It was covered in a cloth. He kept her there, didn't he?"

"Rose kept a lot of things, judging from what Timothy found. But she is now at rest.

We have given her the proper burial she has long waited for at St. Saviour's. The skeleton twins as well. They too deserved the same dignity."

Aurelius grew quiet. "Among the items that Timothy found was a human heart. It was not old, so not a relic. He found it packed in salt inside a box, preparation I suppose for further preservation. There was also a violet ribbon."

Taken apart the two items would not have meant much but taken as a whole the meaning was very different. "Silvia."

"I'm afraid that Florence Suskind was an insatiably jealous woman."

Luce closed his eyes, falling silent. As he thought of Florence, of her flirtations and her fondness, which he took as little more than a warm but harmless flattery, the pieces began to tumble together to paint a dangerous portrait. Florence had attended every show and often found her way backstage. She dressed for him — even Columbine had commented on that. The black crepe rose in her hennaed hair. Ashes on fire.

I only remember the blade.' That was what Silvia had said. She never saw the face of her attacker, only the knife.

"Charlotte."

"In a mind so far gone with one obsession, Charlotte was one more rival. However, that was a rivalry begun long before you came along. There were many secrets in that house, Lucien, the surface of which has only been scratched. Charlotte didn't even know because the Roses kept the truth very close to themselves. They condoned the monstrous acts that started very young in Odilon and I suspect in Florence as well."

"But you saw her. You got her out —"

"The way she fretted over you when she saw you lying there on the floor, she knew then what she had to do."

Aurelius rested his hand on Luce's knee. "Charlotte was the only light in that house and now that light is free, thanks in large part to you."

Luce opened his mouth but whatever words he had wished to say were caught in his throat like birds in a net.

"Until she met you, Lucien," Aurelius continued, "hers was a disfigured life where she had only known cruelty in its varied forms. Her illness affected her body, but what the Roses had done —" he shook his head. "She needed a purpose for being, which you gave her. You showed her that there is genuine kindness in the world, kindness given freely without any extraneous expectations in return. That is an extraordinary thing."

Aurelius rose to leave but stopped. "Choose if you will to never speak of these days, and do grieve for those who are not with us, but do not regret what has passed. It was merely the prologue." He pressed his hand to Luce's chest. "The epilogue has yet to be writ."

"You didn't tell him."

Aurelius paused on the stairs leading from the roof. Harlequin appeared on the step behind him. "Timothy, you are intruding on matters that do not concern you."

"Leaving him to believe that she is dead —"

"I never said any such thing. I stated that she was free. If he interprets her absence as anything else then the onus is on himself. He did not directly ask me otherwise." Aurelius rested his hand on Timothy's shoulder.

"You can't leave things like that. He deserves to know."

"Do you think that telling him the truth would make him feel better? What would be the point in having Lucien worry needlessly? He doesn't need that distraction. He needs only to heal. Besides, I don't believe that he would have approved."

"It's wrong of you, Aurelius. It is cruel. First the lies about his mother and now —"

"It was Charlotte's choice, Timothy. Who am I to have denied her that?"

CHAPTER FIFTY-FOUR

22 December, Paris, France
"There's no cure for circusing, my lad, so you best think long and hard if this is the road you wish to take."

He had first noticed the boy in the striped trousers outside the theater de la Gaite, where the musical talents of Rosa-Josepha, the phenomenal Siamese Twins, drew crowds nightly. For a fortnight, the boy entertained the men and women who waited outside the theater in the chill, juggling one night, performing card tricks and sleight of hand the next, and while he had both an obvious appeal and a skilled hand, he had yet to develop the presence he would need to survive the life.

"Of course with a bit of training, you could be a stage staple rather than a mere street performer. But only if you're willing to work."

The boy sat for a time without remark,

measuring this new prospect as carefully as he had the contents of the glass in front of him.

Linus Noanes knew the look well. It was a common tell worn by any act faced with giving up the freedom of self-employment for that of a troupe. He had worn it himself when he first encountered Aurelius Ashe and had handed the show over to him. He had worn it again when he encountered Odilon Rose and traded the stage for a dubious sense of domestication. It was a look he vowed only to see in the eyes of others.

"You're a long way from London, and you'll find it easier to navigate this business with an eye watching over you. People like us, we look after —" Noanes paused over the memory of the trigger that had killed that philosophy. "I'm looking for acts to build up a new ten-in-one."

"Meaning no disrespect, sir, but I already followed a similar line and that's what's landed me here." The boy's face did not change but his eyes dropped and wandered to the side. "I had a partner, Alfie Richards, who suggested that we take ourselves abroad, move beyond London. I was happy enough where I was, performing in pubs, the odd theater engagement at Wilton's opening for the opener. It weren't the Savoy but it filled the purse for a night. But old Alfie was persuasive and I'd never been to Paris and if the act did prove a success, then who knows?"

The boy downed his dram of rum. "Unfortunately when the time came, he didn't show at the boat. I waited for as long as I could but I couldn't very well afford to waste the fare. I thought he'd show here, but it's been nearly a month and I haven't the money to return home and barely the money to stay."

Noanes smiled broadly and leaned back in his chair. "All the more reason to consider my offer."

The steady drone of voices that had filled the café quickly gave way to a more raucous outpouring as the theaters and dance halls let out and a concourse of the gayest and best-dressed young men made their way to the brasseries for refreshment and comely company, should luck be with them and the waitresses willing.

"We should perhaps take this discussion somewhere quieter," Noanes said, scanning the crowd. "I've been keeping a room here."

He nodded toward the proprietor, who was seated in his own snug near the back of the café where a hallway led to a series of rooms. Settled in his little nook, he was well out of the way of the doors that swung on a draft every few minutes but near enough to keep an eye on his girls when they left their table with a customer. He returned Noanes's greeting as the two men passed.

"Bring us a drink, darlin', on your way back," Noanes said, pinching the heavily powdered, beauty-marked cheek of one of the waitresses as she brushed past him in the hall.

"There's some things in Paris that are quite agreeable." Noanes flopped down in the chair of his rented room. Despite the closed door, an impartial chorus of noises from the café and the smells from the kitchen distributed evenly through the room. Underlying both was the unmistakable scent of perfume, slightly soured, which only served to prove that no amount of cleanliness in one room could withstand the want of such in the next.

The room itself was a Spartan and utilitarian space consisting of a bed, a small table, two chairs, and three hooks on the wall that currently held what could only be considered Noanes's best coat and perhaps third-best shirt. These rooms if anything encouraged short stays, best if the time spent lasted no more than an hour or two.

"So how many acts do you have together so far for this proposed ten-in-one? I want to know the plan before I sign up," the boy said.

"I've two. A Thin Man and a knife thrower."

"They been with you a long time?"

"Does it matter?"

The boy smiled. "In the case of business, loyalty matters a lot."

"Well then, you needn't worry. They have been with me nearly as long as I have been circusing. I have them currently looking for locations to set up the show. Brighton, Brixton, Islington, perhaps. London's a bit crowded, easier to start where the shows aren't as frequent."

"Then, sir, you have yourself a third act."

"You've made the first step on a long and profitable journey, my lad." He leaned back in his chair. "And with that settled, let's see what you can really do."

The boy nodded and pulled from his green brocade coat a small silk bag, which held three painted balls. One red, one blue, and one yellow. He began to juggle. All three balls spun in his palm, gliding over his hand, along his fingers and back, never once losing contact with his skin. It was a graceful and fluid manipulation and it was easy to see how an audience could be spellbound.

"Now let's see what you can do with a fourth." Noanes tossed another ball to the boy, who took it smoothly in hand, spinning it in his free palm before transferring it to the others, not once breaking rhythm as three objects became four that he kept in constant motion.

"Good, good, keep it up."

There was a quick knock before the door swung open and a young waitress entered, carrying a tray with a bottle of gin and two glasses.

"Put it down here," Noanes said without turning his eye from the boy. "Have you ever seen such juggling, *ma petite*?"

"I did learn from the best, Mr. Noanes. From the very best," the boy said.

Noanes felt a hand sweep through his hair. The quick edge of a fingernail scraped his scalp as his head jerked back. His eyes widened as he found himself looking up into the last face he ever he expected to see.

"You . . ." he hissed as the cold blade touched his skin.

"We always look after our own, Mr. Noanes. Mr. Ashe sends his regards."

Noanes tried to respond to the pressure of the steel but the knife hand was quicker. A thin arterial spray shot from the wound followed by a stream of heat as his blood spilled and the face, which was only inches above his and half hidden beneath the shadow of a hat, faded as quick as his life.

"You can stop now." The knife landed on the table with a thud. "We need to be quick."

The boy returned the juggling balls to their bag and the bag to his pocket.

"Do you have it?"

"Yes." From the pocket of his waistcoat, he pulled a shard of black glass. "I can do it if you want."

"No, it has to be me."

It was a simple act. A dip of a finger into Noanes's blood and a swipe across the glass. That was all that Ashe had asked.

"Is that it?"

"That's all that he told me to do, and now we need to go."

"Brighton, Brixton, and Islington. Those are the best places to start looking."

"Excellent. We shall catch the ferry tomorrow. As for now, the quietest way out?"

"There's a back entrance down the hall," the boy said. He pulled from his coat a pair of gloves. They were the brightest shade of virgin blue. The same color as Luce's eyes; eyes she would need to kill twice more to see again.

"Thank you, Michael. Thank you for everything you have done. I am sorry you had to watch this, though. It's not a side of myself I wish anyone to see although I seem to have fallen to it with great ease."

"I'd never deny anything that you asked, miss. He weren't a good man."

"No, Michael. He wasn't."

Charlotte picked up the knife, wiped the blade clean, and slipped it along with the shard of mirror into the pocket of her black dress. Florence had been right, best to wear black as it did hide the bloodstains.

She lowered the veil of her hat, hiding the scar that rode her cheek.

The waters had spared them their rougher edges, which offered an easy night's rest to the travelers as the ship sailed toward the Italian coast. Only the thumping of the engine and the breath of steam gave any clue of life aboard; that and the lone light that burned in the first deck salon.

Aurelius Ashe dropped the drape over the scrying glass in his office, obliterating the image of Noanes's body, dead in the chair, and of Charlotte and Michael's flight from the scene. Everything was done to order and she, both of them, were proving to be ideal additions to the family.

He returned to his desk and sank back in his chair as the orrery clicked once and he felt the cold deep in the pit of his gut. It was the touch of Noanes paying his debt, long overdue at that. One more soul to the legion below.

From the pile of papers on his desk, he pulled an envelope as the black faded from his eyes and he read the familiar refrain.

Dear Mr. Ashe, I do believe that I have in my possession something of interest for you . . .

ACKNOWLEDGMENTS

If anyone had told me that the five little pages I had scribbled in November 2012, featuring a man casting orbs of fire into the sky from a ship on the Thames, would become a full-fledged published novel in 2023, I would not have believed them. Yet here we are and what a journey it has been, and I have many to thank for guiding and supporting me along the way.

First to my mother, Holly Gibbs, who was the first to put a book in my hand and opened the door to the world and all that could be. To Judy Samuels, my first and best reader, who suggested eleven years ago to try writing outside of my comfort zone. You not only embraced those original five pages, you became the biggest fan of Aurelius Ashe and cheered me on every step of the way. Emily Bates, for twenty years of friendship and for enthusiastically talking up the work to anyone who would listen. Amanda

McGuire, a later addition to the group but no less vital in friendship, support, and encouragement. And to Garret Weyr, a wonderful author and teacher, who encouraged my writing with her gentle guidance and words of wisdom.

Colson Whitehead, what can I possibly say? I am forever indebted. It was your kindness and generosity that led to an introduction to my utterly amazing agent, Julie Barer, who not only saw potential in the work, but her patience and passion as a fierce advocate has proven to be a godsend. The same for Nicole Cunningham and Chloe Knapp and the entire team at The Book Group.

To my incredible and indomitable editor, Karen Kosztolnyik, whose insight and vision is matched only by her passion and advocacy, which has proved invaluable at every turn of my publishing journey. And to the entire Grand Central Publishing team: Rachael Kelly, Bob Castillo, Laura Jorstad, Theresa DeLucci, Kamrun Nesa, and Albert Tang, who, with the brilliant artist Chris Buzelli, created the incredible cover art. And a huge thank you to the entire HBG sales group for all that you do for all your authors.

To my PRH family: Jenny Jackson, Lori

Zook, Jaci Updike, Beth Koehler, Kim Shannon, Lara Phan, and Ruth Liebmann. And for always going above and beyond, to Jason Gobble and all of my sales colleagues, I cannot begin to express my gratitude for your support.

I also must take the time to acknowledge the artists whose influence cannot be denied: William Shakespeare, Mary Shelley, Charles Dickens, Seamus Heaney, W.B. Yeats, Edgar Allan Poe, Neil Gaiman, Anne Rice, and Angela Carter, to name but a few whose works and craft and language have inspired me over the years. And to the musicians who created for me the rhythm and mood that became the soundtrack for this work: Robert Johnson, AC/DC, The Cure, Nick Cave & the Bad Seeds, Tom Waits, Nina Simone, Ofra Haza, Coolio, Scala & Kolacny Brothers, and Hozier (whose music I stumbled across well after the book was written, yet whose songs proved a balm during the long nights of final edits).

And finally, to the booksellers, the librarians, and the readers, I want to express my deepest gratitude. Without your knowledge, enthusiasm, love, belief in, and defense of the printed word, we would have neither stage nor audience to share our stories, our worlds, our hopes, our fears, and our dreams. Thank you.

ABOUT THE AUTHOR

Amiee Gibbs grew up in rural Maryland, where she still lives on an allegedly haunted road, but has dreams of running away to Ireland. She has worked for Penguin Random House for thirteen years as a sales manager for independent bookstores across New England, New York, and the West Coast. Prior to that she was an assistant sales manager at Waldenbooks and Borders. She holds an MLA degree with a focus on world literature and creative writing and is currently teaching herself Gaeilge.